I0730415

THE ABCS OF YOU & ME

RIGHT PLACE, RIGHT TIME BOOK 3

MEGAN MCSPADDEN

Copyright © 2025 by Megan McSpadden

All rights reserved.

Cover Illustrator: Ally MacMillan

Edited by: Sarah Pesce (Lopt & Cropt)

Author photo by: Jenn Kavanagh Photography

ISBN Paperback - 978-1-7381040-4-8

ISBN ebook - 978-1-7381040-5-5

No part of this book may be reproduced in any form or by any electronic or mechanical means, including information storage and retrieval systems, without written permission from the author, except for the use of brief quotations in a book review.

No generative artificial intelligence (AI) was used in the writing of this work. The author expressly prohibits any entity from using this publication for purposes of training AI technologies to generate text, including without limitation technologies that are capable of generating works in the same style or genre as this publication.

For Kail, who shines bright even on the dark days.
I love you to the moon and back, little sister.

CONTENT WARNING

This book contains memories of an emotionally abusive past relationship and an abortion. Please take care while reading, your mental health matters to me.

PLAYLIST

Tim Gallagher - Just Friends
OneRepublic - Sunshine
Ryan Mack - Overwhelmed
BANNERS - Someone To You
Andy Grammer - Best of You
Noah Kahan - Passenger
Taylor Swift - Tolerate it
Sawyer - Everywhere
Kelly Clarkson - Mine
Taylor Swift - Vigilante Shit
Forest Blakk - I Choose You
Wingtip - Happiness
BANNERS - Got It in You
Led Zeppelin - Stairway to Heaven
Sleep Token - Shelter
Kansas - Carry on Wayward Son
Styx - Renegade
Paris Paloma - Labour - the cacophony
Oshins - Always On Your Side
BANNERS - Start a Riot

Alex Warren - Carry You Home
Taylor Swift - Dress
Tyler Shaw - Love You Still
Vance Joy - Saturday Sun
Taylor Swift - You Are In Love
Avril Lavigne - Fall To Pieces
BANNERS - Tell You I Love You
Matt Hansen - Where You Belong
Caleb Hearn - Little Bit Better
Roo Panes - I Just Love You
Garrett Kato - Never Alone
Mr. Big - To Be With You
Letters To Cleo - I Want You to Want Me
VOILÀ - Figure You Out
Sleep Token - Give
GIO DARA - Be Mine
Taylor Swift - The Smallest Man Who Ever Lived

Spotify Playlist

ONE

SOPHIE

There is absolutely no way that I'm seeing what I'm seeing.

There is absolutely no way in hell that Foster Walsh is crouched down next to a nine-year-old kid, very patiently explaining something. I cannot believe that when my friends ask how my first day went, I'm going to have to say, *Remember that boy I was in love with from the ages of five to eighteen? Well, he's an educational assistant at the school I've been assigned to. Oh and he's my best friend's older brother. Did you hear that, Cass? Your brother is an EA in the same building I'll be spending the majority of my time in. Thanks for the heads-up, my now-former best friend. Also he's even hotter than I remember, so... awesome.*

When Foster looks up at me, frozen in the doorway, he doesn't seem to register who I am. It feels like a punch to the gut when he immediately looks back down at the student's work.

"Jessica Morris, I'd like to introduce you to our new social worker, Sophie Hore. She's stepping in for Hazel while she's on maternity leave." I do my best to focus on Jessica instead of on the stupidly hot man behind her. "I'll introduce you to Mr. Walsh later," Principal Wong says, gesturing for me to follow her.

I glance back as Foster's eyes find me, and his lips quirk in a barely there grin. Heat spreads across my face as I stumble over my feet turning to follow the principal. I know that grin. I saw it many times when I was younger. He definitely recognizes me.

There isn't much for me to do today other than get myself acquainted with my office and the files Hazel left behind. But the minute I sit down, my mind immediately goes back to Foster, as I knew it would. He hasn't changed much in the last eight years. His dark red hair is perhaps more styled than it had been in our youth, and he's filled out his tall frame well—a little too well.

Sighing, I pull my glasses off and set them on the desk before hiding my face in my hands and releasing a groan that can probably be heard in the hallway.

Those amber eyes, always glinting with a bit of mischievousness, flash in my mind. And my memory starts flipping through all the times he looked at me growing up. We'd played together as young children, but as we got older we didn't hang out because we thought the opposite sex was carrying some horrible disease. Eventually, Foster came back around as a teenager, but it was usually to tease Cass and me or dare us to do ridiculous things. Then one day he was packing and heading off to university. I stood beside his old black Honda Civic with his family as he said his goodbyes. After he'd hugged them, he stood in front of me and opened his arms wide. We'd hugged before, but this one had lasted longer than usual. I kept expecting his arms to loosen, but they remained wrapped tightly around me. It would have been so easy to melt into him, but his family standing there only made me hyper-aware of all the places our bodies touched.

"Good luck," I whispered as he stepped back, my fingers itching to tuck the piece of unruly hair that flopped across his forehead. I loved his hair. Next to his face, it was my favorite thing about him.

"You two behave," he said, amber eyes flicking between Cass and me.

Cass raised her hand in a Girl Guides salute, except she had her forefinger and middle finger crossed. "Promise."

Foster smirked back before he'd reached out to ruffle her hair.

The last time I'd seen him was that Christmas when he'd brought his out-of-province girlfriend home from school, crushing my fragile eighteen-year-old heart.

School and life had pulled us in different directions in the years between then and now, my heart slowly mending with a relationship of my own, only to be ripped to pieces five months ago.

When the lunch bell sounds, I'm brought back to the present, where I sit alone in my broom closet of an office. I have no clue if I should head to the staff room or stay put. There were no directions on how to engage with the teaching staff outside of dealing with students. Is it customary to eat with them or stay completely separate? This isn't the only school I'm assigned to, but it is my home base, and building relationships isn't exactly a bad thing. For today, though, I decide that I'll hide away here, except when I reach for my lunch bag, it's not there. In my haste to get to my first day on the job, I must have left my lunch sitting on the counter at home. I can already hear my mother. "Of course you did," she would say through laughter before asking how the rest of my day went.

When I've convinced myself that I can survive one day without lunch, my stomach lets me know that that's not an option. I'll have to venture outside of my little office in search of a vending machine. At least I know I'll find somewhat healthy snacks there since the province did away with junk food, not that I'd be upset if I had a bag of all-dressed chips or a Kit Kat. My stomach grumbles again, and I take a deep breath before rising and walking out into the hall. I find a vending machine around the second corridor I turn down.

"That one will turn to sawdust in your mouth." My finger pauses over the P as my heart lodges in my throat. When I turn my head, copper eyes and a cocky grin greet me. "Hey, Soph." Cool as a fucking cucumber.

I drop my hand and fully turn to him, not sure how to proceed. Adrenaline and something else course through my body. An urge to run away, perhaps?

"Oh, hey, Foster," I manage to squeak. "I was"—I wave at the vending machine—"checking out the options." A slightly too high laugh escapes, and I want to melt into the floor as nervous energy prickles across the surface of my skin.

The grin fades from his face as he looks behind me. "Don't tell me that's your lunch." His eyebrows draw together in concern.

I shrug. "I don't have— well, that is, I forgot my lunch. I made it, so I have it, I just don't have it on my person. It's still at home. It's in a bright pink bag too and yet I left it on my counter like an idiot. " *Shut up, Sophie.*

His face relaxes as he raises a blue nylon bag. "I'm happy to share."

"Oh no, you don't have to—"

"I wouldn't have offered if I didn't mean it, Soph." He

grins, and I give in. I'd be the worst spy. All it would take is Foster grinning at me and I'd spill all my secrets.

The softness of his gaze puts me at ease instantly. *Magic eyes*, I think as I slip my hands into my pockets and rock back on my heels, immediately regretting it when I realize I'm not nearly as close to the vending machine as I thought. My back slams into the glass, and relief rushes through me when the whole thing doesn't topple over. I'm going to pretend I meant to do that and not acknowledge it, or the way Foster's eyebrows are nearly in his hairline.

"I guess it depends what you're offering," I reason, sounding as bored as possible while feeling as far from bored as I have ever been.

"Some japchae, kimchi, and a couple chocolate chip cookies."

I stare back, wide-eyed. I'm not exactly what you'd call an adventurous eater despite my mother's countless attempts to make me one. "All I understood was chocolate chip cookies."

"Japchae is a Korean noodle dish with vegetables and"—his head tilts, his eyes narrowing as he studies me—"you don't know what kimchi is?"

"I think I've heard of it, but I don't actually know what it is," I admit, my face burning with my admission of ignorance.

His face lights up. "Fermented cabbage and some other veggies in a spicy chili paste. It's not always made with cabbage. There are loads of different kinds, but the one I have..." he trails off when his eyes meet mine. "Information overload, sorry. You may like it, just trust me."

My eyes narrow in suspicion. "The last time you told me to trust you I ended up with a nose full of cow shi... manure," I whisper, glancing around. That moment was only marginally more embarrassing than nearly crashing through a vending machine.

"It's not my fault you could never say no to a dare." He smirks back. "Come on, Soph, I dare you to try the food. I made it myself."

"You could be a terrible cook for all I know," I fire back, pushing off the machine and standing at my full height, which usually makes me seem more intimidating than I am. Foster still towers over me, though, and I'm going to pretend I don't like it.

He looks down at his bag, then back at me. "Guess you'll have to try it to be sure. Otherwise you may spend the rest of the day hungry and wondering if I am, in fact, a good cook. Which, spoiler alert," He leans in conspiratorially. "I am."

He's too close now, and there is definitely a little glint in his eye. All the nerves that I'd pushed down bubble back up.

"Fine." I sigh.

"Mind if we eat in your office? I'd love to catch up before the other teachers pounce." My stomach flips at the thought of being confined to such a small space with him. But I nod and lead the way.

"Not a lot of real estate, eh?" Foster observes, pulling out the chair across from mine as far as it can go, which isn't far.

He starts opening containers, and I distract myself by searching for the plastic-wrapped takeout fork I'd seen in a drawer earlier.

"You sure you're not going to still be hungry if you share?" I ask, taking in the containers that don't look like enough food for two.

"I'll be fine. Jessica and I have a stash of snacks in the classroom."

"What kind of snacks?" I ask, watching him spoon out strange-looking noodles onto the container's lid.

He glances up, that glint back in his eyes. "Contraband. Packed with sugar and sodium and hundreds of other ingredients we can't pronounce." He slides half the food toward me. "Go on, try it."

I look down skeptically at the mix of things in front of me. It doesn't look gross, but I've never eaten see-through noodles before. I take a tentative forkful and chew thoughtfully, letting the flavors envelop my tastebuds. Sweet and savory notes explode as I chew. It's unlike anything I've had before, but I'm already craving another bite. When I look up, Foster is watching expectantly.

"So?" he asks, one eyebrow cocked.

"It's really good," I concede. "Like the best thing I've tried in a while." I take another bite, chew and swallow. "It's very moreish."

"Excellent. Now, try the kimchi."

The minute the cabbage is through my lips I want to spit it out, not because it's gross but because it feels like I've stuck a lit match into my mouth.

"Oh my god," I gasp, desperately looking around for a tissue while fanning my mouth dramatically.

"Here." Foster hands over a napkin from his bag.

I grab it and spit the fire cabbage out as delicately as possible before rapidly sucking in air, which only fuels the flames currently destroying my taste buds. "That's the hottest thing I've ever tried," I exclaim, reaching for my water bottle.

"Really?" he asks, looking genuinely shocked. "It's not even that hot. This was a mild batch."

"Nothing about that was mild, Foster," I sputter between gulps. "Should be called lava cabbage."

"We'll have to agree to disagree. Eat more of the noodles, they'll cool you off." I follow his direction and am pleased to discover that it helps. "Can you handle any spice?"

"Mild salsa is too hot for me."

To his credit, he looks apologetic. "I should have asked, I'm sorry."

"I have the spice tolerance of a slug," I say through more nervous laughter.

"Are slugs particularly bothered by spice?"

I think for a minute. "I don't actually know." I giggle. "I think it's salt they have an issue with."

"Well, I'll keep that in mind." He chuckles and takes another bite of food while my brain goes on one of its famous tangents.

Why would he need to keep that in mind? Is he going to cook for me again? Not that he cooked for me today but is he thinking about doing it in the future, on purpose? Do I want him to cook for me? I think I do, but should I? How is he so fucking hot? Does he realize? Am I being weird? I'm definitely being weird.

When my mind stops with the grocery list of questions, we fall into an easy rhythm catching up. He's lived in the city ever since he got home from a year spent teaching English in South Korea. I'm pretty sure Cass had mentioned where he'd gone, but I'd done a good job of quickly forgetting all things Foster-related at the age of eighteen. Self-preservation and all that.

"How did you end up in the city and at this school?" he asks while packing up the containers as we both nibble on our cookies, that he made of course.

"I moved to the city for my undergrad, loved it, and stayed for my master's. After graduation, I got a job in the social work department, which was fine, despite the fact I didn't want to be in academia. I wanted"—I gesture around the tiny office—"this," I say dramatically. "Life changes occurred, and one of my former advisors suggested applying for this position while Hazel went on maternity leave."

"So I'm more of a newcomer to the city than you," he says, leaning back in the chair.

"I guess you are. If you need any tips and tricks, I've got a few."

"Such as?" He quirks an eyebrow, and I'm momentarily distracted by the way it arches.

"If you pace it right, you can hit the green light highway when moving across the city east to west and vice versa," I say confidently.

"That's literally the only tip people give you when you move here," he scoffs, and my heart sinks. He's not wrong; it was one of the first things I was told when I arrived.

"Okay, how about..." My right foot starts to bounce under my desk, and I focus on that instead of the question.

A knock on the door comes before I can refocus. "Come in," I call, glancing quickly at Foster, who is looking at me, another question on his lips. His stupidly perfect lips.

Principal Wong opens the door and immediately looks surprised when her eyes land on Foster. "Oh, Mr. Walsh, we were wondering where you'd gone off to," she greets him before turning to me. "I'm sorry, Miss Hore, I should have let you know you're welcome to join us in the staff room at any time. No pressure of course, but it's as much your space as everyone else's."

"Thank you, I'll definitely join one day." I smile up at her. "Fost— ugh, I mean, Mr. Walsh was kind enough to share his lunch with me. Mine is still sitting on my kitchen counter."

"I can't think of a better person to share lunch with." She smiles kindly, looking down at her watch. "Bell's about to ring, and I've taken Mrs. Walker's yard duty. I'll see you out there, Mr. Walsh." She waves and shuts the door.

Foster stands the minute the door closes. "I totally forgot I was on duty today." He grimaces. "Someone always bleeds when I'm on duty."

"Bleeds?"

"Lots of bloody noses, unexplained cuts, things like that. Last year, a kid fell off the top of the slide and ended up with a compound fracture. I, ugh"—he rubs the back of his neck, looking at the door—"may have fainted."

"Mr. Walsh, do you not like the sight of blood?" I tease.

"Does anyone?"

I shrug. "I'm sure some people do. Vampires, serial killers, some doctors maybe."

"Vampires aren't real."

"There are people who identify as vampires because they drink one another's blood," I correct, and he stares blankly back at me.

"And with that, I'm off." He opens the door, his head shaking. "Want me to bring you some lunch tomorrow?" he asks, turning back to me.

I blink up at him, unable to make my mouth move. Do I want him to bring me lunch tomorrow? Teenage me is absolutely losing her shit right now. *Say yes, you dummy, he's practically asking you on a date.* "While that's very tempting, I'll bring what I had packed for today. Thanks, Foster." I give a little wave when he nods his goodbye.

After Foster leaves, I rearrange the office because I can't focus on my notes while this room doesn't work for me. It shouldn't take me long between the size and what's in here, but I don't like the configuration. In the middle of doing that, I get thirsty and go to fill my water bottle up. Then I get distracted by the art that lines the hallway in the primary wing. I can hear the kids outside playing and wonder how things are going out there for Foster. I can practically see him cheering on one of the kids as they show him how good they are at swinging or something.

I haven't daydreamed about Foster in a very long time, and all it took was one lunch with him to have me falling back into the habit. *You're over the crush, and even if you weren't, you aren't ready for anything.* And while my head repeats that reminder, my stupid heart beats to the rhythm of *he's here, he's here, he's here.*

TWO

FOSTER

Holy moose muffins, Sophie Hore is working at my school.

When I saw her standing in the door, it was like someone erased my brain. I looked back down at Pete's work and did my best to return to explaining the assignment. When I looked back up and found those blue eyes on me, it hit me that this was a real thing that was happening.

All through lunch with her I tried to play it cool. I can still remember when I got home from camp when I was sixteen and she was fifteen. It was like seeing her for the first time.

She'd been sitting on the front porch with my sister, both freshly back from a horse show, decked out in their fancy riding stuff. While I'd seen her in that stuff many times before, suddenly I saw someone else. When she smiled up at me and said hi, it was like I'd been shot up with adrenaline. I'd practically run into the house and hid in my room for the rest of the day.

The day I'd left for camp, Sophie had been eating cereal at the kitchen table. Hair askew, wearing an old band T-shirt and sweatpants, she was the girl who had spent more time at my house than her own. It was like being away for a few weeks had reset my brain.

She'd wiped my memory clean at lunch too, apparently. If Principal Wong hadn't come in, I'd still be in there, happily chatting with her, getting lost in her smile and how it tilts a bit higher on the right side. How I made it through lunch without spilling on myself or choking on my food is beyond me.

I can almost sense the scream before it comes. I was already turning in the right direction. I don't know what the issue will be—it could be an overdramatic kid upset that they slipped and fell, or it could be much worse and involve blood. With my luck, it'll be the latter, because it's always blood when I'm on duty. I see Emily Vanderhelm running over to me, and I know without a shadow of a doubt that I'm about to feel lightheaded.

"Mr. Walsh! Mr. Walsh!" she pants, nearly sliding into me on the slick ground as her legs slow. "Christina J fell into a tree!" She's off before "tree" is out of her mouth, and I follow quickly.

She fell *into* a tree? When I round the corner I can see the tree in question, Christina J on the ground next to it with several girls crouched around her.

"Okay, everyone back up a bit, give her some room," I coax, kneeling on the cold ground. "Christina, can you sit up?" She nods and slowly sits up, and great gorilla goulash, it takes everything in me not to puke then face-plant right into it. The entire left side of her face is scraped up.

The kids behind me gasp, a couple releasing hushed expletives I don't have the mental capacity to reprimand them for. Christina's eyes go wide, filling with tears. "Is it really bad?" she whimpers, her lips quivering.

I swallow, desperately trying to school my face. "It's

going to be fine," I say as calmly as possible, even if "fine" comes out a bit squeakier than I like. "Emily, can you help me get her to the office, please?" I look around, trying to recognize another face. "Becca, can you go let Principal Wong know I've taken Christina in?"

Emily and I get Christina inside as fast as possible, and once our designated first aid person is with her I excuse myself. I walk on unsteady legs toward my classroom, staying close to the wall in case I need to slide down it. Before I reach the room, someone grabs my arm and helps guide me the rest of the way. Once I'm sitting, things start to clear, and I see long legs, a fitted button-up, and then worried bright blue eyes behind glasses.

"I'm guessing there was blood."

I nod. "As I knew there would be."

"You didn't faint, though," Sophie says encouragingly.

"Small victories." I raise a fist in a half-hearted celebration.

"Have you always had this reaction to blood? I don't remember this when we were kids."

"I've never liked it, but it's gotten worse as I've gotten older. I'm fine with my own. It's the sight of others that does this"—I gesture at my face—"to me. Did you know kids bleed a lot?" I laugh warily.

"I did know that, and experienced it a time or two myself." She laughs, and I close my eyes, focusing on the lightness of it, feeling myself calm even more. "Where is the contraband?" she asks, and I point toward the coat closet at the back of the room. If my eyes fall to her ass for a split second as she walks over to it, it's not my fault—it's currently at eye level. Not allowing them to linger there feels like a monumental victory.

She comes back with a packet of gummies and a KitKat.

"Do you raid the Halloween sales on November first?" She holds up the options, and I nod toward the gummies, then watch as she opens them for me. I'm mesmerized by her long fingers and trimmed bare nails. What would they feel like scratching down my back? Digging into my skin?

"I'm not feeding them to you, Foster," she chastises, and I realize that she's waiting for me to take the packet from her while I've been fantasizing about her hands.

"Sorry," I mumble, shaking my head and reaching for the pack, then dumping all the gummies directly into my mouth. "Thanks."

"Seems like a crappy phobia to have when you work with kids," Sophie says, pulling out a chair and sitting across from me.

My teeth are practically glued together so I nod in agreement.

"Have you thought about seeking some kind of therapy?"

I shrug in response. I have, but I also figured working with kids would be like immersion therapy and the issue would resolve itself. Just as I unstick my teeth the bell rings, and I panic. I can't let the kids see the candy wrapper.

Sophie holds her hand out. "I'll destroy the evidence. You go work on getting it out of your teeth."

I head to the mirror that hangs in the coat closet and do my best to remove every bit of gummy from between my teeth. Maybe not the best choice for secret sweets. As I'm finishing up, the kids start filing in, and I catch sight of Sophie's ponytail as she disappears out the door. I'll have to thank her after school.

The afternoon drags, and by the time I've escorted my students out to the buses and get back to Sophie's office, she's gone. I make a mental note to thank her tomorrow and pack up to head home. My friends have set me up on yet another date, and despite the fact I don't want to go, I don't want to stand the woman up. With any luck, she'll do that to me.

ABC

Paullina is nice enough and attractive, but I can't help being hyper-aware of how she looks at my tattoos. There is definitely a flicker of disgust that appears every time her eyes skim across my forearms. I won't change who I am for another person, and I certainly can't undo the art I have paid good money for, nor would I want to. She orders a salad and water and barely eats, and even though I can see her eyeing my fries she shakes her head when I offer her some.

When the waitress asks if we'd like to order dessert, I'm not sure who says "Just the check please" faster. I can't wait to get home to my cat, and she probably can't wait to get home to catch up on the crime podcast she talked about. This may be the first date I've ever left knowing more about some serial killer than the person I was on a date with.

At home, Gary noisily greets me the minute I open the door. My sister showed up with him one day, along with a bunch of cat supplies and said, "Congratulations on adopting your first cat." She'd been there and gone in a flurry of activity, and I had only gotten "But I don't want..." out before the door shut and I was standing there holding a carrier with a pissed-off cat inside. That was three years ago, and now I can't imagine walking through the door and not having him immediately attack my shoelaces.

"Zero for ten, Gary," I announce, bending to pick him

up, walking into the living room and slumping down onto the couch. He climbs up and perches on my shoulder when I shift to pull my phone out of my pocket. If reincarnation is real, I'd wager he was a bird in his last life.

> Paullina was nice but I don't think we have a future.

HEATHER

Shit!

DAN

Miranda is going to be thrilled.

MIRANDA

Why am I going to be thrilled?

HEATHER

You won the pool.

MIRANDA

TBF I'd rather Foster find love than win money.

But I guess I'll take it.

> I think I'm done being set up for a bit, friends.

NICK

No way! Alex and I have the perfect woman for you. Stick with it!

> I really don't want to. Give me a month off, I'm begging you.

Thankfully they all agree, but I know it won't stop them from making their lists and placing bets on my love life. They all act like I want to be single, when in reality I'd love to be in a relationship. I am a relationship guy. Big fan of love and monogamy and all that. But I don't like feeling pressured to find it because it only amplifies those buried feelings of not being good enough that filter in from other areas of my life. It would be great if love simply fell into my lap, or walked into my classroom.

Chills rush through my body as I picture Sophie standing in the door, then smiling as she admitted the food was good and finally handing me the bag of candy.

Standing, I head into the kitchen and preheat the oven. I've got frozen cookie dough from the last batch I made, and I have a feeling Sophie won't say no to thank-you cookies.

THREE

SOPHIE

"Fucking kill me," I mutter when I find the invitation in my mailbox. I knew it was coming; it's alumni gala season, after all. I just hadn't expected to find my name listed as one of the graduates being recognized for my role in the development of the humanities mentorship program.

The Annual Alumni Gala, an event I'd been going to for the past four years on the arm of one of the most well-respected professors at the university. A man with credentials well beyond his years and an ego to match. A man who'd waxed poetic about our future together, especially when we were with my friends and family. A man I'd existed for up until five months ago, when he told me out of the blue that he was out because he needed to be on his own for a bit. "I am feeling stifled" were his exact words. It was confusing because we didn't actually spend that much time together with our schedules, and yet somehow I was stifling him. He told me to move out by the weekend, and seeing as how all the furniture was his, all I had to pack up were my clothes and some books.

The following week, I'd stopped by to drop off a couple

books of his I'd packed by accident, and a woman I recognized from a first-year master's class I had assisted with answered the door. At first I figured she was there for some academic reason, but then I heard Gregory call out from somewhere in the house. "Is that the food, baby?" I'd looked her straight in the eye, turned, and walked right back to my car. I ended up leaving the books in some random Little Free Library down the road from his place.

And now I was being recognized for the mentorship role I took on last year and was expected to attend this stupid gala where he was listed as the keynote speaker. She'd probably be with him, stars in her eyes as he kept her close, guiding her this way and that. Having such a handsome man who was at the top of his field take an interest in you was addictive. I'd ignored every single red flag he'd thrown up, and I'd kept every story that didn't paint him in the best light to myself, convinced that one day he would change, go back to who he'd been in those first few months when he'd love-bombed me so hard I couldn't see the truth through the flames.

I have to go. The connections at the university are still important to me. I just don't know how I'm going to do this and maintain composure when he walks by with her on his arm like we don't have a history. Like he hadn't swept into my life, upended it over the course of five years, and then kicked me out of his. I know I'll weigh the pros and cons about going until the last minute, and I know I'll show up and plaster a fake smile on my face. The worst part is, I know he knows it too.

My grumbling stomach reminds me that I'd had a smaller than usual lunch and after looking between the fridge and my lunch bag still sitting on the counter, I opt to eat the sandwich I'd made instead of making something else.

"This is fucking pathetic, ya know," I mumble to myself as I sit at my kitchen table all alone with a glass of water and my sad day-old sandwich.

I'd had visions of the kind of life I would have when I found a full-time job in my field. A life that involved happy hours and flirting with men in suits. Instead, I'm mindlessly going through the motions of eating while scrolling through Instagram. Cass has posted a couple new reels for the rescue. The first one features old footage of my parents' bull Jason running through the frame, followed by her boss Bennett and his wife Marley shouting and waving their arms. The second is a slideshow of Bennett and Marley on pack walks with their many, many rescue dogs. The final image however has me breathing in bread and meat and gasping for air. Three pairs of hiking boots sit on a log, the log where Bennett found an injured Marley and where he later proposed. Once I get the food dislodged from my airway, I call Marley.

"Hey, Soph!" Marley answers, a knowing tone in her voice.

"A baby!" I screech, unable to contain my excitement. I can hear Bennett's deep laugh clear as day, glued to her side like always.

She laughs. "That's what I'm told."

"How, when...when?"

"Well I think the how is pretty self-explanatory. The first when, well...definitely after I got home from my last trip." She sighs as if remembering it. "The second when I assume means the due date, and they told us August twenty-seventh. Which means I'll be in the last part of the pregnancy during the hottest months. It's going to be awesome," she deadpans.

"Does this mean you're done working for a bit?"

"Damn straight," I hear Bennett proclaim. "The travel stuff, anyway."

"Simon and I are working on a follow-up to our first book so I'll focus on that for the foreseeable future," she clarifies.

"And then?" I know I'm being nosy, but I don't know how Marley is going to ever return to conflict photography at all if she's got a kid at home. Meeting Bennett changed everything for her professionally, not that she's ever complained, but I can't see how this life continues as-is after a baby.

"Undecided. Thankfully there's still lots of time."

"Well, I think this is great. Do my parents know?"

"Your mom is the reason I took a test. They had us over for dinner, and the second I smelled her baked ziti I ran to the bathroom and threw up."

"Oh no!"

"Oh no is right," she whines. "Even the mention of the sauce is too much. Let's move on." I feel awful for her. It's a running joke that my mom's tomato sauce is actually what she'd come back to Bennett for five years ago.

"Wait, does this mean Bennett can't have any, um, stuff either?"

"It is considered contraband and no longer allowed in the house or within smelling distance of Marley," Bennett says, and I can't help but think of the contraband I secured for Foster today.

"You started work today, didn't you?" Marley asks, changing the subject.

"I did."

"And?"

"So far I haven't done much beyond forgetting my lunch, eating half of a coworker's, and rearranging my broom closet-sized office."

"Well, I'm glad someone shared their lunch with you at least." Marley yawns.

"I'll let you go. You sound tired."

"It's my new normal, sadly," she says through another yawn.

"I'll be up there in a few weeks for Easter break. I'll pop round to see you at some point."

"Well, we are having brunch at your parents' place so we will definitely see you. However, you know you're welcome here whenever, especially if you want to talk about things that aren't safe for Karl or Nancy's ears."

"I definitely will. Night, you two."

They wish me a good night in unison, in perfect harmony as always. No love story has ever made my heart as happy as Marley and Bennett's, and it feels nice to have been a part of it, even if it was incredibly minor. I once had a brief spark of hope that I had found my own love story with Gregory, only to realize there was no love there to build a story with. Now I'm back to thinking about that fucking gala again.

My phone lights up as I'm getting ready for bed, and I see Cass's name pop up in my notifications.

CASS

A little birdy told me you and Foster are now coworkers.

Was that little birdy Foster?

Foster is anything but a little birdy. He's a sturdy birdy —a very sturdy, very nice to look at kind of birdy.

It may have been! I didn't know you were going to be at the same school!

I didn't even know he worked in the city.

Yeah for like 4 years. Have I never told you that?

Not even once.

Well surprise he lives and works there! It's not fair that he gets to see you all the time.

You could always find a job down here. I'm sure there are loads of businesses looking for good communications people!

I love you, I like Foster, but I am not leaving Bennett's to move to some smelly-ass city to work some corporate job!

Speaking of Bennett, I saw the reel then had to immediately call them. Why didn't you tell me?

Exciting eh? I was sworn to secrecy. You should see them though, B was already a doting husband but holy shit it took some convincing that M could walk to the barn without him right next to her.

Well considering how she was when they first met this doesn't surprise me at all. He's a caretaker by nature. Things should be fun!

Indeed!

I've gotta go, we've got a new litter and
they are getting hungry!

Night!

Today may have been my first day, but tomorrow is when I actually get to work, and when I get into bed, I do my best to mentally plan. But the second I envision the orange folder sitting on my desk, planning goes out the window. I end up thinking about a certain redhead who, even after all these years, still sets my heart racing.

I bet Foster has a life. He probably met up with friends to do something fun tonight. He was always surrounded by a big group of people and was never short on women vying for his attention. Maybe I could ask him to come to that stupid gala with me. He's the complete opposite of Gregory, he'd be a nice distraction, and no one from my academic life knows who he is. Unless he's dating someone, which he probably is, but I could ask. The worst he can say is no, which would leave me no worse off than I am now. Although a no would be humiliating and I'd have to see him every day knowing he didn't want to accompany me to an event and I'd end up spiraling trying to figure out what it is about me that made him say no.

I could sell it as a night out with an open bar and free food. I just have to think positively. If I ask him to go with me as a friend, he's going to say yes. He's going to say yes because he's the kind of guy who, at fourteen years old, tied the skates of his sister's friend because her arm was in a cast then skated beside her for an hour in case she fell. The kind of guy who drove us to the mall with a smile on his face the first day he had his license. The type of man who becomes an EA, gets woozy at the sight of blood, and shares his lunch with flustered forgetful coworkers. *He will say yes,* I repeat until I drift off.

FOUR

FOSTER

I stifle another yawn as I stand in front of Sophie's office. I got to school early, wanting to make sure I had time to adequately thank her for what she did for me yesterday, but I seem to have forgotten that me being early doesn't make anyone else early. Now here I stand shifting from foot to foot, holding a Christmas tin full of chocolate chip cookies, practicing how to say thank you like a normal person whose breath isn't immediately stolen away by the other person.

I've lived so much between the last time I had seen Sophie and now, but I may as well be sixteen again.

When she finally comes around the corner, her head is bent as she searches for something in her bag. Just before she reaches me, she throws her head back, mouths a word that has no place in these halls, and turns, retreating in the direction she had just come from. Checking my watch, I see I've got about eight minutes before I need to be outside to greet my students so I stay where I am. I just have to hand the tin over, I don't need to stick around making small talk.

Five minutes later, Sophie scurries around the corner again, this time seeing me immediately. I won't pretend the smile I get from her doesn't do things to my insides. Saying hi seems inadequate. She deserves more than a two-letter greeting.

"Morning, sunshine!" comes flying out of my mouth before I even realize what I've just said.

She blinks back in surprise. "I haven't been called sunshine in years."

I'd have called you that every day if you'd been in my life. "Guess I'll have to make up for it."

"Go bananas," she says, unlocking her office and beckoning me to follow. "I forgot my fu– ugh, my lunch in the car." She looks apologetic. "I've really gotta get my language under control, sorry."

"It's okay. There are people who have been working here for years who still struggle. I've gone in the opposite direction."

"What's the opposite direction?" she asks, setting her bag down on her chair and turning to face me.

"Instead of saying the f word, I say something like..." I can't even say it now in the presence of an adult, as if my tongue has its very own censor. I don't plan what I say, so it takes me a minute to recall something that has escaped my mouth recently. The first thing I thought when I saw Sophie immediately pops into my head. "Holy moose muffins."

"'Holy moose muffins'? Are those muffins for moose or muffins made from moose?" she inquires.

"You know what, I've never thought that deeply about it, and surprisingly not a single one of my students has ever asked. Speaking of students." I sigh, glancing at my watch. "I've gotta get out to them. I'll see you later."

Sophie offers a small wave, and it's not until I'm walking outside that I realize I'm still carrying the tin.

"Mr. Walsh!" Pete happily calls the minute he's got himself balanced on his crutches. Despite the challenges that come with cerebral palsy, he's always got a smile on his face, a go-getter attitude, and way too much stuff in his pockets, which I can see are already bulging with today's treasures.

"Pete McGee!" I hold my fist out, and his much smaller one connects softly with it as he balances on one crutch. "What did you get up to last night?" I ask as we make our way into the school.

"I had a swimming lesson and then we got pizza."

"What did you get on your pizza?"

"Pepperoni and green olives," he says, looking up at me with a sly smile. He knows he's going to get a reaction out of me.

"Eeeeeewwwww," I whine. "Green olives are the worst green things."

"Worse than brussels sprouts?"

"A zillion billion times worse."

"Agree to disagree, Mr. W." He shrugs. "What did you do last night?"

"I had a swimming lesson too," I say, enjoying the shock on his face. He doesn't need to know that I was swimming through the dating pool.

"But you're old!"

"Hey now, I'm only twenty-eight. To some that's very young."

"But you're too old to learn how to swim."

"Not true. You're never too old to learn new things."

"Mr. Walsh, did you really have a swimming lesson?" Pete asks as he slides into his chair and begins to empty the contents of his pockets onto the desk. A few hockey trading cards, three game dice, some crumbled stickers, stegosaurus and triceratops figurines, and six individually wrapped Life-Savers. Less than I expected.

"Nah, I stayed home and baked cookies." I hold up the tin, dragging my eyes away from today's collection of pocket treasures.

"Are they for the class?"

"They're for Miss Hore, the new social worker."

"Why?"

"Because she did something nice for me yesterday so I made them as a thank-you."

"If I do something nice for you, will you make me cookies?"

"If I can find a good recipe for egg-, flour-, and butter-free cookies, I will definitely make you some."

He looks at me skeptically. "Never gonna happen. Mom gave up trying."

"Well, now that sounds like a challenge, and ya know what?"

"What?" he asks, his eyes narrowed.

"I love a challenge." I wink before going to hang up my coat and stash the cookies at the top of the closet.

"Any Oreos today?" Jessica asks as we walk our class to the gym for an assembly.

"I think I saw some crumbs, but nothing whole. He did have six peppermint LifeSavers, though."

"Wrapped?"

"Surprisingly, yes." We laugh, remembering the mess that a couple vegan caramel candies had made back in October.

"Well, I guess if I need to freshen my breath at some point today I know who to go to," she says as we file into the gym.

The assembly is not overly interesting, and Jess and I spend most of the time giving kids the stink eye for talking. The best part is when Principal Wong introduces Sophie and asks the kids to give her a warm Dundurn Elementary welcome. She looks nervous until the kids erupt. I think everyone in the gym falls a little in love with her when she smiles out at us. I whistle, and when her eyes find mine, I swear her smile gets bigger while my palms definitely get wetter.

"Miss Hore, he made you cookies." Pete points at me when he sees Sophie in the hall on our way back to class. Her eyes go wide.

"Me?" she asks, slowing to walk beside us.

"Yeah!"

"Just as a thank-you for yesterday," I say quickly.

"Oh, you didn't have to do that."

"Are you saying you don't want them?"

"You can give them to me." Pete looks over hopefully.

"Pete, stop being nosy," I scold. "Scoot!"

"I'm going as fast as I can." He pouts.

"You're moving at half your normal speed, buddy."

"Fine," he grumbles and picks up his pace. He's still not going as fast as he can, and he's not overly subtle about continuing to eavesdrop.

"So, sheep eat grain, and frogs like rain, and I hate

poison ivy," I say and watch as Pete stops and turns, looking confused. "See!" I exclaim. "Nosy!"

When I glance over at Sophie, she's looking at me like I've hung the moon. "What?"

"You're really good at this." She gestures between me and Pete.

"I hope so, or else I'm in the wrong profession."

"True." She reaches out like she's going to touch me and my skin preemptively tingles, but then she seems to think better of it and slips her hands into her pockets.

"I'm winning, Mr. Walsh," Pete cackles as he swings his crutches faster, starting to move at a decent clip.

I look at Sophie one last time, let my eyes roam over the side of her face as she looks down the hall at Pete. "I think he may just win this one." She peers over at me with a tiny smirk on her face. I don't know if it's a challenge, but that's how I take it.

"I'll stop by at lunch. Now, you'll have to excuse me, I've got a race to win." I wink at her before walking quickly after Pete who immediately speeds up.

"No way, Mr. Walsh," he shouts.

The hour between the end of the assembly and lunch drags like no other hour before it. Pete excels at math, which means I end up helping some of the other students who have a harder time with the subject. When the bell finally goes I practically run from the classroom, Pete's eyes on me and a knowing smile on his lips.

FIVE

The hour between the assembly and lunch flies by, and I'm left wondering how late I'm going to have to work in order to update the files I have on the go. I've only seen a quarter of the kids I have to meet, but at least only a few of the students will have regular sessions. I'll need to meet with teachers and the EAs as well. Hazel's notes are great, but I like doing my due diligence. Starting on a Thursday was not well planned, though; I'll have to wait until next week to get into any kind of rhythm now.

There is a knock at the door, and I instantly feel my face heat in anticipation of seeing Foster.

"Come in," I call out, sitting up straighter and brushing invisible hair off my face, looking up just in time to see the door swing open, revealing the man who has starred in way too many of my daydreams over the course of my life.

"Hey!" Why the hell do I sound out of breath? I've literally been sitting at my desk, exerting very little energy. *Calm the hell down, Soph. He's a friend, or he could be a friend. He's just an acquaintance now. Chill the fuck out.*

"Hey, sunshine," he says, stepping in and closing the

door. Why does he have to smile like that when he says sunshine? He says it like someone who has seen nothing but cloudy days for months. Had he said it like that when we were younger? When he'd said it this morning, he almost looked shocked, like he hadn't planned on using his old nickname for me. But goddammit, I hadn't realized how much I'd missed hearing him say it. No two syllables have ever sounded so good.

He holds up a Christmas tin and wiggles it. "Cookies?"

"You really didn't need to do that," I chastise while reaching eagerly for the tin.

"Same as yesterday, but I baked these last night."

"You never liked being in the kitchen when we were kids," I say, somewhat distracted by the pile of golden chocolate chip cookies before me.

He laughs. "Weird, eh?"

"Well, if this whole working-with-kids thing doesn't work out, you have a backup." I take a cookie and hold the tin up to offer him one.

He holds his hands up, politely declining my offering.

"Oh, come on, I feel rude eating in front of you."

"Fine, but you'll have to let me eat my lunch first. I'm a strict savory-then-sweet person."

"Okay, I definitely remember the opposite as kids," I say, pulling my sandwich out of my insulated lunch bag.

"I am a strict savory-then-sweet person post twenty-five," he amends, taking out three containers from his own bag.

"You've changed," I tease as I remove the lid from my sandwich container while watching Foster reveal his own lunch one container at a time. I have no idea what I'm looking at, but I know it's going to be ten times better than my turkey, mustard, and lettuce on whole wheat. "What did you get up to last night, other than preparing a gourmet lunch for today?"

He releases a deep sigh, and I see exhaustion settle into his features. "My friends are hyper-matchmakers. And I"—his *very large* hand splays dramatically across his chest—"am chronically single." A deep red blush spreads across his face at his admission. "I've been on roughly ten dates in the past month and a half with women they say are perfect for me. Last night's spent most of the date glaring at my tattoos in disgust."

"Tattoos?" Foster didn't have tattoos the last time I saw him, not that I could see anyway. Maybe they're in places that you can't see unless you reach that specific part of a date. The thought of Foster hooking up with some woman last night turns the cookie to dust in my mouth.

"Yeah, I've got a few," he says, pushing his sleeves up to reveal two formally bare arms covered in intricate designs.

"Holy sh– sugar cookies,"

He chuckles as I lean forward to study his arms. One is all *Lord of the Rings* scenes and characters seamlessly woven together. Nothing surprising there—on movie nights as kids he always suggested a *Lord of the Rings* marathon. I, of course, would have watched the weather channel if that's what he had suggested, but Cass never wanted to partake. The odd time she gave in, I spent most of the movie with my eyes on Foster, his eyes glued to the screen, his lips moving along with the characters. I was always stuck somewhere between desperately wanting him to look at me and dreading him catching me watching him.

His other arm is more random. A rabbit, teddy bear, and a tree I sort of recognize but can't place. Not a single one looks like it was done on the spur of the moment or as the result of too much alcohol.

"That's art!" I say indignantly. "How dare she not see that?"

"It's fine. She wasn't really my type anyway." His eyes dip to my lips, and I reach up to brush away the crumbs he's obviously noticing. "What about you? Have a hot date last night?" He looks genuinely pained asking me, probably just because he knows how crappy dating can be.

"Um, no, I won't be going on any of those for a while. I need to do a lot of inner work before I'll be ready for a date," I confess before stuffing the rest of my cookie into my mouth.

"Bad breakup?" he asks. I'm kicking myself for creating a choking hazard because the way he looks at me makes me want to tell him everything.

I swallow once I'm sure choking won't be a possibility. "It was," I start to say and then realize I don't care to sugar-coat the whole ordeal. "He's a professor, a wunderkind basically, and we were together for five years. I lived with him." *For him* goes unsaid. "Until he told me to move out because he didn't love me anymore and he didn't want to be in a relationship."

"He wasn't in love with you anymore?" he repeats slowly, as if trying to make sense of the words.

"I'm not sure he ever was, but he sure moved on fast."

"But he didn't want to be in a relationship anymore..." The words trail off as his expression hardens. It's not one I'm used to seeing on Foster. Anger and disbelief settle into his brows and his lips.

"Not with me. Apparently I was 'too old' for him."

"You're *twenty-seven*. Wait, were you dating Leonardo DiCaprio?" he asks, his face lighting up.

I snort. "No, definitely not Leo."

"How old is he?"

"Thirty-eight."

"And twenty-seven was too old for him?" His eyebrows arch so high, they nearly hit his hairline.

"Well, technically, twenty-six at the time of our breakup."

His lip curls. "That's...that's gross."

"The age difference? Because I was not opposed to that part," I admit.

"No, how at twenty-six you were too old for him."

"To be fair, he never actually said that, but his new girl-friend is four years younger than me. And I learned after the breakup that I was three years younger than his previous ex."

"Well, he clearly doesn't deserve you. There will be better things on the horizon," he says confidently, despite not making eye contact with me.

Better things, like going to a gala with you? I want to ask so badly, but it doesn't feel right yet. We may need a few more quiet lunches in this tiny space before I work up the courage. At least I know he's not in a relationship right now. Doesn't mean he won't be by the time I bite the bullet and bring this favor up.

Foster takes off five minutes before the bell goes so he can head out for yard duty, but before he goes, he insists on bringing me lunch tomorrow. Apparently my sandwich made him sad. And I am not in the habit of making hot ginger men sad.

SIX

SOPHIE

"Messy cabbage rolls." Foster swings the lunch bag back and forth as he enters my office three weeks to the day he shared lunch with me the first time.

"I love cabbage rolls," I exclaim as I start shoving things to the side of my desk so we have room to eat. One day I'll figure out a system where I'm not constantly having to do this. But clearing off my desk feels as ritualistic as Foster bringing me lunch at this point.

He never says anything about the mess or my perceived lack of organization, but I do know where everything is on my desk. No one else ever would, but I do, and that's what's important. My new pair of glasses on the other hand—well, those are lost somewhere between my house and this desk.

After a week of hiding in my office at lunch, I ventured into the staff room. It's nice to socialize a bit, but I find that I can't concentrate there if my life depended on it. So many conversations happening at once is a tad overstimulating, and my misophonia gets a bit out of hand in large groups between the smacking, slurping, and crunching. By the end of lunch, I find myself longing to be shut away in my broom closet. If Foster is closed in here with me, even better. He's also a quiet eater, which is a bonus.

"Did you watch *Top Chef* last night?" I ask, collecting cabbage and mince on my fork.

Foster nods but waits until he has swallowed to answer. "The blindfold challenge is one of my favorite ones."

"Would you want to do a challenge like that? Be blind-folded?" His hand stops in mid-air, his food forgotten in front of his lips, and the words finally make their way to my brain. *You're asking for taste purposes. He's not going to think you mean in bed. Right?* Not that I'm thinking of him in bed, except I definitely am now. Is that something he'd like? Is that something I'd like? You can do taste tests in bed. Lots of tasting can happen between the sheets, or on the couch, or in the backseat of a car, or the shower—oh my god, I'm off in sexy Foster land and can't seem to locate the exit.

"Truthfully, I'd like to do a lot of the challenges you see on cooking shows. Like..." He tips his head back, thinking and I zero in on his throat and the way it connects with a jaw sharp enough to cut glass. That's new. His jaw wasn't always that sharp. I wonder if he uses one of those jaw trainer things I've seen on infomercials at three a.m. "Boxes with ingredients. You know?"

Nope, I don't because I zoned out of the conversation and directly into that jawline. I don't need multiple conver-sations to distract me.

"I mean, they all sound fun to watch rather than to do," I admit, assuming I'm even close to answering what he asked.

"I'm sure a lot are way more fun to watch than do, but I have this weird desire to try them all." The grin he flashes isn't hiding anything other than an admission that he wants to try cooking challenges. *He is talking about cooking, Sophie, nothing more.*

"Hana Pearson"—Foster points at a little girl with her hair in long braided pigtails sticking out of her toque—"goes for tutoring three days a week before school. When she started the year she really struggled with reading, like three grades below where she should be."

"That's hard at this age," I say as I watch Hana throw a handful of fresh snow into the air and run under it as it falls.

"She's now doing better than just about every other kid in her fourth-grade class."

"Just from tutoring?" I ask in shock.

"Her tutor is a retired teacher, and she just uses a different style of teaching. It's been amazing to watch her grow." The pride in his voice is undeniable and annoyingly attractive.

The bell rings, and we stand at the side door as kids filter back into the school. I've been joining Foster on his yard duties when I have some time.

"Anything exciting planned for tonight?" he asks as we do a final sweep of the yard to make sure there aren't any rogue kids.

"I've got a Pilates class, and then I may visit with some friends. It depends if I can convince them to come with me or not."

"You like Pilates?"

"I do. I tried yoga for a bit, but I think my mind is a bit too active for an activity that isn't. Every time the instructor would tell us to quiet our minds or something, it was like a challenge to make mine even louder. I'd get stuck going down rabbit holes of lists and creating wild scenarios for things that will never happen."

"Like what?"

"What scenarios?"

He grins, his eyes flicking to the top of my head as if he'll be able to see something currently playing. "Yeah? What wild scenarios does that brain create, Sophie Hore?"

Why does he have to say my name like that? Why does my name sound like a luxury good coming out of his mouth?

"Oh, anything unrealistic, really. Like, it's supposed to snow tonight, and what if it snows to the point where I can't open my front door to leave? Do I have enough food to survive for days on end? Maybe I should go to the store and buy a bunch of random things and then I'll have all my cravings covered. What fruits or vegetables last the longest because I wouldn't want to get scurvy from eating only junk. But if I do get stuck in the house, that would be a great opportunity to sort through stuff. I could do a full cleanout of all the things I accumulate. Or I could finally sit down and watch *Game of Thrones* because I've been meaning to for a decade."

Foster is staring at me, mouth slightly agape. "And you're thinking all this while in downward dog?"

"I'm thinking all this *transitioning* into downward dog. Those thoughts are just the beginning."

"No wonder yoga didn't work for you. I can go on ten-mile runs and only think about the song that's currently playing, and even then it's like, 'this is a good song.'"

"Wow, you must get a lot done in a timely manner," I say in awe.

He shrugs. "I don't want to brag, but I can procrastinate pretty well."

"Oh yeah?"

"Oh yeah." He opens the door and gestures for me to go first.

I slip the minute my foot hits the floor beyond the now-soaked mats, and strong hands wrap around me.

"Careful." Warm breath brushes the side of my face, and I'm suddenly glad he's holding me up. "Wet floor." Foster lets me go once I've proven I'm not a fawn taking its first steps, and part of me wants to replay it over and over.

"Thanks." I smile awkwardly back at him.

"Any time, sunshine."

UNKNOWN

It's Foster, Cass gave me your number, I hope that's okay.

Foster Walsh is texting me, holy crap, like the holiest of craps. I see him nearly every day and yet seeing his number at the top of the message has me on the verge of a meltdown. A happy meltdown, but a meltdown nonetheless.

Of course!

I somehow manage to complete those two words without adding in unwanted letters or thirty exclamation marks.

Figured this way you can reach out if you get snowed in and need someone to dig you out. Or bring you food or watch Game of Thrones with you.

As if I'd be able to watch the show if he was sitting there with me. I'd be sitting there like, *oh my god, Foster Walsh is sitting beside me, in my house.* Then he'd ask if I liked the episode and I'd be all like, "oh yeah, it was great," even though if you asked me what happened, my only answer would be "well, Foster was there and I think maybe there was a dragon or something?" It would be like *Lord of the Rings* all over again. Must have something to do with fantasy.

> Good thinking! Just having someone to help shovel the driveway would be amazing!

I'd shovel your driveway any time, Soph.

That sounds like a euphemism for about seven other things, none of them involving snow removal.

> I wouldn't say no!

I add and then remove a winky emoji. This already feels like unsafe territory for reacquainted friends to be venturing into.

> What are you up to today?

Went for a run, now I'm being lazy.

> I think the run negates any claims of laziness. I am revoking any rights you think you have to laziness.

I look out the window at the miserable February weather. It's too gray, too slushy, too unwelcome on every level. Who runs in this? I bet he's cold. I bet I could help warm him up. *Oh, stop it, you delusional cow.*

SEVEN

I have a list on my fridge now of things I want to make for lunch. Recipes that will be good for dinner and then transition well for two lunches. Food that is interesting enough for me, but not too out there for Sophie. Who, to her credit, has eaten every single meal I've put in front of her and seems to have only struggled through the eggplant parm. I learned after that she thinks eggplant has the texture of an old crusty sponge, or what she thinks the texture would be like. I did confirm that she has not actually tried to eat one.

"What do you think Gary? Taco bowls for Monday? Maybe dumplings for Tuesday..." I trail off as I close the fridge finding Gary eyeing me from his perch on the counter stool. No doubt judging me for talking to a cat.

I get the beef started before beginning the prep on the veggies. Sophie was pretty insistent that I didn't have to make her food, but I'd told her that this sort of thing brings me joy. The me of ten years ago would be shocked by this development, but then again he'd be shocked by just about everything. He'd be pretty thrilled by all the Sophie time, though.

My phone buzzes on the counter, giving Gary an excuse to overreact and jump down from where he's been watching me for the last twenty minutes.

Dan's name appears, followed by Heather's.

DAN

I know you said you needed a break from the setups but our friend's daughter just got home from Korea and I think you two would hit it off.

HEATHER

If we are allowed to throw our hats back into the ring I've got the PERFECT person.

Weird, I didn't think Heather knew Sophie. Sweet potato fries, where did that come from?

I'm sure your friend's daughter is lovely and no one is perfect, H. I may have met someone but it's early days.

Bouncing belugas, what am I doing? I'm actively complicating a situation that's not even real.

HEATHER

WHO?

When????

Like I said, early days. That's all I'm going to say.

That's all I'm going to say because I have nothing else to say. I'm a liar, a spinner of tall tales.

DAN

Bring her to the BBQ.

HEATHER

Yeah, or else we won't believe you.

I roll my eyes and lock my phone. I don't have the desire to discuss this any further. Mainly because lying makes my stomach roll. When they find out the truth, I'll feel like a bigger fool than I already am.

Asking Sophie to go with me could be fun but how would that conversation even go? And why would I be inviting her? Have we settled into an easy routine in a short time? Yes, it feels a lot like old times. But I think if I asked her to go she'd feel like she had to say yes because that's the kind of person she is and my friends can be a lot.

"Mr. Walsh?" Pete says, looking up at me from the diagram of states of matter.

"Yes, Pete?" I reply as I struggle to get his pencil sharpener to actually sharpen a pencil.

"I want to run a marathon." I look up expecting to see his classic gotcha grin, but his face is set in a determined grimace. Like he's ready for me to tell him that's not possible.

I have to make sure I don't immediately write off this new aspiration. "Oh? What makes you want to run a marathon?"

"Cody Daniels said I couldn't."

"Well... that's probably one of the better reasons I've heard to run one."

"Have you run one?"

"No, but I've thought about it. I've run a half marathon.

Maybe you should—" He's already shaking his head before I finish.

"I want to run the whole thing."

"Well, okay. Do you know what it takes to run a marathon?"

"Big lungs," he says with conviction. "And a big heart," he adds.

Pete is one of those people who doesn't look at his disability as a barrier to anything he wants to do. The more someone tells him he can't do something, the more likely he is to try and prove them wrong. There's genuinely no point in telling him he can't do it.

So, instead of dousing the flames, I add fuel to them. "How can I help?"

"Pete said you're going to help him run a marathon," Sophie says from the doorway of the empty classroom where I'm pulling my jacket on.

I turn to see her leaning against the door, her long black winter coat hanging open, revealing a green button-up and black pants. I try and fail not to notice how good she looks in green. Her head tips to the side as she waits for me to answer.

"I did. I have no idea how I'm going to manage it, but I don't know, the kid's hopeful about everything. I couldn't bring myself to tell him that kids typically don't run marathons, let alone kids..." I don't finish the sentence, letting the reality of it hang in the air.

"I get it. He knows himself. He's one of the most self-aware kids I've ever met. Hell, there are adults who don't have that level of self-awareness. So," she asks as we head down the hall together, "how are you going to help?"

"For now I guess I'll just do a bunch of research. There have got to be people with CP who have run marathons and triathlons right?"

"Many. Several Paralympians and world champions too."

"You looked it up?"

"I did. The second Pete was gone, I got real down and dirty with Google." I look over to see her smiling brightly at me and feel an odd sense of jealousy toward the Google search bar. "It wasn't a comprehensive search by any means, but I was curious. Also, CP presents in a lot of ways. I don't think that's what will hold Pete back, if I'm being honest."

"I know it won't," I assure her. "What will hold him back is his age, and that's about it."

"Well." Sophie sighs as we walk through the door to the parking lot. "How can I help?"

During the first week of March, another blast of winter blows through, dumping two feet of snow on the city. I'm standing on the basketball court with Pete and a couple other students, stacking giant snowballs.

As I prop the third ball at the top, I see Sophie walking across the yard, something orange in her hands.

"Someone told me there was a snowman contest today so I brought adornments," she says, holding up two carrots.

"Two?" I ask, my eyes automatically going lower on the snowman.

When I look back up at her she rolls her eyes. "Men," she mouths. "I brought a nose for each team."

"You brought full carrots to work with you today?"

She laughs, the sound tinkling through the air like sleigh bells. She reminds me of that Disney princess. I almost expect cartoon rodents to appear.

"No, I had some time, and Jess mentioned what was happening this afternoon so I ran out to grab some."

I gesture at the head. "Go for it."

Sophie steps in front of me and twists the carrot into place. "You know what this snowman needs? A Twiz—"

"Twizzler," I finish and earn a big smile.

"You remember that?" she asks with wide eyes.

"Hard not to. My best friend ate half of them that night, and Cass was distraught the next morning when she discovered half the mouth missing."

Her eyes widen further. "It was you?"

"I just said it was my friend." I laugh, flicking snow at her.

She doesn't flinch, just steps closer. "You swore you didn't know what happened though. You swore on your PlayStation if I remember correctly."

I stand my ground, even though the smell of her hair hits me so hard I'd be wise to step away. "I really liked my PlayStation." I grin down at her. "I recall you liked it too." There were many nights that ended with Sophie and me on the basement couch, the sound of rapid clicking, grunts of frustration, and hushed celebrations the only evidence that we were down there.

We stand like that for a few more seconds until the sound of laughter breaks us apart. Pete is flat on his back giggling like a mad man. "I slipped," he squeals.

"You sure did," I laugh, walking over and helping him up. "You good though?"

"I'm grrrrrreat!" he cackles as he slips his left arm back through the ring on his crutch.

When I look back to where Sophie was, I see her back as she walks to the next snowman and pulls another carrot out of her pocket.

EIGHT

I slept like absolute shit last night because today is the day I'm doing it. I'm asking Foster to be my fake date to the gala. He'll be here in—I look up at the time on my monitor—six minutes. I have six minutes to panic and pull myself together. I can do this. I can do hard things, and on the scale of hard things, this isn't actually that hard. It may just be very embarrassing and make things extremely awkward for the foreseeable future.

There's a knock and a creak as the door opens and I look up in horror as Foster Walsh enters my office three minutes early.

"Hey," I say nervously as he sets our lunch on the desk.

"Hey?" He eyes me suspiciously while he unpacks everything. "What's up, Soph?"

Okay, Sophie, here it goes, remember the worst thing he can say is no. "So, I have a favor to ask and it's totally fine if you say no, don't feel like you have to say yes. I mean it's kind of bananas but I figured I'd at least ask because you're kind of the only person I know who would possibly do it and it's not like you're a stranger, I mean, I've known you since I was five and you were six and just because we haven't seen each other in years, anyway maybe I—"

"Soph," he interrupts, and I look up from where my eyes have landed on the Tupperware to see a soft smile on his face and I'm instantly calmer. "Just ask me."

Just ask me, he says, as if it's not a big deal. "Would you be my friend-date to an alumni gala in a couple weeks, on March thirtieth?" I say it so fast that I'm not sure he understands. "Again, you can say no—"

"I'll do it." *Holy shit, what?* "On one condition," he continues. I knew that was too easy. "My friends are hosting this stupid April Fools' barbecue and I could use a— what did you refer to it as? A friend date?" I nod. "Okay, you be my friend-date to the barbecue, and I'll be yours for the gala."

"Why do you need a date to a barbecue?"

"Remember those hyper-matchmaker friends I told you about?" I nod. "Well, they'll all be there. But if you come with me, maybe they'll actually give me a break."

"Wait, they won't know we're just friends?"

"Well, I was thinking that maybe we could pretend to be dating. I may have told them I was seeing someone, but didn't give them any information beyond that. I just needed a break from their relentless need to pair me off. But you don't have to agree to that. I'll still come with you regardless. I didn't mean to make it conditional."

"Actually, I wouldn't mind if that's the approach we took at the gala too. My ex will be there, and I'd really prefer not to go alone."

"Now, what are you wearing to this gala? Is it black tie?" Foster asks as he packs up our empty lunch containers.

"It's formal, not black tie. I don't even know why they call it a gala when it's really just a shameless attempt to get more money out of people. People talk, get awards, I'm being recognized—"

"Wait, what?"

"It's just a pat on the back for helping set up a mentorship program in the department. Nothing groundbreaking. And I don't even know what I'm wearing yet."

I swear his eyes sweep down my body, or maybe I just imagine it because now he looks like he's going to call me a silly goose or something equally adorable. "Recognition is a big deal, Soph. I can't wait to celebrate with you."

I believe those words. Then again, if he told me the moon was made out of cheese with that tone and expression, I'd believe that too.

I have to look away because it feels like my heart is going to beat straight through my chest. "I guess I need to get a celebratory dress then," I mutter.

"Yeah, you do. I've got a blue suit I can wear if that helps at all."

Keep your eyes on his. Keep your eyes on hi— dammit. I reprimand myself as eyes trail down to his trim waist and back up.

"That's good to know," I mumble so it sounds like one word. I'm screwed if just the *thought* of him in that suit is scrambling my brain.

"What about this one?" my friend Maya asks, holding up a strapless black satin gown.

I study it for all of three seconds before shaking my head. There's nothing special about that dress. Nothing that will fill Gregory with regret. Nothing that will fill Foster with— *No, do not go there. You're doing this for you,* I remind myself.

The need to do unspeakable things to you in the coat closet, the little voice rushes to say, my body heating at the thought.

We've been at the mall for an hour, and I've gone through every dress rack in every store that sells dresses. I haven't found a thing. Maya, on the other hand, has three bags dangling from one elegant hand while she uses the other one to flip through another round of dresses.

A gasp draws my attention in her direction as she pulls out an emerald green gown that has every hair on my body rising. "That's the one," I say without an ounce of doubt.

When I come out of the dressing room, Maya's face says it all. She motions for me to spin. The minute my back is to her she cackles maniacally. "He's going to come in his pants when he sees you in that."

"Maya, geez." I shush her but laugh when I see her face. She looks like an evil genius. "So I should get it?"

"If you don't, I'll never speak to you again."

"Yes, you will." I roll my eyes before going back into the change room.

"Okay, yes, I will, but I'll bring this up constantly as the day you damaged our decade-long friendship."

"Sure," I murmur, swaying slowly back and forth, admiring myself in the full-length mirror on the back of the door. Foster is going to be in blue; we'll look good together. Like two people who stood next to one another in the bathroom doing our hair. Like two people who woke up sharing the same pillow.

"Stop staring at your ass and get out here. We're going to be late for the movie." Maya's voice filters through the door.

"I'm coming, keep your panties on!"

"I'd say the same to you, but there's no way you'll be able to wear any in that dress."

Shit, she's right. I'll be going commando while going out with the hottest man I've ever met .

I wake up every single day and mentally slide a line through the date on the calendar. I'm a ball of nerves. It's like one of those balls made out of elastics, and each day I add another one.

Foster makes me nervous, but it's a good kind of nervous. The kind of nervousness that has me jumping out of bed in the morning and giggling when he compliments me on one of my patterned blouses.

During my second week I'd been wearing one with bees, and talking about various bees had been a gateway to a productive session with one of the kids. I went home and ordered a bunch of blouses with different flora and fauna. Foster telling me the idea was smart had me flying high for two weeks after.

"How many of those cows can you name?" one of the teachers asks me when I sit down at the table across from her in the staff room.

I look down at my blouse. "Six."

"Which one is stumping you?"

I point at the bright pink one and hear Foster laugh beside me. "She's good with cows."

"Oh yeah?"

"I grew up on a dairy farm," I admit.

She stares back at me as if the longer she looks she'll be able to smell the cow. "I would have never guessed it."

I don't know what to say to that so just offer a smile before stuffing my mouth with a garlicky roasted potato Foster brought as a side today.

The comment is still rolling around in my mind though. Should I be acting a different way? Be dressed in head-to-toe Wrangler jeans? I knew farm kids who were deeply entrenched in the life. They were born to work with their parents and then one day take over. I never once saw that as my future, nor was I ever pressured to make that my future. One of the reasons I loved going over to Cass and Foster's house was that I got to go to bed late and sleep in. There were often times I'd stay up even later than Cass just because Foster did. We'd play a game on his PlayStation or gossip. More than once I'd wake up on the couch in their basement with a blanket over me. I knew who put it there, even though we never acknowledged it.

The night before the gala I have a sudden worry about what I'll hyper-fixate on once I'm home tomorrow night. What if it's a disaster? What if I make a fool of myself? What if I cry? What if I lose it on Gregory's new girlfriend? What if people want to know what happened? Will Foster still want to be my friend if any of those things happen? What if the dress was a bad idea? Is it too low in the back? You can see the top of my ass. What was I thinking? I can't wear that around a bunch of academics. What if I trip walking up onto the stage to receive the pat on my back and bare my ass for all to see? Tears sting my eyes as a wave of dread overwhelms me.

Breathing slowly, I squeeze my eyes shut, trying to pull something out of my mind to focus on instead. Pete's new dedication to using his crutches less. My dad laughing over the phone last night when he was telling me about Mom mistakenly using salt instead of sugar on top of scones. Foster's smile every time he sticks his head around my office door. Foster's eyes lighting up when he talks about any of the students accomplishing something. Foster's voice when he's doing an impression of Pete. Foster.

NINE

Sophie had said she'd meet me at the gala, but I reminded her that if we wanted people to buy that I was her date-date and not her friend-date, it would look better if we arrived together. I've been super anxious about tonight but in a good way. Walking into an event like this with Sophie Hore on my arm? My god, dream come true.

I take three deep breaths before knocking.

"Hey, just give me one second," Sophie says, opening the door and immediately disappearing from sight.

"What if it was a murderer and not me?" I call out.

"No murderers are out at this hour," she hollers from somewhere toward the back of the house. "Oh, fucking fantastic!" I hear her curse, followed by the sound of something crinkling.

"Everything okay back there?"

"Yes, sorry!" She rounds the corner, looking down at the coat she's buttoning up, hiding most of her outfit from me. I can see that it's long and green, the fabric cascading below the hem of the coat. "The dry cleaning tag was pinned to the dumbest spot, and I ripped a button off when I pulled at it."

I step back to take her in. "I can't tell."

"Well, that's good. I guess it's not like I'll be wearing the coat for long, right?"

God, I hope not.

"Shall we?"

"Yes, please!"

I wait for her to lock her door then offer my arm. At first she looks at it like I've offered her a carrot. "Figured we should get into character sooner rather than later."

"Right." Her cheeks redden ever so slightly. "Because we are dating."

"That's the story I'm sticking to."

"Yeah, same, me too." She looks nervous, and I don't know if it's the thought of dating me, of pretending or just overall nerves about seeing her ex. But Sophie is going to enjoy her night if it's the last thing I do.

I watch her fidget for the entire twenty-minute drive to the gala. Her left foot in particular is keeping a beat I can't make out. Almost like it's at a rave for one. At some point I reach over and take her hand. I only mean to give it a squeeze to hopefully help calm her nerves, but when she squeezes back I can't bring myself to let go. So I just hold on, my thumb eventually drawing circles across the back of her hand. When we arrive and I have to let go, all I want to do is take her hand again, and so when we're both out of the car, that's exactly what I do. She even moves in closer as we walk toward the entrance, and when I offer to take her coat she lets me.

As the fabric comes away from her body, it feels like I'm opening my Christmas and birthday gifts all at once. Every time I think the skin will stop it doesn't. Once the coat is off

I can't bring myself to move. I am met by the sight of Sophie Hore's entire back, the dress starting again right above her perfect ass.

"Ticket, sir?"

"Wha... sorry?" I say, blinking away from Sophie's back and looking at the coat room attendant holding a ticket out for me, his other hand outstretched waiting for her coat. "Yes, sorry." I shake my head and make the exchange before repeating the process with my own.

"The blue suits you," she says, her eyes roaming over me.

"The blue suits that green," I say, following her lead and letting myself look at her. It's a good thing I've reached an age where I have some control over my body because sixteen-year-old me would be running and hiding in the bathroom right about now. Sophie looks like she was poured into the emerald green gown. From the front she appears fully covered, even her arms, but then she turns and it's all skin. And for all people know, all that skin on display is just for me. And tonight, I guess it kind of is.

"Let's do this, sunshine." I hold my arm out for her to take again, and she does without hesitation.

The ballroom is huge and teeming with people. I wouldn't be surprised if we go the whole night without running into Sophie's ex. That is until I hear her name being called and turn to see a man approaching, practically dragging a much younger woman behind him. Sophie tenses, and I move my hand to her back, momentarily forgetting that I'm about to place it on her bare skin. I slide it down her back and then possessively curl it around her hip so no one will question who she's with. I've never been one to play a game without plans to win it.

The guy seems to be coming in for some kind of physical greeting so I pull Sophie in tighter and angle us so if he tries for a kiss on the cheek he's going to get air or my shoulder. He bails almost as fast as he tries it, and when I glance at Sophie she's looking at me with relief.

"I was told you weren't going to make it. It's lovely to see you," the guy says, tugging the woman behind him so she is standing closer to us. He's posturing, trying to show Sophie who he replaced her with. And no offense to the poor woman, but she doesn't hold a candle to the goddess in my arms. When I look back at Soph, she's not looking at her ex but at the woman. She doesn't look upset or angry, just worried, and I don't blame her. Anger surges through me, imagining him dragging her around like that too.

"I changed my mind," she says, now looking up at me, a giant smile on her face. Her right hand lands on my chest, and the combination of the smile and her touch makes it hard to breathe.

"Dr. Gregory Dickson, keynote speaker for this evening," the guy says, holding his hand out in greeting. I spare it a glance before my eyes return to Sophie.

"If you'll excuse us, Soph and I were just going to find our seats." Ignoring his proffered hand, I let Sophie guide me around them toward the table we've been assigned to sit at.

"I won't lie," I say quietly, my lips nearly brushing her ear. "I've never felt the need to punch someone in the face for simply existing. What a hodenkobold."

"A what?" She stops dead and looks up at me.

"Hodenkobold?" She nods. "German for testicle gremlin."

She glances back to where we left Gregory and laughs. "He is definitely a hodenkobold with a very punchable face."

"I commend you for lasting five years without giving in." I look around and notice people are still mingling. "Do you want to sit now, or is there anyone you'd like to connect with, preferably someone a little less punchable?"

She smiles softly at me before looking around. "My friend Edwin is over there, let's go say hi."

She turns toward the group, worrying her lip. I reach up with my thumb and drag it out from between her teeth. "You're going to ruin your makeup, sunshine." I want to tell her that I'd like to be the one who does that, but I keep that to myself.

I hold my hand out and watch her transform from an uncertain person to one who's about to own this room the minute her fingers slide between mine. It's hot, and I have to remind myself that it's an act, albeit one I'm glad to participate in.

"Goddamn, girl!" The guy Sophie pointed out as Edwin says the minute he sees her. "I know what you're doing, but I have a feeling it's working too well. He hasn't taken his eyes off your sexy ass since you walked in." Sophie rolls her eyes and drops my hand to pull him in for a hug.

"I didn't know you were going to be here. Last I heard you were on the west coast trekking through rainforests searching for bears."

"I was, then I found one." He points at the man standing behind him. "Nolan, this is a former student turned friend, Sophie. And?" He turns toward me and looks at Sophie expectantly.

"Oh, sorry, Edwin, Nolan, this is Foster. Foster, Edwin and Nolan." We all shake hands, and once the greetings are out of the way, I wrap my arm around her waist again and relish the way she relaxes into me. Pretending to be into this woman is almost too easy.

TEN

Foster is proving to be an incredible actor. I think I may be too, but only because he's making it easy for me. When he slid his hand around my waist and rested it on my hip, leaning into him more seemed like the thing I'd do if this was real. Watching Edwin's eyes track the movement and then the smile that he tried to hide sends a shiver of triumph through me. We are nailing this.

"So what do you do, Foster?" Nolan asks, grabbing a passing appetizer and tossing it in his mouth.

"I'm an educational assistant," Foster replies, his thumb slipping under the edge of my dress where it opens at my hip. An entirely different kind of shiver runs through me this time.

"Cold?" he asks, moving his attention from Nolan and Edwin to me.

"Nope." I smile innocently back at him.

"My cousin is an EA. You people are saints," he exclaims.

Foster shrugs. "Just patient. I'm definitely not a saint." And fuck me sideways, upside down, and right-side up because the little grin he includes has me thinking things a friend should not be thinking.

Nolan looks over at me and bounces his eyebrows. "Lucky lady!" Okay, so I'm not the only one who read a bit more into that.

I laugh, probably a bit too loud, before looking up at Foster to find those amber eyes already on me. He's too fucking good at this. At this rate I'm going to be his first cult follower.

"Yes, definitely lucky." I pull my lip back between my teeth, looking up at him through my eyelashes and he does exactly what I hoped he'd do.

His featherlight touch somehow reaches to the back of my knees as he pulls my lip free with his thumb again. "Only I get to mess up those lips, babe." He grins again. *Yes,* I think, *I want that.* I just hope he never calls me Gregory's preferred term of endearment again.

I somehow manage to keep it together and play along. "I do like when you do that." We haven't looked away from one another, and it's as if the room has entirely faded away. Until Nolan or Edwin clears his throat. "Would you believe he bakes me cookies?" I say almost giddily, turning back to them.

I watch as Edwin does a full-body scan of Foster with his eyes narrowing. "No one that looks like you should be able to bake and be good in bed. It's not fair."

"Hello! If everyone could take their seats, dinner is about to be served." The announcement saves us from further discussion on what else Foster is too good-looking for. It doesn't stop me, however, from wondering just how good he is at all the things.

As we make our way back to the table my heart plummets. Gregory, always a gentleman in public, is pulling out his girlfriend's chair. Foster squeezes my hand again and as we reach our seats he pulls me closer, his lips settling next to my ear.

"You've got this, sunshine, and I've got you." His whisper sweeps across my skin, sending more tingles to far more intimate areas than the back of my knees.

I draw back a little so I can look him in the eye. "I'm going to owe you cookies after this."

"You haven't met my friends yet," he says, pulling my chair out. "You'll probably be expecting cookies for life."

"You say that like it's a bad thing." I sit, doing my best to keep my focus on him. I can feel the asshole's eyes on me, and it turns my stomach. "Just no raisins. I had a bad experience as a child."

I see his shoulders shake in a silent laugh as he sits next to me, sliding his chair a bit closer so he can rest his arm on the back of mine. Every movement he makes seems so natural, to anyone else it would look like he does this all the time.

"That time you sneezed while eating an oatmeal raisin cookie and a raisin got lodged in your nose?" he says it so casually, as if he didn't just pull a memory from when I was ten out at the drop of a hat.

"You remember that?"

"Hard not to. Cass thought you were going to die."

"She has always been the dramatic one," I say as his finger trails over my shoulder, sending sparkler-tinged chills down my arm. *Now who's being dramatic?*

"I remember Cass freaking out, then my mom running out of the house expecting to see blood everywhere or something and there you were, eyes watering and looking worried. She had you blow your nose really hard and out came the raisin."

"Then Cass gagged for about half an hour." The entire scene is becoming clearer now. "And you wanted to see it."

"It was disappointing. All that fuss for what was essentially a wet raisin." He tips his head back and laughs, and I am momentarily mesmerized by the way his throat moves. "I don't think Cass has ever recovered. You were pretty chill, though."

"Well, a wet raisin doesn't really hold a candle to the sight of calves being born. That being said, it took all the joy out of eating raisins."

His left eyebrow arches high, pulling his lips up on one side. "I'm more surprised you ever found joy in eating raisins."

A sudden flurry of activity distracts us both, and I realize that while we were discussing the great raisin extraction of yesteryear servers have placed bread and big bowls of salad on the table. Several other people have joined us as well, and I'm happy to discover that the woman sitting next to Gregory has pulled his attention away from me.

"Don't judge me too harshly, but I love a banquet-style salad," Foster says, holding the bowl out for me so I can serve myself.

"Why's that?"

"They always have those little hot peppers." I look down at my plate, and sure enough, a pepper is peeking out from below some shockingly pale iceberg lettuce.

"Do you want mine?" I spear it with a fork and hold it out to him. Instead of plucking it off and putting it on his plate he drags it off my fork with his teeth, pulls off the stem, and chews like he's in heaven. How the fuck is that so seductive? "Good?"

"Judging by the lettuce, that will probably be the culinary highlight of the night," he whispers while passing the bowl to his right.

"The food at this thing has never been spectacular." I shrug and move the salad around my plate.

"Be careful with that one," I hear Gregory say, and the hairs on the back of my neck stand on end. "The salad has chickpeas. Might be too exotic for our girl Sophie."

Before I can say anything though, Foster's hand gives my knee a squeeze. "Huh," he says thoughtfully. "Ya know, I've never had a problem with making her food she likes. Hell, we had Korean the other night, and she had seconds. Then she thanked me for..." He stops, pretending to think. "What was it, like two hours?"

"Oh, at least," I confirm. "But you're forgetting the balcony, I think." I watch Foster bite the inside of his cheeks, trying not to laugh.

A choking sound comes from across the table, and we look over to see Gregory dab the corners of his mouth. "I guess one is never too old to learn to like new things," he says with a sneer.

"You've made that quite obvious," Foster mumbles, earning a glare from my ex and a confused look from his date.

The exchange between them seems to have ended Gregory's desire to engage further, and we spend the rest of the meal talking to the people on either side of us until the speeches. Gregory stands at the podium looking out across the ballroom before his eyes land on me. He looks at me the way he did when we first got together, when he wore a veil to hide the kind of person he really is, and I feel sick.

"I'm just going to run to the washroom," I whisper to Foster.

He turns back to me looking concerned. "You alright?"

"Oh yeah, fine," I lie before rising and walking briskly from the room.

In the washroom, I stand in front of the mirror trying to calm my mind. I hate the effect he still has over me. I thought I'd show up here and power through, and I think I'm pulling it off, on the outside at least. On the inside, it feels like bugs are crawling beneath my skin. Just as I feel like I can go back out and face him the door opens, and his date walks in. I don't mean to stare at her, but once my eyes lock on her, it's like I'm in a trance.

"Um, are you okay?" she asks, looking partly concerned but mostly terrified.

I bet everything with him is wonderful, right? He showers you with gifts and praise. I bet you've eaten at all the best restaurants in the city and you feel lucky to be on his arm. He's probably jumped enthusiastically into your life, taking an interest in everything that means something to you.

I blink several times, slowly realizing not a word came out of my mouth and I've just been standing here staring with my face on fire.

"The left sink isn't working," I stammer before brushing by her and rushing back to the table, to Foster.

Gregory is still talking, and I hope for his girlfriend's sake he didn't notice her leave during his time in the spotlight.

"Good?" Foster asks when I sit down, concern etched on his handsome face.

"Um, I'm just a bit nervous," I admit, forcing myself to take a sip of my lukewarm wine.

The rest of Gregory's speech is a blur of soft touches from Foster, as if he's reminding me he's there. When my name is called from the stage, I desperately wish I could grab his hand and bring him with me. I don't want to be up there with Gregory. I don't want to be anywhere near him ever again.

I rise slowly and look up to find Foster standing as well. He pulls me gently into his body and drops his head to whisper in my ear. "You've got this. You've earned it, sunshine."

He gives my hand a quick squeeze and I turn to the stage with my head held high.

"I knew this program was a good idea, and I can recall many nights of talking Soph into it. So in a way you have me to thank as well. Sadly, there is only one plaque, and my walls are pretty full as it is." I keep the smile plastered on, but inside every muscle tenses as I cringe at his narcissistic diatribe. The crowd laughs, of course; they always do. He's the golden boy, the favorite son. They clap and cheer and throw funding at him, and his ego grows and grows.

On the stage, Gregory hands me the plaque with one hand but pulls me against him with the other. "Maybe you can thank me for this in my office later, baby," he whispers. "Like old times." The fake smile falters for the briefest moment, but he's made sure I'm the one on the outside, I'm the one everyone can see, so I force it back into place.

When he backs away and lets me step to the podium, I thank my colleagues who helped make the program possible. I keep my eyes on Foster the whole time, loving the way his hard gaze remains squarely on Gregory as if he heard what he had said. Foster is so often smiling that his expression halts me mid-sentence. As if me stopping snaps him out of it, he turns his eyes to me and a soft smile appears. I finish my little speech, leaving Gregory out of it entirely and then brush off his attempts of guiding me off the stage with as much grace as I can muster.

Back at the table, Foster stands as I approach and pulls me in for a hug before I can sit down.

"What did he say to you?" he asks quietly, his voice so deep I can barely hear him.

"Nothing," I say, leaning back and smiling at him. "Nothing important anyway."

He looks like he's going to push me, but he just gives a single nod and lets me sit down without any more discussion.

When the dance floor opens, Foster pulls me to him and we sway slowly together. "Remember the senior dance in elementary school?" he asks, his mouth right beside my ear.

"The one where you danced with a group of us because the other boys pretended they wanted to, only to then ignore us for the whole night?"

He pulls back, looking confused. "There was a whole group?"

"Yeah, and you danced with each of us. You made a big show of it too. Bowed when you offered me your hand." I laugh, remembering the flourish of it and the anxious anticipation of laying my hand in his. I'd been jealous of the other girls he'd offered his hand to until it was my turn.

"I hope my skills have improved since then."

"Definitely," I sigh, laying my head on his chest. His cheek comes to rest on the top of my head, and I catch a thumbs-up and okay signal from a couple of my former colleagues at the university.

I see Gregory look at me a couple times. See him chatting to Edwin and gesturing toward me and then the look on his face when Edwin says something with a knowing grin. I know he's trying to get intel. Trying to find out who this man I turned up with is.

Foster's arm tightens a little more, and I slide my hand

down his back, stopping just above his ass, and a loud, somewhat nervous laugh bubbles out of me. Gregory wouldn't recognize it; it was always forced with him.

"Thank you for going with me tonight," I say, turning in my seat toward Foster when he pulls up in front of my house.

"I had fun, despite the hodenkobold, of course. Did you have a good time?"

I take in his hopeful expression and realize that while the night was tainted, I did actually have a pretty decent time. "Thanks to you. What time should I be ready on Sunday?"

"I'll pick you up at 11:30 if that's alright?"

"Should I be prepared for hijinks and tomfoolery?"

"Absolutely." He flashes me a mischievous grin.

"Excellent," I say, stepping from the car. "I love me some tomfoolery."

I've been nervous about our little arrangement, but after how easy being with him tonight was, I'm already very much looking forward to Sunday. Even if it confuses my heart more.

ELEVEN

FOSTER

I'm baking cookies at three in the morning because I can't sleep. Every time I closed my eyes I could see his eyes on her, could feel her tense beneath my touch when she felt them. It wasn't the playful interactions or the feel of her skin beneath my fingertips that kept me up. It was purely her discomfort. Eventually, I gave up trying to sleep and got up to focus on something else.

My phone lights up just after I put the first batch in the oven.

SUNSHINE

What does one wear to an April Fools' BBQ?

Why are you up?

Why are you?

Couldn't sleep.

Same! So I'm planning what to wear.

Whatever you want!

> So if I show up in a bikini that's okay?

I stare at my phone for a bit trying not to imagine Sophie walking out to my car wearing nothing but a bikini. I fail.

> You may be chilly but I won't stop you.

> HA! So a sweater and jeans is acceptable?

> That's probably a better choice. Should we coordinate again?

> Surprise me!

> Deal!

I'm about to ask what she'll do once she's picked her outfit out, but before I can she's calling.

I hit accept, and her face fills the screen. "Good morning, sunshine!" I say as cheerily as I can manage this early.

"Barely morning." She yawns. "So who are you thanking this time?" I don't answer right away because I wasn't ready for three a.m. Sophie and I'm a little mesmerized by the messy hair, glasses, and makeup-free face. Even at this hour she's the sun breaching the horizon.

"Thanking?" I stammer.

"With the cookies. Or are they 'just because' cookies?"

"Ah. They're 'it's three in the morning and I can't sleep' cookies."

"Why can't you sleep?"

"Why can't you sleep?" I turn the question around.

"I kept replaying what I didn't say to his girlfriend in the bathroom." She groans. "I don't think I should have actually said anything, but I just stood there staring at her for way too long."

"How did she react?" I ask as the timer on the oven goes. "Just a sec." I pull the cookies out quickly and turn my attention back to my phone. "Sorry, continue."

"She looked worried." She shrugs and wiggles her nose. God, she's adorable. "So, why are you awake so early, Mr. Walsh?"

I can't say *because I was worried about you* so I play dumb. "No idea. Maybe I could sense you worrying and I have sympathy insomnia." Okay, so I've basically just admitted it. I turn away from the screen to transfer the cookies to the cooling rack and then begin putting raw scoops onto the pan. When I turn around, she's eating a cookie.

"Are you bringing cookies on Sunday?" she asks, brushing crumbs from the corner of her mouth. I don't know why the action has my tongue sneaking out to the corner of my own.

"Ugh, no. Dan wants people to bring booze. If you show up with food, you won't be invited back."

"Wait, seriously?"

"Seriously. He takes it as an insult, like we don't think he can cook. And truth be told, sometimes he can't."

"Any bad experiences in particular?" She takes another bite and leans forward, ready for some hot gossip.

"Let's see..." She's turned my brain to molasses by simply existing, or maybe it's just the early hour. "He once baked bacon on a pan with holes. I think it was a pizza pan. He thought it would crisp up better to have 'more air flow.'" At first I think the screen is frozen because Sophie is sitting there with her mouth open.

"Is he a bad cook or just dumb? Should I bring a fire extinguisher, or have 911 at the ready? I have a friend who's a firefighter. I could call her so she's prepared."

"Definitely reach out to the friend. He tends to get experimental with the menu for this one. I suppose that makes us all the fools for still showing up."

"I'm genuinely looking forward to it." And by the look on her face, I don't doubt it. "Any asshole exes I should know about?"

"Thankfully no, all friends."

"Oh." She yawns again. "Excellent, less drama that way."

"Do you want to try and get some sleep?"

"I'll try when you're done baking, unless you want to be alone."

"Nope, it's nice to have some company for pre-dawn baking." Would it be better if she was here in person? Absolutely, but I'll take whatever time I can with her when we aren't squished in her tiny office or surrounded by coworkers.

"Do you ever eat any of the cookies you bake?" Sophie asks, taking a bite of another cookie.

"Probably too many of them," I admit. "I bike, run, and box to make up for the cookie eating."

"You box?" She looks surprised.

"Don't I look like a boxer?"

"Honestly? No."

"I'm not sure if I should be offended," I say, holding up my arms and flexing. "These things can throw some punches."

She giggles, dare I say adorably. "You don't look like you've ever been punched in the face," she says and then seems to realize what she's been implying. "I don't even know what I mean by that. I guess when I think of boxers they have obvious signs of sustaining some kind of trauma." She waves a hand over her face.

"Maybe I'm just really good at dodging fists?"

Her eyes narrow at me. "Are you?"

"I don't box seriously, so there are no headshots allowed. Most of my time is spent punching the stuffing out of a bag."

"Really? You punch the stuffing right out of it?" she teases.

"Well, I am good at shifting it." I grin and watch as she yawns again. "Hey, when these cookies are done in"—I look over at the timer—"four minutes, I'm going to try to get some sleep, so you should probably do that too." She opens her mouth to argue with me. "Don't let him rob you of one more second of sleep, sunshine."

She watches me for another minute then nods. "You're right. He's fucked up enough of my nights." Sophie's sad eyes are endless pools of despair, and I have this need to coax the light back into them. Before I can say something to lighten the mood though, I see her eyes widen. She's looking behind me so I turn just in time to see Gary grab a cookie from the rack. He doesn't get far with most of it before it breaks apart.

"Chesapeake Bay! Gary!" I scold, chasing after him. I don't even know if cats can have chocolate, but I don't feel like paying a vet bill to find out. He doesn't get far because my apartment isn't large, but by the time I get him he's licking his lips.

"You have a cat?" Sophie asks, when I step back in front of the phone.

"Yeah, he was Cass's idea of a housewarming gift."

"Did he come from Bennett's?"

"He wasn't there for long, but yes."

"Oh yeah, they don't like to keep cats for too long. With all the dogs, it can be stressful for them." "Them" is elongated as she fights another yawn.

"Okay, seriously, go to bed," I insist as the timer goes.

"Good night, Mr. Walsh." She smiles and waves before the screen goes dark and I'm left looking at my reflection.

I begin cleaning up while Gary weaves between my feet meowing at me. "I know, man. I'm screwed. I don't need a lecture."

I do eventually fall asleep while I create a mental list of how to keep the light shining brightly in Sophie's eyes.

TWELVE

SOPHIE

I manage to sleep through brunch with friends, but Maya isn't going to let me stay at home in my pajamas all day, which is why I'm now standing outside of a home goods store waiting for her.

"It would be so much more acceptable if you'd bailed on brunch because you were wrapped around a tattooed ginger giant," she yells from an inappropriate distance.

I tip my head back and take a deep breath. *I love her,* I remind myself. She opened her home for me when Gregory kicked me out. She's a good friend. She wants only good things for me.

She greets me with one of her bone-crushing hugs. "You were missed," she huffs. "Yas could have used your smile. I can tell she's nervous about Miguel's recovery."

Yasmine has been there for me since I got lost on campus my first week of university and guilt gnaws at me. Her fiancé had a heart transplant two weeks ago, and I haven't seen her yet. "I'll call her later to see when a good time to stop by will be. What are we looking for again?"

"New bedroom lamps. "

"What's wrong with the ones you have?" I'd been with her a year ago when she had moved into her new place and had raved about the vintage lamps she'd found for her side tables.

"Davis happened."

"Davis?"

"Hinge date. He was..." She looks at me and grins. "Acrobatic."

"Gotcha." I nod in understanding. "So are we looking for Davis-proof replacements or..."

"What a fun indirect way of asking me if I'll be sleeping with him again." Maya laughs but doesn't elaborate, so I drop it.

"So did the alumni people buy your fakeship?" Maya asks while we browse a row of new lamps made to look old but with a price tag of an original Van Gogh.

"We deserved an Oscar for our performance. I was so nervous, but I really had no reason to be. Gregory spent most of the night glaring at him."

"Oh, we love a jealous ex!" She smirks while flipping over the tag of a pair of blue and gold lamps. "What do you think of these?"

I walk over to examine them closer. "I think they will break even faster than the other ones."

"Ugh, you're right, but all the durable lamps are repulsive," she insists.

"I mean, you could find someone who's less... what did you say? Acrobatic? Or forego bedroom sex altogether to avoid the risk of breaking another lamp."

"I'd rather break another lamp." She flips the tag over again and sighs. "I think I have to get these."

"Why don't you think about it for a day, and if you still want them after a few hours, come back tomorrow?"

"Sophie, you know the rules at this place. If you don't buy it now, it's... poof, zap, dab."

"Dab?"

"Gone!" She throws her hands out dramatically.

By the time we walk out, Maya is carrying a bag with two new lamps and a basket she claims she has to have to keep her throws in.

"So date number two tomorrow?" Maya asks after she slides into the passenger seat.

I glare over at her. "Your car is fine, isn't it? You wanted a ride home so you could get me alone to ask me questions."

She looks over with a huge smile. "Guilty! Also I wanted more than one mimosa at breakfast, and also, climate change. It was a win-win-win."

"*Friend* date, outing, whatever number two is tomorrow, yes. I have no idea what to expect. Who the hell has an April Fools' barbecue?"

"Full disclosure, it totally seems like something your dad would have."

I snort because she's right. "He totally would. Just to be different."

"I say embrace the different. Especially when it's the kind of different that gets you more time with Foster. And I know, I know, you're not ready. But there is nothing wrong with testing the waters. Consider this practice for what a healthy relationship looks like."

"Maya, we are *pretending* to be a couple. I'm not sure that's healthy."

"It is if it's for your own sanity. His friends stop throwing women at him, and Asshat McPrickface thinks you've moved on and he hates it." She does have a point there. Although I've been wrestling with some not-so-great feelings since last night. He may be annoyed that I appear to have moved on, but seeing him had a negative impact on me both mentally and physically. It felt good being out with Foster, but the happy mask slipped off the minute he drove away. It's exhausting to act fine. It's hard to feel extreme happiness because I'm with one of my favorite people while also feeling like I have to be on guard for certain behaviors and fearing that I'll miss the signs again because someone is making me feel good.

"Listen." Maya takes my hand. "I know there's a lot you haven't told me, but if you are ever ready, I'm here and I promise to keep my judgments locked up, unless you want them."

"I love you, do you know that? Like a whole lot."

"Yes, I do. You're not capable of half-love, Soph. You love with every atom of your being."

That's one of my fucking problems.

At home I flop down on the couch and let my mind wander instead of tackling the two laundry baskets of clean clothes that need to be folded and put away. I'm tired. Between the lack of sleep the past couple of nights and the anxiety of preparing for the gala, it feels like my entire body is about to shut down.

I'm swamped but nowhere near as swamped as the educational assistants. I'd heard how bad things were, but I don't think it sunk in until I witnessed it. There are sixteen students who require physical or mental assistance. Many require both, and there are only six EAs. My tiredness is nothing compared to theirs.

Last Wednesday, I ran into Principal Wong in the hall after walking with Pete back to class. She caught me lingering outside the classroom as I watched Foster welcome him back. She told me that when Foster had arrived at the school two years ago Pete was drawn to him immediately. Foster claims it's because they're both gingers, I think it's because Foster has that something. When he's around, it feels like things are going to be okay. I don't think I realized how badly I was in need of that until recently.

In our session on Friday, Pete told me he's scared about leaving the school or Foster changing schools because he makes it easier to be there. Pete's teacher informed me one day at lunch that his self-confidence has improved notice-ably since Foster's arrival, and for math and science he was confident enough that Foster was able to go assist other students. The other EAs seem just as passionate about ensuring their students get to experience school as normally as possible. And despite being short-staffed, I've been amazed at how they come together to support one another.

I wake up on the couch with every muscle screaming at me. Blinking sleep from my eyes, I flip my phone over. It's six thirty, and I've missed two calls from my mom. I'll call her tomorrow morning, probably bright and early since I've fucked over any chance I have of sleeping tonight. *You get to hang out with Foster tomorrow,* a little voice cheers. I let myself sink back into the couch with that thought soothing me.

THIRTEEN

Sunday morning arrives, and I finally feel the past week in my body. A decent sleep last night was helpful, but one night of sleep is not going to make up for several busy days and restless nights in a row.

Forcing myself out of bed, I change into my sweats, slip on my running shoes, grab my headphones, and head out into the dawn of April first for a quick five-kilometer run. Up with the sun in five-degree weather. I really am the king of fools today. When I turn back onto my road, Styx filters through the headphones and I slow my pace to "Renegade." My sister says I have the playlist of a middle-aged man, but it's what gets me moving.

My phone vibrates while I'm stretching, and when I see who it is, I stop immediately.

SUNSHINE

What kind of booze should I bring? I picked up a bottle of red, white, rose, and Prosecco. Or is that not boozy enough?

> You don't have to bring anything. I've got us covered.

Foster, I can't show up without a sacrificial bottle of something. I want to be invited back.

She wants to be invited back.

Before I can answer, a text from Cass pops up.

LILWALSH

I have to bail on a concert I have tickets to with Sophie. I'm going to suggest she asks you to go. DO IT.

> What concert?

Does it matter?

Of course not, but I'm not telling her that.

> Yes.

Nyx Avalon on Thursday night.

A pop artist with a dumb name on a school night. I could not think of anything worse—but going with Sophie *does* sweeten the deal.

> What are you going to do for me?

Other than give you a free night out with my amazing best friend to go see one of the best live shows out there?

> I don't know any of her music!

You have the internet, use it!

> Come on, she can't go to a concert alone,
> that's just sad.

> She has loads of friends, one of them
> would probably go.

> You don't think I reached out to them first?
> Hate to burst your bubble bro but you were
> not my first choice.

> Fine. But only cuz you asked so nicely.

> You're second best!

> How am I still second best?

> Sophie will always be the best.

Well, she's got me there.

Before I get in the shower, I select a "Best of Nyx Avalon" playlist, and my crash course in Nyx's entire catalog begins while I wash my workout and another busy week from my body.

"I am bringing all the options. Dan is going to love me." Sophie holds up three slender gift bags.

"You really don't need to. I've got a bottle of rye for him."

"Dan will love us both then," she says matter-of-factly and hands me the bags while she locks the door. "Unless," she says, whirling back around, "three bottles makes me look desperate and that I'm trying to compensate for being your fake date." She snatches two of the three bags back, opens the door back up, and sets them to the side before repeating the locking-up process. "Prosecco it is."

"No one is going to know this"—I gesture between us—"is fake."

"I mean, we did a fantastic job on Friday, but that was a busy event with hundreds of people. There wasn't as much scrutiny as there will be today," she says, paling. "These people *know you*, know you. You aren't just a person they saw at work."

I reach out and take her hand as we walk to my car. "Hey, if they find out the truth, it's not the end of the world. I'll take their meddling over your discomfort. If at any time you feel like you can't carry on the charade, just say the word, okay? Regardless, it's going to be a good time." The look Sophie gives me is a mix of relief and awe, like she cannot believe I would release her from our deal.

Then her eyebrows pinch together. "What word?" she asks seriously.

"Oh, not a word-word, just say you're done."

She comes to a stop on the sidewalk and her hand slips free of mine. "But now I think we should have a word."

"Snuffleupagus," I suggest.

She thinks for a moment, then nods. "That's a good one. People don't tend to bring it up too often."

Nyx Avalon blares through the speakers when I start the car, and my hand flies to turn the volume down. "Sorry about that." I laugh nervously.

Sophie leans forward and scrutinizes the screen before looking over at me, her blue eyes wide. "*You* like Nyx Avalon?"

"Um, she's growing on me."

"When did she start growing?"

I look at the time. "About three hours ago."

"I'm going to see her on Thursday with Ca... Wait." She holds up a finger and turns her attention to her phone. "You?" she asks, turning slowly toward me.

"Apparently." I shrug. "Cass texted me this morning saying she couldn't make the concert and begged me to take her place."

She's staring at me in disbelief, and I focus on the drive instead of on her expression.

"You don't have to go with me, ya know. I am sure I can find someone who'd take the ticket. In fact, I know a few people at the board who would probably fight for it."

"You'd rather go with someone you barely know over me?" I pout.

"I barely know *you*." She puts emphasis on the "you" to really stick it.

"Ouch!" I lay my hand on my chest. "And here I thought we were going steady."

"You know what I mean." I can actually hear her eyes roll.

"I haven't changed much since the days you spent half your time in my house."

"That guy cursed and couldn't stand kids," she counters.

"That guy turned into this guy," I say, pressing my finger into my chest. "A guy who curses creatively and enjoys working with kids. But otherwise, he's still the same guy."

"Well, you better not complain or make fun of how into the music I'm going to get."

"Sunshine, I am looking forward to how into the music you're going to get." I flash my flirtiest grin and watch as her cheeks pink.

By the time we pull up in front of Dan's house, I think

I've got one verse of a Nyx song down. I'm not going to throw myself on the altar of Nyx Avalon yet, but I'm starting to see the appeal. Watching Sophie bop to the beat out of the corner of my eye may have been the most appealing part.

There's a sign on the door that tells us to walk in.

"So it begins." I take Sophie's hand, open the door, and we are immediately hit with the smell of latex as we walk into a wall of yellow balloons. It's not only a wall, though—the balloons continue in every direction and I'm immediately disoriented.

"Which way?" Sophie asks from beside me, and when I look down at her, her hair is standing in all directions from the static the balloons are causing. The yellow is reflecting off her hair, and she has never looked more like sunshine than at this moment. "Foster." She gives my hand a tug, and I blink out of my stupor.

"I have no idea." I chuckle.

"Marco?" Sophie yells, catching me completely off guard.

Moments later, a disembodied voice comes from somewhere to our left. "Polo!"

Sophie pulls me in the direction the response came from and calls out "Marco?" again. After a few steps, my shin connects with something hard and stationary.

"Figgy pudding!" I curse, reaching down to rub my leg.

"You okay?" Sophie's other hand wraps around my forearm, her eyes full of concern.

"I'll live." I wince, the pain dissipating immediately when I see how the balloons cast a brilliant yellow across her face. Sunshine.

We eventually make it through the cloud of balloons and are greeted by Dan and his wife Maria who each hand us a drink in greeting. "Happy April Fools'!" they say in unison.

"Um, Happy April Fools'," Sophie says back with some uncertainty.

"You need to move whatever is in there. I smoked my shin off it," I inform them, pointing behind us.

"You shouldn't do that, it'll hurt." Dan grins at me before sticking his hand out to Sophie. "Welcome, I'm Dan. This is my wife Maria."

"Hi! I'm Sophie, but you probably already knew that. Thanks for having me," Sophie says, shaking both of their hands and then looking down into the glass she's holding.

I ask the question I know she's wondering. "So what's this year's drink?"

"That there is Joker Juice. Take a sip and tell me what you think is in it."

Sophie is still looking inquisitively into her cup so I take one for the team. Except when I tip the cup only a dribble of liquid comes out. The remainder of the green substance stays firmly inside the glass. "It's Jello!" Sophie looks up smiling. "With"—she smells inside the glass—"water?" When she looks up she freezes as both Dan and Maria are staring at her. "Did I ruin the prank? I did, didn't I? Oh my god, I'm a walking party pooper."

"I'm actually impressed," Maria proclaims, smiling brightly at Sophie, who starts to relax. "What gave it away? You didn't even attempt to take a sip."

"Well, it is a pretty heavy glass." Sophie shrugs. "It also doesn't feel like a glass of liquid. It's a solid prank, though. Sure fooled this one." She bumps me lightly with her elbow.

"I'm not sure if this makes me gullible or an idiot." I sigh. Thankfully no one confirms that I'm an idiot. Although no one denies it either.

If Sophie is surprised that Dan and Maria clearly aren't from the same generation as us, she doesn't let on. Instead, she falls into easy conversation with them while we wait for others to arrive.

Within ten minutes, more cursing comes from the entry and we all watch as people slowly emerge from the balloons. One of them, noticeably angrier than the rest.

I thought it was Miranda who'd released an angry curse when her shin had connected with whatever immobile object I had run into earlier. "That better be a real drink and not some fucking prank nonsense," she grumbles in place of a traditional greeting, her hand instantly reaching for the glasses Dan and Maria have ready.

Maria looks quickly over at Dan with a look that screams "I told you so," but because Maria is the nicest person alive, there's a "love of my life" tacked on at the end.

"Don't mind her, she had a late night." Heather yawns. "Me too, come to think of it."

"Was it fun at least?"

"Well they lost so it could have been better," Miranda grumbles, waving off the fake drink. "No, I'd prefer a real one, please. The twins had us up at five, and then Mike's parents called to say they were sick and couldn't babysit. Hence"—she waves at the empty space beside her—"no Mike."

"How fun for Mike. Babysitting them last night and again today." Dan laughs.

The laugh dies on his lips as he takes in Miranda's expression. "They are his children. It is not babysitting when they are your offspring. If I was home with them, no one would say a thing. But oh, dad is staying home with the kids, what a sai—"

"Oh no, fucking no, just no. Dan!" Nick yells from the

entry, silencing Miranda immediately. "I'm leaving. I'm going right back to my car and never speaking to you again."

Miranda's anger seems to vanish, and she disappears into the balloons. The door opens and slams, and we're all left standing there in stunned silence.

"I didn't mean anything by it. I stayed home with our kids." Dan winces.

"She's exhausted and hungry. She'll be back to her usual self the minute she gets some food in her."

The back door opens, and we all move further into the house. "Real great prank friends, stellar." Nick looks shaken, and his partner Alex rubs his back, looking concerned.

"He's got globophobia," they say like any of us know what that means.

When no one says anything, Sophie whispers, "That's a fear of balloons."

"Oh shit!" Dan exclaims. "I had no idea, Nick. Why have you never mentioned it?"

"Well, I've never been so aggressively confronted with the fear. I've only ever had nightmares of being in that"—he points toward the front of the house—"kind of situation."

"So this year's festivities are off to a grand beginning." Maria sighs. "Dan, perhaps we should get the drinkable drinks flowing?"

"Oh," Sophie says, startling all of us as she reaches around me to grab the bag I'm still holding. "I brought you this." She holds up the gift bag, and Maria takes it.

"You did not need to— Oh, bubbly!" she squeals, pulling the bottle from the bag and doing a little shimmy. "You," she says, pointing at Sophie, "are welcome anytime."

FOURTEEN

To say that getting to know Foster's friends is an education is an understatement. They all met while teaching English in Korea, which explains the wide range of ages. Nick explained that it was like being in university all over again. You make fast, strong friendships with people all in the same situation. In their case, expats living in a new country with a different language and customs.

"Dan and Maria were the senior teachers at the English academy I was at, then I met Miranda, Heather, and Nick in Korean class," Foster explains. "One day I invited everyone out for dinner after class and asked if Dan and Maria wanted to join us."

"The rest is, as they say, history." Maria beams over at Foster. "We were simply happy to be included. People think once you hit a certain age, you don't know how to have fun anymore. The reality is you start having more fun because you stop giving a cat's caboose about what anyone else thinks of you."

"Cat's caboose?" I repeat, glancing over at Foster as things start to click.

"So, it turns out kids are really good at repeating things you say, and I learned very quickly that they were particularly proficient with curses."

"Kid cursed like a sailor when he first arrived," Dan guffaws.

"Yeah, and he was apparently unable to shake the cutesy cursing habit when he got home," Heather teases.

"Well, I still work pretty closely with kids so..." His shoulders rise and fall with a sigh.

"I have kids and don't censor myself," Miranda says.

"Yeah, but you're expected to teach your own kids bad words. No parent is going to walk into a school, shake my hand, and thank me for teaching their kid how to swear."

"I don't know," I say, "I'd say your language is more colorful than the usual stuff. It's definitely more interesting." I reach over, threading my fingers through his. "I like it."

"The question is, does that language come out in the bedroom?" Nick asks. I immediately feel heat rush to my face.

"Nick," Foster warns, his hand tightening around mine. "Too far."

I think of the way Foster touched and held me at the gala. How he helped sell the illusion that we were together. "All I'll say is that in the bedroom, Foster's vocabulary is the last thing I'm thinking about." The room erupts in laughter and hoots, and Foster's face goes nearly as red as his hair.

Lunch is delicious, and Maria pats herself on the back for keeping Dan from straying too far in the experimental direction. "He was going to grill absolutely everything, and that's when I put my foot down, especially since the dessert is pudding-based."

"How the hell do you grill pudding?" Heather queries.

"I found a recipe. I was willing to try it, but this one"—he gestures toward his wife—"said it was dumb."

"But now I want to know," Miranda whines.

"I'll send you the recipe." Dan grins over at her.

"Oh no, I don't want to make the recipe, I just want to know if it's possible." She waves off his offer. "If you're going to send it to anyone, send it to Foster."

"Is the end result a hot pudding?" Foster asks, leaning forward, and I can't tell if he's actually interested or simply concerned.

"You serve it warm," Dan says.

Now I can definitely tell that Foster is not, in fact, interested. "I think I'm good never knowing what it is," he says confidently, leaning back into the couch and letting his hand rest on my thigh. It feels like a rogue firework, sparks going in every which way, and I have to consciously stop myself from squirming. Not because it doesn't feel good, but because it feels *too* good and I'm not in the type of situation where I want to be feeling this good. Ultimately feeling good is making me uncomfortable.

Amazingly, Foster seems to pick up on my discomfort and moves his hand from my thigh, opting to take my hand instead. This has the same effect as a good hard hug, and the anxiety that was building begins to deflate.

"So you two have known each other since you were kids?" Maria asks, walking around with a pitcher of sangria and refilling half the glasses in the room.

"Yeah, since I was five and he was six," I confirm.

"And it took you until now to realize you had feelings for each other?"

"We were..." I start to say as Foster says, "Oh no, I knew when we were kids."

I look at him wide-eyed and then remember this is fake. He's selling a backstory we had foolishly not planned out.

"I mean, I guess I had a crush, but I would have never guessed he did too," I say bashfully.

"Took me a while to figure out why my heart didn't turn into a jackhammer when my sister had other friends over. It was only when Soph was there."

There are *aww*'s from around the room and I'm stupidly allowing myself to be dragged into this alternate reality. "Well, you never let on."

He looks at me, those amber eyes so intense I have to actively remind myself this isn't real. "I'm a very good actor." And there it is, the reminder of what this is.

"You are indeed. Fooled me completely."

"Dan, why do you have a picture of Ray Romano on your wall?" Miranda asks, coming back into the room.

"Excuse me?" Dan asks, standing up and heading in the direction Miranda had come from. He stops in front of one of the framed pictures in the hall. "That's my uncle Gabriel," he says coyly.

"That's Ray fucking Romano and you know it. And that's Jennifer Aniston," she says, pointing at another picture.

Foster stands and walks over to the framed pictures on the mantle and starts to laugh. "I had no idea you two were so close to this many famous people including"—he leans in —"Queen Elizabeth from like 1960. When were you born again, Danny Boy?"

"Nineteen sixty-nine."

"Did you invent a time machine between then and now?" Nick asks, joining Foster at the mantle.

"If so, you should send Foster and Sophie back so they can share their feelings in a more timely manner," Heather says absently while studying more pictures. "No one from your family is even in this one, it's only the BeeGees. Wait, is it the BeeGees? I don't know, I'm so young."

Everyone is laughing, and I'm lost in a daydream of what it would have been like if Foster and I had actually confessed having feelings for one another long before Gregory. Would I have gone to Korea with him? Would we have made it until now? It's silly to wonder—there are no time machines, and one of us is acting while the other is trying desperately not to fall for it.

By the time all the pictures are studied, thirty-two famous faces are discovered pressed between real family pictures and their glass covers. One of them has five versions of Jon Stewart, which throws the friends into a lighthearted argument about which expression correlates with which famous quote.

"That one is from the episode where he rants about deep-dish pizza," Foster says before quoting him in a terrible New York accent. I struggle to hold in my laughter.

"Didn't you say you were a good actor?" Alex scoffs.

"I never said I was good at accents, but I do have a fantastic memory. and that face is definitely the pizza rant face."

"I'm not saying this because of the whole being with him thing, but he's right, that's pizza rant face. I must have rewatched that episode a hundred times in the Walshes' basement." I go on to quote the next part of the line.

"Now that is acting," Alex exclaims, with a flourish of jazz hands.

I bow dramatically. "Thank you. I've been training my entire life to be a Jon Stewart impersonator."

"Hate to break it to you, sunshine, but you're way too beautiful for that," Foster says.

I roll my eyes before looking up at him. "You have to say that."

"I don't have to say anything," he says quietly, moving closer. He wraps an arm around my shoulders and pulls me gently into his side. "When it comes to you, I want to say it, yell it from the rooftops actually." And then he bends and plants a kiss on my forehead.

Holy shit, holy shit, holy shit, Foster's lips are on me. Sure, they aren't on my lips, but they are on my face, and that's a step in a direction I've only ever dreamed of.

FIFTEEN

My lips have been burning since I kissed Sophie. Sure, it was only her forehead, but my lips were on her skin, and it turns out I like that more than my lips not being on her skin. When I moved away, she acted like the kiss was nothing new. Which was good, to everyone else in the room. To me on the other hand, it felt like I'd crossed a line—or blurred one. And now I was pulling into her driveway and this whole act was about to end.

"Would you mind if I drove on Thursday?" she asks before she gets out of the car.

"Something wrong with my driving skills?"

"No, you are an excellent driver, no notes." She giggles. "I was thinking it's a school night and you just might be tired by the end of the concert."

She's not wrong. Work has been intense of late, and the thought of not only going out after work but going somewhere that's going to be hours of high energy is already making my eyes droop. "I won't fight you on this. Are we going to leave right after school?"

"Yeah, probably for the best. We can grab food near the

arena first, but we can figure that out later." She doesn't jump out right away; instead, her eyes focus on something out the windshield, her fingers tapping nervously on her thighs.

"Everything alright?" I ask, focused on her hands.

"Today was fun. You've got some great friends."

"They are weird, though, right?"

She looks over, a wide smile on her lips, and I clench every muscle to keep myself from reaching for her. "A little, but weird is good. Weird is welcome."

"Weird *is* good. It definitely keeps things interesting. They liked you, so if you want to pretend again with me, you're welcome to do so at any time." My heart drops when I see the smile fade from her face.

"It may be hard to explain if you find someone to actually date. Although this will probably be a fun story one day."

"Soph," I start to say, but she's already opening the door.

"Yeah?" She stops her escape and looks back at me.

Things are good right now, I remind myself. She's not going anywhere. She told me from the start that this was ideal because she wasn't ready for anything real yet. She's still coming to terms with what her ex did to her. And I have a feeling that what she revealed to me only scratches the surface. If I confess how badly I want this to be real, she may run, and I wouldn't even blame her.

"Thanks again for coming with me. I'll see you tomorrow."

"See you tomorrow." She gives me one last brilliant smile, although it doesn't reach her eyes, and heads toward her front door.

I turn up the Nyx song, and her voice fills the car, singing about how we have a lot of time to make up for. "No kidding," I mumble, backing out of the driveway and heading home.

Monday and Tuesday are two of the busiest days I've ever experienced in any area of my life. By the time I get home I don't feel like doing anything other than crashing.

SUNSHINE

Heard you had a bit of a situation today. I
hope you're okay.

I had basically nodded my hello to Sophie Monday morning and then hadn't seen her again. It felt strange to be so invested in each other for three days to then not even say the word hello.

I've got a nice bruise but it's nothing I can't
handle.

We have a couple students who can have violent outbursts, and today I was in the wrong place at the wrong time. It was a fluke, really. Justin hadn't meant for his fist to connect with my jaw; that's just how it played out. And I'd much rather be sporting a nice tiny fist-shaped bruise than see one of the students with one.

I bet you look really tough with all those
tattoos and a bruised face.

I fear little old ladies will no longer accept
my help when crossing the street.

Nah they'll probably want to take care
of you.

> Time will tell.

> Listen, I'm going to pass out any minute, but maybe I'll actually get to say hi tomorrow.

> Kids first, hellos can wait. Sleep well!

Wednesday comes and brings with it a tornado of drama. I don't know a thing about astrology, but I can't help but wonder if Mercury is in retrograde. I have absolutely no idea what that even means, but at this point I'm willing to put money on that being the reason things have gone topsy-turvy.

By the end of the day, we had one student run away from class which then inspired three more to make a break for it. Another student cried hysterically for the entire day, making us all worry about dehydration. Pete had an anxiety attack, which broke my heart. One of the other EAs fell and hit her head on the basketball net post, and the student she'd been out with was so distraught he hasn't talked since. That's on top of the normal amount of work we have on any given day.

If tomorrow is anything like the last three, I don't know how I'm going to make it through a concert. I'm pretty sure I could fall asleep next to a space shuttle about to launch. No offense to Nyx, but her concert may be white noise at this point.

I'm mindlessly preparing to leave for the day, wondering if I should maybe not be behind the wheel, when I sense someone watching me. Turning, I see Sophie leaning against the door frame, holding her coat and bag, forehead drawn in worry.

"You look about ready to drop," she says, pity tinting her words.

"You should see everyone else." I laugh humorously.

"I did, that's why I stopped by. Principal Wong said the board is 'looking into getting more help.'"

"They say that every year, and then the following year it's worse," I scoff as I shoulder my bag and walk slowly toward her. I'm so tired I barely register how stunning she is, even after what I assume was an equally long day for her. She's got her hair pulled back in a sleek ponytail and she's wearing slim green pants and a blouse with... "Are those toadstools?" I ask, gesturing at her top.

"Sure are." She grins. "Are you going to be okay to drive home?" she asks when she sees me fighting off a yawn.

"Yeah, I'll wake up when I breathe in some fresh air." I watch as her eyes narrow in disbelief. "Honestly, it's only a ten-minute drive, I'll be fine."

We walk out together, and the minute the cool air hits my face, I sigh. "Waking up?"

"A little... enough, anyway."

"Don't feel like you still have to come tomorrow. I am sure I can find someone, or I can go alone. I know most people are resistant to that sort of thing, but I'm an only child and I'm excellent at being by myself. Plus, I'll be surrounded by rabid Nyx Avalon fans so I'll just—"

I put my hand on her arm to both stop her forward motion and her mouth. "I've been listening to Nyx Avalon nonstop since Cass asked me. I haven't been studying to bail on the exam. But don't hold it against me if I fall asleep."

"Alright, if you're sure."

"I wouldn't be saying it if I wasn't." If it were anyone else, I would have bailed already. In fact, I wouldn't have agreed to go in the first place, but I'm going to take every single opportunity I can to spend time with this woman.

She walks to my car with me, as if she doesn't truly believe I can make it there on my own before telling me to drive safe and heading for her own. I watch her walk away in my side mirror and then tip my head back. I am dreading and craving tomorrow night.

Gary demands my attention the minute I walk into my apartment, and I pick him up on the way to the couch. I'm drifting off to the rhythm of Gary making biscuits on my chest when it hits me that tomorrow is our third friend date and we're going to a concert, something starting with C. Date one was an alumni gala, two was a barbecue. I bet I can convince Sophie to go through the alphabet with me.

I fall asleep with a smile on my face and brainstorming what we could do for D.

SIXTEEN

SOPHIE

Thursday moves at a snail's pace, but isn't that always the way when you're looking forward to something big?

After my final session on Thursday, I quickly change into my concert outfit and head to the staff room to wait for Foster. He's meeting with one of his students' parents and said he'd find me here.

"Hey Sophie," one of the primary teachers says when she walks in. I think her name is Chanel, but I'm terrible with names of people I don't deal with on a regular basis. "What are you still doing here?"

"Waiting for Foster." Her eyebrows go up, and a knowing smile crosses her face. "It's not like that. His sister is my best friend and gave him her ticket for the Nyx concert tonight. He's being a good friend, stepping in at the last minute."

"Foster is going to see Nyx... Avalon? Foster Walsh, that Foster?"

"You know another?" I cross my arms and lean against the counter.

"I'm starting to think I don't know this one," she jokes.

"He's a staunch classic rock guy, or at least that's how he's always presented. Maybe he's a closeted pop fan."

I shrug. "No idea. He's been 'studying' Nyx's backlist, apparently."

"Please film him so we have evidence," she begs.

"Will do!"

She washes her mug and sticks it in the drying rack before turning back to me. "He's a really good guy."

"Yep." I nod.

"Like too good, ya know?"

"Can a guy be too good?" Everyone has their faults and their ugly sides, I'm sure even Foster. He sort of used to anyway, although at the time I was drawn to the rebellious side of him.

"Foster's the kind of guy who goes out of his way to shovel snow from his neighbors driveways, walks old ladies across the road, volunteers at every school event, bakes for every kid's birthday in his class in case they forget to bring something in..." *Agrees to be your fake date to an alumni event so your ex doesn't think you're still a little broken.*

Foster walks in while she's still listing things really good people do. I've missed most of the list as I escape back into a world where Foster's thumb slips beneath my dress and gently caresses my skin, comforting me during one of those good guy moments.

"Ready?" He's wearing different clothes too. Tight distressed black jeans, a white T-shirt, white Converse that match my blue ones and the same dark green bomber jacket he wore to the barbecue.

"Yep!" I say a little too enthusiastically, and I catch Chanel hiding her smile by turning to wash something else.

"You two have fun," she calls after us.

"Was Chantel talking about me?" *Chantel.* I was close.

"She was listing all the ways you're too good," I reply, walking through the door Foster holds open for me.

"Oh yeah? Did she mention my work with blind elephant seals on the ice floes of the Arctic?"

"She had not gotten to that one yet."

"Pity." He sighs, shaking his head. "It's some of my most selfless work." He's so serious-looking it takes way too long for me to realize that he's fucking with me.

"I'll be sure to mention it first whenever you come up. 'Oh yes, Foster Walsh, you know he works with blind elephant seals in the Arctic, don't you'?"

"Don't forget all the work is done on ice floes, it's very important." He flashes me a crooked grin, and my brain short-circuits.

"Riiight." I nod. "It definitely sounds more dangerous with that additional information."

"In this climate, it actually is," he ponders solemnly. "Wow, nothing like climate change talk to kill a joke, eh?"

"Climate change kills, it's a well-known fact," I say, straight-faced before tossing my bag into the back of my car. "Now, let's forget about our demise by singing along with a blue-haired woman as she jumps around an arena."

I probably shouldn't put too much thought into the fact that we're wearing the same shoes. Converse high-tops aren't exactly rare, especially at concerts. Yet, as Sophie drives us toward the city, I can't help my eyes from journeying to her feet. I don't even attempt to stop them from taking the scenic route on their way. She looks as stunning in the dark blue jeans and a simple light blue T-shirt as she did in the gown.

I pull my attention away from her outfit and stare out the windshield.

"Do you ever use cruise control?" I ask, noticing that the current driving conditions would have me turning it on in a heartbeat.

"Not if I want to arrive somewhere alive," she says, and I'm not sure if she's being serious. When she sees my expression her smirk fades, and she looks back at the road. "I used it once right after I'd gotten my license, and I ended up getting distracted. Let's say it's a good thing the cows weren't in the south pasture because I renovated the fence with my mom's car. In second year, I was diagnosed with ADHD and a lot of things started to make sense."

I peek down at her feet and notice her left foot tapping to its own beat. I work with kids everyday with ADHD, but just because someone fidgets doesn't mean they have it. I try and think back to when we were kids. I remember Sophie being very active and chatty, but nothing really stands out.

"You can close your eyes and sleep, you know. I won't be offended."

Fat chance. I change the subject. "So did you know that we have managed to go on three friend dates in alphabetical order?"

I watch her forehead scrunch. "What?"

"A, alumni. B, barbecue. C, concert." I count on my fingers.

"Interesting," she says, sparing a quick glance in my direction.

"I kind of want to see if we can get through the entire alphabet." And when we finish the alphabet, we'll start at the number one and go from there, and after we get bored of numbers, we can do nouns.

"We've also managed to switch off every other one. Are we accidentally really good at this?"

"Nothing accidental about it, sunshine. So, what do you say? Should we go for the D?"

"That sounds kind of dirty." She laughs.

"It does, sorry. Let me rephrase: shall we attempt the letter D next? I dare you to do this with me."

She groans. "What did you have in mind?"

Sex. That's literally all I have in mind now.

I pretend to think for a bit, but I already knew what I was going to suggest the minute I woke up today. "My friend Lucas is performing in a drag brunch this Sunday."

I watch her light up immediately. "I've never been to a drag show! I'm in. I guess that leaves me with E."

"I do believe that letter comes next, yes."

"I'll have to give it some thought." Her face suddenly falls, "Shit, can you open my calendar. I think I've got plans with friends on Sunday."

"Password?"

She lifts her hand off the steering wheel and moves her finger as she recites, "369870."

Her screen unlocks, and I'm instantly distracted by the background picture. A cow's head lays on the grass and a smallish white dog is asleep with its head on the cows nose. "That's Lloyd and Yogurt," she says when she notices me staring at the picture. "Cass's boss's dog and the cow he raised for his first year after my father forced him to take him in."

"Wait, what?"

"A few years back, Bennett, my parents' neighbor and Cass's boss, was all sulky because he let the love of his life leave without telling her how he felt. So my dad showed up at his house with a calf that had been rejected by his mother. Literally walked into the man's kitchen with him. Yogurt, the dog, is Bennett's, and the two have basically been best friends ever since."

"I think Cass may have mentioned a cow when she started the job, but she's always throwing out random names and I can't keep track."

"I don't blame you. I know a lot of them personally, and I still can't. Half the time I don't know if someone's talking about an animal or a new employee."

"They do love giving them generic human names, eh?"

"Or food. Marley was on a roll a couple years back. They had a fat tan tabby come in, and she named it

Biscuit. A wiener dog that she named Frank, but she always mentioned that it was short for Frankfurter. Let's see." She purses her lips while she thinks, and I have the urge to lean over and kiss her. "Chowder, Waffles and Jellybean have also all been used. Waffles was adopted by someone who owns a breakfast place so that name proved to be useful."

"I guess you'd see that as meant to be." I yawn.

"Destiny," she agrees. "Speaking of food, do you feel like anything in particular for dinner?"

"Food."

"But what?"

"I honestly will eat anything, just don't make me pick. I need to save all available energy for belting out 'Let's Just Pretend.'"

She laughs as if I'm joking, but over the last week I have gotten very into that song, and I do not plan on sitting quietly by when it's performed tonight.

"That would make my whole night to see," she declares. Sophie Hore is not prepared for how made her night is going to be.

"How about we flip a coin five times? Heads, we take the first turn on the left. Tails, we take the first turn on the right. Then after five turns we eat at the first restaurant we see."

I watch eyes slide sideways before snapping back to the road. "For someone who doesn't want to use any energy deciding on where to eat, that is a very elaborate way to decide."

I shrug. "But an interesting one, right?"

"Yes. I think there is a coin somewhere in my bag."

I look down and then back up at her. "As in you'd like me to find it?"

"If you wouldn't mind. Unless you're afraid of tampons or something," she teases.

"I'll have you know," I say, picking up her bag and plunking it on my lap, "that I have not only seen tampons before, I've purchased them."

"I bet you got nominated for Boyfriend of the Year for that move."

"Well, it was for Cass so she may have put my name in for Brother of the Year," I reply with my face practically in Sophie's bag, which is a lot like Pete's pockets. I push aside multiple chapsticks, a loose piece of gum, a half-eaten granola bar, countless receipts, two pens, and a hair elastic. My fingers brush a coin buried in the corner as I'm about to give up. I hold it up triumphantly and set her purse back at my feet.

"Okay, call it."

"Heads."

"It's tails, so the first right we take when we get off the highway."

Thirty minutes later, we are making our first right followed by another right and a left which leads us to a dead end. It takes ten minutes to back out of the alley and we decide that maybe we should verify the following turns using GPS in order to avoid that happening again.

"Alrighty," I say after we make our last turn, "keep your eyes peeled for a res—"

"There!" Sophie shouts, swerving into a parking spot in front of what looks like a great place to get tetanus.

I get out of the car and reach the meter before Sophie realizes what I'm doing. "Foster Steven Walsh, you put that card away right now," she yells as she rounds the front of the car.

"Too late." I grin over my shoulder at her, joy bubbling

away in my chest over the fact she remembers my middle name.

I hold the door open for her and stop inside when I see the interior of the place. "Colonel Mustard's marsupials." The place is absolutely covered in paper. Post-it notes and ripped paper scraps adorn the walls and ceiling. Even most of the tables look to have a fair amount under their glass tops.

"Well, if all these people have eaten here, that's probably a good sign, right?" Sophie asks, squeezing by me and walking to the hostess stand.

"How many?" the woman behind the stand asks, already picking up two menus.

"Two," Sophie tells her.

"Table or booth?"

She looks back at me with her eyebrow raised. It's not that busy in the place, but the booths offer a bit more privacy. "Booth, please," I tell the woman who leads us to a table near the back.

"Your server will be right over, enjoy," she informs us before walking away.

Sophie is lost in the wall immediately, leaning in close to read the notes. "'The love of my life died yesterday. I'm drowning my sorrows with fries and margaritas.' My god, that's fucking sad," she murmurs before reading the next one. "'I was here, and now so are you.' Deep." She laughs.

While she looks at the notes on the wall, I begin reading the ones on our table. They are a mix of wise words and ridiculous observations. "Here's a good one. 'People don't talk about their good days enough.' I am definitely guilty of that. Ha!" A laugh bursts out of me. "Yes, I've heard of Jesus, have you heard of Google?"

"I have a friend who has that taped to their mailbox."

"And?"

"People still knock and leave pamphlets. Want to write our own?" Sophie holds up the stack of paper that is sitting against the wall, a cup of pens beside it.

"Maybe after. I need to think of something clever."

When our server arrives to take our order, we decide that if the fries are good enough for a grieving person they must be worth getting, and because we can't decide on mains, we order four other appetizers.

"A meal of apps, solid," the server drawls before taking our order to the kitchen.

"I'm going to wash my hands." Sophie slides out of the booth and walks to the back of the building.

I use the opportunity to write a note. I'll write another later, but there is a secret I've wanted to share since I was a kid and now seems like a good time to do it.

At 16, I fell in love with a girl.
I'm 28 now and still falling.

EIGHTEEN

"I'm not sure if these fries are things I'd turn to if I was grieving the love of my life," Foster ponders, holding up a fry and studying it. "They aren't bad, they just aren't good enough to be grief fries."

"Grief fries?"

"Bereavement frites." I try to hold in my laughter, which is a mistake because it causes the sip of margarita I just took to shoot out of my nose.

"Oh my god." I grab frantically for a napkin. "That fucking burns!"

"Here." Foster hands me his, and I dab at my nose and chin while he tries and fails to hide his laughter.

"Let's never speak of this again." I glare at him.

"So I shouldn't write a detailed account of the events of the past two minutes as my contribution to the wall?" he teases.

"Only if it paints me as an innocent party," I say matter-of-factly, balling up the napkin and setting it to the side.

"It was with my deepest shock and horror that I

unknowingly caused my stunning companion to spew a neon-green beverage out of her nose. Even with the filtered drink dripping down her face her beauty was ten times that of anyone else in the room. I can only hope that one day she will forgive me for my outrageous sense of humor," he says as if performing a Shakespearean play, and despite knowing he's putting on an act, I cannot help my mind from snagging on "stunning" and "beauty." If crushes die hard, mine is an expert at evading its execution.

"That was excellent. You may have a future on the stage."

"If I didn't have stage fright, that would be fun."

"You have stage fright? But you're so confident," I marvel.

"In a small group, sure. In front of a large one, not so much."

The rest of our meal is fine, but certainly nothing to shout about. Before leaving, we both write notes and find a place to stick them on the wall. He wouldn't show me his, so I hid mine as well. It seemed only fair.

The first half of the concert is electric, and while I spend most of it completely captivated by whatever Nyx is doing, I cannot stop myself from noticing the way the woman beside Foster keeps peeking over at him. I can't blame her; I'd be looking too if he were a stranger. His hair is stylishly messy, and his T-shirt doesn't leave much to the imagination. He's clearly someone who treats his body well, plus all those tattoos aren't so bad.

His amber eyes are wide and seem to look at everything with wonder. He catches me watching him and smiles, and for a split second I'm twelve again and Foster's teasing Cass about something and then smiling at me the same way, except back then he had a mouth full of metal. I need to write a Yelp review for his orthodontist because that smile is now commercial-worthy.

"She's ridiculous," he shouts, leaning in closer so I can hear him.

"Her performance is something, eh?" He nods back, but his attention is already back above the stage as Nyx is now suspended fifty feet in the air playing a piano.

I'm still distracted by the other woman. She's becoming bolder, moving closer to Foster and eventually leaning in to say something to him. He turns briefly to her so I can't see if he's smiling the way he smiled at me. I hate the little bubble of jealousy that builds somewhere deep inside. *You have absolutely no claim on him. We're friends. Let him have his fun.*

When Nyx gets to the section of her slower, more acoustic guitar songs, I see the woman lean into Foster again, and this time I know exactly what she's doing as she bites her lip, gives him a full-body scan, and turns to leave. Foster's head is turned, watching her go, and when she looks back and sees that his eyes are on her still, she bounces her eyebrows at him before disappearing down the aisle toward the exit.

"Go on, have some fun," I force out.

His head snaps back to me, brows furrowed. "What?"

"She clearly wants you to follow her. Go on, go have some fun."

"We're here together," he shouts back. "This is fun." He gestures between us.

"Well, not exactly together," I correct even though it sucks to say out loud.

"Well, I am here with you and because of you." He

leans closer so I can feel his words brush my ear when he says them. "And I don't want to go hook up with some random at a concert because she made eyes at me. That's not my style, Soph."

My name sounds like a plea, but it's loud in here and that could be all in my head. I'm afraid to look at him, afraid that I'll see my own longing reflected back at me, terrified that I won't. So I nod, keeping my eyes on the stage.

"I do have to pee, though, so that's where I'm going now."

About ten minutes later, the flirty woman returns looking more than a little put out, and if the look she gives me is any indication, I'm the reason she's feeling that way. When Foster comes walking back, I see the woman panic and switch places with her friend. He's carrying two drinks and wearing a new T-shirt. The official concert tour T-shirt, to be exact.

"It's ginger ale," he yells, handing me a cup. Ginger ale is a weird choice to randomly bring someone who isn't feeling ill—or it would be if the person it was being brought to wasn't me. The bubble of jealousy begins to morph into something else as it hits me that even after all these years, Foster remembers what my favorite fizzy beverage is.

"Thanks," I yelp, trying to hide how in awe of this little gesture I am.

"And that's not all." He turns and shimmies, drawing my attention to his butt, more specifically to where a T-shirt is hanging out of his back pocket. I give it a little tug, and once it's free, he takes my drink back and gestures for me to put it on.

I slip it over my head and snort, I haven't worn a shirt this big in a while. "They only had extra-larges left," Foster says, grinning down at me. "You can do one of those knot things."

"It's okay, I like a baggy tee." To sleep in more than wear out and about, but I love that he not only got me a shirt, but he got himself the same one.

His lips part as if he's about to say something, but the first notes of the next song begin and a huge smile lights up his face right before he throws his head back and yells "This is my soooong!" I watch, spellbound, as he gets right into it, singing along to every word with Nyx. It's not until he sings, "You're the sunshine after a rainy day, I wish I knew how to make you stay," bringing his face right down to mine so that even in the dark I can practically count every eyelash, that I snap out of it and join in.

We jump and sing, and by the end half our drinks are on the floor from toasting. Foster's lips return to my ear in time for the last line, offering it up for my ears only. And no offense to Nyx, but his version is way more impactful.

"Hands-down best concert I've ever been to," Foster proclaims, as his head falls back against the headrest. "Also, brilliant parking so far from the venue. The worst part of any concert is getting out of a parking lot."

"It does kill the vibe of a concert pretty quickly. I figured getting you home sooner rather than later was key."

"I appreciaaa–" His sentence is interrupted by a yawn. "Gah, sorry. I appreciate it. Now that the adrenaline is gone, I can feel the energy draining from my body."

"I'll get you home as fast as I can." I wink at him. Why the hell did I wink at him? That wasn't even a wink-worthy comment. What the fuck is wrong with me? I can't even bring myself to look at him again until I hear a soft puff of air. When I peek over he's asleep, his lips parted in my direction. It's probably a good thing that I need to keep my eyes on the road because the urge to stare at him is strong. But I don't want to be creepy about it, even if the desire to do so keeps leading me to slide my gaze to my right. Whatever the complicated feelings I have for him are, there is one that stands out, and it's happiness. He calls me sunshine, but he's always been the reason she comes out.

NINETEEN

From the moment we leave the concert, I start counting down to Sunday's brunch. I'd consider myself to be a pretty happy person, but Sophie brings a different kind of happy out of me. The kind of happy that makes life a bit lighter. She's always had that effect on me, I just didn't realize it until she stepped back into my life. My sunshine is back, and I am reaping all the rewards of a healthy dose of vitamin D.

When Sophie stops in front of my building, I have the urge to invite her up, not because I want to move this relationship out of the friend zone into a romantic one. Even though I would in a heartbeat if she said the word. Looking over at her, I want to ask, *Do you want to come up for a bit? I've got cookies. You could meet Gary. We could debrief about the concert over some decaf or tea or water.* Her eyebrows rise as if she's waiting for me to speak, and I realize I'm only thinking things and not saying them. I don't need anything else to convince me that I am in no shape to host anyone at this moment.

"Tonight was a blast. I'm glad I could fill in," I finally manage to say.

Sophie's eyebrows drop, and she smiles softly. I watch as her hand lifts toward my face, and I automatically move my head toward it. Only it lands on my shoulder a split second later.

"I hope you're able to sleep tonight. You don't even look like you'll make it to the door," she teases.

How about I sleep here? You can keep me company. With your hand on my shoulder and your sunshineyness surrounding me.

The hand on my shoulder gives a squeeze, and I realize I've started to drift off again. Pulling away, I throw the door open and go to step out, only to be pulled back into the car by the seatbelt that is still very much buckled.

"The universe seems to want me to stay put," I mumble, hearing a click and then watching as the belt slides across my body.

"I don't think your body would appreciate that in the morning," Sophie muses.

I look back pathetically. "Can we forget how tired I was?"

"I won't mention it to anyone, but I don't think I'll be forgetting about it any time soon."

I nod because, fair. "Thanks again, Soph. I'll see you tomorrow."

I don't hear Sophie pull away, and as I open the door to my apartment I wonder if I should text her to let her know I made it all the way without falling asleep or getting trapped in anything.

Gary is sitting by the window when I flick the light on and I walk over to join him. Sophie flashes her lights and drives away. I lift my hand in a delayed wave only to have Gary move his head toward it.

I watch him nuzzle in. "I think we spend too much time together, Gary," I tell him as he succeeds in doing what I had automatically done in the car.

"Why do they call dogs' bits their privates?" Pete asks Friday afternoon during gym class.

I should be used to him asking random questions by now, but I'm not sure I will ever be. "Excuse me?" I ask, dodging a rogue basketball.

"A dog's bits," he says emphatically. "My mom called our dog's bits his privates last night. 'Dougie, put your privates away.'" Pete's impression of his mom is phenomenal. "But his bits are on the outside. There isn't anything private about them."

The kid has a point. "Well, I think it comes from calling, um, well, humans'…um…bits?" I ask and he nods, "privates so we use that term for dogs too."

"Hmm," he ponders while squinting up at me, and I know I'm about to have an even harder time not laughing because I've seen that face before and something ridiculous is coming. "I think we should call them their publics, since they're out swinging around"—he leans in and whispers—"in public."

I'm about to tell him that we should use the proper terms for body parts, but I'm clocked in the face by a stray basketball before I've even opened my mouth. "Fudgesicle," I grit out, grabbing my face.

"I'm sorry, Mr. Walsh." I hear one of the kids yell from across the gym, and I wave away the apology.

To say I'm counting down the hours until I can go home is an understatement. I'm probably going to crash through my door and then sleep for days right there on the kitchen floor. Not even Gary's incessant meowing will be able to wake me.

The only thing that could make this day better would be seeing Sophie, but she spends Friday afternoons at a different school now, so I won't see her until I pick her up for brunch on Sunday. Probably for the best in my state. I'm embarrassed enough by my failed car exit from last night.

"Oh, Foster," Jessica frets when she sees me after gym. "That's going to bruise. Go grab some ice. I'm sure Pete and I will get along fine without you for a few minutes."

I know Pete will be fine. My main concern is that if I go to the staff room to grab ice, I'm probably going to sit down, and if I do that, the likelihood of falling asleep in there is high.

I brush off her concern and start gathering the art supplies Pete's going to need for the paper mâché globes the class is working on. Mixing art with geography is brilliant.

"How'd it happen?" Jessica asks after I get back from the bus pickup line.

"Rogue basketball," I mutter as I help put away the pieces of art that need to dry before the next step.

"Been there." She chuckles. "However, not my jaw. You're going to look super tough."

"That's why I got these." I raise my arm so it peeks out of my sleeve. There are no specific rules about covering my tattoos, but I know they'll distract the kids, and a lot of these kids don't need that.

She looks over at me with pity. "Foster, I don't mean to be rude, but nothing about those tattoos screams tough guy."

I look down at my arm, now hidden under my sleeve again. I don't need to see it to know what's there though. I have no tattoos of skulls, roaring lions, severe Roman gods, or snakes. I have my full nerdom tattooed on my body for the world to see. My left side is all *Lord of the Rings,* and my right represents my favorite books as a kid. No one is going to look at a guy with a tattoo of the Velveteen Rabbit or the Giving Tree and think, *oh, watch out, he's a live wire.* And now with what I imagine will end up being a nicely bruised jaw, I'm going to look like the guy who's easily punched.

She takes my silence as though I am indeed offended and starts apologizing. "Really, they are fantastic tattoos. Ten out of ten on design and execution. Just, well, nothing screams tough guy like a stuffed rabbit."

"I have layers, Jess," I object. "Many complicated layers, and within those layers is indeed a tough guy."

Her eyes narrow as she studies me. "I think if you were defending someone else, I'd be worried for the bad person," she concedes. "Any plans this weekend?"

Even the word plans has my eyes growing heavier. The thought of having to do anything tomorrow is too exhausting, so I'm glad I don't actually have to think. "Going to a friend's show on Sunday, but that's it."

"What kind of show?" she asks as she grabs our coats from the closet.

"It's a drag brunch."

"Shut up, at Triple C's?"

"Yeah," I answer slowly.

She hands me my coat. "I'm going to that with a bunch of friends. Have you been before? It's my first time."

Alarm bells start going off in my head. If I show up with

Sophie, Jess is going to see, then she's going to speculate and ask questions. She's the gossip goblin of the school. She's going to wonder how the hell someone as accomplished as Sophie is out with a guy like me.

"I've been a couple times. It's alright," I lie, and my stomach tightens with guilt. "You definitely don't go for the food, that's for sure." I don't know why I'm saying this. I doubt me saying the food isn't great isn't going to stop them from going. And on Monday she's going to point out that the food is in fact delicious, because it is. There isn't a single thing about the Triple C's drag brunch that I'd change.

She looks puzzled. "Huh, the friend who planned it is a chef. Her partner is the head chef at Triple C's." *Shiitake mushrooms.*

"Maybe I was there on a bad day. The second time I only had mimosas."

We walk toward the parking lot together and I'm glad that she doesn't ask any more questions. "Well, have a great Saturday." She waves when we reach my car and continues on to her own. "And see you on Sunday!"

Slumping into my car I wonder if I can come up with a new date while still attending the brunch to support my friend. But then I think about how excited Sophie was when I'd mentioned it, and that goes out the window. We're going to have to come up with a story. Maybe she can know Lucas too, and we're simply two supportive friends who happen to find out the other one was going. Or we can be honest that we've known each other since we were kids and she's my sister's best friend.

I'm already hiding my true feelings, feelings that are rising to the surface far faster than I'd expected. If I add in more pretending I may let something slip. And for Sophie's sake, I can't allow that to happen.

TWENTY

SOPHIE

Both of them?

Can confirm.

Acrobatic guy?

Yes.

I mean if it's worth it I guess you'll have to factor in a lamp budget. Or remove the lamps before you get going.

Oh it's worth it. I'm learning a lot about myself.

I stop midway out of my car. Maya and I have been close since I walked into my university dorm room for the first time and she greeted me with a big hug. And right now I'm torn between wanting to know what exactly she's learning and never knowing.

> As long as you're being safe and having fun.

I'm so much bendier than I ever realized.

If she'd come to Pilates with me, she'd have realized that long ago. I grab my yoga mat and bag of groceries out of the car before making my way to the house.

> I'm very happy for you!

And I am. Maya is notoriously hard to please in just about every aspect of her life, so if she found someone who does it in an area she happens to really enjoy, that's terrific.

My relationship with sex changed drastically from the start of my relationship with Gregory to the end of it. Looking back, it's so easy to see the pattern. In the beginning, he centered me. Then gradually it became all about him. His pleasure, his desires, his moods, his kinks. He'd do what he wanted, then clean up and go to sleep or carry on with whatever his plans had been. I know looking back and berating myself isn't the answer. I'm trained in this, and yet that's what I do.

Lost in thought, I jump when my phone rings. I never have the ringer on, so I must have hit the switch by accident.

Mom's face takes up the screen, and I immediately feel a bit better.

"Hey," I answer with as much pep as I can muster. My parents don't know a thing about what happened with Gregory. They just think the relationship had run its course.

"Hey, Soph," Mom's voice comes through clear as a bell, which means she's standing on the third step of the porch.

"What's up?" I ask, walking to the front door to hang

my grocery bag on the handle. If I don't do that I end up buying a new bag every single time I go shopping.

"I was wondering if you'd like an overnight houseguest tomorrow?" she coos sweetly.

"Um..." I start.

"Unless you're busy, I can stay at a hotel," she adds quickly.

I'm not going to let my mother stay at a hotel when the only reason I live in a house rent-free is because she and my dad bought it as an investment property when I was a kid.

"No, don't be silly. Of course you can stay here."

"If you have plans, though, keep them. I'll entertain myself," she insists.

"Why will you be in the city?" I throw myself down in my favorite armchair.

I can practically hear her deciding whether or not to tell me. "I've got an appointment in the morning, and I'd really rather not have to drive down right before it."

"Is everything okay?" I ask, sitting up.

"Yeah, no worries, it's probably nothing." She's being overly cheerful and I want to call her on it, but I also don't want her to decide not to come.

"When do you think you'll get here?"

"Probably late afternoon? We can do dinner. I'll make your favorite." Which means Mom's bringing lasagna.

"Well, if that's on offer, come whenever you'd like and stay for however long you think is best."

I feel her chuckle in my bones. That soft barely there laugh she's always had. "I'm not sure your father would like me to stay too long."

"I don't think he'd like that either," I agree.

My parents are attached at the hip and have been since I can remember. My mom's sister told me once that they only ended up together to spite her family. Sometimes I think my mom's whole family makes things up because they still aren't thrilled with the marriage. Dad was always seen as less than by my grandparents, and even if they treated me well, I picked up at a young age that they were never overly welcoming toward him.

"Okay, my dear, I'll see you tomorrow around three probably. I love you."

"Love you too, Mom. See you tomorrow."

"I'll have the 'shrooms on toast with a side of bacon please," I say, handing the server my menu.

"And you, sir?" they ask Foster, who has been switching between the Epiccc Waffles and the shakshuka.

"I'll have the shakshuka, please, extra spicy. Thanks."

Well, there goes any chance that I'll try it now, I think as he hands over his menu.

"Oh, actually, is there any way I could have chilis on the side instead of in it?" The server lets Foster know that it won't be a problem, and he beams over at me. "Now you can try something new today."

He has no idea how many new things I've already tried since he walked into my office.

Foster lifts his freshly squeezed orange juice. "To reconnecting with old friends and new experiences."

I lift my grapefruit juice and clink our glasses before taking a sip, my lips immediately puckering as the juice hits all the sour taste buds.

"Sour?" Foster laughs.

"Yes, but in a good way," I assure him. "So, what did you get up to yesterday?"

Foster suddenly looks sheepish. "Would you believe me if I told you I didn't even change out of my pajamas? I basically slept all day."

"Did you forget we work together? That doesn't surprise me at all."

"What about you?"

After I had talked to my mom, I'd did some laundry that I still haven't put away, chatted with Cass a bit, and spent way too long scrolling through every social media app I have. "Not much. Recovered from the week." I shrug.

Foster tips his head back and groans, the bruise on his jaw more obvious with the change of angle. "I hope we get a break next week. Because if this is what we can expect for the next three months, I don't think anyone will survive it."

"Foster!" I hear a woman's voice call from behind me and watch as his face goes red.

"Jessica is here," he grits out right before she leans down on our table, her ample cleavage on full display in a way it never is at work.

"Oh my god, Sophie!" she squeals when she notices me. "Foster didn't say you'd be coming." If I had to guess, I'd put money on Jessica pre-drinking before arriving this morning. "Are you two on a date?" she whispers loudly.

"No!" we both say at the same time.

"Just two friends supporting another friend," I say, really emphasizing the 'friends' part.

Thankfully the server arrives with our food, and Jessica recognizes it's time to go back to her table. "I'll see you two tomorrow. Have fun!" She raises both hands and gestures while mouthing "Nice work" as she backs away with me shaking my head at her, desperately trying to tell her she's got it wrong.

"Tomorrow is going to be fun." I giggle nervously, cutting into the poached egg sitting atop a mountain of buttery mushrooms.

"Hey," Foster says, reaching over to touch my hand, pulling my attention back to him. "We're allowed to be friends, Soph. Half the staff knew we were at the concert the other night."

"I know, and I'm very happy to be friends with you." I wonder how many more times I can say that we're friends before it starts sounding like I'm trying too hard.

He gives me a strange look that I almost miss before looking down longingly at his food and back at me. "Do you want to go somewhere else?"

"And make you wait even longer for food? No. Besides, have you seen this?" I point down at my food as the yolk spills down the mountain of mushrooms like a luscious volcano. "I can't remember the last time I wanted something so badly."

I'm practically drooling as I jab my fork into my food and take a bite. I think I moan while I chew with my eyes closed because when I open them Foster's lips are slightly parted and he's staring at me, hunger blazing in his eyes. His mouth closes, and I watch him swallow before blinking rapidly and looking down at his own dish.

"I can't remember a time either," he says quietly and I have to assume he means the food. He has to mean the food because we are just friends and he's very hungry.

It soon becomes easy to slip back into our pre-Jessica conversation which doesn't last long because the opening bars to "Poker Face" by Lady Gaga blasts through the speakers.

"Here we go." Foster grins right before I look up to see a queen stomp out in a silver-sequined bodysuit and what looks to be an entire peacock on her head.

"That was incredible," I say to Foster's friend Lucas, drag name Della Licious. "I don't think I'll be able to eat brunch any other way going forward."

"Turned another one." Della shimmies with joy. "The bigots are going to be very upset."

"That's my favorite way to see them," Foster quips, leaning back in his chair and taking a long sip of his third coffee.

"What are you two beautiful humans doing after this?" Della asks, running her hand through Foster's hair. While I know they're friends, jealousy pings from somewhere deep inside.

"I was actually going to see if Foster wanted to come for dinner. My mom's in town and is making lasagna." I watch Foster's eyes widen for a split second before he leans forward. Della's hand falls away as he does, leaving his hair a little messy. It's a good look. It would be an even better look if my hand had been the one to mess it up.

Stop it.

"Does she still make that tomato sauce?" he asks dreamily.

I nod. "Every year."

"Well, Della, I have a date with layers of pasta, cheese, and sauce."

"How does a queen get an invite to such a dinner?" Della asks, eyelashes batting at me.

Della is lovely, but hell no, Foster is mine tonight. For dinner. Just for dinner. "I'll see if my mom will make one when I go home for Easter, and I'll host a dinner," I say to Della, who does a little happy clap.

"Should we get going?" Foster asks.

It's now two, which means my mom should be arriving soon, and knowing her, she'll be early.

"Yeah, probably best, I'd like to be home when my mom arrives."

"Should I come now or..." Foster asks, standing in front of our cars.

"Oh, well..." I hadn't really thought about the in between now and when we'd actually be consuming lasagna.

Foster starts to say he can go home as I tell him to come on over.

"Okay, so I'll follow you then." He nods toward my car, and I have to actively suppress the need to squee about Foster Walsh coming over to my house.

TWENTY-ONE

FOSTER

Sophie's house is very her. All fresh decor but with touches of warmth everywhere. Pictures of her with her parents and friends and even cows line the walls. More throws than one person needs are draped over the couch and armchair and spilling out of a cloth basket. Well-loved books fill the shelves surrounding the TV.

"So you're a real grownup," I say, walking over to the bookshelf to see what she's got.

"I am pretending to be one, somewhat successfully," she chirps, joining me.

She has the entire JRR Tolkien catalog, and I pull out the special edition of *The Hobbit*. I read this book every summer. I wonder if she remembers that. Cass used to tease me about it, but Sophie never did.

"Oh, are you a fan of his?" she asks innocently.

"He's alright." I shrug, slipping the book back in its place. "A bit long-winded at times."

"No one could describe a tiny insignificant detail like he could," she says solemnly.

"Can I have a tour?"

Sophie spins and waves for me to follow. "This"—she turns back to the living room—"is the living room."

"Ooooh," I revel. "It's very green. Very chic."

"I like green," she says, turning to admire the walls. I like *her* in green, surrounded by it, wrapped in it. "This way."

I follow through the living room and into an open, modern kitchen with pale green walls, white counters, and dusty blue cupboards. A vase of cherry blossoms sits on the counter, adding to the fresh spring vibes. Sophie stands in the center with her arms out like a showroom model. I'd buy anything she was selling.

"This is where all the magic will happen tonight," she jokes, dropping her arms and turning toward the dining area.

I have to remind myself that she means that there will be delicious food served from this room, and not that we'll be acting out one of the dreams I used to have about her when I was a teenager. Dreams that have begun to slowly creep back in, except now they're more intense, more detailed than anything my teenage brain could come up with.

"Is this where the eating happens?" I point toward the table that is the focal point of the room.

She smiles brightly, indoor sunshine. "I see you've been in one of these before."

Running my fingers across the white table, I offer a small shrug. "Once or twice."

Next, we head down the hall to the bathroom, a spare bedroom, and then she stops and points at a closed door. "And that's my room, but I didn't clean it so we won't be going in there."

"Why do I feel like that room is cleaner than ninety percent of bedrooms out there?"

"Because you're looking at how clean the rest of the house is and applying logic. I cleaned all night after my mom called to tell me she was coming, but I didn't touch my room. That is where all the mess moved to." She points at the door. "It's amazing I got the rest of the house done, but nothing cures avoidance like company coming over."

I give her a once-over. She's flawless in her dark denim and green sweater. Her hair is up in one of those messy ponytails that looks effortless but I know from my sister takes forever to look fashionably messy. I'm pretty sure she's only got mascara on, like usual.

"You don't look like you were up all night."

"That's because I'm used to functioning on very little sleep."

What I would give for a sleepless night with Sophie Hore.

The front door swings open as we're heading back to the living room, and I hear a voice I haven't heard in years sing hello through the house.

"Hey, Mom," Sophie sings back.

Mrs. Hore sweeps Sophie into a hug, and her eyes widen comically when they land on me. She quickly guides her daughter out of her way and has me pulled into her arms a second later.

"Foster Walsh," she exclaims into my sternum. "My god, it has been forever since I've seen you." She takes a step back and she studies me. "Sophie, why didn't you tell me you had a handsome man over? I could have gone elsewhere."

Sophie rolls her eyes as a pretty blush spreads across her

cheeks. "We work together, Mom, and I figured you might want to see him."

"Oh, that's right, Cass mentioned that, and that you went to a concert together. Odd *you* hadn't." Mrs. Hore's tone is inquisitive, like she thinks there is more to it than Sophie forgetting. "You're an EA, right?" she asks.

"I am."

"I never would have guessed that's where you'd end up." She laughs.

"Me either," I agree. My parents certainly wish it wasn't where I'd ended up.

"He's really good at it," Sophie says softly, glancing quickly over at me. "His students adore him."

It's out before I can stop it. "Thanks, sunshine."

Mrs. Hore's expression softens. "Oh, I'd forgotten you called her sunshine. Karl was so mad that he had never thought of it." She looks up at her daughter approvingly. "She is sunshine, isn't she?"

Sophie is totally red now, avoiding looking at either of us as we appraise her.

"She is," I agree. I have no idea what my face looks like, but in my head I'm wearing a dreamy expression that screams *you are the best part of every one of my days.*

Sophie shakes her head and skirts around her mom, heading out the door. "Okay, well, now that we have established that I am a ball of fire, can we help you with anything?"

"So, have you two been spending a lot of time together?"

Mrs. Hore asks, setting a massive slab of lasagna on my plate.

"I mean, not a lot of time, but catching up," Sophie tells her.

"You went to the Nyx Avalon concert together." A statement, not a question.

"Well, Cass couldn't go, and so she asked Foster, who graciously put his taste in music aside to attend the show with me."

Mrs. Hore glances over at me as she hands Sophie back her plate, which has a slab equal to mine. "What kind of music do you enjoy?"

"Oh, classic rock, mostly."

She sighs. "I remember when that was just called rock. One day Nyx Avalon is going to be classic pop, and you'll understand," she says to Sophie.

"One day, but not today." She smirks back.

Once Mrs. Hore has food on her own plate, I dive in. When the flavor hits my tongue, I'm fifteen again, sitting in my parents' dining room with Cass and Sophie eating lasagna Mrs. Hore had sent as a thank-you for something I can't recall. They were talking about Matt, some guy in their riding lesson that Sophie had a crush on. Two weeks before I wouldn't have cared, but now I was suddenly interested in what it was Sophie liked about him. Apparently he was tall and cute and a bit of a rebel. Sophie liked that he bucked the rules and was totally fearless.

I was tall and had been told I was kind of cute, but I liked rules. I was always home by curfew, cleaned my room, did my homework and the dishes, and I had a healthy fear of things that could kill me. But if that was the kind of guy Sophie was into, then I could probably break a rule here or there and, I don't know, try something a bit more daring at the skatepark. A few weeks later I was grounded and had pins in my arm after I lost control of my friend's dirt bike.

The whole ordeal did spark something in me, though. I suddenly found it thrilling to not do exactly what my parents wanted, something I'd watched Cass do since we were kids. But as the eldest, I always toed the line—until I jumped right over it.

"This is incredible," I moan once I've swallowed the first bite. "I can't believe I went so long without this stuff."

"Foster is a great cook," Sophie tells her mom.

"Oh? What do you cook?" she asks me.

"Pretty much anything." I shrug. "I like to make Korean food because it's hard to find around here, and I bake when I need to clear my head."

"His thank-you cookies are pretty good," Sophie says, glancing at me.

Mrs. Hore looks from me to Sophie and back again. "Thank-you cookies?"

"Chocolate chip cookies that I made as a thank-you."

"Definitely better than a card," Mrs. Hore agrees. "Certainly tastier. How was that event for the alumni you went to?"

"It was fine," Sophie says as I blurt out, "She looked amazing."

Mrs. Hore's head swings my way, and when I notice the look on Sophie's face I realize I should have kept my mouth shut. But I couldn't help it; she was breathtaking.

"Are you an alumnus too? I thought you went to Waterloo?"

I look over at Sophie, but she's back to eating her food. "Um, no, I went as Sophie's date so Gregory didn't treat her badly." Sophie's head snaps up the minute her ex's name is out of my mouth and she looks horrified and I think angry? It's not a look I've ever seen on her before.

"Why would Gregory treat you badly?" her mom asks.

Sophie's eyes are glued to me, and the lasagna loses all flavor in my mouth. "Sophie?" her mom asks again.

Sophie slowly turns toward her and puts her fork down. "Because he always treated me badly, Mom."

"What do you mean? He was always a perfect gentleman."

The scowl that forms on Sophie's beautiful lips physically hurts to see. "In the beginning, sure. In front of other people, absolutely, he'd never want anyone to think poorly of him. He had a reputation to uphold. But the minute we were alone..." Sophie's words fade, and she stares down at her plate.

"Soph, I..." I start to apologize but she cuts me off.

"Not now. I've had a really nice day, and I'd rather not do this right now." She turns to her mom. "If you don't mind."

Mrs. Hore reaches over and takes Sophie's hand, her face a portrait of concern and confusion. I can see the questions bubbling at the surface. *What did he do? Why didn't you say anything? Do I need to hire someone to take care of him?* Thankfully she doesn't vocalize any of them.

"So what did you get up to earlier today?" she asks instead.

"We went to a drag brunch," I answer, my eyes still glued to Sophie who seems to be a million miles away. All I want to do is crawl under the table and pull her down with me to hide from the world. Hold her until the clouds break and the sun comes back.

"How fun. So," she says slowly. "Alumni gala, drag brunch... what else have you two gotten up to?"

I keep my mouth shut, attention still on Sophie so I see the exact moment the mask slips back on, smiling at her mom. "Oh, well, like I said, Cass couldn't go to the Nyx Avalon concert with me so she gave her ticket to Foster. Ultimately, it was better than going on my own. He even learned some of the songs." She smiles over at me, and I'm almost convinced it's real.

"She's no Zeppelin, but I can't deny that her songs are catchy," I admit.

"You and Karl would get along well." Her eyes slide back to Sophie who's pushing her food around the plate before looking back at me. "What are you doing for Easter, Foster?"

"My parents host a breakfast so I'll be back home for the day." Easter is my most hated of the holiday meals. Between the overcooked eggs and my uncle making passive-aggressive remarks about my chosen profession, hair, tattoos, and general existence, I'd rather bathe Gary with my tongue.

"Well, if you're able to slip away, you're more than welcome for brunch or leftover brunch that we end up eating for dinner."

I can't read Sophie's expression. There is maybe hope there, but also some dread. Hope I'll go? Dread that I'll say yes? "Thank you, I'll keep that in mind," I say.

"You should drive up together. Makes sense with gas prices being what they are these days," Mrs. Hore suggests, pushing her chair back and starting to clear the table.

I rise to help but not before offering Sophie a reassuring smile. Her responding one is far more tense than I'd like. It's one I've seen once before, at the gala, and I'd prefer to never see it again.

Between the three of us, we get everything cleaned up and packed away in no time. While I'd like to spend every possible second I can with Sophie far from the halls of school, I get the sense that if I stay much longer I will outlast my welcome.

"Soph," I murmur, pulling her gently toward the front door. "I'm going to take off and let you and your mom spend some time alone."

"You don't have to go," she stammers as her hand lands on my bicep briefly.

"I'll see you tomorrow," I insist, slipping on my shoes.

"Oh, no, not tomorrow. I'm at Bishop all day. I won't be back at school until Wednesday."

Nuts. Days with a zero percent chance of seeing Sophie in the halls are the worst.

"Right, well." I hold up my phone. "I'm a text away if you get bored or can't decide which pattern to wear one morning."

I love how she uses her clothes as a way to put the kids at ease. Last week, Pete came back from meeting with her and went on for about ten full minutes about the different mushrooms that were on her shirt and how he once ate a morel but didn't like it because it was too spongy.

Sophie opens the front door, leaning against it stiffly. "I'll be sure to reach out if I'm having trouble deciding." The storm clouds from earlier are still too dark for my liking, but I keep that to myself. I'm not going to force her to open up to me, standing in her doorway while her mom makes "I'm not listening" noises in the kitchen.

"Thank you for dinner, Mrs. Hore," I call, stepping across the threshold. I hear the door click shut before I even have a chance to offer Sophie one final wave.

On the drive home, I replay the entire day, but the minute I get to dinner it's as if there's a glitch and I keep saying the same thing that called the storm into the room.

No matter how badly I want to take those words back, I can't.

Gary greets me noisily when I walk into my apartment, and after feeding him I sink into the couch with a frustrated groan, feeling like an absolute buffoon.

Monday and Tuesday drag, a fact that is exacerbated by the fact Sophie hasn't reached out. The simple laughing emoji taunts me from her last message. A cruel little reminder that I got way out in front of my skis by saying anything about the gala in front of her mom.

"Mr. Walsh?" Pete shouts next to me, causing me to juggle my phone wildly and thankfully catch it before it hits the floor. "Do you think Miss Hore will like this?" He holds up the watercolor he's been working on since the start of class.

It looks like a painting someone would have done if they were tripping on acid. Saturated non-mushroom colors jump from the page. *Happy shrooms*, I think.

"I think she'll love that, bud." And I mean it. Sophie will be adding that to her tiny office cork board that already has an impressive number of student artwork. She'll light up the school with her smile when he hands it over. "Did you pick mushrooms because of her shirt?"

Pete nods, blushing. "Also, I love mushrooms."

"You've mentioned that once or twice." Pete is the only kid I know who regularly brings whole button mushrooms in his lunch.

"Mr. Walsh?" he asks again.

"Mmm?"

"Why are you so sad?"

Shiitake, I must look about as awesome as I feel right now. "I..." I stop and try to figure out what I'm going to say. I can't tell him the truth but I can't tell him nothing. "Had a busy weekend. I'm tired."

His left eyebrow raises skeptically and his eyes shift down to my phone. "Who is Sunshine?" He points with his brush.

"Are you being nosy?" I question.

"It's your fault for having your phone out in class," he counters.

"Fair." I slip the phone into my back pocket and lean back in the chair with a sigh. "Just a friend."

"Is that why you're sad? Did you have a fight?"

No, even if it feels like we did. "I never fight," I say with a tight smile.

"Not like this." Pete punches the air with both fists. "A feelings fight."

"A feelings fight?" I repeat slowly, and he nods. "No fight with fists, feelings, or fungi," I assure him.

"Mr. Walsh?"

"You know you don't have to keep saying my name if I'm the only one you're talking to, right?" I tease.

"Mr. Walsh?" he says seriously.

"Yes, Pete?"

"What is your favorite mushroom?"

I'm relieved he has moved onto favorites. This is one of the things I love most about working with Pete. The kid loves to discuss favorite and least favorite things, and I've been surprised to learn a thing or two about myself in the process.

"Enoki," I say without hesitation.

He scrunches up his face, his upper lip curling slightly. "Enoki? Did you make that up?"

I shake my head. "Nope. They're long skinny white mushrooms."

He grabs a pencil, and as fast as he can manage, he draws what looks like a very elongated sperm, or very skinny penis and I have to bite my cheeks to keep from laughing.

"Not quite. Here." I take the pencil and draw a less phallic mushroom.

"Huh," he says, his head moving this way and that as he studies it. "What does it taste like?"

"Not much, actually," I admit after taking a minute to think. "They have a fun texture, though."

My phone vibrates, and I look down, hoping to see Sophie's name. My heart sinks when I see that it's only a message from my sister.

SOPHIE

You're being ridiculous, I scold my reflection in the microwave. It's Wednesday night, and I haven't seen or talked to Foster since he left my house on Sunday. Today, I was back at the school and managed to avoid him all day. Five minutes ago, his name popped up on my phone, and I haven't had the nerve to open it yet.

It's not his fault that my parents don't know the full extent of my past relationship or breakup. It's not his fault he doesn't, either. I know if I told him, he'd go to the ends of the earth to protect me from future pain. I think he'd do that anyway, even without the full story, because that's who Foster Walsh is.

The microwave beeps, and I'm pulled out of my little spiral.

Three days of no Foster has not been fun. And not because I miss his face, which I do—he has a very nice face. But I miss how I feel when he's around, like the world isn't tilting and I'm racing to keep from falling off.

I abandon my reheated lasagna, suddenly disgusted by

the sight of it after multiple days of eating it hot or cold for every meal. Flopping down on the couch, I stare down at my phone, willing myself to see the message without actually opening it. If he sees I've read it then I don't respond, it will be worse. And I *do* want to respond. I just don't want to get into all the shit with Gregory and my parents and me quite frankly. I'm not ready to show Foster what an idiot I was for five years of my life.

The phone screen blurs as I stare at it until it goes dark. Cass's name appears moments later, lighting it up and causing me to blink rapidly to clear my vision.

CASS

I'm coming to Easter!

Aren't your parents doing something?

Obvs, but my uncle will be there so fuck that.

I remember meeting her whole family a couple times when I was a kid and wondering how Foster and Cass were related to some of them.

My mom invited Foster too.

Why?

I mean, awesome but how the hell did that come about?

He was over for dinner when she was here on Sunday night. He said he was going home though.

Well now I feel bad.

He can still come.

> He'll make an appearance at home
> regardless. He feels obligated to and shit.
> Plus our grandmother will be there and he
> feels bad that he doesn't see her enough.

Damn, I love their grandmother so much. I'd be going too if I were him.

There seems to be no escaping thinking about Foster so I finally open his message. It's a meme of two chocolate bunnies, one missing its ass and the other missing its ears. A classic.

> Never gets old.

I watch the three dots of his reply appear and then disappear over and over again, my anxiety amping up in the meantime.

> I'm sorry I've been MIA.

I fire off after the dots disappear again.

> I was busy with work and needed a couple days.
>
> I hope you don't think I was mad at you.
>
> Now I sound full of myself...
>
> Anyway, I am sorry. I haven't been a good friend.

I reread my barrage of texts, zeroing in on "friend."

He hasn't read the texts yet, and the dots haven't returned. I could delete them and pretend like I never said anything, but then maybe he'll see that I deleted them and wonder what I wrote. What if he thinks I was telling him off and then was too chickenshit to own up to it?

I stuff the phone under the couch cushion before I let myself do another thing. A knock on the door makes me jump out of my stupor. The curtains are closed so I can't see who it is through the living room windows. So I sit still, hoping whoever it is goes away. After ten minutes of silence I creep to the door and peek through the window at the top. Seeing that the coast is clear I slowly open it and stick my head out to look around. As I'm about to close it I happen to look down and see a small tin with an envelope taped to the top.

Bending to pick it up, I pull the note free.

Soph

I'm sorry I made things awkward on Sunday. I know these won't erase it, but hopefully they'll help you forgive me.

F

I open the tin and reveal a mountain of mini chocolate chip cookies. He made me "I'm sorry" cookies. Backing into the house, I don't even remember shutting the door before my back hits the wall and I slide down to the floor, still staring at the cookies.

I force myself to put the cookies away after I've swallowed the final bite of the fifth, and then I go dig my phone out from the couch.

FOSTER

Sorry I was out for a run.

Did you run to my house?

Guilty.

Can I FaceTime you?

I just got home, I'm gross, need to shower.

I don't care.

My phone rings, and I hit accept. Foster's slightly blotchy face fills the screen, and I pull my lips between my teeth to keep my smile at bay. He looks good like this. His usually artfully coiffed hair is sticking up in all directions where it's not plastered to his face. Little dots of sweat cover his forehead and temples, and his lips are parted as he still works on catching his breath. I have to remember to breathe myself as I take him in. *I want to make him sweat like that.* My face heats at the thought.

"Hey," I greet him quietly. "Thank you for the cookies."

He tilts his head, eyes narrowed. "How many have you eaten?"

"Two."

I watch his eyebrow rise. His eyes narrow further, and I lift my hand spreading out my fingers to reveal the real number. The deep warm tone of his laugh reaches places it has no business reaching, and I try to cover how flustered I feel with an eye roll.

"It's your fault for making good cookies. If they were half as good, I could have stopped at one."

"You eat as many as you want, sunshine, they're all yours." Warmth washes over me.

"I'm sorry," I blurt out.

"You mentioned that in your texts. You've got no reason to be sorry," he says gently as he sits.

"I do, though. I disappeared and that wasn't cool."

"As you said, you've been busy."

I shake my head. "I haven't been that busy. I just didn't know what to say after Sunday. I've been avoiding you." I clamp my jaw shut so nothing else escapes. I know once I get talking about things I won't be able to stop, and I've never been someone who likes to have honest conversations on the phone. I need to be in the same room as the other person, otherwise I become hyper-focused on what their body language could be saying. Which, let's be real, I'm going to do regardless, but at least if I can see all of them, I do a lot less spiraling.

"Are you done avoiding me now?" he asks slowly, leaning forward.

"I am," I confirm.

"Do you want to talk about it?" It's so easy to see why his students adore him. Even the ones who have outbursts eventually come around when Foster is the one sent in to defuse the situation.

"One day, but not today."

"Well, I'm here whenever you want to."

We sit there for a few seconds looking at one another, and it's then that I see that underneath the sweat and wind-burned skin, Foster looks as tired as he had the week of the concert.

"Rough week?"

"Do I look that bad?"

"Not bad, just tired."

"Same thing," he counters. He runs his hand through his hair, the sweaty strands sticking up at new angles. "I haven't been sleeping well, and we're down two EAs this week."

It seems selfish to feel guilty—the not sleeping well may have nothing to do with me—but guilt seeps in all the same.

"I didn't know."

Foster shrugs and then stretches his neck. "It's not like you could fix it, Soph. No need to apologize."

"I know, but I could have at least been a sounding board for you."

He stops stretching and stares through the camera. I can feel the heat of his gaze. "And I could have reached out. Should I be sorry that I didn't?"

"No."

"So no one needs to be sorry." His expression relaxes and his lips turn up at the corners. "Cass told me she's going to Easter at your parents this year."

"Yeah, she told me too. Does that change your plans?"

"No, I want to spend some time with my grandmother, and my mom told me she's been complaining about forgetting what I look like." He chuckles as he stands, the lighting changing and shadowing his face. "Sorry, I've gotta get out of this shirt. It's drenched, and now I'm freezing." He tosses the phone, and it bounces a bit so I assume it landed on his bed. When it settles, I can just make him out. I freeze when I realize what he's about to do. I should look away, give him some privacy. He likely doesn't realize that the phone did not land flat.

But I don't look away. Instead my eyes are glued to him as he reaches over his shoulder and pulls his shirt up and over his head in one fluid motion. Why is that maneuver so fucking hot? I haven't seen Foster's body since we were kids, and while I can't really get a good look now, I can see that his arms are not the only area tattooed. He picks the phone back up and I'm greeted by his face again. No complaints, but lord help me, this is going to be such a distraction whenever I see him in clothes now. I'm going to want to study every line he has drawn on his skin.

I can see some dark lines right below his collarbone and realize he didn't put a shirt back on. "I thought you were cold?" I tease.

"I'm not putting something on when I'm about to go shower."

My mind is spinning out of control. Probably because I haven't done anything sexual in months. But one tiny glimpse of Foster shirtless, and I'm ready to scream "fuck it" while running to his apartment, stripping as I go.

Because my mind is fracturing in real time, I don't know how I manage to piece a sentence together, let alone the one that leaves my mouth. "I can come with you to Easter, if you want. Then we can go to my parents' after. It'll knock E off our list."

Foster's smile is radiant. "Really?"

Sure. Maybe. No. Yes. Absolutely. "Why not? E is for efficiency."

He frowns. "You wanna get through the alphabet faster, sunshine?"

A nervous laugh bubbles out of me. "What? No, but now I'm curious what you're going to pick for some of the letters."

"Oh, I've got those figured out, don't you worry." Why does he sound flirty? Why are my nails digging into my thigh?

"I'm not worried," I counter.

His eyes travel behind the phone, and he sighs. "I am working through my own daily alphabet, though, and I've done R so need to do S."

Sex? Suck? "Shower." It comes out a bit too dreamily.

"Nothing like getting clean," I squeak, cringing at myself in the process.

He smirks back. "It does make getting dirty more fun." His eyes widen comically, and all the nerves and mortification I had been feeling disappear.

"Go shower, Foster, you probably stink. I'll see you tomorrow."

"Night, Soph." He gives a little wave before hanging up, and it leaves me fucking breathless.

TWENTY-THREE

FOSTER

LILWALSH

Heads up, I told Mom that you were bringing your new girlfriend to breakfast.

CASSANDRA she's picking me up in 5 minutes.

And she's not my girlfriend!

Hey, this way Uncle Phil won't go on and on about how you're a deadbeat that can't even get a woman. You walk in with smokeshow Sophie and you'll be laughing all the way over to the Hores for brunch.

She's not wrong, but now I have to ask Sophie to lie about us again. She must think I'm supremely pathetic.

Also, I told her she has to play the girlfriend part already and she's fine with it.

Well, that makes things a bit easier.

> Can you at least run stuff like this by me
> before hard launching devious plans?

Pfffff nope, the surprise is half the fun!

Don't say hi to the relations for me!

SUNSHINE

I'm here

> Coming

"You really don't have to do this you know," I say as Sophie pulls into my parents driveway and parks behind my uncle's obnoxiously large pickup.

"Do you not want me to? Is it going to be harder for you to be here if we pretend again?" Yes, but not for the reasons she thinks. Because it's hard enough to keep my hands to myself when we aren't pretending. Pretending means I get to touch her and then it's nearly impossible to reprogram my brain when we're alone again.

"No, pretending is very easy. And having you here will make everything more tolerable."

She pulls her phone off the charge cord and swings the door open. "Excellent. Let's do this, boyfriend." *Call me boyfriend again. Call me whatever the heck you want, just don't stop.* She doesn't, but she does twine her fingers with mine when we meet in front of the car. *This is equally nice,* my body hums.

The front door swings open before we've even reached the end of the sidewalk, and my uncle Phil blocks the view into the house. Phil married into the family and brought with him his ignorant ideas and vocabulary. He's such a walking stereotype that it's almost boring at this point. Cass got sick of listening to him lecture her on her own sexuality and fully skips out on most functions he attends now because it stresses her out too much, and she's the most unflappable person I know.

"Well, would you look at that, he does indeed have a woman with him," he bellows, his gaze dragging hungrily from Sophie's head down to her feet and back up again. "Looks like a bona fide one too."

"Phil, give him a break," Mom scolds halfheartedly, squeezing past him and rushing out to hug me. "Oh, I've missed you, baby," she murmurs into my neck, and I reluctantly drop Sophie's hand to hug her properly. When she pulls back, she finally looks over at Sophie, and the look of shock on her face makes me laugh.

"Sophie Hore, you're the girlfriend?" She drags Sophie to her before she has a chance to answer. "When?" she asks, leaning back, her hands still on Sophie's upper arms. "How long has this been going on for? And why the hell didn't you say something?" She smacks my arm playfully.

"About a month, maybe?" I say, looking at Sophie for confirmation.

"About that, yeah." She offers me a knowing smile that may seem flirty to those observing the interaction, but really it's just an acknowledgment of the inside joke.

"I'd make him keep it quiet too, blondie," my uncle remarks gruffly, giving me a look that can only be described as scathing before turning to go back in the house.

Sophie watches his retreating back with wide eyes, her mouth open slightly. "Why would I want to keep it quiet?" she asks, turning to me.

I shrug. "My uncle thinks I'm a failure because of my

job." Sophie doesn't even try to hide her disgust. "That, and my hair color makes me less of a man or some nonsense."

"He doesn't think you're a failure," Mom says. "You know how he is." She shrugs off his insult for the thousandth time.

It's easier for her to pretend that he means nothing than to confront the problem. Everyone has let him get away with this stuff since my aunt passed five years ago. And my mom hates an uncomfortable family gathering.

"He's the best EA at the school," Sophie says, slipping her fingers back between mine. I feel like I could take on the world with her hand in mine. Certainly my uncle at the very least.

"I bet he is, dear." Mom smiles tightly at Sophie as she leads us into the house.

My mom has never said she's disappointed in my career path, but she does like to make comments about how it's not too late to go to teachers' college. There seems to be a general consensus that only women choose to be EAs.

Before we get to the door, I pull Sophie to a stop while my mom disappears inside.

"You sure you want to do this? You could go straight to your parents and avoid the roasting of Foster Walsh."

Sophie looks from me to the open door and I see the minute she makes up her beautiful mind. "No, I think I'd rather be here with you. At least I can try and help control the temperature. Perhaps keep it to a light grilling rather than a full-on roast."

If this was real, if she were mine, I'd pull her to me and kiss the ever-loving daylights out of her.

Sophie is working the room like she was made for it. And it's not hard to spot her in the crowded space. Despite being the most beautiful woman I've ever seen, she towers over most of the others here. All the men in my family are over six feet while all the women are under five six. Three of my cousins have given me a thumbs-up when they walk away, and there has somehow been less talk about my lack of a real profession than usual by this time in a gathering.

"You know," my grandmother whispers, while handing me a stack of plates, "I always knew you'd end up together." I watch as her gaze swings to where Sophie is talking animatedly to my dad.

I should tell her the truth, but I'd really like to know what she thinks she saw. "Oh yeah? How'd you know that?"

"Well, when she was a kid, she only had eyes for you. She always smiled a little bigger, laughed a little louder, blushed a shade darker when you were around."

"I am pretty great." I wink at her.

"Then there was you." She dips her chin and looks above her glasses at me.

"Me?"

"You. I want to say when you were about fourteen you were having a conversation with your grandfather, and she walked by with your sister. Your grandfather said you stopped speaking mid-sentence to watch her. 'That boy's got a bad case of the love bug for that string-bean friend of Cassandra's,' he'd said while we were driving home." She reaches out and squeezes my arm, looking around me to where Sophie is still standing. "I'm glad she caught the bug too."

I shake my head, not remembering this at all. Not believing I ever looked at her that way before I got home from camp. I think I'd remember if I had. Sophie was always at our house, so I obviously saw her a lot, but I didn't really *see* her. But as I take the plates to the head of the buffet my mom has set out, I start thinking back.

A lot of my memories before I went away for school have her in them, and a lot of those memories aren't of anything major. Sophie laughing in the kitchen with Cass, taunting me while she crosses the finish line in Mario Kart first, or playing road hockey with us and a couple other friends, friends I can't even see the faces of.

"You just gonna stand there holding the plates, Foster? Maybe that girlfriend of yours knows how to reboot you. Although she may not want you. May want to find someone who's a bit more of an equal, if you know what I mean," my uncle sneers, roughly grabbing a plate off the top and immediately serving himself food before my mom has called anyone to help themselves.

Doing my best to ignore him, I set the plates down as gently as I can and head back into the kitchen to see what else I can help with only to find Sophie laughing with my grandmother.

"I was telling Sophie how your grandfather caught you staring at her." Sophie looks at me with an eyebrow raised and a tiny smirk on her face.

"What can I say?" I shrug, walking up to her and pulling her into my arms. "I knew what I wanted from a young age."

Sophie leans into me in response, and I swear my heart skips several beats. Nothing about this feels fake right now.

Easter breakfast is a chaotic affair at my parents' place. It's a "feed yourself and find a place to sit" kind of situation. My plate is sparse aside from the extra-large helping of my grandmother's Swedish tea ring. My uncle eyes my plate with contempt; he's allergic to pecans, and despite never admitting it, I'm convinced my grandmother refuses to change her recipe to spite him. As if I need another reason to love the woman.

Sophie smiles and does a little happy wiggle as she takes her first bite of the pastry. When she looks up and sees me watching her, she shrugs.

"It's really good," she mouths before going in for another bite.

Before I know it it's time to head to the Hores' for brunch, and for the first time in as long as I can remember I'm a little sad about leaving a family gathering. Sophie made the whole experience tolerable, enjoyable almost. The only thing that wasn't was the way my uncle's eyes would stay on Sophie for a little too long.

"Check your coat pocket," my grandmother says as she squeezes me harder than anyone her size should be able to.

"Why?"

Her answer is a simple pat on my arm as she turns to give Sophie an equally tight hug. "It was so nice to see you again before I die," she says with unnerving joy.

"Oh." Sophie laughs nervously. "I'm glad too." She looks up at me over my grandmother's head, and I shake my head. I'm pretty sure this is a dig at me for avoiding family stuff.

"I'm sure you'll see her many more times before that day, many years in the future."

"Especially if whatever that thing you made is

involved." She smiles brightly down at my grandmother who pulls her back in for another hug.

"Your uncle is a real hodenkobold, eh?" Sophie says as she's pulling out of my parents' driveway.

"He does have certain hodenkobold qualities, yes," I grumble.

"Hey." She reaches over and squeezes my hand, her touch instantly making everything better. "You don't believe anything that man says, right?"

I shrug because sometimes I do. "Sometimes I think I should have gone to teachers' college or pushed myself to study something more like, I don't know, engineering or medicine."

Sophie looks like she smelled something bad. Her face is set in a grimace—a beautiful grimace sure, but a grimace nonetheless.

"Well, I can't see you in something like engineering, and you hate blood so medicine is out."

"Why not engineering?"

"Don't you hate math?"

"You remember I hate math?" I ask, surprised.

"Don't flatter yourself, Mr. Walsh. Throw a dart, and you'll hit at least three people who hate math." She smirks out at the road.

"True. Do you hate math?"

"Math to me has always been a bit like spinach or broccoli. I see the benefits and I use it, but that doesn't mean I like it."

"You don't like broccoli?" I ask.

"I have a complicated relationship with broccoli," she says as she concentrates on turning onto the road to her parents' place.

"Go on," I encourage.

She sighs. "Well, I don't like when it's in a stir-fry because it's always overcooked and mushy. But I do like it in a soup where it is arguably mushy. I like it lightly steamed so it's bright green, but I hate it raw."

"So the cook on it has to be extremely precise?"

"Exactly. There is a fine art to cooking broccoli to my very exacting standards." I file the information away in the mental folder I have for things about Sophie Hore.

She pulls into her parents' driveway, and we are immediately greeted by several dogs. A small white one I recognize as Yogurt goes absolutely bananas when he sees Sophie.

I wish I could show affection like a dog, I think as I watch her drop down to fully absorb the canine love.

"Sophie Elizabeth Hore, you're going to be covered in mud!" I hear Nancy shout from the porch.

"That's the goal, Mom!" she calls back, cackling as another dog pulls her attention away from Yogurt.

Two seconds later, she's on her butt and five more dogs take the opportunity to get in on the action. Her hand shoots straight up, and I take it as a sign she'd like help so I grab and pull. Except in my enthusiasm I pull her so hard she loses her balance and falls into me.

Deep breaths, I tell myself as every part of her body connects with me. *Abort!* Deep breaths mean I'm overwhelmed by the smell of her. Citrus and honey flood my nose, and I find myself pulling her in a bit tighter.

She's got a small smudge of dirt on her forehead, and I reach up to wipe it off. As I do that, her eyes meet mine, and everything stops. My thumb on her head, my arm around her waist, blinking, my heart—heck, the earth probably stops spinning too.

"You don't have to pretend here!" Cass yells from the porch.

Sophie blinks, and a small smile appears, so small one might call it sad. That's what my delusional mind tries to convince me of, anyway. Her smile is reflecting my feelings about this all being pretend and also not getting to pretend a little longer today.

I reluctantly let her go and step back, missing the feel of her instantly.

"I'm going to have quite the bruise, I think," she murmurs as we make our way to the house, the dogs circling our legs the entire way.

"Where?"

"My right cheek," she says, and when I look over her face, she laughs. "Not that cheek."

I feel the blood rush north and south as I realize she's talking about her ass.

Don't say you'll check it for her, I warn myself. *And stop thinking about her asking.*

"How's the fam?" Cass asks.

"They're fi—" I begin to say, but the second I cross the threshold into the Hores' home, I'm bowled over by the delicious smells wafting from the kitchen.

"He's about to learn the real reason I skipped out on family Easter," I hear Cass say, but she sounds far away. Can smells dampen sound?

The scent of warm spices fills the air along with pastry, butter, and bacon. I have to swallow again and again to keep from drooling.

"I think we've lost him," Sophie murmurs.

The sound of her voice brings me back, and I look over only to discover she's not next to me as there's a tug on my foot. She's kneeling in front of me, untying my shoes, and god help me I wish the sight of her down there didn't do what it's doing to me. There is nothing sexual about untying someone's shoes in the presence of family, but that doesn't stop my mind from trying to make it a thing. When her gaze meets mine, my knees literally wobble.

"Um, you don't have to do that," I stammer, quickly dropping to one knee to take over the task.

"My mom's breakfasts tend to have a paralyzing effect on first-timers," she whispers, her face level with mine.

So does that darn smile.

"Cass has bragged about her breakfasts for years. I should have been prepared," I say as my brain starts to acclimate.

Sophie releases my laces and stands as I finish my right shoe and stand to toe each one off. I need to pull it together.

A high-pitched squeal has me nearly jumping out of my skin as a dark-haired woman steps into the foyer and enthusiastically embraces Sophie.

"Oh my god, I shouldn't hug you so hard," Sophie says, stepping back, her hands hovering over the other woman's abdomen. "May I?"

The woman, who I now realize must be Marley, the Hores' neighbor, shrugs. "I mean, not much to feel right now, but go ahead."

Sophie lays her hands gently on Marley and smiles serenely. "I can't believe there's gonna be a li'l Bennett or Marley running around soon."

Marley bursts out laughing. "You can't? I still can't believe I'm married and love it, let alone over the moon about becoming a mom."

A look I can't quite identify replaces Sophie's joy briefly before her mask slips back on.

Marley looks up at me and holds her hand out. "You must be the brother and fake boyfriend, right?"

"Shit, sorry," Sophie says, gesturing toward me. "Marley, this is Foster. Foster, Marley. I can't believe you two have never met."

"Feels like we have," Marley says, gripping my hand tightly.

I'd have to agree with that. Cass gave me a play-by-play of how Marley and Bennett came to be shortly after she'd started working at the rescue. Since then, she talks about them more than she talks about anyone we're related to. I don't actually know Marley and Bennett, but I do know I like them more than almost everyone I share DNA with simply by the way they've treated Cass. The fact that Sophie speaks so highly of them doesn't hurt either.

A call to come eat comes from somewhere deep in the house, and I follow Sophie and Marley as they talk about potential names.

In the dining room the table is piled with copious amounts of food, every dish more mouthwatering than the last.

"Foster?" a deep voice asks from beside me.

I look up from the food to see a guy nearly my height but who looks like he'd crush me easily if the chance arose.

"Bennett?" I dare a guess.

We shake hands and are then ushered to our seats before we have a chance to exchange more than names.

When Sophie sits down next to me, I clasp my hands to keep myself from reaching for her. It has become a habit now in the presence of other people where a meal is involved.

Being here feels right, but not touching her feels wrong.

TWENTY-FOUR

SOPHIE

Foster looks far more comfortable at this table than he did at his parents' place. He's in the middle of telling Marley and Bennett about Pete and his love of storing things in his pockets, and the two react the way you'd hope people would—engaged, taken in, genuinely curious. No one is sneering or judging him because of his job.

I don't realize I'm staring at him until Cass clears her throat, pulling my attention from the conversation.

"So, how terrible was my uncle?" she asks, her lip curling in disgust.

"From what I've heard about him, he was in fine form," I grumble.

Cass rolls her eyes and chews a piece of cinnamon roll thoughtfully, her gaze sliding to her brother for the briefest moment before looking back at me and mouthing, "Thank you."

I shrug in response. I don't need to be thanked for being there for him. Friends show up for the tough times too.

"So, Soph, it's wild that you got placed somewhere with someone you know, eh?" Marley says enthusiastically.

"Even wilder that I had no idea that it was a possibility." I glare over at Cass, who is suddenly very interested in a smear of ketchup on her plate.

"Do you two get to hang out much during the day?" Bennett asks, leaning back and wrapping his arm around Marley's shoulders. She relaxes into him, her hand automatically going to his thigh.

I've never seen two people who need to have constant contact with one another and yet have it look so natural. I don't even think they realize they're doing it. Even before they were officially a couple, they were like this. It's a level of intimacy I worry I'll never understand.

"Most days we see each other at lunch," Foster says. "But some days we don't see each other at all." I hate those days. Not only because seeing him is a highlight but if we don't see one another it's usually because something has gone wrong.

"Those days always seem extra-long," I admit shyly. I can feel my face heat and then turn into an inferno when I see the way Marley looks over at Cass.

"I remember those days," Bennett says as his hand tightens on Marley's upper arm.

"So, Bennett, any new additions?" I ask, changing the subject before anyone else can try to interpret what I said.

"We've got a couple boarders," he says. "Temporary residents," he amends forcefully, smiling down at Marley who's looking at him like she doesn't believe a word of it.

"Oh? You've learned what 'temporary' means?" I tease.

Foster looks from me to Bennett, confused.

"Believe it or not, Soph, I've become somewhat of an expert on the word."

"He has," Cass confirms. "The three temps are from Teddy's place."

"Teddy's place? It's official then?" I ask.

Cass's former coworker Teddy and his partner Nellie had gone up to Marmot Point five years ago and had bounced between Bennett's and Spencer Lake Rescue while the owners were dealing with some health issues. The bet had been that it wouldn't be long before Teddy and Nellie would be permanently changing their address.

"It is. Spencer Lake Rescue is officially their home," Marley says sadly. "I'm so happy for them, but I do miss seeing Nell more." Bennett and my parents burst out laughing. "I know, I know, it's a role reversal." She rolls her eyes.

"Aren't you two going up next week?" Dad asks.

"We are," Bennett confirms.

"And weren't they here two weeks ago, to bring the dogs down?"

Bennett nods, avoiding Marley's glare.

"And before that..." my mom begins.

"Okay, I get it," Marley huffs.

I feel the heat from Foster's body before his arm brushes into mine. "I don't get what's happening," he whispers.

"I'll tell you later," I assure him.

He nods and pulls away, making me wish we were pretending to be dating here too.

"Ya know," Marley says as we begrudgingly take part in the annual "I'm too full for this shit" Easter walk, "for two people who aren't pretending to be together, you kind of look like two people who are together."

I slow my pace, putting some distance between everyone else and us. "We get along well. We always have."

"No offense, but the vibes are more than two people who get along well. Is there something there?"

"No," I say a bit too quickly.

"Do you want there to be?" she pries.

"When did you become such a romantic?" I ask.

"You've met my husband? Oh, and this slightly overbearing, if not well-meaning, incredibly meddlesome couple, the Hores? I had no choice. I had to conform or lose my mind. And conforming has way better benefits," she says coyly.

"How's the new book coming?"

Marley looks at me as we walk and I can see her wanting to push for more out of the corner of my eye, but she gives her head a small shake. "It's going well. I've submitted everything I need to for the outline, and now it's up to Simon to fill in all the blanks."

"Well, I'm excited for it. Let me know when pre-orders are available."

"I'm sure your mom will before I have a chance." She chuckles. We ended up with nine copies of the first one between my parents and me because we all ordered a copy for ourselves and each other. A fact that thoroughly embarrassed Marley.

"Any new cravings or aversions?"

"Sadly, only your mom's sauce still. I was hoping I'd start craving things that are super healthy, but so far nothing. I guess I should be happy I'm not craving really specific things that are hard to get."

"You know Bennett would find any way he could to get them here."

"I do know that." She smiles dreamily at her husband as he talks with Foster.

Foster picks that moment to look over his shoulder. His eyes find me, crinkling with his smile.

Marley makes a tiny contented sound before she hurries ahead of me to take Bennett's hand. Foster is instantly forgotten and he slows for me to catch up.

"Good conversation?"

"Yeah, he was telling me about Spencer Lake's new barn."

"Riveting," I joke.

"It is in a way. I appreciate people who are into the minutiae of their jobs. I mean, the dogs are clearly the best part, but he seems equally as enthusiastic about fixing a barn door as he does about taking them out for a walk."

"That's how you sounded about your job today."

"It's easy with your family." I love that he calls them "my family" despite the fact I'm only technically related to two others here.

"No," I say, resting my hand on his arm as we both slow to a stop. "That's how you sounded with your family. Despite all the nasty things some of them think and even say about your job, you still sounded as passionate about it with them as you did with everyone here."

I register the look of surprise on his face at my words.

"I guess I'm so used to being on autopilot when I'm around them I didn't even realize. Thank you."

"For what?"

"For telling me. For going with me. For keeping me sane. For encouraging me to be myself." His eyes track across my face, the world around us quieting and fading away as they land on my lips.

"You don't need to thank me, Foster," I assure him, stepping closer. The urge to kiss him is like none I've ever experienced before.

"It's what friends do, right?" he says.

"Absolutely," I force out.

"Are you two coming or what?" Cass calls from the front of the group, breaking the spell.

"Still as impatient as ever." Foster grins toward his sister before turning and continuing on while I stand there trying to remember how to walk.

"I'm sorry, you're what?" I gasp, sitting up so quickly that the hot chocolate in my mug sloshes over the side.

"We're retiring. Or I'm retiring, at any rate," my dad says.

"Is something wrong?" I look up at the mantle where my parents' wedding photo sits. Mom in a vintage blue polka-dot dress and Dad in a button-up vest and jeans as he holds her in his arms above the snow. They're practically kids compared to the people sitting in front of me now. It's like I didn't register how much they've aged until "retiring" came out of my dad's mouth. Come to think of it, he does look a bit more tired than usual. Maybe it's just the late hour; he's usually been asleep for a few hours by this time.

"Why does anything have to be wrong?" Mom asks, setting her mug down on the table beside her. "You're not taking over the farm. Our herd is half of what it was. We don't have a bull anymore. It feels like the right time."

"Besides, the deal your mother got will—" My dad stops talking abruptly when he sees the look on my mom's face.

"What deal?"

"I should..." Foster says from beside me, rising slowly

but not getting far before my arm shoots out and I pull him back down. "Or not," he says slowly.

"What deal?" I ask again, calmer this time.

Mom takes a deep breath and straightens a little before answering. "I signed a brand deal for my tomato sauce."

"Holy shit," I say under my breath. "With who?"

"Simmons."

"Whoa," Foster breathes out. "They're everywhere."

"And..." my dad says encouragingly.

"A book deal," Mom says sheepishly.

"Why do you sound embarrassed, boop?" Dad asks while Mom glares at him. He never calls her boop in front of anyone other than me, but he let it slip in front of Foster.

"I'm not embarrassed. I'm bloody overwhelmed with pride, but I'm still coming to terms with the fact it's real."

"Can you explain so I too can come to terms with the fact it's real?" I ask.

"About three months ago, some TV executive was eating at The Blind Shepherd and he had a dish with my sauce." It's rare that I see my mother flustered but she's well on her way trying to tell me about this news. "He wanted to know where to buy it, and when they told him he couldn't, he wanted to see how he could make buying it a possibility. There were talks and lawyers and now I have an agent and—"

"Slow down, dearest," Dad says, taking her hand and squeezing. I watch as she looks at him and takes a couple steadying breaths.

"Turns out I'm pretty good in the kitchen." She shrugs.

I sit there staring at her, in complete shock.

"I'm sorry I didn't tell you sooner, but I was worried it wouldn't happen and then I'd be a disappointment to everyone."

"Excuse me?" I say in disbelief. "A disappointment to everyone? Who is everyone? Mom, this is amazing!" I squeal, jumping up and going to hug her. "I'm so fucking proud of you," I murmur as I pull her up so I can squeeze her tighter.

My dad's arms wrap around us next in a family hug.

"Get over here." I hear him say before another set of arms join the fray.

Notes of patchouli and leather hit my nose, and I let myself enjoy the sensation of being held, albeit somewhat awkwardly by Foster.

When we separate, my mom announces that they're heading to bed. "Oh, one tiny thing," she says, turning back to us at the bottom of the stairs. "It totally slipped my mind with all the hosting duties that the new mattresses for the guest bedrooms were supposed to be delivered on Thursday but were delayed."

"Oh," Foster says, the warmth from his body impossible to ignore as he steps beside me. "I can... I can see if Cass has room, or maybe borrow the car and go to my parents'?"

Mom is already waving off the suggestions like they're the most ridiculous things she's ever heard. "Cass only has her bed and a small sofa. It's very late, and there are lots of deer out. And Marley had that look in her eye when they left, so no point in calling them. Thankfully, Sophie's bed is a queen so there's plenty of room."

My mouth drops as my dad hides a chuckle by clearing his throat and guiding my mom up the stairs.

Slipped her mind, my ass.

FOSTER

"I'm really glad you came," Sophie says. "Sorry about the sleeping arrangements."

She's on her side, head sinking into a downy pillow and apologizing to me for the thirteenth time since we found out about the bed situation. I'd told her I was fine sleeping on the couch but she wouldn't hear it.

"It's okay, Soph, really," I assure her, rolling onto my side so we're facing one another.

It's dark, but I can still make out her features. Not that I need the power of sight to actually see them. Her face has been seared into my memory.

"I can't believe my mom's sauce is going to be out there like... Prego," she whispers in wonderment.

"I don't think you should say that brand and your mom in one breath." I chuckle.

"You're right, that was insulting. Please don't ever tell her."

I slide my hand toward her with my pinky raised. "Pinky promise." She rolls her eyes, but she reaches out and wraps her pinky around mine.

My body reacts like she's straddled me. Every ounce of blood rushes south, and I pull my hand back quickly. It would be so easy to reach for her and pull her to me. So easy to guide her lips to mine and sink into her. So darn easy to give in to this gnawing need I've had for weeks now.

"Night, sunshine," I whisper before rolling over.

"Goodnight, Foster," she hums, and if I allow myself to get sucked into the delusion, I'd tell you she sounded disappointed by that sendoff.

I wake to the smell of something baking and coffee. A guy could get used to waking up to someone else creating the delicious smells in a house.

A guy could also get used to waking up with Sophie Hore's hand on his chest. She's still on her side of the bed, but her arm is stretched across the gulf between us, like she had reached for me in the night. The thought of Sophie reaching for me at any time, let alone in a bed has me standing at attention just in time for her eyes to open.

"Good morning." She yawns, and my god it's the most beautiful sound in the world.

"Morning, sunshine," I murmur, rotating my hips, trying to hide myself from her.

She stretches, and the noise she releases makes everything worse. "Something smells amazing." She rolls over and slips her legs off the bed, sitting with her back to me, and I take a minute to study her from behind.

Her hair is mostly in a bun, but strands have escaped the elastic. She's all long lines and lean muscle, same as she has always been. As beautiful as she has always been.

I watch, captivated as she pulls her hair out of the band and gathers the blonde locks back up to redo it. I don't know what it is about watching a beautiful woman do her hair, but I can't seem to move. I should get up, at least get my legs over and hope the change of position hides the morning wood I'm sporting. But instead I remain motionless running over the fact that I got to share a bed with the woman I've loved most of my life without fully realizing it.

"I'll see you down there, okay?" she says without even looking over at me.

Wicked, I've made her uncomfortable. Chased her from her own bedroom.

I sit up and take in the room in the daylight. She hasn't lived here full time in years, and yet she's everywhere. My parents put away all our stuff the second we moved out. Not Nancy and Karl, though. This space is a time capsule of their daughter.

Along the wall across from the bed is a string of horse show ribbons, more red than any other color. Below the ribbons are pictures taped to the wall. Lots of her and Cass smiling. Cass's hair is a little different in each one while Sophie's remains the same—long, straight, golden. My eyes snag on one at the bottom right of the collage.

Getting up slowly, I walk to the wall. I see caramel eyes and the hint of a smile on the face of a younger me. I hated my picture being taken back then—I don't know why, too cool for it maybe, or at least I thought I was. But I can see it there, the joy I got from Sophie being beside me. The hint of a smile was all because of her, and how I managed to contain it at all was a testament to my teenage stubbornness and nothing else.

I pull it from the wall. It's us, sitting on the couch at my parents' house, game controllers in hand, Sophie radiant as always.

"If memory serves me right, that was taken during a Mario Kart marathon," Sophie's silky voice flows from the doorway. "And I do believe you were losing." She snatches the image out of my grasp and studies it. "It's a lifetime ago."

"You haven't changed much," I say.

"You haven't either," She reaches up and threads her hand through my bedhead. "Your hair is even the same." We freeze when her fingertips make contact with my scalp.

Tension seeps out of every crevice in the room, and its tendrils wrap around us. Easing it could be so sweet. I could just slip my arm around her waist and pull her into me. Lean into her touch and silently beg for more. Drag it out as I tip my head and run my nose along hers. Breathe her in and breathe out all the things I wish we could do.

It takes a Herculean amount of effort to take a small step back, moving toward where my phone sits on the bedside table on my side of the bed. No, not my side—it's not our space, it's hers.

"What smells so good?" I ask, slipping my phone into the pocket of the sweats I'd opted to sleep in. Sophie's eyes follow my movement, stopping on my legs before they meet mine again.

"Maple scones."

"I love scones," I exclaim with more enthusiasm than I mean to, and she laughs, the tension immediately dissipating, much to my relief.

"Yo!" My sister's voice comes from somewhere downstairs. "Can you two stop being cute and come down here, please?"

"Cute?" I ask, one eyebrow raised as I catch myself in the mirror above the dresser.

Sophie steps closer, tilting her head as she studies our reflections. "Yeah, it works. Only because of the morning hair, though. Otherwise 'hot mess' is how I'd describe this" —she gestures between us—"situation."

"Hot." I let the word linger and take a small amount of pleasure in the way her eyes widen. "Mess," I finish, grinning over at her. "Let's go be hot messes with scones."

"We've got the space, so we figured why not. Bennett and Marley didn't even hesitate."

"What are you talking about?" Sophie asks, sitting next to her father, her plate piled high with breakfast.

"Bennett's rescue. Expanding operations, again." Nancy says, setting down another basket of towel wrapped scones, fresh from the oven. "We don't usually have this much food. I'm testing out some variations in my original recipe and then different ways to serve them to see which way is best for a crowd," she explains when she sees my expression.

I nod. "That makes sense. So you'll include tips beyond the recipe itself?"

"I want to make sure that after the recipe is completed, the end result is as good as it is coming from my own kitchen."

"Nothing will ever be as good as it is coming out of your kitchen, dearest," Karl says confidently, pulling Nancy onto his lap. "Unless you're cooking in someone else's kitchen. Then I suppose it would be." Sophie watches her parents over her coffee and rolls her eyes.

"I swear he's still trying to win her over with flattery," she says.

"Lifelong goal, kid," Karl murmurs without taking his eyes off his wife, her own expression calm as she looks back. *That.* That right there is what I want.

"Feel free to come to my kitchen and bake anytime," I say before popping a piece of scone into my mouth.

"You don't need any help in the kitchen," Sophie scoffs.

"Oh?" Cass looks up from her plate, "What does that mean?"

"Nothing."

Sophie's eye roll is directed at me this time. "He's very good in the kitchen," she says, leveling me with a look that dares me to contradict her.

"I'm fine in the kitchen."

"He's being humble. I'm going to make him go to the farmers' market with me soon to buy ingredients, then beg him to teach me how to use them."

What she said was innocent, but she may as well have admitted that she wants me to drag her to bed and do unspeakable things to her all night long. Beg me to.

"I don't understand how you grew up here and still can barely fry an egg without messing it up," Cass teases.

Sophie looks over at her mother. "Listen, someone has lightened up considerably when it comes to sharing the kitchen."

Nancy smiles sweetly at her daughter and slips off Karl's lap to sit in her own chair. "The kitchen was a bit of a retreat for me, and not having to worry about busy little hands around burners and knives was always nice."

"Hey, I couldn't help it," Sophie huffs.

"Well, we know that now," Karl insists. "But at the time

we were worried about your safety. And your mother's sanity." He grins at Nancy.

"Pfff," Cass scoffs. "No one is sane here. It's why I fit in so well." We all laugh.

"So, Bennett's expansion?" Sophie asks, circling back to the conversation we entered during.

"Oh, it's so good," Cass exclaims, and I see Sophie flinch before a tight smile appears.

Nancy doesn't miss the expression. "We didn't want to bother you while you were getting situated in a new job. We knew you'd worry and focus on us rather than yourself."

"I'm not worried," Sophie says. "I know you two aren't impulsive... anymore."

"Be impulsive one time, and it sticks with you forever." Karl throws his hands up dramatically.

"I mean, it was kind of a big thing to be impulsive about, Dad."

"Marrying your mother wasn't impulsive, it was unavoidable. Kismet. Fate. Everything. Besides," he says indignantly, "why waste time calling her my girlfriend when I could call her my wife?"

I have no idea what is happening. I want to ask for some kind of backstory, but I'm enjoying the banter too much to interrupt.

"It's not for everyone, kid. We got lucky. That being said, when you do it you expect everyone to. I kept expecting you to walk in with a ring on your finger with an announcement with Gregory." Karl chuckles.

Sophie stiffens, and before I can even think my hand is on her knee, squeezing. Her hand slides across my fingers, and I flip mine palm up and thread our fingers together. I brace for the zing of touching her, but nothing comes. I'm too focused on keeping her grounded. Desperate to keep her light from dimming. This isn't a romantic gesture, it's a caring one.

"Well, I guess it's a good thing we never took that step," Sophie says coldly, and I squeeze her hand tighter. *Stay with me*, I think.

Karl stares at her for a beat, concern etched on his weathered face. "Indeed." His eyes slide to mine, and I see a question there. A reminder that she hasn't shared everything with anyone, not even the ones she's closest to.

I desperately want to know. I want her to tell me everything so I can hold all the hurt Gregory caused for her. I'd start a riot for Sophie. Burn the world to the ground and put her heart back together with the ashes.

TWENTY-SIX

SOPHIE

"I did not expect an Easter basket," Foster says, sorting through the literal basket on his lap. He ripped into it the second we got in the car. "I don't think I've had one since I was like"—he stops to think—"ten, maybe."

"I'm not convinced my mother realizes I know the Easter Bunny isn't real."

"Never tell her you know," he says, popping a jellybean into his mouth.

The weekend was interesting. The difference between Foster around his family versus mine was stark. He walked on eggshells around his, his body language tight, buttoned up, on guard for whatever attack one of his cousins or uncle were ready to launch.

At my parents' place he was open, his smiles wide and genuine, not a single worry lingering behind his eyes. Meanwhile, I was on guard with my family. Ready to divert any mention of Gregory that I could. Ready to avoid letting them in on how not awesome things had been for years, yet again.

"You okay?"

I glance over as I pull to a stop at the end of my parents' road. "Yeah." I force a smile. "Just." I swallow. "Nothing."

"You know you can talk to—?"

"I haven't shared a bed with a guy since him. I also haven't told my parents everything. There's a lot they don't know because I don't know how to bring it up. I... you saw my mom at my place. We have never had secrets from one another. It's going to take me time to open up. I'm still figuring things out, still trying to understand how I missed so much."

He doesn't respond, just reaches over and gently squeezes my arm as I turn right and head for home.

"Good Easter?" Principal Wong asks when she walks into the staff room to fill her coffee mug on Tuesday morning.

"Yeah, you?"

"Oh, you know, the usual. Too much food, kids hopped up on sugar." She sighs. "I'm glad I caught you, actually."

My heartbeat intensifies. I'm not doing something right. I've told a kid the wrong thing. Something awful happened to one of the students. I'm being transferred to a new school.

"I heard you and a certain EA are seeing one another socially." I swear my heart stops. It resumes only when I see the smile on her face. The relief that I'm not about to be reprimanded is immense.

Foster and I haven't talked about this. We are definitely friends, but are we still fake dating for certain people? Are we broadening the net to include people beyond the ones we were initially trying to fool? Panic begins to rise as my heart beat quickens. We should have discussed this at length. Should have set more rules and boundaries.

"Sophie." Principal Wong's hand rests lightly on my arm. "Don't panic, it's not against the rules or anything, and the fact no one really knows tells me you're both professionals."

"We are, yes," I say. I didn't confirm or deny anything other than the fact we are professionals. That should be okay. Unless she finds out that it's all fake and then is upset with me for lying. *You didn't.* But didn't I? I omitted the truth; that may as well be lying. *It's a victimless lie.* Hardly. I'm going to be a casualty of this lie. The gravitational pull of Foster is powerful, and I'm afraid of being pulled in so violently that my entire existence breaks into a billion pieces when he moves along to something real.

You're doing it again. You're making your entire life about a guy.

She's still talking, and I'm barely listening. No, I'm panicking.

"I'm sorry," I interrupt. "I have a call in a couple minutes so I need to get back." The lie comes too easily. Or maybe this is me now, Sophie Hore, expert liar. Gregory gave me one skill, I guess.

I slip out of the room and hurry back to my office, avoiding every person on my way, hoping Foster doesn't pop around a corner.

In my office, I lock my door and pace around the tiny space before grabbing my phone and calling Maya.

"What's up, buttercup?" comes her cheery voice.

"Hey," I squeak. Fuck. I wanted to sound fine. I don't want her to worry, I just need to talk to my friend.

"Soph?" Maya sounds instantly concerned. "Is everything okay?"

I take a deep breath and then another one until I'm practically gasping.

"You get your shit together, and I'll be right here okay? Slow breaths, Soph."

After a few minutes I've slowed my breathing down enough that I don't feel like I'm chasing air.

"Tell me something ridiculous," I gasp.

"Sure thing." I can practically see her lean back in her desk chair. "So last night, Davis came over, and my god, Sophie, this maaaan. He shows up with a goddamn mustache. A mustache!" she shouts. "You know, the thing I said I'd never ride." My breathing changes again as I start to laugh. "But like, here's this guy who has rocked my world and ruined a bunch of lamps in the process, so I figured why not. I'm going to marry this man, I can feel it. I'm going to be married to a guy with a mustache, and I'm going to be fine with it."

"Trying new things keeps life interesting," I say, my breathing back to normal, my heart rate, almost back to normal.

"Davis keeps life interesting," she cackles. "So, what's up, Soph?"

"I don't know—"

"Nope," Maya cuts in. "Don't give me that shit. You know but you don't want to face it. So let me ask one more time: what's up, Soph?"

"I think I'm making my life about a guy again, and I'm afraid."

"What guy?"

"Foster."

"Fake boyfriend friend date Foster?"

"Mmm."

"Have you moved in together?"

"No," I huff.

"Are you doing his laundry?"

"No," I say quietly.

"Canceling plans with friends because he wants you to hang out with him?"

"No."

"Are you planning on changing your career path because he thinks you should aim higher than your dream job?"

That one still hurts. I put so much on hold to appease him.

"Are you wearing clothes he picked out for you?" she asks before I can answer.

I bristle at this one. "No."

"Letting him get off on you without getting you off?"

"Maya!"

"What, didn't you tell me that's how it was?"

"Not in those words."

"Is the meaning the same?"

I hesitate for too long, and she makes a noise of disapproval.

"Do you enjoy his company, in a non-romantic way?"

"Yes, of course I do."

"And you're definitely not dating?"

"No, we are *just* friends. We're just really good at pretending and I think I'm having a hard time separating the two sides," I admit. "And I think I should be able to."

"Maybe take a step back?" she suggests.

But I like spending time with Foster, and he makes it easier to forget. He makes me feel worthy of his time.

"What's going through your head, Soph? You called me, so talk."

"I... I don't want to take a step back."

"Why not?"

"Because." I pick up a pen and roll it between my fingers. "I want to spend time with him."

"Okay, so you are afraid of... what? That you're developing feelings? Rediscovering feelings you've always had?"

"Yes."

"And you're scared that he won't share them? That it's too soon? That he's going to be like Gregory?"

I hang my head. "Yes," I say softly.

"Right now, at this moment, is he anything like Gregory?"

"Not one bit."

"Alright, so let's stick to that for now. He's not Gregory."

"Gregory wasn't Gregory in the beginning either," I say quietly. He was charismatic and kind. Always giving me his time, constant gifts, compliments. He built me up and then without me realizing it he began to tear me down.

"Yeah, but this is so different, Soph. You've known Foster since he was a kid. I want you to ask yourself one question, okay?"

"What is it?"

"What do you want? Don't focus on the negative shit. I want you to narrow it right down. Don't think about the future right now. What do you, Sophie Hore, want?"

"I... want Foster in my life."

"Great. Then keep doing what you're doing and use that intuition of yours to guide you."

"I used that with Gregory."

"No, you didn't, Sophie."

"What?"

"He used fear. We saw it, even though at the time it wasn't obvious."

"I'm so stupid," I whisper, fighting back tears.

"Stop it. You weren't stupid. You aren't stupid. You were young, and he abused his power. You aren't at fault here."

The timer on my desk goes off, letting me know I have five minutes before I need to pick up a student for a meeting.

"I've gotta go, Maya. Thanks for the chat." I can hear her say my name as I end the call. I'll apologize later.

It's hard to be in this line of work while coming to terms with how I allowed Gregory to treat me. *No*, I scold myself. *You allowed nothing.* He used everything in his arsenal to always turn things on me and he did it so gradually, so fucking effectively that I didn't see it happening.

"Do you feel angry right now?"

"No," Lily, a grade three student I've been meeting with regularly, huffs.

"How do you feel right now?"

"Tired." I can see that. I've never seen a kid with bags that rival a first-year medical resident.

"Are you having trouble sleeping?"

She glares at me. She says she's not angry, but her body language is screaming at me right now. I can see the rage simmering below the surface.

"No." Her tone is defensive.

"It's not your fault if you're not sleeping, Lily." I try to comfort her.

"My mom says I'm not trying hard enough to sleep."

"Why do you think she says that?"

Lily stares back, unblinking. She thinks I'm an idiot. I can read it all over her face. But I want her to tell me. I'm not going to tell her what I think is going on. I maintain eye contact until she looks up and out the high library window.

"She says I'm sneaky."

"How is being sneaky making it hard for you to sleep?"

"She thinks I'm listening to her for my dad. She thinks I'm his spy."

"Why would she think you're spying on her?"

"I got up to pee and heard her talking to someone."

"Did you stop and listen?"

"No!" she snaps. "I'm not a spy."

I can see her body coiling, like she's ready to jump up and run out of here.

"I don't think you're a spy, Lily. I'm trying to understand why your mom may have thought that." I watch as some of the tension leaves her body.

"She yelled at me when she heard the toilet flush." I wait for her to collect herself. "She told me I was lying and I didn't have to go to the bathroom. She said I was hiding and listening."

"But you just had to use the bathroom," I confirm. "Do you have to use the bathroom a lot at night?"

Her gaze is trained on the window again, and I can almost see her going somewhere else. Her lips purse and relax again and again, an inner battle showing on her face. She's not the first kid struggling to tell me, and she won't be the last. Hell, I'm an adult and trained in this stuff, and I can't seem to get my feelings out.

The bell goes, and she jumps and runs out of the library so fast I don't even have time to say a proper bye. The last two sessions with Lily have been silence or grunts. I may not have gotten everything out of her, but I got something and it feels like a win. And after my little breakdown earlier, I'll take any win I can.

TWENTY-SEVEN

FOSTER

"What are you doing on Saturday?" Sophie asks quietly while we're standing at the back of the gymnasium. The kids are enthralled by the presence of a couple hockey players from the local junior team.

"I was going to try and give Gary a bath," I say as casually as possible.

"Wait, seriously?" She pulls away, her eyes narrowing skeptically.

"Yes. When I say try, I mean try and make time. The guy loves a bath."

"Huh," she says, looking back at the front. "So how long does it take to bathe a cat? Like is this an all-day thing, or would you have time to go to the farmers' market with me?"

"I'm sure I can squeeze you in. I'll have to check with Gary, though. He expects to be fully pampered. Nail clipping, massage, tail fluff, the whole shebang."

"Okay." She smiles back. "Check with the cat-in-chief and report back. I figured... Who are you call—"

I lift my finger up to stop her while raising my phone to my ear. "Hi, yes, Gary, I know... yes, I'm aware I've interrupted prime squirrel hour. I... go on... No, that was a one-time thing, I promise. Listen, I know Saturday is bath day... Excuse me? I'm a week ahead? No, that can't be right... Well, alright, if you insist. So you wouldn't mind if I go to the farmers' market with Sophie? Of course I'll get something for you. Geez, you act as if I don't feed you ever... Go back to glaring at your nemesis. I'll see you tonight... Love —" I stop speaking abruptly and pull the phone away from my ear to look down at it. "Well, that was rude," I murmur before turning back to Sophie. "Turns out I'm a week ahead and definitely have time for a trip to the farmers' market."

She's got both lips sucked between her teeth, clearly holding in a laugh.

"I'm glad you were able to confirm with Gary."

"So, farmers' market. Is this our F date?" I ask, stepping back beside her just inside the gym doors.

"It's lame, isn't it?" she asks sheepishly.

"Incredibly," I assure her. "But I love a lame trip to the farmers' market. Especially with a friend." Her smile falters the tiniest bit, and I try not to let myself wonder why. She's made it clear she can't do more than friendship. I'm doing my best to respect that. "How about we do a two-for-one?"

"What do you mean?"

"Shhh." A student turns back to the front leaving us speechless.

I gesture with my head for Sophie to follow me into the hallway.

"Did we get shushed by a student?" Sophie asks in disbelief.

"We did. I don't know whether to be insulted or proud," I say, leaning back to look back through the door. "What I was going to say before I was so rudely and appropriately interrupted, was we can do a two-letter date night. Friend-date night," I quickly amend. "We'll get whatever you were going to get, then I'll get stuff to make a meal starting with G."

"You're going to make me dinner?" she asks.

"Well, I'm going to make us dinner."

"G." She crosses her arms and tips her head back in thought. "G... g...g...g...g. Gnocchi? That's a G, right? Or... Gonorrhea." Her eyes go wide. "Oh no, god, sorry, definitely don't make that."

"I don't even know where to get the ingredients." I grin back.

Sophie slaps her hands over her face, and I can't tell if she's crying or laughing.

"Hey." I wrap my hands around her wrists and tug them gently away from her face, "Don't worry about it, we all mix up STIs and food sometimes." I can't even get the words out before I'm laughing, thankfully along with her.

The kids erupt in applause and Sophie leans toward the door, raises her finger to her lips, and gives an exaggerated "Shhh," which has us laughing even harder.

That laughter carries me through the afternoon. It gets me through one of Pete's meltdowns, which are thankfully rare. It gets me through a lengthy negotiation at the end of the day with a student who doesn't want to wear their winter coat despite the light snowfall simply because it's April. It gets me through arriving home to discover three of my hanging plants smashed on the floor in front of the window. I'm guessing I can blame the squirrel for this.

"I hope it was worth it," I say to Gary as I sweep up the massacre.

My phone lights up with Heather's name, after I finish dumping the soil into the trash. It's unusual for her to text outside the group chat so I'm instantly nervous.

HEATHER

Yo, the team is into the playoffs. We need a couple extra sets of lungs cheering at the game next week.

What night?

Tuesday is the second game, at our rink.

I'll see if Soph can make it. I'll be there regardless.

Love you and all but make sure she comes.

Unless you messed things up already?

Hey! That's not fair.

What? It's not like you've got a great record. Besides, she's way too good for you.

Wow... I mean I know but WOW!

Foster, you're supposed to stand up for yourself. This was a test and you failed!

See you Tuesday at 7:25.

"So," I say as we get out of the car on Saturday afternoon, "what vendor are we going to first?"

Sophie looks at me like I have three heads.

"What?"

"I haven't been here before. I've always wanted to, but I'm a bit overwhelmed by all the face-to-face stuff."

"You're great with people."

"Yeah, but if I'm looking at their stuff and don't really want anything, I'm going to feel really bad if I walk away without buying anything."

"Seriously?"

"Yeah, I don't want to let them down."

I stare at her for a minute. She couldn't let anyone down if she tried. "Soph, they're used to that. Hell, there are like three people in there selling dried flowers. Does that mean you'd get something from each of them?"

She shrugs, looking guilty. "Probably."

"Oh, so this is so much more than shopping for a gonorrhea dinner."

She guffaws. "Don't call it that."

"I don't know," I say thoughtfully, "I think it has a nice ring to it."

"It really doesn't. It sounds like a dinner that's all army green or like... something that's going to give you diarrhea."

I take the tote from her and throw it over my shoulder. "Stick with me, sunshine, and you'll only go home with one bunch of flowers." If this was a real date, this is when I'd reach for her hand.

I can feel Sophie's discomfort ripple through the air as we walk away from the first table in the market building. It only builds as we do the same at the second.

"If you were selling milk from your parents' farm here and someone came up and left without buying any, what would you do?"

"Nothing," she says as she reads the label on a jar of honey.

"Okay, how would you feel?"

She puts one jar down, then picks up another. "I guess I'd think that they weren't looking for milk."

"Right, so that's what all these people are thinking, if they're thinking anything at all."

"Hmmm, that's probably true," she says, preoccupied by the third jar she has picked up. "Excuse me," she says to the vendor. "I'm sorry, I don't know what the difference is between these three honeys. Do they actually taste different, or are they only named after the seasons?"

"Honey that's produced from the pollen of different seasonal flowers actually have really unique flavors. Would you like to try them?" the woman asks, producing tiny spoons from a container behind the display.

Sophie beams. "That would be amazing."

We're both handed a spoon with spring honey. It's light in color and sweet on the pallet with a hint of floral.

The next is summer, which is slightly darker than spring and gets a reaction out of Sophie immediately. "Oh, this is delicious."

"You like it more than the spring?" I ask.

"You don't?"

"I like them both pretty equally."

Fall comes next, and there is absolutely no doubt that this one is not going to dethrone summer on Sophie's list.

The vendor laughs. "Fall honey definitely isn't for everyone."

"I'm surprised it's for anyone," Sophie says before looking horrified. "Oh my goodness, I didn't mean to say that out loud."

The woman leans toward us conspiratorially. "Full disclosure? I feel the same way."

Sophie buys a summer honey and we make our way to the next table, which is various goat cheeses.

Maybe I can do something with goat cheese for dinner. That would take care of the G component of the evening.

"Care to sample our pepper goat?" the man says, gesturing to the glass cloche.

"Oh. that's okay." Sophie backs away. "I've never liked goat cheese."

"What don't you like about it?" I ask, taking the spoon from the man and sliding it into my mouth. The pepper hits first followed by the rich creaminess of the cheese. It's the perfect combination as the pepper stands up to the mustiness that goat cheese usually carries.

Sophie leans into me. "It's how I imagine a goat would taste."

"Have you had goat before?" I have and can't figure out how someone could think the meat and cheese taste alike.

"Not the meat," she says, leaning closer still. "The fur, like if you walked into a barn and licked a goat. That's how goat cheese tastes to me."

The visual makes me laugh instantly. "I promise you this may change your mind about that. It's not as strong as some. And the pepper helps. Try it. If you don't like it, I'll never make you try anything again."

She looks at me for a minute before turning to the man and asking for a sample. I watch as she slowly raises the spoon to her lips and slips it through. Then I revel in the way her expression reveals pleasure and not the disgust I think she had expected to feel. Her eyes close, and a tiny smile appears on her lips.

When her eyes open again, she rolls them immediately. "Okay, that is delicious."

"You know what it would be good with?" I challenge.

"Crackers?"

"The honey you bought."

She looks at me skeptically. "You think?"

"I know," I assure her. "But also I think I'm going to use it for dinner tonight."

"Goat cheese over gonorrhea. I support that."

The goat vendor clears his throat, looking uncomfortable. I guess out of context that is a bizarre sentence, but also? Not an incorrect one.

In the end I've selected broccoli, onions, goat cheese, fresh pasta, parmesan, lemons, chicken, and a loaf of Italian bread.

"What are you making?" Sophie asks as we are walking back to the car.

"It's a surprise." It's a surprise for me too, I don't have a clue what I'm making, but I know these flavors will all work well together. It's some kind of pasta, that's all I know.

Sophie buys flowers, honey, a German chocolate cake, and in the end some goat cheese for herself as well.

"Can we have the cake for dessert, or does that ruin the G theme of the meal?"

"I think between the starter and the main, we'll have G covered," I quip as Sophie pulls the car onto the road.

"I'm excited to meet Gary."

"He's looking forward to meeting you too. No promises that he'll keep his feelings to himself that you stole me away for the day."

"Hardly for the whole day. It's only been a couple hours. I'm sure he's fine."

"You'd be surprised how needy the guy is."

ABC

Gary is making me look like a liar. The minute he sees I have Sophie with me, he turns and trots to my bedroom. When I go to get him, he wedges himself under the bed, letting me know without a shadow of a doubt that he has no interest in socializing.

"Maybe he knows I'm more of a dog person," Sophie whispers when I come out empty-handed.

"Don't tell him, but I am too," I concede. "Want a tour?"

"Absolutely."

"Well, you're standing in my formal dining room, kitchen, and foyer. I"—I gesture at my feet—"am standing in the living, family room combo." I walk to my bedroom, and Sophie follows. "The bedroom, also Gary's refuge."

"May I?" Sophie asks before stepping inside when I nod. She takes in my mostly blank walls before stopping at the foot of my bed and staring up at the large piece of art I have above my bed. I let her take it in, wanting to know how it makes her feel.

I'm not a great admirer of art or anything, but this one did something to me when I saw it. An abstract forest that seems to lead to eternity. It's a print, of course, but I had it professionally mounted which elevates it.

While she looks at my room I look at her. Hair up, light green sweater, jeans that make her legs look even longer than normal. I'm convinced at this point that green only exists for her to wear.

"Not what you expected?" I ask when she makes a tiny noise of approval.

She turns to me, shaking her head slowly. "It's not that I

was expecting racy images of scantily clad women or anything. She shrugs. "It's... so grown-up."

"I am grown-up." I grin back.

"I know." She laughs. "I remember your old room being very— well, you had *Lord of the Rings* posters and video game stuff everywhere."

"You can say it, I was a nerd."

"Are you saying you're not a nerd anymore?"

"Nope, definitely still a nerd. I just wear those posters on my body now."

Her eyes assess me slowly before meeting mine. There's an odd softness to her expression, yet something heated in her eyes. She can't be looking at me like that while we're standing in my bedroom. She can't be looking at me that way because we're just friends.

TWENTY-EIGHT

SOPHIE

I don't know what's come over me, but standing in Foster's room, surrounded by the essence of him, him standing next to me talking about having all that nerdy shit on his body makes me suddenly desperate, ravenous to see what he's covering up.

I drag my eyes up his long lean body, my imagination going wild, pulling from the glimpses I've seen. When my gaze meets his, I see my hunger reflected back.

"Soph." My name is only a whisper, but it snaps me out of whatever haze I'm in. The heady fog lifts rapidly, and I quickly look away.

"We should start on dinner."

He doesn't answer me right away, only smirks back. "We?" he asks.

"You?"

"Mm-hmm."

"Will you be a good friend and teach me something?" There's no hunger in his eyes now.

"You wanna know how I learned?"

"Trial and error?" I suggest.

"I watched the Food Network endlessly. Keyword there, 'watched.'"

"So, I can watch, but I can't..." I know what I'm doing. I'm testing the waters. I'm seeing how some flirting feels for me and how he reacts. "Touch?"

"No touching unless I say so."

I swallow and try not to react as chills race across my skin. The idea of not being allowed to do something unless I'm told, of not having to think about what to do, of *Foster* telling me what I'm allowed to do is something I never expected to want. But fuck, right now, that's all I want. I need to pull it together. I keep saying friend and then my imagination goes to very unsafe places.

"Okay." I tamp down the desire that's bubbling up. "I won't touch unless you give me permission."

He leads me back into the kitchen, and my head instantly clears. It's not quite as Foster-y out here and I can think straight again.

Sitting on the lone stool at the peninsula, I do as I'm told and watch.

I watch Foster steam and then blend broccoli with parmesan, garlic, lemon, and olive oil. I watch him slice onions so quickly I keep one hand on my phone, ready to call 911 in case he chops off a finger. I watch as he flips those onions in a hot pan with oil and butter, his forearms distracting me. I watch him dump pasta into boiling water. I watch as he strains the pasta and stirs in the broccoli mixture before adding in a knob of the goat cheese then carefully adds in reserved pasta water. I watch as he twirls pasta onto a fork and brings it to my lips.

"Open," he commands, and I do so without hesitation.

He smiles as my lips close around the fork, leaning in a little more, gaze intense as he pulls the fork back. Bright flavors burst on my tongue, and as badly as I'd like to keep looking at his smile, my eyes close as I sink into the taste dancing across my taste buds. "Good?"

I nod.

"Tell me, sunshine. What do you taste?"

I swirl my tongue around and concentrate. "Lemon, garlic, and something sweet."

"That's the onions. What else?"

"I don't know," I open my eyes to find Foster leaning in close. "Broccoli, but tamed. The cheese is less..."

"Goat-y?"

"Is that the technical term?"

"I believe so." He pulls back and starts arranging bowls and cutlery. "Have I convinced you?" I hear him, but I'm lost in his hands as he expertly plates the pasta. He has long fingers and the veins along the back of his hands shift as he works. "I'll take that look as a yes."

He definitely caught me staring. No doubt he knows what I'm thinking, although that doesn't seem fair because I barely know what I'm thinking.

He's not Gregory.

"Am I allowed to take the plates to the table?" I ask, slipping from the stool and rounding the counter before he can answer.

"You may," he says, handing over the cutlery, his fingers brushing my skin as my fingers wrap around it.

At the table we eat quietly, sneaking looks at one another and smiling. This feels like a first date. But looks instead of words aren't us. We talk; we always talk. *You don't tell him everything, though. He'll think you're pathetic if you tell him.*

Foster puts his fork down and stares at me. "What's up, Soph?"

I have a hard time meeting his eyes. I'm afraid of what I'll see there. "Nothing."

"You know you can talk to me about anything right?"

I finally look at him. Soft eyes under slightly furrowed brows. Concern wrapped in something else.

I set my own fork down and lean back, trying to appear more relaxed than I currently feel. Hiding in plain sight.

"I guess..." I need to give him something. He's been so patient with me. I know he isn't the way he is to earn rewards, but I need him to know that when he says things like that, that I do believe and trust him. "I really appreciate what you did today. You challenged me in a fun way, made me step out of my comfort zone, but never once made me feel like if I didn't, you'd hold it against me. Gre—" I stop abruptly because I don't want to ruin the taste in my mouth with his name. "He always held it against me. Guilt and gaslighting were everyday tactics. So I appreciate you not taking that approach. And of course for not insisting I talk about it."

"I'm not going to force you to talk, for the record. But you'll tell me if I do something that makes you uncomfortable or... feel anything other than good."

I want to scream that he makes me feel better than anyone else. That he makes me want to jump straight into something new and exciting. That he alone has fanned a spark into a flame I thought was forever extinguished. But I can't, because if I start talking, I'm going to tell him that I want to hold his hand for real. I'll confess that I want to feel his long fingers skim across my skin and sink into me. I'll wax poetically about how I've loved him since we were kids. I don't want to make things awkward or uncomfortable for him. I don't want him to walk by me in the hallway and avoid looking. I want to be the one to hand him candy when he's woozy from the sight of blood. And I don't want him to think he needs to fix me.

"I'll tell you, I promise."

TWENTY-NINE

FOSTER

Tonight was weird. It was like Sophie and I were dancing to the same song, and then suddenly her beat changed. I sat there trying to keep time with her but kept losing it.

The only thing I can think of is that I made her uncomfortable with what I thought was some innocent flirting. Not that I was trying; it just comes out when she's near me.

"You were no help," I say to Gary who is lounging lazily on the window ledge in my bedroom. "You couldn't be polite to her?"

Gary yawns and turns his attention out the window. He never cares about what I'm saying unless it's food-related.

I know things ended poorly with her ex, and I find myself wondering how badly things had been at the end. Or perhaps things had been bad for a while. She wouldn't be the first person to stay in a toxic relationship far longer than they should.

I roll on my side and close my eyes, but I'm greeted by my imagination playing an alternate reality version of tonight. I should open my eyes, but I'm curious to see where this goes.

Delicate hands lift my shirt up and over my head. Her voice, clear as day, asking if she can touch me. When I nod, she moves closer. I watch as her hands trail across my skin, over the artwork, admiring each unique piece.

I feel myself getting hard and clench my fists. I can't touch myself while I'm thinking about her. I won't be able to look her in the eye on Monday if I do that. But it is taking every bit of strength I have to not give in. If I come with her name on my lips, there will be nothing fictional about it.

Rolling onto my back I let out a frustrated sigh and try to think of something that resets my body. *Gonorrhea?* Sophie's voice cuts in, and I chuckle. Nothing like an STI to break the tension.

"Horse hockey," I grit out as Gary lands on my chest. I sit up. "Hockey... H." I forgot to bring it up while Sophie was here.

> I forgot to ask tonight, do you have plans for Tuesday night?

> Heather's hockey team is in the playoffs and she invited us.

"Us" jumps out at me. Us as friends, us as nothing more than that.

SUNSHINE

> I have a meeting after school with my supervisor. What time?

> 7:25.

> Can I meet you there?

> Absolutely!

Would I rather us go together, yes but I can keep some things to myself.

See you tomorrow. X

She put an X. She put an X. What does that mean? Did she mean to put an X? She hasn't done that before. I scroll back through all our previous conversations, and there is a definite absence of Xs. Maybe she does this for all her friends but didn't feel comfortable doing it with me until this moment. Like I'm a friend worthy of an X.

I keep waiting for her to message again and say it was a mistake, but no such message comes. The X grows and multiplies in my head. It becomes something it's probably not.

Did those looks she gave me tonight mean something? Did the slight flair of her nostrils when I told her she wasn't allowed to touch trigger something inside of her, something good? Slipping back into the movie that had paused in my head, I hear myself tell her to lay back and keep her hands to herself. I tell her she can't touch me. She has to watch as I worship her. And in the process I lose control, the angel on my shoulder loses the battle to the devil, and despite how good it felt, I'm instantly filled with regret.

"Mr. Walsh?"

"Yeah, Pete?" We're walking well behind the rest of the class around the track. Some days he doesn't want to partake, but today he said he felt like a walk, so here we are.

"Are you okay?"

"Yeah, bud, why?"

"You look..." He stops and squints up at me, studying every inch of my face. "Tired but...I don't know, different?"

It's shame, kid is what I want to say. "I didn't sleep great last night, that's all."

"Bad dreams?"

Bad? No, the best, actually. "Yeah, you could call them that."

"What were they about?"

"I was being forced to eat pizza after pizza covered in green olives." I gag.

"Mmm," he says in delight, stopping to rub his stomach dramatically. "That sounds like a dream come true."

"I bet it does." I chuckle at him as we continue around the track.

"Mr. Walsh?"

"Yes, Pete?"

"Do you think Miss Hore is pretty?" I stumble a bit as I look down at him, speechless. "You smile a lot when she's around. She's away today."

"I told you, I'm tired, buddy."

"But do you?"

"Do I what?"

"Think she's pretty."

"I think she's beautiful inside and out."

He stops abruptly and looks up at me in horror. "You've seen her insides?" he whispers, looking around as if I'm about to admit something scandalous.

I chuckle at his horrified expression. "It's a saying," I assure him. "It means someone is a good person."

His face cracks open in a big smile. "I know, Mr. Walsh,

I'm only joshin'." I love this kid. "So, have you told her that?"

"That I think she's beautiful inside and out?"

"Yeah. I told my mom she looked beautiful the other day, and she said it made her whole day."

"That was nice of you. Are you going to tell her more often?" I ask, hoping to redirect the topic of conversation to his mom rather than Sophie.

"Depends." He shrugs.

"On?"

"If she looks beautiful. I don't lie, Mr. Walsh."

"Well... Lying isn't great, but what if it makes her whole day again? It's kind of a victimless lie."

"But what if she gets a big head? She could die from that, you know."

"I don't think anyone has died from too many compliments, Petey Bird. Real or not."

"No one has yet, but I don't want my mom to be the first."

"Wow, okay. Well, you've got me there. Stick to what you're doing, I guess." I shove my hands in my pockets. "Do you know what you want to write about for your story this afternoon?"

"I think so."

"Are you going to tell me?"

Pete looks up at me with his lips pursed. "I think I'm going to surprise you, Mr. Walsh."

"Cool, I'm looking forward to it."

When Pete stands at the front of the room reading his short story, I want to immediately melt into the floor. It's about a tall redheaded man who can see into people's bodies to determine if they are in fact beautiful inside and out. The body he's looking into in this particular story is a tall blonde woman in a mushroom-patterned blouse.

THIRTY

SOPHIE

"I'm a fucking disaster," I admit to Maya as we wander the aisles of yet another home goods store, looking for sturdier side lamps.

"I know, but this too shall pass," she says absentmindedly as she picks up a dark blue lamp.

"I want to be in your state of mind right now."

She looks up at me, mock pity on her face. "Honey, if you looked like me right now, that means you'd be sleeping with someone, and you're not ready for that. You have made that pretty clear."

She's right, I'm not at all ready for that. I mean, if Saturday was any indication, I may actually be ready for that, but I'm also terrified. I don't want to sleep around to ease this need bubbling away inside of me. "I don't know..." I trail off.

"Foster?"

"He's, I don't know, nice, and..."

"I get it."

"You do?"

"Sure I do. He's nice and not bad on the eyes." Not bad

on the eyes seems like an insult to how gorgeous he is. "He's the perfect rebound from snoozy Gregory."

He's the only rebound from Gregory.

"He makes me feel good."

"Mentally, you mean?"

"Mentally..."

"Wait, did something happen?" I have her full attention now.

"No, we had this moment. Like if I'd stepped closer, something would have happened."

"Did you *want* something to happen?" she questions in a low voice as another customer slips past us.

"Yes? No? Maybe?" *God, yes.*

"Classic trifecta of doubt. Do you think *he* wanted something to happen?" I think of how his face looked after I'd studied him in his bedroom. How he told me I wasn't allowed to touch anything. His eyes on my lips after I'd finished the bite of pasta he'd fed me.

Maya's laughter brings me back to the lighting aisle of the store. "I'll take everything that happened as a giant yes." She cackles as she pulls me into the pillow aisle. "Why don't you get down in the sheets with him to see? Be honest about what it is. You need a good railing, but you want to do it with someone you trust."

I'm aghast. Agog. "Maya." I look up and down the empty aisle, half expecting to see someone looking equally shocked by what she just suggested.

"What? No one heard me. Pillows dampen sound."

"Are you suggesting I propose a friends-with-benefits kind of relationship?"

She shrugs. "Sure, if you wanna label it."

"Those never work!" I hiss.

"Sure they do."

"Give me one example."

"Well, there's..." She thinks for a minute. "Trav and Kyle, and... Darren and Steph."

"Trav was heartbroken when Kyle got a boyfriend, and Darren and Steph are married with a kid now."

"Well, then I'd argue that Darren and Steph's worked great."

"I mean, someone usually gets hurt."

"Or you end up getting married. It's the same risk you take in any relationship."

When I don't answer. Maya rolls her eyes and makes a frustrated noise.

"Listen, what are you going to do if he finds someone and moves on and you don't get any time? You either do something now or you risk staying in the friend-zone forever. That's something you're going to have to come to terms with eventually. You can't keep going on these dates forever."

She's right, of course.

"They aren't dates. They're outings. They're... I don't know, a series of challenges to see who can come up with something next."

She glares back. "Can I come on one of these outings? Seeing as how they're not dates and all."

No! It's my time with Foster. "Sure," I say nonchalantly, adding an exaggerated shrug.

Lying to Maya is virtually impossible if she asks me something outright and I can see the words liar flash back at me in her gaze. "I don't think this place has Davis-proof lamps," she says, walking toward the front of the store.

Sleep evaded me last night, and I felt like I let my kids down in every single appointment. I also haven't seen Foster since Saturday, and I miss his face and his voice. I miss him in his entirety. How would I feel if he started seeing someone? I'd be devastated.

Now sitting in my car outside of the community rink where his friends are all waiting inside for me, I can't seem to move. It's five minutes after he told me to arrive, and I'm sitting here staring at my steering wheel wondering if I should propose the arrangement Maya seems set on for me. The thing is, I'm not even sure if it's sex I need from him, or anyone. I think what I'm after is deeper, what I was starved of for years. Sex was always there, and it's not what I miss. It's not what I'm craving.

A knock on my window causes me to jump. A pair of amber eyes peer at me through the window.

"Sorry, I was lost in thought," I confess, stepping out of the car.

"You're allowed to be." He steps back, giving me space before turning and walking beside me toward the building.

"Sorry I'm late," I apologize.

"You're not late. Heather gave everyone an earlier time so we could get seats. You wouldn't believe how many people are here to watch a beer league game."

Just before we reach the front door, I reach for his hand and slide my fingers through his easily.

We fit.

The concourse is busy with people mingling and lining up for food. A few older kids are running around playing tag while their parents talk. Foster effortlessly guides us through the sea of people.

The rink itself is buzzing with activity as players warm up on their respective nets. Two goalies stretch on either side of center ice, clearly deep in conversation, while pucks hit the boards in all corners of the rink.

"If this is beer league, it's not Coors or Budweiser," I murmur, gripping Foster's hand a little tighter.

The place is jammed with people, many wearing the colors of the team they're cheering for.

"Definitely something European," Foster agrees, smiling back at me. The smile disappears quickly as I see a man running after a small child, and I yank our hands back. His forward motion is disrupted, and he practically falls into me. Thankfully his reflexes are quicker than mine and he keeps us upright, albeit pressed together.

"Sorry!" the father calls as he rushes by yelling for Martin to slow down. Martin cackles maniacally as he continues on, dodging people left and right, outmaneuvering his dad with ease.

"Kid's got a future as a receiver," Foster says in wonder.

I can feel his chuckle through his chest, and it stops my breathing as I tense. He steps back instantly, breaking all contact. I hate it immediately and grab his hand before he has a chance to put any more distance between us.

"Gotta sell it."

He swallows and searches my eyes before nodding and turning away, continuing on to where his friends are sitting.

"Sophie!" several voices call when they see me.

"They've been counting down the minutes until your arrival." Foster grins at me.

"Hi!" I wave lamely with my free hand, the other still firmly entwined with Fosters.

"Still going strong, eh?" Dan says, only to be elbowed by Maria.

"Leave them alone," she hisses at him. "It's nice to see you again, Sophie."

"You too." I lean around Foster to smile at Nick. "The whole gang's here."

"There may have been some bribery involved," Nick says.

Foster's forehead crinkles. "What kind of bribery? I was told to be here."

"That's because you'll do anything people tell you if you think it will make someone else happy." Nick laughs.

No touching unless I say so. Flames crackle across my skin.

"Mike, this is Foster's girlfriend, Sophie. Sophie, this is Heather's husband, Mike." Maria says, and we nod at each other in greeting.

Foster leans back, our hands still clasped together, with the back of mine resting on his thigh. This is going to be so distracting.

Heather and Alex's team wins easily, and I'm suddenly agreeing to go to the next game too. I got way more into it than I thought I would. Only three fights broke out in the stands, which wasn't a lot according to Dan, and Foster held my hand for the entire thing. His thumb occasionally brushed the side of my palm as if reminding me he was still there and still aware.

"Oh my god, Alex, you're disgusting." Nick jumps back as his partner attempts to haul him into their arms.

"Drinks at Carl's!" someone shouts, and everyone hoots and hollers.

"You two in?" Heather asks, sliding her arm through her husband's.

Foster looks at me, and I give my head a tiny shake. I really like his friends, but I feel ready to burst with the need to talk to him. And now that I've decided that I need to, I don't want to wait another second.

"We're going to bow out, friends. It's a school night."

"Mm-hmm," Alex gives a knowing look. "You two have fun doing whatever activity you're going to get up to on a school night."

Please open up and swallow me, I think, looking down at the floor.

"See you two Thursday!" Maria calls as they all head for the door. When they leave, we stand there for a little longer, hands still clasped, sides pressed together.

"You don't have to come to the next game," Foster says.

I give his hand a squeeze. "I know I don't have to do anything."

I only recently learned this lesson. I don't have to have dinner ready at a certain time, even if I'm not going to be around. I don't have to roll over because he says so. I don't have to wear my hair down because that's the way he prefers it. I don't have to drive the car he bought me and then reminded me of daily.

"I want to come," I finally say. "I, um..." I drop his hand and regret it instantly. "I have something to talk to you about. You told me I could talk to you about things if I was comfortable and I am but I just don't know how to bring this up, not really. It's a bit awkward. It's nothing bad, at least I don't think it is. Fuck, now I'm not sure if this is..."

Fingers grip my chin gently, and he guides my face from the current position of looking back at the floor, to look at him.

"I meant it, Soph. What's up?"

"Can you come over? I don't want to talk about this here. It smells like sweat and stale coffee."

"I can do that."

I pull into the driveway a second before Foster, and as his headlights illuminate my garage, my heartbeat slows down for the first time since I parked at the rink.

Foster follows me into the house silently. Inside the air feels charged, and I put space between us. It would be so damn easy to turn and kiss him. To give into these primal feelings that have been omnipresent since seeing him again. But that's not what I want from him. Well, it is, and it's not. There is something else I need first, something I need much more.

"Do you want something to drink?"

He doesn't answer, and when I turn to look at him he's got his hands in his pockets, studying me.

"What?"

"I'm trying to decide if I should tell you to get to it or if getting me a drink will ease your nerves."

"Do you want a drink?" I ask again.

He steps toward me. "I want to know what's up."

"Okay, let's." I gesture at the couch.

Once we're sitting, I do my best not to fidget.

"Breathe, sunshine," Foster says gently. Foster's calming easy presence washes over me.

"So I was thinking of what we could do for I, and I—" I laugh, losing myself in all the I's. "I was wondering— oh god, I don't even know how to ask this, so whatever comes out of my mouth next, well, I'm sorry for it. I know how to have sex," I rush to say only to realize what I said. "Oh no, obviously, wait." I put my hand up, preemptively stopping him from saying anything while also hoping to slow myself down. "Oh, this is not going how I thought, or maybe it's going exactly how I thought it would, I'm so sorry."

Foster reaches for my hands and scoots closer. "I'm not going anywhere."

He has the kindest eyes I've ever seen. They're not the eyes of someone who's going to hear my request and run from the house. They're not the eyes of someone who will laugh at me. They're not the eyes of someone who will use my next words as a weapon later on when he wants to hurt me.

"For I, I was wondering if you could maybe help me with intimacy. Not sex," I clarify. "Sex, I've, well, probably not mastered, but I know the ins and outs." A slight blush appears on his face, and I am suddenly so grateful for his gingerness. Seeing that blush gives me a bit of a boost. "In my last relationship, my only one really, what was missing most was intimacy. I don't really know what it's like, but I know that I never want to experience another relationship without it. It was lonely. But I don't really know what it is I'm missing, does this even make sense?"

"It makes sense."

"Perfect. And I don't know, doing this with someone I trust, a friend, feels doable." I breathe out in relief.

He swallows and looks away for a minute. I watch as he breathes out before his head slowly turns back to me. "So," he asks, his head tipping in question. "When does this start, and what are the boundaries? You said no sex, which makes sense with us being friends." He says "friends" slowly as if letting it sink in. "What about other physical things? Or do you only want emotional intimacy?"

"Shit, I hadn't really gotten that far yet. I should have waited until I knew." I can feel myself begin to spiral. I'm such an idiot for not thinking this through more. I have a master's degree. A fucking master's degree and I'm charged with helping kids navigate tough shit, and I didn't even think of what my boundaries would be when I broached this subject.

Ripping my hands out of Foster's, I stand and begin pacing.

"Hey." He's up a second later and pulling me to him. One minute I'm walking and the next he's got his arms around me, pulling me tightly into his body. "We'll figure it out together, okay? You can tell me what you're not into or what you would like. You don't have to have a list prepared right now. We'll get you to wherever you need to be."

THIRTY-ONE

I'm doing my best to stay calm. But it's taking every bit of strength I have because Sophie Hore just asked me for... well, I'm not even sure what. Intimacy lessons? I told her we'll figure out what she needs together, but I'm totally in the weeds here too. It's not like I teach this kind of thing. I help kids manage emotions and get their schoolwork done. Now I'll be helping Sophie manage her libido? No, that's not right. This is about more than sex, something deeper, and she's asking me because she trusts me.

She relaxes in my arms, and I step back while maintaining contact, my hands sliding over hers.

"Is this okay?"

She looks up at me like I've lost my mind. We've touched more than this when we are around other people. She's probably wondering why I'm asking if now it's okay.

"Yes, this is fine. It's nice."

When she doesn't look like she's questioning all her life choices anymore, I guide her back to the couch, sitting a little closer this time and keeping our hands locked.

"So I can hold your hand. And I can hug you?"

"Yes," she confirms. "What about you?"

"What about me?"

"What are your boundaries or needs or…" That blush again. Pure torture.

"It's not about what I need, Soph. This is about what you're asking for."

She shakes her head, her expression hardening. "No, I won't use you like that. You have to be getting something out of it, or I won't be able to get into char—" She trails off. "No, that's not the right word. I won't be able to absorb anything if I'm constantly worried that you're not getting something out of it."

Good lord, her ex really did a number on her.

I slide my hands to the sides of her face and into her hair. "What I get out of it is helping you, giving you something you need and have been starved of." *Being with you, touching you, maybe kissing you, tasting you.* "I'm not totally selfless, sunshine. Trust me."

I watch those pretty blue eyes dip quickly to my lips and fight the urge to pull her to me. Instead, I tip her head down and give her a soft kiss on her forehead. It's the second time I've kissed her on the head, and it's somehow the hottest kiss I've ever experienced.

Her hand comes up and gently wraps around my right wrist, my lips break contact with her head as she twists and lays her own kiss to my palm. Scratch the head kiss—this, this right here is the hottest kiss I've ever experienced.

"I should go," I force out, even though I want to stay like this for the foreseeable future.

She sits back, and the space between us suddenly feels like the Marianas Trench. "School night, I guess."

Leaving is hard. It feels like we are moving into something, and the last thing I want to do is walk away from it right now. But at the same time, I need to do that. What she's asking for isn't what my body is desperately asking for. So we say our goodbyes, and I force my feet to move out of the house and to my car. I don't remember the drive home. All I'm thinking about is how I'm going to make this work so when she's ready to move onto something real with someone good enough for her, I don't end up with my heart broken.

"Do you have any good date ideas starting with J?" I ask Jessica through a yawn the next afternoon while the kids are reading. I spent most of last night reading about intimacy online and coming up with a game plan. It's not something I can really plan for, though. Just go with how she's responding or recognizing what she may need, including listening if she needs to talk. Basically what I've been doing, but with some extra physical contact if that's what she needs.

"For you and Sophie to do?" she asks without even looking up from her marking.

Apparently everyone in the school thinks we are dating, something Sophie seemed fine with, so I'm going along with it. Probably because I'm fine with it too.

"Yeah."

"Why J?" she says, looking over at me. "Wait!" She sits up straighter. "You're not doing alphabet dates, are you?"

"We may be doing that," I concede.

"That's the nerdiest damn thing I've ever heard," she says in a hushed tone. "What have you done for all the other letters?"

"Um, an alumni gala, barbecue, concert, drag brunch, Easter, farmers' market, goat cheese," I count off using my fingers.

"Goat cheese? You had a goat cheese-based date? Like you learned how to make it, like a cooking class?"

"No, I got some at the farmers' market and then taught her how to make a dish with it."

"What did you make?"

"A pasta dish."

No touching unless I say so.

"Did she like it?"

I remember the look on her face as I pulled the fork slowly out of her mouth. How her eyes closed and the tiniest moan escaped. I felt it through my entire body like a shockwave.

"She did," I admit without going into more detail.

"You wasted no time getting to know her, eh?"

"Well, not really. We've known each other since we were kids. She's my sister's best friend.

"What?" Jess's mouth has dropped open, and she looks elated.

"What?" I ask again.

"You're her best friend's brother?"

"That would be the other way of putting it, yes."

"Oh, this is too good!"

"What is?" I'm so lost.

"This trope," she huffs.

"Trope?"

"Like enemies-to-lovers or friends-to-lovers in books and movies."

"Best friend's brother is a trope?"

"Yeah, it sometimes carries a forbidden quality with it. Like 'Oh, I can't fall for him, he's my friend's brother, what if things go wrong, now things will be weird with my bestie.'"

"Okay," I say slowly. I don't know what else to say to this. I don't want this to be seen as a trope. I want this to be just Sophie and me spending time together without some weird trope-y expectation hanging over our heads. I also don't want things to go wrong and it messes up Sophie and Cass's relationship. I hadn't even considered that. "But do you have an idea for J?"

"Juggling lessons? Jokes? You could go to a comedy club. Jousting? I don't think that's a thing people do outside of Medieval Times so never mind." She sits back and crosses her arms, lost in thought. "Jigsaw puzzles. J... J... J... Jazz? A jazz club? Jogging? You run, right?"

"I'm not sure I want to..." I was going to say I don't want to get all sweaty, but a vision of Sophie post-run has me shutting up real quick.

"Jacuzzi? Oh, jumping! Go to a trampoline park," she squeals enthusiastically.

"Sounds like a good way to injure ourselves."

"You've gotta live a little before you're thirty, Foster."

"I've lived plenty without risking breaking my neck on a trampoline, thanks."

"Fine. Junk? Thrifting or food, or a combination of the two?"

"That sounds like actually not a terrible idea."

"I am somewhat brilliant occasionally, after having the right amount of coffee." She smirks and goes back to marking before her head pops up, eyes narrowed. "What did you do for I?"

"Hmm?" I play dumb. "Oh, ice cream. We, uh, went for ice cream."

Wednesday night I cancel drinks with a friend so I can do some more research. I want to be more prepared for when I see her tomorrow.

I find a list online with ways to improve intimacy in your relationship and realize we're already working through it. Do new things together, check. Reminisce, check. Be present, check. Cook together, check. Hug daily? I can do that.

The list evolves into more physical intimacy, and while I tell myself that's not what we're doing here, I can't seem to stop from reading through the list. An adult version of Go Fish that leads to physical closeness. It sounds a tad corny, but I wouldn't say no. Pausing while sexually intimate to look at one another or share an intimate detail is further down the list. The last thing I want to do is imagine Sophie with her ex, but I know for a fact she didn't get that from him. He's probably the type of guy that the expression "wham, bam, thank you, ma'am" was invented for.

"Pfft, I doubt he ever got to the thank-you part," I mumble to myself.

Gary jumps on the couch beside me and wails. I've been neglecting him a little bit since Sophie walked back into my life, so I set my phone aside and lean back. He immediately climbs up my chest to rub his face against mine. Getting to this point took forever, but here we are, two gingers cuddling on a couch.

"Sorry I've been a bit distant lately," I murmur into his

fur once I've got my arms around him. He purrs and starts making biscuits on my right pec. "I'll take this as forgiveness."

Sitting in my apartment with a cat, I never would have believed it if someone had told me this was my future. Then again, I wouldn't have believed them if they told me I'd be pretending to date Sophie Hore either.

THIRTY-TWO

SOPHIE

"I even left a tip," Cooper says with a defeated shrug.

"You left a tip for the Tooth Fairy?" I ask, uncertain that I heard him correctly.

"She does good work," he claims.

"Oh, well, yeah, sure, that's true." Tipping the Tooth Fairy seems a bit like tipping an ATM, but I don't share that. "Did you ask your dad?"

"He got home late. Melissa was babysitting." Melissa is Cooper's older half-sister and babysits a lot when their dad is working a later shift at the hospital. He probably didn't even know about the tooth.

"Has the Tooth Fairy ever missed a pickup before?"

"No, she's always on time. I hope nothing happened to her." He looks at me with wide eyes filled with concern.

"She probably had a busy night. There are a lot of kids losing their teeth right now."

"Maybe she should hire some help."

"There's an idea. But also maybe tell your dad. Sometimes parents have a direct line to the Tooth Fairy."

"Really?" He perks up. "Santa too?"

"Oh." Shit, I'm digging myself into quite a hole here. "I'm not sure, to be honest. Santa is a pretty big deal."

"But the Tooth Fairy is busier. She works every night." His voice rises as his enthusiasm grows for the work habits of fictional entities. "And everyone loses teeth, but not everyone celebrates Christmas." He's got me there.

FOSTER

Hey! You good if I pick you up tonight?

My body fully relaxes when I see Foster's message. Interesting.

Yes! Same time?

Thought maybe we could grab dinner?

Sure, where?

Little place I know.

Two hours later, Foster is standing at my door looking better than any man has the right to look in a simple blue crew neck sweatshirt and jeans.

"Hey!" His face lights up when he sees me, his eyes doing a quick sweep of my outfit before stepping over the threshold. "So, I was thinking we could try something." My heart rate spikes when he stops directly in front of me.

"Oh?" I swallow as his hands slide down my arms. I hold my breath when I feel him wrap them around my wrists and lift my arms to his shoulders before his slide around my waist. He's not touching my skin, but you'd think we were both naked by the way my entire body reacts. I'm almost expecting his lips to meet mine, but instead I find myself pressed against his body as he hugs me.

Hugging is new. It's not unwelcome, but it's new.

"Hi," he murmurs, his lips right next to my ear.

"Hi," I whisper back.

It doesn't last long, but when he releases me it takes all my brain power to drop my arms. When I do, he steps back, scratching his neck and looking nervous. "So, was that okay?"

"Hugging me?" I ask, slipping on my shoes and grabbing my coat.

"Yeah, it's a more intimate step than, ya know, well, not hugging," he stammers, the tips of his ears turning pink. It's the cutest thing I've ever seen.

I could tell him that, yes, hugging is fine. That I am actually a pretty big fan of hugging, but I would much rather show him. This time I am the one to step forward and slip my arms around his waist. His arms wrap around my shoulders the minute our chests connect, and I release a sigh that I hope doesn't come off too intimate. Although that's what we're doing, isn't it? Being intimate?

"I love a hug," I say, giving one more squeeze before stepping back. "I'm starving. What's for dinner?"

Fifteen minutes later, Foster pulls up in front of his apartment.

"Is this the little place you know?" I laugh, stepping out of the car.

Foster meets me at the front of the car and reaches for

my hand, which I take without hesitation. "You wanted intimacy, sunshine. Cooking dinner together is an easy way to achieve that."

"Together? You're going to let me touch?" I catch the grin and tiny shake of his head before he tips his face to the sky and breathes out. "What?"

"Nothing. Yes, I'll let you..." He looks at me, his eyes dipping to my lips before he swallows. "Help."

"Well, lucky me."

We don't say much on the walk up to his apartment, and when he unlocks the door I definitely stand a bit too close, but I can't seem to help it.

Gary weaves around our feet meowing as soon as we step through the door, and I watch Foster bend and pick the orange tabby up. He starts licking Foster's exposed forearm instantly, his yellow eyes zeroed in on me.

"Don't worry, buddy, he's all yours," I assure the cat, scratching behind his ears. He doesn't ease up, though, if anything his licks become more intense.

"Okay, I think that's enough," Foster says, setting the cat back on the ground. "I'd like my tattoo to remain intact, thanks." Gary scampers to the window and starts chattering at something. "That'll be his nemesis," Foster explains, heading to the fridge. "Drink?"

"Sure, what do ya have?"

Foster opens the door and starts naming things off. "Water, orange sparkling water, aloe..."

"Aloe?" I ask, confused.

"Aloe juice." He holds out a bright green bottle of liquid.

"Are those... what's floating in there?" I ask, squinting into the bottle.

"Bits of aloe," he says as if it's the most normal thing in the world, and I physically recoil.

"I think I'm good with water."

"You don't even want to try it?" He waves the bottle in my direction.

I take it from him and swish the liquid back and forth, feeling queasy as the bits bob around, suspended in the liquid. "Maybe another time."

He grins at me, making me want to say or do anything that keeps it on his face. "Flat or sparkling?"

"Let's go wild and have sparkling."

"If this is you going wild, we need to get you out more." That grin is still there as he opens the can and hands it to me.

"If you get me out anymore," I say, taking the can, our fingers brushing as I do. Chills spread up my arm. *The can is cold*, I tell myself, *that's all*. "My house is going to forget I exist."

"Your house? You'd rather remind your house about you than spend time out and about with me?"

I'd never go home if it meant spending more time with you. "I didn't say that." I take a sip of the water but maintain eye contact. "So, what are we making?" I ask, redirecting the conversation.

"Apricot-glazed pork, mashed potatoes, and chili green beans."

"Sounds spicy." I wince.

Foster shakes his head as he pulls ingredients out of the fridge. "The beans are more garlicky than spicy, don't worry. I wouldn't do that to you, sunshine."

The things I'd let you do to me.

What the fuck is it about this apartment?

He stops midway to the counter, staring at me, and I'm filled with dread that I vocalized that very internal thought.

Panic sets in. "What? Is there something on my face?" I stammer, lifting my fingers to my cheek, watching his eyes track my hand. Trying to ignore the way the muscle in his jaw ticks.

He clears his throat. "No, sorry, you looked..." He blinks rapidly and looks away. "How do you feel about cleaning up these beans?" he asks, his back to me.

I take the bag he holds out. "I think I can do that without cutting or burning myself."

"If you do either of those things, I will be incredibly impressed," he teases as he begins mincing garlic.

Foster moves seamlessly around the kitchen, prepping and cooking while I meticulously trim the beans. We work side by side for a while, chatting easily about our day, the blip of awkwardness fading and eventually disappearing completely. It feels incredibly domestic, like we do this every single night. When he moves around me, his hands rest momentarily on my hips, innocent, purpose-driven movements that feel like more in this confined space.

"Pete leaves the Tooth Fairy a thank-you note," Foster tells me after I finish the story about Cooper.

"Does she ever write back?" I ask, throwing the final bean into the steamer.

"Apparently she writes very lengthy replies." He laughs as he forms the pork into patties. I watch his hands work, gently packing the meat before he shapes it and places it on a parchment-lined tray. "Soph?"

I snap my head up and see he's looking at me, his brow furrowed the tiniest bit. He was definitely talking while I was being hypnotized by his hands. It's not my fault. "Yeah?"

"Everything okay?"

"Oh, yeah. I was totally expecting you to make balls." I feel the burn in my cheeks when that grin I like so much reappears.

"I find patties are better for this recipe. Balls work for some things, but not all."

Oh my god, we need to stop talking about balls when he's grinning like that.

"Good to know. What did you say after the part about the long replies?" I'm not doing a great job of showing I can pay attention while in the kitchen. But to be fair I'm still not prepared for how distracting his hands are. Or for how the tattoos shift as he flexes. I'm not lost in my mind, I'm lost in him.

He hands me a jar of apricot jam and a spoon. "Put two heaping spoonfuls into that bowl and stir in the leftover garlic." He walks by me and sets a frying pan on the stove. "I was saying that when I was a kid, there wasn't any pressure to do anything aside from losing a tooth. And parents certainly didn't go above and beyond."

"I had a pillow. Like a little heart pillow with a pocket. I'd stick my tooth in there, and when I woke up there would be a shiny loonie."

"You got a loonie? Cass and I got quarters."

"It's amazing that we didn't figure it out earlier. Imagine the drama had we discussed how much we were making on our teeth."

Foster pours a bit of oil into the pan and leans against the counter, crossing his arms. "It's kind of creepy, if you think about it. A fairy trafficking in body parts, basically."

My eyes are locked on his arms, is he flexing or are his arms always like that? Somehow my mouth conveys the one non-horny thought that I've got going. "I hadn't thought about it before." I shudder. "Although," I say, dramatically flourishing the apricot-covered spoon, "my mom said it was fun to have a harmless lie to partake in."

"Do you want to partake in the lie?"

"What do you mean?"

"Like with your own kids."

My stomach drops at his words.

THIRTY-THREE

FOSTER

I could kick myself for bringing up kids. Things were going well until I mentioned her own. Maybe she doesn't want them and she's over telling people that.

"I think the oil is ready," she nods toward the pan.

I look at her for a second longer before I turn back to the stove and start adding in the patties. I watch as she stirs the jam and garlic together and then hand her a bottle of soy sauce. "About ten shakes should do."

She counts as she shakes the bottle, eyebrows drawn together in determination. I pull out my Microplane and a knob of ginger from my freezer and begin grating it into the bowl of sauce Sophie's back to mixing together.

"That's good," I tell her, taking the bowl and setting it next to the pan before turning back to her. "What's up, Soph?" I lean next to her fighting the urge to cross my arms or pull her into them.

"Nothing," she says, smiling at me quickly before turning on the sink and beginning to wash things.

She's lying. Something is clearly wrong, but I'm not going to force her to tell me. Instead of pressing, I carry on like nothing is wrong. I grab another frying pan and add it to the stove top. The sound of the meat cooking and garlic hitting hot oil are the only sounds in the entire apartment. Sophie and I don't have trouble talking. We haven't since the day we met as kids. Even on our first day together as adults, we filled the silence with words and laughter.

"Do you want to do the beans?" I ask while she's drying her hands.

She looks over at me and then down at the pan. "If you think I can handle it."

I roll my eyes and hand her the steamed beans. "I think you can handle anything. Add these into the pan and give it a stir." She does as I instruct, and I hand her a jar of dried chilies followed by a small bottle of sesame oil. "Once there's a bit of wrinkle to those beans, add in a drizzle of the oil and pull off the heat."

While she does that, I finish the pork, dumping the sauce she made into the pan and spooning it over the caramelized patties.

"That smells amazing," she says, leaning a bit into my space with her hand resting on my lower back.

The tension I caused seems to have evaporated, and we move around one another with ease with me plating our food while she sorts out the cutlery.

"Holy mother of mercy, this is incredible," she moans after taking a bite of the meat and mashed potatoes. "Can you cook for me every night?" she asks in a tone that makes it hard to tell if she's serious or not.

"No, but I will cook *with* you every night." I mean it as a joke—well, kind of—but it comes out seriously, and I watch as Sophie's chewing slows and her gaze moves up from her plate to my face. My god, she's pretty.

"I can think of worse things than cooking with a friend."

No one has ever hit me as hard at the gym as the word "friend." It's a knockout punch.

"Sophie!" my friends call out as we arrive at the game.

"I guess I've been replaced," I jest, following Sophie into the row.

"Jealous?" she asks over her shoulder.

Wrapping my arms around her from behind, I bend to kiss her neck. "There's no one I'd rather come second to," I murmur against her skin, and I swear I can feel goose bumps rise beneath my lips. *It's cold in here, that's all,* I tell myself.

"You two are so damn adorable," Maria coos, smiling over at me like a proud parent.

We sit, and Sophie immediately slides her hand into mine, bringing them to rest on her thigh. "Oh, we know." I think about how amazing it would feel to be able to lean in and kiss her. Not on the cheek or the neck, but right on those perfect rosy lips.

I won't, though—that's my boundary. A line I can't cross for my own sanity. I know that if I do, there will be no coming back from it and putting that on either of us isn't fair. So I'll press my lips to her neck and that perfect jaw. I'll hold her hand whenever it's near, and I'll wrap my arms around her and keep her close. But I will not kiss those lips.

Watching Sophie get into the game this time is mesmerizing. It's like the concert all over again, but she's yelling things, the odd obscenity slipping out when she disagrees with a call or lack of one.

"You're very creative with the words, sunshine," I say

when she sits back after one particular turn of phrase that has many of the shoulders in our section bouncing with laughter.

"I learned everything I know from my mother." I try and imagine seeing Nancy Hore standing and hollering at the field of play and can't seem to. But then again, I also would have a hard time believing that Sophie was so good at it if I wasn't witnessing it with my own eyes.

"You're full of surprises, eh?"

Her reply comes in the slight tilt of her lips and the bounce of an eyebrow and it leaves me shifting in my seat. I force myself to think of Gary attacking my foot before dawn this morning. Anything to avoid trying to figure out what that look means. Because if I allow myself an inch of space to think about what it means, I may come up with all the ways this woman could surprise me behind closed doors. All the little things I could discover in the name of intimacy.

"Oh shit!" I hear from beside me and look up to find Nick standing there with a tray of drinks. "I didn't know you two were here, or I would have grabbed you hot chocolate too."

"All good. I'll run up to get us some," I say as Sophie and I stand to let him pass. "You want one, right?"

"Oh, yes, please."

Everything about her response is innocent. There is nothing suggestive in her tone or smile, and yet I'm desperately reaching for thoughts that take me away from her. That container in the back of my fridge I'm afraid to open does the trick.

You're going to mess this up, the little voice I've been good at ignoring whispers. And what exactly am I going to mess up? Our friendship? My heart? Too late for that one; my heart has been all-in since she walked into that classroom. She's going to walk away from this, and no matter what I'll be a bit broken. But if she walks away feeling a bit more put together, then every crack I sustain will be worth it.

ABC

"Tonight was fun," Sophie says as I pull into her driveway.

"Even though they lost?"

She rolls her head so she's looking at me and I sit back and do the same. Sitting like this in the dark car feels more intimate than about every touch we've shared yet. I don't want her to get out and go into her house. I want to stay here like this, Sophie and me.

"Yeah, which I guess is a testament to how awesome you and your friends are." Sophie liking my friends lights something in my chest. Hope, maybe?

"Well, you make it easy for them to be awesome." We sit smiling at one another, and I wait for it to get uncomfortable. But as I watch her watch me, it gets easier. Like sinking into a hot tub after a long run, or that first sip of the most delicious hot chocolate. Looking at Sophie fills me with only good feelings.

Her eyes travel to my lips, and a soft sigh leaves through hers. "I should go in. Tomorrow is going to be a long day." She doesn't move, though, and neither do I. "What's on the docket for J?" she asks after a couple minutes of silence.

"Junk," I reply.

"Junk? As in?" she prompts.

"Sunday yard sales. If you're around Sunday."

"I have brunch with my friends, but you can come if you want. I feel like I'm always with your friends."

"I want you to be there," I admit.

"I want you to meet mine. We can never have too many, right?"

"I've heard that," I say as I get out of the car.

She steps out, and automatically her hand slips into mine when she meets me at the front of the car. *This is too easy. It's too natural,* the voice taunts.

I look at our hands as we walk up her front path. So close. *Fake. Fake. Fake.*

She drops my hand when we get to the door so she can slip her key into the lock. I watch as she turns and casually leans against the door frame. She's so effortlessly elegant, even in her casual clothes. I'm amazed anyone buys us as a couple. She's out of my league in every single demographic.

"What?" she asks, her head tipping to the right, sharp blue eyes narrowed in concern.

I shake my head, feeling a bit dazed. "Nothing, just wondering how to say goodnight to you in an intimately appropriate way." I step forward and lower my forehead to hers. "I'll see you tomorrow, sunshine." I kiss her forehead and tuck a lock of hair behind her ear, letting my hand slowly trail away from her body as I step back.

That look is still on her face, and I hate that I've caused her any worry. "See you tomorrow, Foster," she says quietly before stepping through the door and closing it. I don't move until I hear the sound of the lock sliding into place.

I'm so screwed.

THIRTY-FOUR

SOPHIE

"It's so amazing to finally meet you." Maya extends a hand to Foster when we arrive at the restaurant, hand in hand because it's easier to pretend at this point than to not. "Fuck, you're tall. Soph didn't mention how tall you were."

"I've heard lots about you." Foster looks over at me with a smirk. "And I'm shocked, that's usually the first thing people mention. That or my—" He gestures at his red hair.

"I like him," Maya says approvingly as her eyes do a full scan of him. It makes me want to demand she stop looking at him like that or immediately scratch her eyes out so she doesn't even have the chance to.

"Is lamp man joining us?" I ask, looking around, hoping to draw her attention away from my... my what? My friend?

"He'll be here soon." She blushes. It has been three years since she was in anything that resembled a relationship, and even then it took her twice as long to introduce us to the guy. The fact we're meeting Davis after about a month is a big deal. "Do me a favor, though, don't mention the lamps? He's not aware how free I am with information."

"He probably knows," Foster says.

"No way," Maya scoffs.

"Most guys assume women are like the characters on *Sex and the City*. It's why a lot of guys have performance anxiety these days."

"Do they also still think we have pillow fights in our underwear?" I ask.

"You don't?" Foster asks, eyebrows raised, eyes wide, and I'm momentarily stuck in those sharp eyes.

"There he is," Maya practically squeals, pushing past us to greet a guy. A very short guy.

"That guy breaks lamps in bed?" Foster whispers, his warm breath brushing against my skin.

Davis is topping the height chart at max five five.

"Maybe it's got nothing to do with, um, length of anything. He does look bendy."

"Sophie, Foster, this is Davis. Davis, this is my friend Sophie and her... ugh, what are you exactly?" Maya asks, squinting up at Foster.

Foster looks down at me, his eyes wide in question. "He's my friend," I say slowly. Because introducing him as my friend who is also helping me out with intimacy doesn't really roll off the tongue quite right.

Davis smiles brightly and taps his nose. "Friends." He looks down at our hands that are clasped back together. "Right."

"Good friends. Lifelong, some might say," Foster adds, giving my hand a little squeeze.

"Holy shit, you are tall." Yas practically skips over to introduce herself to Foster, barely looking at the rest of us.

"So I've heard," he replies like the good sport he is.

"Yasmine." I watch as they shake hands, but unlike Maya, Yas looks over at me, her grin letting me know she approves. "And you must be Davis?" She pulls her hand from Foster's and offers it up to the much shorter man.

"Nice to meet you."

Yas steps back and sizes the two men up. "You know, you two have all the hallmarks of a buddy cop duo." She waves at their obvious height difference.

"I have been looking for a really tall buddy." Davis looks up at Foster. "You wanna audition for the role?"

"Depends. What's the role entail?"

"Watching a game here or there, the odd trip to a bar to not talk about feelings, and occasionally reaching for something on a high shelf."

"Hmm," Foster contemplates. "Can we throw in you reaching for stuff on the ground?"

"Seems fair." Davis shoots a hand out, and they shake.

Yasmine and Maya look over at me, absolutely beaming. "It's going well," Maya mouths.

"I wish Miguel was here." Yas sighs. "Soon though," she adds happily.

I wasn't worried about things not going well. Foster is one of those guys everyone likes. The kind your friends beg you to stay with so they don't have to choose between the two of you if it ends. I had to try so hard with Gregory despite the accomplishments of my friends. They weren't at his "level," and he always seemed a bit like he smelled something off the entire time we'd be out. But heaven forbid I didn't invite him. I'd hear about it for days. About how I should want him there with me, that's what couples do, they go out together. And every time I'd feel awful and invite him the next time, and with each outing my friends said less and less while the looks became more and more concerned. It wasn't only me walking on eggshells around him, it was everyone.

"Hey." Foster's light touch on my cheek has me turning and blinking in his direction. Visions of Gregory fade, and in their place it's just Foster.

"Hi," I say quietly.

"You okay?"

"Mm-hmm," I hum, forcing a smile.

"Great, tell the poor guy what you want to eat," Yas says, and I look up to see our server smiling awkwardly at me.

"Oh, shit, sorry. I was miles away. I'll have the eggs Florentine, please."

"With breakfast potatoes or greens?"

"Serious question." I lean forward. "Does anyone ever say the greens?"

He thinks. "Happens occasionally."

"Well, today isn't going to be an occasion."

"Good choice. And for you, sir?" He turns his focus to Foster.

"I'm going to have the chicken and waffles please, but with the hot sauce on the side."

"Sure."

"Also, I'll get a side of the potatoes. I'm assuming they're great since everyone got them."

"You'd assume correctly."

Once the server leaves, Yasmine updates us on her wedding and how Miguel is doing.

"That reminds me, will you be back to two for your RSVP?" Yas eyes Foster.

"Oh, um, I don't know. Do you want to go to a wedding with me?"

Foster looks at me like I've lost it. Like I've done the impossible and asked a stupid question. "I want to go every-where with you," he says matter-of-factly, tucking that stubborn lock of hair back behind my ear, causing everyone at the table to sigh, including Davis. The combination of his words and the graze of his fingers has me tightening my hand around my water glass as my body reacts in a not-so-appropriate manner.

I can feel my face heat, and I know my blush is visible to everyone around me. There are probably satellites registering it this very minute.

He plays his role well. Some woman is going to be wildly happy one day.

Could be me, a hopeful little voice comes to life.

"It's at a winery in Niagara," Yas says dreamily. "We wanted to keep it small and simple. Good food, good wine, no pressure. Miguel has even seen me in my dress," she laughs.

"Wait, what?" Davis sputters, mid-sip.

Yas smiles. "We don't waste time. There's no guarantee of tomorrow for Miguel. Even after a successful transplant, things could go downhill quickly. I wanted to see his reaction now."

"I like that," Foster says. "It should be about what works for you and not about superstitions."

When our meals come, Foster immediately offers me a bite. Gregory did that in the beginning too. But he wouldn't have asked for the hot sauce on the side. He would have goaded me into trying it and then smirked as I battled the unpleasant burn in my mouth, chastising me for something I had no control over. Foster, on the other hand, dips each forkful into the hot sauce. He doesn't have to say that he's welcoming me to help myself; it's as clear as day in everything he does.

After I finish my potatoes, he slides over his side plate still stacked high with the seasoned crispy delights, while chatting with Yasmine about Miguel's transplant. It's the fact he's very much engaged with my friend while also aware of me that has me rising and practically running to the washroom. Yet again.

Standing over the sink, holding onto the sides, I take deep stuttering breaths. Foster's goodness. His attentiveness. The way he touches me and listens to me shines a light on what my life had been like for so many years. It illuminates all the deep cracks of toxic behavior I either couldn't see or refused to acknowledge.

The door opens, and I look up to see Maya.

"I'll be out in a minute." I force a smile, and I'm met with a skeptical look.

"There's no rush." She shrugs, joining me at the sink and catching my gaze in the mirror. "He's special," she says.

"I know."

"Is that why you're hiding in the bathroom? Because you know he's special?"

I shake my head, my shoulders dropping. "I'm hiding in the bathroom because it hit me how fucked up my relationship with Gregory really was."

"Just realizing it, eh? You spent a lot of time in denial, my friend."

"I didn't want to see it. I didn't want to, I don't know, fail."

Maya pulls me into her arms without a word and squeezes me tightly. "Staying in a relationship that is not good for you isn't succeeding, my love. Leaving it was not a fail."

"But I didn't leave it." I pull back as tears finally break through. "He did. I didn't have a choice. I would have stayed."

"You don't know that," she insists, rubbing her hands up

and down my upper arms. "You would have still met Foster."

I shake my head slowly. "No."

"What do you mean, no?"

No, because I never would have applied for that job if I'd still been with Gregory. I'm doing what I always wanted to do now, but for years he'd convinced me that my calling was to be the head of some agency or another. He wanted us both to be the head of something. Equals, he'd said countless times. But when I look back, I'm not so sure he actually realized what the word meant.

"Sophie?"

"My path changed when he kicked me out, that's all." I wash my hands, if only to do something with them. "I don't want Foster to worry. Let's go back." I dry my hands and head for the door, only to have Maya's hand wrap around my arm and pull me back.

"Promise me one thing."

"Maybe."

"Be honest with yourself when it comes to whatever this thing is with him."

"I am."

Her expression screams bullshit. "You're not, and we both know it. You're not there yet, not ready to be."

We stand there, staring at each other until her hand drops, a silent understanding reached before we head back to our table. I know exactly what I want. But I also need to respect what it is I need.

The minute we come into view of the table I sense Foster's eyes on me, concern etched across his handsome face.

I am fucked.

THIRTY-FIVE

FOSTER

Sophie's friends are wonderful and clearly think the world of her, and that alone wins them points in my book. I do find myself on the outskirts of all their conversations though, awkwardly putting in bits and pieces from my work life when it feels appropriate.

I am proud of what I do and I love my job, but my uncle's words have worn away at me over the years. People making comments about how I've somehow lost my way and ended up in a female-dominated profession also haven't helped. Sitting here, I have to remind myself that ultimately what matters is how *I* feel about my life. But it's hard while sitting between people with advanced degrees and ambitions I can't even begin to fathom.

Sophie's been crying. I see it immediately when she walks around the corner from the bathroom, and I have an intense desire to rush to her, pick her up, and carry her home, shield her from the world. When she sees me staring she forces a smile, it does nothing to abate my desire to get her out of here.

"You okay?" I ask quietly when she sits back down next to me. It's not lost on me that she doesn't sit as close as she had been. There's a full hand width between us now whereas before her thigh was pressed against mine.

"Yeah," she lies. I see the no in her eyes, but I don't push it.

I look over at Maya, who plasters on a smile when she notices me. Everything that's happening right now feels contrived, and the tension in the air feels thicker than it should at a brunch with friends.

By the time we leave, Sophie seems more herself. She holds my hand as we walk to the car and takes it again once we're buckled in.

"Sorry I keep running to the washroom every time we're out. I promise it's not you."

"You never need to apologize," I say before placing a kiss on the back of her hand and her responding sigh has me smiling against her skin. "Now, let's go look through someone else's junk."

"How about this?" Sophie holds up what appears to be the artwork of a child.

I take it from her to study. "Imagine selling your kid's artwork."

"Can't you see the genius in the brush strokes?" she says, leaning into me and pointing at the one thick red line that extends across the canvas.

"I'm pretty sure this was done with fingers."

"Oh well, I've never claimed to be good at judging art." She laughs as she walks away toward an antique trunk.

"This is— Oh, oh god no." She slams the lid down and sits on it quickly.

"What's in there?"

"Nope, don't even think about opening this thing."

"Come on, let me see." I drop to my knees in front of her. "Please, Sophie," I beg.

She blinks a few times before swallowing. "Foster." She looks at me, her face pure seriousness. "You do not want to know. Trust me."

"I do trust you, but I also want to know what caused your reaction."

She shakes her head. "I'll tell you one day, I promise."

"Fine. I won't look. But if there's a body in there, you should probably report it." I stand and hold my hand out to her.

She takes it and stands. "Not a body. Well... no, not a body."

I tilt my head suspiciously. "Parts?" I whisper.

She shakes her head again, eyes wide, lips pressed together so tightly they're almost white.

"Alright, well, let's go look through the kitchen stuff over there." I gesture behind me.

She holds my hand until we get to the table, but once she lets her guard down and loosens her grip, I drop it and run back to the trunk.

"Foster, no!" she shrieks, her desperation only adding to the need to see what's enclosed in the trunk.

When I open it and see the contents, my jaw hits the ground. "Are those..."

"Yes," she confirms.

"So when you said they weren't body parts..." I trail off and peek over at her. Her face is three shades redder than usual, and I find myself unable to look away.

She finally meets my gaze and shrugs. "They are representations of a body part I guess, but they're not a body part."

"Do you think they know they're in there?"

"How could they not?"

"There are so many," I say, looking down at the closed trunk.

"So many," Sophie agrees as a laugh bubbles out of her, and within a few seconds we're holding each other up as we make our way back to the car.

"I think I need a minute," I gasp, leaning my head back against the headrest.

"No one is going to believe us," Sophie says as she wipes her eyes. "I wouldn't believe us."

"I wonder what treasures the next stop will have," I say, pulling away from the first sale. "Perhaps a bag of vibrators?"

"Oh, some of those probably vibrated." Sophie erupts in a fit of giggles, and they wash over me like sea-foam, tiny bubbles popping gently as they touch my skin.

The second sale does not reveal any interesting, disturbing, or even useful findings, so we move onto the next.

"Wyatt Earp! Look at this." I can barely contain my excitement as I lift the dark blue Le Creuset dutch oven off the table.

"My mom has one of those," Sophie says, brushing her finger over the enameled cast iron pot. "How much is it?"

I lift it above my head and find the sticker. "Five dollars," I whisper in awe.

"Why are you whispering?" Sophie whispers back.

I look around to make sure no one is listening. "Because I'm afraid I'll sound too excited and they'll say it's a mistake."

"How much are these things normally?"

I look at her in shock. I know she's not much of a cook, but she was raised by a tremendous one. "Seriously?" I ask.

"Seriously."

"One this size is about six hundred dollars."

Her jaw drops. "No way."

"Way! Quick, look to see if there are any other ones."

"Here." She reaches for an orange pot about half the size of the one I'm holding and never parting with. "Oh, but this one doesn't have a lid. Is that a deal-breaker?"

"Not even a little bit." I have the urge to throw cash at the teenager sitting scrolling through his phone and running to the car.

Sophie seems to notice my nervous excitement. "Is this a 'start the car' moment?"

"A what?"

"You know that old commercial where the woman gets such good deals she wants her husband to start the car before someone comes out and tells her it's not real?"

"Ikea?" I recall, and she nods. "Yes, this is definitely one of those moments."

I drop a ten on the table in front of the teen who barely acknowledges us and then Sophie and I speed walk back to the car with my new favorite kitchen accessories.

"So, what are you going to make me?"

"Whatever you want, sunshine."

"French onion soup," she says as if it's a challenge.

"Done."

"Coq au vin."

"Easy."

"Boeuf Bourguignon."

I glance over to see her grinning back.

"I've seen that movie with Meryl Streep. I know what it is, but my French is très terrible."

Dare I say I found something Sophie is not good at? Although even hearing her butcher the French language is a bit of a turn-on. Perfectly imperfect.

At the last sale we stop at, conveniently around the corner from my apartment, Sophie finds *Lord of the Rings* placemats and buys them. My heart skips several beats when she says our meals will taste even better with them on the table. At least that's what I think she said. I'm stuck on how she brought up collective meals, plural.

Once at my place, we each open our food delivery apps, pick a cuisine, scroll once, and where our finger stops the page, that's what we order. I landed on a barbecue place and then picked pork with baked beans and mac and cheese. I have no clue what Sophie got because she refuses to tell me.

While we wait, we scroll through all the streaming services until we find a movie that some may call junk, but we've decided to call a guilty pleasure.

"I think we're starting to play a bit fast and loose with the alphabet now," Sophie says as she sets her bag of takeout on the counter.

"Is that sushi?" I ask, surprised.

"It is, and three of the kinds I've never even had before. You're rubbing off on me, Mr. Walsh." The minute the words leave her mouth, I see them register. "Oh, no, well, shit. That's not... Can we maybe just forget I said that?"

"Absolutely not," I tease. "That's getting filed up here for later." I tap my head and wink.

"Oh my god, Foster, ew!" She cringes before covering her face, her body shaking with silent laughter.

Sophie, completely uninhibited, laughing in my kitchen, surrounded by takeout. I can't believe this is my life.

THIRTY-SIX

SOPHIE

Foster is groaning on the couch next to me. His long legs stretched out on the floor while his hands rest on his stomach.

"Why'd I eat the second bowl of mac and cheese?"

"Because it was delicious?" I reply from my spot on the couch.

"It was really good," he agrees, grinning over at me.

I try to sit up only to flop back. "I don't think I'm ever going to be able to move again."

"You'll have to live here with me."

"I don't think there's enough room on this couch for the two of us to live on," I tease.

He looks over and then down at the couch. "Well maybe if I just"—he bends forward, grabs my legs, and in one fluid motion has me flat on my back across the couch—"then..." He mirrors my position except he's so tall that his feet are right at my mouth.

Looking down at his toes, I crinkle my nose. "Not the most ideal position."

"Fair," he mumbles, shifting, and suddenly his face is

where his feet had been. He has to lie on his side, but he fits next to me. "Better?"

My eyes go directly to his lips. "Yes," I purr, my body automatically turning into him.

"Good."

"You move pretty fast for someone who is *so* full," I sass.

"I have a really fast metabolism," he whispers, lifting his hand and dragging his thumb across the corner of my bottom lip. "Sauce," he says, bringing that same thumb to his own mouth. My tongue sneaks out to where he touched me, and I watch his eyes heat when he catches the motion.

He cannot be comfortable that close to the edge, but I can't seem to move. I don't want this moment to end.

"So, how did I do with J?" he asks.

"Mmm," I hum, trying to think of an appropriate word. "Joyous? Jovial? Jolly?"

"Are you asking me if it was those things?"

"I'm just trying to stay on theme."

"And overall, how was your experience?"

I laugh, shaking my head as he switches into serious mode. "This is starting to sound like a customer satisfaction survey."

His gaze drops quickly and a tiny grin appears. "Your satisfaction is our number one priority here at Foster Inc."

"Would you say it's guaranteed?"

His arm slides around my waist, and my skin erupts in full-body chills when his fingers brush the skin where my shirt has ridden up. "Yes."

I could lie like this forever, just looking at him. Watching how his eyes subtly move around my face. The way his lips tip up every now and then. How his gold-flecked eyes seem to catch every emotion I feel even when I don't think I'm showing them. He's still the boy I fell for as a kid, just with sharper lines, several more inches, and way more muscle.

"I should head out," I say quietly as if saying it quietly enough will make it not a thing I'm about to do. If I say it quietly, I won't hear myself, and then I can stay here longer.

Foster manages to roll off the couch gracefully and ends up on his knees. I want him to tell me not to go. That I don't have to go. But I respect him even more when he stands and reaches down to pull me up. I love him a little bit more for holding my hand as we walk to the door. I appreciate him most when he insists on driving me home rather than letting me call an Uber. I melt when he takes my hand the minute we're both in the car. And I cherish the soft kiss he drops at the corner of my mouth at my front door.

"More sauce?"

"Night, sunshine," he says, my hand falling out of his as he backs away.

Standing in the doorway I watch as he slips back into his car, backs out of my driveway, and waves before heading back home. I touch the place his lips had been as I walk into the house, the tension of the evening finally easing as I close the door.

EDWIN

Have you seen this?

I click on the image he's attached to enlarge it and see a pregnancy announcement.

Dr. Gregory Dickson and Ms. Stephanie Norman
are pleased to announce they are expecting a baby
boy in October. This is the first child for both.

I read the announcement six times before it hits me.

"I don't want kids, Sophie. I thought I made that crystal clear." That's what Gregory had said to me when I showed him the two lines on the test. Except he had claimed to want kids in the beginning. I remember that very clearly, but my excitement died immediately at his disgust, like I'd done it on purpose, as if I chose not to take my pill that one time. I started to question whether I had thought he had because it's what *I* wanted.

"You're so fucking stupid sometimes. How hard is it to wake up and take one of those pills every day?" he'd spat at me while practically throwing around papers. I got blamed for that too when he couldn't find one of the pages that had slid to the floor during his tantrum.

I'd stood there and let him list all the ways I had let him down. Looking back, it's easy to say I should have walked out right then and there. But at the time I'd been ashamed of letting him down. And as I made an appointment to terminate the pregnancy, I'd told myself that it was for the best. That I wanted Gregory and this life more than I wanted to be a mother. Except I wanted to be a mom, desperately.

I cried alone in the waiting room and felt numb through the procedure. When asked if I had someone at home, I smiled and said yes. But at home, he never even asked how I was. I had convinced myself that it was because he thought it was too hard for me to bring up, so he went on as if nothing had happened. That his silence was for my benefit.

Walking to the living room, I sink down onto the couch, my hands sliding over my flat stomach. Remembering the joy I'd felt for a short time at the thought of having a baby. It had been the right decision in the end. But that doesn't mean I don't still wonder what could have been.

When Foster had brought up kids the other day, he'd done it so innocently, and I'd shut down. I hate that I reacted that way, especially because he'd never mean anything malicious by it.

I sit here, my imagination replacing the unpleasant memories. Foster swaying back and forth in front of the big front window, talking softly to the newborn in his arms. A tuft of red hair poking out of a tiny hat. Foster running down the street after a little kid on a bike, laughing as he smiles back at me. Foster telling me he's got it when the baby cries in the middle of the night. He'd be such a good dad. He's never said that's what he wants, though. Just because he works with kids doesn't mean he wants kids of his own.

Do you want kids?

I text before I think better of it. I may as well get this question out of the way, before letting my mind spend a second longer in imagination land.

I watch as three dots appear and disappear over and over again until a simple answer finally appears.

FOSTER

Yes

Then I stare at his reply until the letters become illegible.

THIRTY-SEVEN

FOSTER

I thought about Sophie's text until sleep finally took me into dreamland. But even there I couldn't escape it. Sophie beaming at me telling me she's pregnant, me crying and sweeping her off her feet. A slideshow of beautiful possibilities until I woke at four a.m. wondering how the hell I was going to afford a baby, hypothetical or not, on an EA's salary. *You should have gone back to real school,* I can hear my mom saying.

I'd gotten up, put on my running stuff, and hit the pavement well before the birds had even begun to sing. And now as I turn the corner back to my apartment, I feel like Sophie has thrown a big ol' wrench in my plan to not get too attached. Although I'm delusional if I think I'm not attached. She had me hooked from the first smile she sent in my direction.

Gary doesn't greet me at the door, and something immediately feels off. I don't bother taking my shoes off as I walk further into the apartment. He's by the window, in his usual spot, but he's flat on his side. I can see that he's breathing, but the squirrel is sitting outside and Gary doesn't seem to care. I've never seen him not take issue with his nemesis, so alarm bells start going off in my head. Without thinking I pull my phone out of my pocket and immediately dial Cass's number.

"Someone better be dying," she croaks. "Or dead."

"It's Gary. I think something's wrong?"

Now fully awake, she fires off questions, "What's he doing? Is he puking? Does he have the runs? Lethargic?"

"He's breathing, flat on his side. But the squirrel is at the window, and he's not losing his mind like he usually does. He also didn't meet me at the door, and he always does."

"Did he eat something he shouldn't have? Anything new missing?"

I look around unsure of what he could have eaten that would cause him to be sick or in pain, or both. "Not that..." I stop abruptly and walk to the coffee table. Sophie had taken her hair out of an elastic last night because it was giving her a headache. She'd left it on the table, but it's gone now. "I think he may have eaten Sophie's hair elastic."

"Get him to the emergency vet right now, Foster." Cass's tone is serious, and because it's rarely serious I'm already pulling his carrier down from the closet before she even gets to my name.

When I pick him up, he yowls at me. "Sorry, bud." I wince as he lets out another sorrowful meow.

"That's an unhappy cat," I hear Cass say from where my phone is sitting on the chair next to me. "Okay, there's an emergency vet on Rymal. I sent you the address. I'll call and tell them you're on your way. Are you going to be alright?"

"Thanks. I'll be fine." I'm a bit calmer now knowing there is somewhere I can take him.

"Keep me updated."

"Will do," I say before hanging up, grabbing my keys and running out of my apartment.

It's six thirty a.m., and I'm the only one sitting in the waiting room. The magazines are all from at least six years ago, everything and everyone within their pages already old news. I've paced so much my watch has congratulated me on reaching my step goal for the day and then suggested I take a break.

I'm about to get up and start pacing again when the front door opens and Sophie rushes in. Her hair pulled back and lopsided, pieces of it coming out everywhere. Pajama pants with little stars peek out beneath her long coat, like she'd gotten the call and come here straight from bed. My heart stutters at the thought of her rushing to be by my side for my cat.

"Oh my god, how is he?" she frets breathlessly, sitting in the chair next to mine.

I blink back stupidly. "What are you doing here?"

"Cass called and said there was an emergency with Gary, then she sent me the address and"—she looks around as if realizing where she is for the first time—"I guess I'm here now."

"You didn't have to come," I assure her even though I'm the farthest thing from upset that she's here right now.

She scoffs, rolling her eyes. Why is that so sexy? "As if —" The door to the back opens, and a tall man wearing scrubs and a lab coat walks toward us.

"Mr. Walsh?"

I stand, Sophie joining me. "Yes?" I ask anxiously.

"I'm Dr. Jacobs. Gary has a bowel obstruction." He turns the iPad he's holding toward me. "Right here." He points at the X-ray. "Unfortunately, it looks like our only option for treatment will be surgery."

"Okay, do whatever you need to do," I confirm.

He looks back toward the receptionist who rounds the counter with a clipboard. "We'll just need you to sign a few things." I must look like I'm about to puke because Sophie squeezes my arm while Dr. Jacobs assures me that it's a pretty standard procedure when it comes to cats. But it's still a surgery and therefore involves risks. "Gary appears to be in excellent condition aside from the obstruction, so I'm not overly concerned about how he'll do under anesthetic."

"Okay." I nod, sitting so I can begin filling out the form.

"Do you know what the obstruction is?" I hear Sophie ask.

"I can't really make it out, but if I had to guess it's string or an elastic." Sophie's gasp has me adding an extra-long line to the cross on the end of "street."

She's got her hands on her head, looking horrified. "I left my elastic at your place." Her eyes immediately fill with tears, and I can't get rid of the clipboard fast enough as I pull her into my arms. "Oh my god, this is my fault," she murmurs into my chest.

"No, Soph," I say, sliding my hand into her hair and pulling her tighter against me. "He's never done anything like this before. I saw it there and didn't think anything of it."

I look over at the vet only to realize he's gone. When Sophie pulls back, I don't hesitate to take her face in my hands, running my thumbs over her cheeks to wipe her tears away.

"You didn't do anything wrong, sunshine," I say as soothingly as I can.

"I'm sorry."

I pull her back in and rest my lips on the top of her head until her breathing returns to normal. "I really need you not to be sorry." I have a feeling she was blamed for a lot in her relationship with Gregory. He doesn't strike me as the kind of guy who takes responsibility for much.

"At least let me pay the bill," she pleads.

"Yeah, not a chance, sunshine," I argue as we sit back down and I pick the paperwork back up. I don't miss the look on her face when my words land. Indignant mixed with shock, and I can't help but chuckle as I complete the form.

I know this is going to be pricey, but I'd saved everything I made in Korea and have some inheritance left from my dad's parents. It's not going to last forever, but it means I can afford to keep my cat alive without going into debt. As long as he doesn't make this a habit.

When I give the form back, I'm told that I can go home and they'll call me with an update later in the morning. When I let Sophie know she can go home, she insists on driving me because apparently I look "done in."

"Why don't you come up?" I suggest when she pulls up to the curb.

"Oh, you should probably get some sleep."

I look over at her skeptically. "Do you really think I'm going to get any sleep while I don't know what's going on with Gary?"

She studies me for a minute before shaking her head. "No, I suspect you'll pace or go for a run."

"I already had a run today. If you come up, you'll keep me from running myself into the ground. You'd be doing me a favor." I reach over and squeeze her hand and watch her look down at where we are connected. "I insist."

She peers up through her lashes as she worries her lip. "Well, if you insist."

I take her hand the second she rounds the car, threading my fingers through hers, relishing the feeling of her skin against mine. I hold it in the elevator and as I unlock my door, and the minute we're through it I wrap my arms back around her and laugh at the little yelp of surprise.

"Thank you for coming to check on me and for coming back with me," I whisper.

"Of course. I wasn't sleeping anyway."

I step back, resting my hands on her upper arms and really look at her. She looks more tired than she had under the lights of the vet's office. She offers a sleepy smile and then fights a yawn.

"Come on." I take her hand again and lead her toward my bedroom. I expect her to slam on the brakes, but she follows without any hesitation. We stop at the end of the bed, and I turn and unzip her coat before sliding it off. She's got a thin long-sleeved henley on, and I have to look away immediately when I realize she isn't wearing a bra.

Tossing her coat on my dresser I gesture for her to lay down. Again she does so without hesitation. After removing my own coat, I join her.

"I should shower," I say. "I probably reek."

She shakes her head. "You smell surprisingly good."

"Liar," I tease.

"I'd never lie to you."

I take a chance that if I ask her something right now she'll be upfront. "Why couldn't you sleep?"

"It's dumb." She shakes her head and rolls onto her back.

"Talking about dumb stuff is as important as talking about the serious stuff."

I watch as she swallows, eyes glued to the ceiling, and I think she's about to shut down. "Gregory's girlfriend is pregnant," she blurts out. "Due in October. It's a boy."

Her question from earlier makes sense now. "That's not a dumb reason, Soph."

She blinks rapidly, and I see a tear slip down into my pillow. I want to wrap myself around her but I stay put, giving her space to collect herself.

"Three years ago, I got pregnant." The words tumble out of her. "It wasn't planned, but I was so excited. I've always dreamt of being a mom. But Gregory insisted I terminate the pregnancy because he didn't want kids. He acted like I'd gotten pregnant on purpose and twisted it so much that at the end I almost believed he was right. That I had somehow tried to trap him with a baby."

Like with your own kids?

Do you want kids?

Crap.

THIRTY-EIGHT

SOPHIE

Once I start, I can't seem to stop talking. I tell Foster about every shitty thing I can remember Gregory saying to me or doing during the five years we were together. Things I've never told anyone else and never planned to talk about. All the ways he didn't know me, always obvious in the gifts he gave or the way he touched me. Gifts and touches I accepted with a big smile on my face or a perfectly timed moan. Bits of my story that leave me wracked with shame for staying and anger for allowing him to control so much of my life.

I'm a solitary figure standing in a field of waving red flags in every single chapter Gregory was in. If I knew my friend was in that kind of situation, I would have forcibly removed them. Instead, I dug in because there was no way the logical part of my brain could be right about any of it. I was studying this kind of thing; obviously I'd know better.

Foster hasn't said a thing, and he hasn't moved a millimeter. When the last word finally leaves my mouth, he looks as if he's going to set fire to the world. Like he's going to avenge my lost years and somehow bring them back to me to redo.

I wait in the silence of the room for him to say something, but he just stares at my shoulder. It's not until I finally roll onto my side that he looks up at me. I expect to see wet eyes, but I only see the anger burning within.

"I never wanted to be this woman," I admit. "I was that woman on campus with a sign, yelling 'fuck the patriarchy.' Then I let the patriarchy fuck me. I think I've stayed quiet because I'm embarrassed."

Foster's eyes snap to mine, somehow hardening even more and causing me to recoil. When he notices, his face immediately softens.

"You have nothing to be embarrassed of. You're human, and you're going to be impacted by the same stuff as the rest of us. Your education doesn't negate that. Life still happens, and it's always harder to see and admit things to ourselves." His left hand cups my cheek, and it warms me to my bones. "Thank you for telling me. I wish you had nothing to share, but I'm honored you felt comfortable enough to share things about your past with me."

I sigh, feeling suddenly lighter for sharing things that have been weighing my heart and mind down. Pieces of debris left over from an emotional atomic bomb finally swept away.

Reaching up, I mimic him by laying my hand on his cheek, which earns me a tiny smile. "Thank you for being a safe place for me."

"Always, sunshine. I'll always be a safe place for you."

"Can you do me a favor?" I ask.

"Anything." He may regret that.

"Tell me something I don't know about you? Or don't, you don't have to, I just—"

"I feel like I'm never going to be good enough for my family or..." he says, quickly before trailing off when his gaze meets mine.

I'm confused. I know his uncle has issues with him, but his family seems fine. "What do you mean?"

"My parents make comments here and there about how I could have been a teacher. How I *should* be a teacher, because men are teachers, not"—his fingers curl into air quotes—"'helpers.' They act like I've settled into a job because I'm incapable of being more."

The audacity of the fucking patriarchy.

"More than what? Someone who makes the lives of kids easier? And the lives of teachers, for that matter? Someone who shows up every day and ensures that no child is forgotten or feels invisible? Someone who not only encourages dreams but dedicates himself to helping a kid achieve them? I don't know how you could ever be more when you're beyond enough."

He's looking at me like he wants to kiss me. His eyes keep dipping to my mouth, and his breathing is more ragged. It would be so damn easy to roll into him and press my lips against his. Let all our feelings of inadequacy, shame, and anger evaporate. But I don't want him to kiss me while my face is stained with tears and he looks about ready to implode with too many emotions. I don't want him to kiss me while we carry the faint smell of a vet's office, all antiseptic and sterile.

I want him to kiss me while I'm laughing at something silly he said because he can't hold himself back any longer. I want him to twirl me in a circle and then hold me in a way that feels like forever. I want all the things he's done to make me feel good, wanted, and safe to be real.

Scooting closer, I wrap my arms around him and tuck

my head under his chin, breathing in his scent and laughing when the faint odor of sweat hits me.

"I told you I stink." He laughs, pulling me in tighter.

"I don't mind," I whisper, my lips moving across his chest, only the thin fabric of his shirt separating us.

He starts playing with my hair, and the simplicity of the action has a few fresh tears slipping down my face. I asked him to show me what intimacy could be like, and he has managed to do it at every step. I spent years missing out on the most mundane yet pleasurable things. I never knew it was possible to feel like the center of someone's world simply by the way they touched you, at least not until Foster opened my eyes to all the could-bes.

"Soph?" I wake to the smell of coffee and gold-flecked amber eyes. A girl could get used to this. "The vet called."

I sit up so fast that Foster has to jump back to avoid a broken nose. "Is he okay?"

He nods, a soft tired smile stretching across his face. "He's still out of it because of the drugs, but they got the elastic. Apparently they won't know how things are until he poops."

"Classic." I yawn and rub my face. "When do you get to pick him up?"

"Tomorrow after work, most likely. They'll keep him a little longer for observation."

I study him for a minute. His hair is damp, which means he showered. Which means he was naked. Which means he was naked in the same space where I currently am. I'm woozy for a second as all my teenage fantasies come roaring back.

"Coffee?" he asks, and I rip my gaze from his hair back to his face. My god, his face. How is it even better now than it was back then?

"Coffee, yeah. Coffee would be great."

"Did you have plans today?" Foster asks as I stir some cream into my mug.

"Well, yes and no," I admit. "I was going to tackle the mess that is my bedroom. Remember when I said that was the room I hadn't cleaned? Well, it's still the room I haven't cleaned."

He shrugs. "We all have one of those."

I look around and scoff. "Foster, this place is pristine. Like your bedroom as a kid."

An eyebrow goes up as his mouth is pulled to the right in a cocky grin. "You remember my bedroom as a kid?"

I remember every inch of that room. Including the time I saw him reading on his bed in only his boxers when he was seventeen.

"Barely," I lie, taking a sip and immediately burning my mouth. Anything to avoid admitting my obsession with him for most of my life.

"I don't have one of those rooms because I don't have space for one of those rooms." He spreads his arms toward the rest of the apartment. "It's three rooms and a closet."

"Three *clean* rooms and a closet," I tease.

"Breakfast?"

I turn back to him and shake my head. "I came to support you, not to have you feed me."

"I like feeding you," he confesses, with his head inside the fridge. "It's way better than feeding only myself." He pulls out a carton of eggs, a brown paper bag, and the rest of the goat cheese we got last weekend. "I'm going to make you the best omelet you've ever had."

"Big words." I pull out a stool so I can sit and watch him cook for me, yet again.

"Do me a favor?"

"Anything."

"Think up a K date for today. Make me forget about Gary."

Kiss. No, that's not a date, that's a thing I want to do. But we could kiss in different places. Maybe try different kinds of kissing in different places. Kiss in the kitchen. French kiss at a crepe café. Butterfly kisses at the botanical garden. The possibilities are endless. A kissing scavenger hunt could be fun. Kissing also seems like a good way to forget about the cat, especially if we do a really good job and get lost in them.

"Okay, but I'll have to get home and change first."

"Oh wow," Foster says in awe. "I didn't even know these existed here."

We're standing outside a twenty-four hour karaoke bar. I can't sing, and the thought of doing it in front of anyone, let alone Foster, has the partially digested omelet in my stomach doing loop-de-loops.

"In Korea, we'd go into one of these at like ten at night after drinking for a few hours and emerge after seven a.m." He mimes walking out of the darkness into the sun. "Just a bunch of hungover people staggering out onto the quiet street to drag ourselves home."

"Sounds... fun?"

"It was actually," he assures me, leading me through the front door into a sleek reception area with black leather couches and shiny surfaces. This place would be a nightmare to keep clean. They probably go through more Windex in a week than most people go through in an entire lifetime. "Hey, we'd like a room for two, please," he tells the receptionist.

I hand over my card, and then we're being led down a narrow hallway with doors on either side. It looks like a place where nefarious deeds would be carried out, not just terrible singing.

"If you want anything from the menu, hit the call button beside the door," the attendant says. "The catalog is all digital, and the remote is here." They pull it off the wall and hand it to Foster. "You'll be given a five-minute warning. If you'd like more time, select the option on the menu. And"—they suddenly look uncomfortable—"no sex."

Great, now all I'm going to think about is all the things Foster and I could do that are not sex exactly but definitely sex-adjacent.

THIRTY-NINE

FOSTER

"Does that happen often?" I ask.

"You'd be surprised," they sigh before turning and leaving me and Sophie standing alone in the quiet room.

Sophie takes in the space, glaring at the L-shaped couch that lines two of the walls. "Do you think it's sanitary?" she wonders aloud.

I lean closer to inspect the surface. "It's not a porous material, so probably." I shrug and sit and stand quickly. "Not even sticky." I grin at her and then watch in delight as she bursts out laughing. The urge to kiss her is getting harder to contain.

"Such a gentleman, checking for bodily fluids for me."

"I think if we refrain from getting naked, we'll be fine," I tease only to immediately regret it. We'd stopped at her place before coming here so she could change, and while sitting in her living room I kept thinking *she's probably naked in there right now*. I've seen her entire back, and I'd be a fool not to want to see every other inch of her.

As much as I try to tell myself that this is all fake, all for show, all a lesson in being with someone who treats her the way she should be treated, it's more on every single level. Being with Sophie is more than any lie I whisper in the dark before I fall asleep.

"What song do you want to sing first?" Sophie asks, sliding the remote out of my hand and pointing it at the screen.

"You don't want to go first?" Her head swivels in my direction, and I'm met with wide terrified eyes. "Sophie, why did you pick karaoke if you don't want to do karaoke?"

She winces. "I panicked?"

"We can go... kickboxing? Knife throwing? Keg? Oh, we could go to The Keg." I breathe out, mouth watering at the thought of a perfect steak. "Let's do that, then we can go to a comedy club where we can laugh, for L."

Followed by making out for M, I think but don't dare say.

"Knock off a bunch of letters in one day?"

"Why not? There was no rule that said we had to do them all separately."

There were no rules at all, from what I recall. Boundaries had been brought up but not set, and so far she hasn't named a single one. She's been receptive to every question, every touch.

"No rules," Sophie says quietly, her gaze dropping briefly.

"I do have one request, though."

"Shoot."

"Let me sing one song."

She immediately sits, crossing her legs and looking at me with anticipation. "Oh, please do."

I scroll through the songs, passing by all the usual ones until I get to "To Be With You" by Mr. Big. She may read into it, but so what? I'm not planning on singing it to her exactly, so it may be subtle, especially if she doesn't know the song. It's not exactly a hit from our generation.

Peeking over, I don't see the opening bars register. Through the first line, however, I watch her face transform from indifference to something else. With each line the words don't just pass over her, they begin to register. Her eyes close as her lips begin mouthing the words, a tiny smile appearing there.

Reaching down I take her hand and pull her to her feet, holding the mic between us. I'm almost surprised as she actually starts to sing. And wouldn't you know it, this stunning woman who is just about perfect in every single way cannot carry a tune to save her life. That doesn't stop her from getting into it, though. For someone who didn't actually want to participate, she's not holding back. It's like the concert again except I can hear her. And despite her ability to hit every note sharp, I'd pick singing in private with Sophie over listening to one of the best singers in the world, any day of the week.

An hour later, we've made a decent dent in the top songs of the nineties, all of which have been about eternal love. She's breathing heavily as the last chords of Letters to Cleo's cover of "I Want You to Want Me" fades. Flushed and smiling, her head tips back with a light thud against the flower print wallpaper.

Kissing her throat right now would be intimate. Running my tongue from her collarbone to chin would be sensational. My eyes are still glued to her when her chin drops back down, her eyes wide as she takes in my attention. I should look away, maybe make it less obvious how badly I want to show her a whole other side of intimacy. It takes several blinks and a slight shake of my head to pull my gaze from her.

"Um, so," I stutter, trying to get my brain restarted. "What should we do next?"

"It's your letter, rock star." She bumps her hip into mine, and I fight the urge to wrap my arm around her to keep her pressed firmly against me.

"L..." I hem and haw for a few seconds before grinning over at her. What I'm about to suggest is going to get a hard no really fast, but I'm going to say it anyway. "Line dancing."

"Line dancing?"

"Yep."

"Like..." She starts shuffling her feet. "Line dancing, line dancing?"

"Is there another kind?"

"I don't think so, but maybe you know something I don't."

"There's nothing I know that you don't, sunshine."

Her brow furrows as she sets me with a hard stare. "You know how to calm Pete down when he's having an anxiety attack. You can make all the kids laugh when they're having a bad day. You can take a bunch of random ingredients and make an incredible meal. You make me feel seen," she almost whispers the last part as she looks down.

Taking her chin between my thumb and forefinger, I tip her chin up so she's looking at me. "Everyone sees you, Sophie. You're impossible to ignore."

She shakes her head, and I watch as her eyes fill with tears, rain clouds darkening her irises. "No. People see what they want to see. And it's easier to see a smile as something it's not than it is to ask what's going on behind it. I got so good at hiding things. But I know you see me by the way you look at me and speak to me." I freeze as her hands cup my face, and I fully stop breathing, afraid that I may wake up and this will all be a dream. But no dream has ever felt like her hands on my face. No dream could produce the way her eyes search mine. "By the way you touch me."

I've got my hands clenched at my sides because I'm not sure if I could touch her right now in a way that reflects everything she's saying. If I touch her now, it will be desperate and careless, and the very last thing I want to do is touch her with careless hands. If I get the opportunity to touch Sophie Hore, to really touch her, every single graze of my skin on hers is going to be intentional.

"I'm sorry."

Confusion spreads across her beautiful face. "Why?"

"I'm sorry people haven't seen you." She wraps her arms around my neck, hugging me tightly, halting my words as I finally move my arms to wrap around her waist. She calms me. Grounds me.

"Foster?" she says, her lips, an inch from my neck.

"Mm-hmm?" I hum back.

"Take me dancing." She pulls back beaming.

"Yes, ma'am," I try a western accent which leads to a snort and a laugh from her. Sunshine.

FORTY

"What are you doing over here?" Foster asks when he joins me where I'm sitting at the bar, examining my feet.

"I'm checking to see if I have two lefts."

"No way, you were killing it out there," he assures me, but when I look up at his face I can see him trying to hide his grin. He's failing.

"Nearly killing others is more like it," I scoff.

"Nah, you weren't—"

"Foster, let's not play the game where we pretend I'm good at something I'm not. I'm okay with not being good at things. Especially things that are, well—" I wave at the floor where six couples decked out in various levels of western wear are boogying around the dance floor. "Will you please go back out?"

"I don't want to do it alone."

"You won't be. That woman's partner bailed." I point at the only single woman on the floor who's now awkwardly shuffling around. "He took a phone call. Probably won't be for that long."

He looks down at me and back out at the woman. When

he looks at me again, I think he's about to say that he actually doesn't want to do it without me, but he doesn't. "Just a dance or two, then I'll be back. Start thinking about M."

Foster approaches the woman whose blush I can see from here, and I'm instantly filled with regret. Is this when it happens? He finally finds the woman he's going to bring to all the silly friend barbecues and hockey games? Is she the one who's going to go to the emergency vet with him at three in the morning and eat the food he makes?

It's fine if that's what happens. This was never a real thing anyway. It's fun, I won't deny that, and he has made me feel all the things I've heard people talk about, but it's not real. If he comes back and says he's actually going to head out with her, I'd be fine with it.

You're a fucking liar, Sophie Hore, I can hear Maya hiss. Look at how sexy he makes line dancing look. See how his hips move. He can probably do so much with those hips, and you're sitting here trying to tell yourself that for the past two months what you've been doing is purely friendship-based. Bullshit wrapped in horseshit, deep fried in a big old vat of denial.

I keep one eye on Foster as I pull my phone out.

> I think I'm in trouble.

MAYA

> Because you're in love with the jolly red giant?

> I'm not in love with him.

> Soph, you're so head over heels for that man that Simone Biles is going to be asking you for tips.

> What do I do?

I don't know. Do you FEEL ready for
something real?

I don't know.

Can I be honest with you?

Please

You've been dating the guy for two
months. Like one hundred percent in a
relationship without the sex and if that's not
some serious edging I don't know what is.

I have nothing to say to that so I stare as Foster twirls
another woman seamlessly around the dance floor.

Like, when he touches you, you're going to
come immediately just from sheer relief.
And when you decide to go for it you may
want to have backups for all the lights in
your place because you two are going to
be feral.

MAYA!

You said I could be honest with you! I'm
being honest.

...

You're only uncomfortable with it because
you know I'm right. I saw you two together.
I've seen you talk about him. I've seen him
watch you when you didn't realize it. He
got the hot sauce ON THE SIDE Sophie!

Seriously though you may want to check
your vacation days because the fuckfest
you'll be engaged in will be

Shoes appear in front of me, and I quickly lock my

phone before I can finish reading Maya's message. Foster is standing in front of me, a bit more disheveled than he had been earlier. His hair looks like he's run his hands through it a few times, and I fight the urge to jump up and do the same.

"I wanna ride the bull," I blurt out. I don't actually want to, but I can't admit to what I'd really like to ride right now. Stupid Maya.

He looks to his left where a middle-aged man is staggering to the gate after being thrown off. "Are you sure? I've seen like six people get whiplash on that thing since we got here."

"I'm sure. You too chicken to try?"

"No, I think I've got too much length to center myself on that thing."

Don't think about his dick, don't think about his dick.

He instantly looks mortified. "Length was the wrong word," he stammers. "I mean height."

Dick, dick, dick. Oh my god, Sophie, stop it right now.

"Well, you can watch me. I don't have your, uh, length." What the actual fuck am I saying?

Foster's whole face turns the color of his hair, and I suddenly find myself unable to care what left my mouth because he looks adorable right now. He's always so damn hot, but adorable isn't his standard look. Turns out it's a nice one, though.

"It'll start slow and speed up quickly, so be prepared," the attendant tells me as I swing up onto the headless bovine. Odd considering I grew up with a real one outside my door, but I never once thought, *I should ride that thing.*

I peer over at Foster as the bull starts to move and grin as I let my hips match the rhythm under me. *This is a mistake,* I think as our eyes lock. I shouldn't be looking at him while moving like this. He looks hypnotized, his eyes locked on me as he visibly swallows, lips parted slightly. *He got hot sauce on the side.* Maya's words hit me as the bull goes left and I go right, landing on my back on the padded ground.

A hand appears above me, and I reach up so Foster can pull me to my feet.

"You're not supposed to be in here, man," the attendant scolds. But Foster doesn't even acknowledge him. His attention is fully on me, and it's heating me from the inside out.

I need air.

Without letting go of his hand, I drag him out of the building and into the parking lot. Once I'm free of the music and people in cowboy hats, I feel a bit more like I can breathe.

"You okay?" Foster asks after I let go of his hand so I can redo my ponytail. I look up in time to see him smiling at my head. Smiling at my hair, maybe? Like he's happy I'm putting it up. Gregory hated my hair in a ponytail, told me I had too much of a pinhead to carry one off. I've worn one almost every day since he kicked me out.

"I'm fine, just stuffy in there." I spin to see where we are in relation to the car. "I guess that could be M? Mechanical bull?"

"Yeah, that works. Can I interest you in Nigerian food for dinner?"

"Four letters in one day? We are wild," I gasp. "I've never had Nigerian food."

"I haven't either," he says enthusiastically, and the idea of trying something with him for the first time has me agreeing immediately.

FORTY-ONE

FOSTER

Two hours later, we're sitting in the parking lot at the vet's so I can get my car. The last thing I want to do though is get out of Sophie's. I don't want today to end. I don't want to go home alone or for tomorrow to come. I want to go back to sitting in the restaurant with her while she smiles around the fufu and okra stew she's got in her mouth. I want to take her home and get her to make those sounds she was making during dinner, but without the food.

"So I won't see you much this week, I'm guessing." She's going to the other school tomorrow and then has a conference Wednesday to Friday.

"Think you'll survive?" she jokes.

No? Barely? Maybe but it's going to be hell?

"Seems unlikely." I watch as her hands trace the steering wheel. How is she making that so hot? Am I getting turned on by a steering wheel?

"I was thinking that maybe on Friday night you'd want to go see *The Magic Flute* with me? Yasmine is an assistant to one of the directors with the Canadian Opera Company, so I can get tickets. I had a recording as a kid and was obsessed with it."

"Papa..." I start to say.

"...geno," she finishes.

"You used to talk about them like they were real. I think I thought you were talking about a horse." The sound of our laughter fills the car.

I watch as she collects herself. The sun ablaze through the window behind her, making her even brighter than she usually is. She turns to me, a shy smile on her face. "So, wanna come with me?"

Picking up her hand, I keep eye contact as I bring it to my lips. "Yeah, sunshine, I'll go watch an opera with you."

Her responding smile puts the sun to shame.

I'm still thinking of that smile when I let a very unhappy Gary out of the carrier. He doesn't even look at me as he scurries to the bedroom.

Gary is home. Thanks for the help.

LILWALSH

Good!

Are you going to Dad's party on Saturday?

Dad's party... I'd completely forgotten. Probably makes me a terrible son, forgetting his dad's sixtieth birthday party. I'll have to blame my infatuation with a certain beautiful blonde. Poor me.

I forgot.

Well, unforget, and bring Sophie. It's going to be at Bennett and Marley's now.

Why?

More people RSVP'd than Mom thought would. They don't have room.

Well that's nice of your boss.

They're gone up north for the weekend.

Wait, do they KNOW?

LOL yes Bennett suggested it when I mentioned how stressed Mom was.

How are things going btw

With what?

Soph

Amazing? Confusing?, I wake up full of nervous excitement every day I know I'm going to see her?

Fine

Have you told her yet?

Told her what?

That you're in love with her.

I'm... not *not* in love with her. But I can't exactly say anything. It feels like a betrayal of what she asked from me if I pull her aside like, *hey Soph, I know this was all for fun and all, but you're the only one I've ever wanted a happily ever after with.*

When I don't answer, my phone rings. But I don't feel like listening to whatever lecture she's going to give me so I let it go to voicemail.

"What's up, Pete?" I ask Thursday morning as he sulks at his desk.

He looks over at me and shrugs. "I feel… not good."

"Like your stomach? Head?"

"I guess my head. That's where the not good feelings are." Oh.

"Can I do something to help?"

He shrugs again.

"Do you want to go for a walk?"

"No, my legs are tired."

"Too much training for the marathon?" I tease.

"Mr. Walsh." His eyes meet mine, and I see it then. The truth. "We both know I'm not running a marathon."

I've been working with Pete for two years. Two years of banter. Two years of calming him down when his anxiety becomes too much. Two years of building up his confidence wherever and however I can. This is the first time I've seen him look defeated, and it's by far one of the worst things I've ever seen.

"What brought this on?" I wish Sophie were here. She'd probably be a good person for him to talk to right now. She'd definitely be able to approach this conversation in a more impactful way.

"My mom."

To say I'm shocked would be an understatement. Aside from myself, Pete's mom is his biggest cheerleader. She's one of those moms who looks at everything as an opportunity. She's also a single mom with a full-time job and two kids, one of whom is eager to do and try everything.

"What happened?"

He peeks around to make sure no one is listening. "She said I couldn't do it." His eyes fill with tears. "She told me to stop bothering her to take me running because she doesn't have time right now."

I can't even imagine this conversation happening. "What if I took you running?" I ask without really considering what it would mean.

He shakes his head. "I don't want to be too much for you too."

What ten-year-old thinks they're too much? I didn't think that set in until your twenties. "I hate to break it to you, bud, but you'll have to work a lot harder if you're gonna be too much for me. I'm very tall, remember? I've got room for more than most people." That gets a smile out of him. It's small, but it's there. "I'll talk to your mom, okay? And if she says yes, I'll take you out on Saturday morning for our first training session."

"Really?"

"If she says yes, really."

SUNSHINE

I'll pick you up tomorrow around 6? Show starts at 7:30.

I've never been to an opera. What should I wear?

Formal.

The last time I wore formal wear was our first "date," and Sophie nearly killed me by wearing that dress. I can't imagine she'll be in something like that dress again.

I have the chance to speak with Pete's mom on Friday after school. While Pete is in the hall waiting, she lets me know she's been under a lot of stress at work and that Pete, who she calls the best thing in her life, has been nonstop lately.

"He's got ten-year-old energy in a body that doesn't allow him to expel it efficiently. I'm... I'm so tired," she admits as she runs her hands over her face. "My entire life is working and then being a mom, and I love my kids but I feel..." she trails off, shaking her head. "Never mind. It's just a lot, and when he came home a couple nights ago and told me what you'd said, I nearly cried."

"Is that a good thing?"

"I don't want you to feel like you have to do this, Mr. Walsh. He's my kid, and I should be the one doing this marathon thing with him. I, well..." She shrugs and looks toward the door. "The thought of seeing him fail is almost too much. I'm scared of what the reality will be like."

"He won't fail," I say confidently. "Some way, somehow, we'll get him across whatever line there is to cross."

By the time they leave, we've agreed that I'll come over tomorrow morning so we can start and we'll plan from there. I race through the door at home, barely sparing a moment to scratch Gary behind the ears as I strip and jump into the shower.

I've just pulled my shirt on when there's a knock at the door.

FORTY-TWO

SOPHIE

I've got my fist up to knock when I start second-guessing everything. The dress, the hair, the whole look, a repeat from the gala. I remember Foster's expression when he saw me in this dress. How his eye color changed in front of my eyes. The way he bit his lip as he took me in. I don't think he even realized what he was doing. I'd never felt so sexy in my life, and I don't even think it had anything to do with how I was dressed but rather the impact I was having on him.

I pull off my coat, draping it over my arm. I want to see his face when he sees what formal wear I chose. "Get it over with," I whisper before my knuckles finally connect with his door.

It swings open, and he's standing there in his suit pants, his feet bare, and his shirt wide open, revealing black ink across his chest. Dumbstruck, that is what I am. I don't even notice his expression.

"Hey," he breathes out, backing up so I can step inside. Except I don't. My feet seem to be glued to the floor. "Soph?" I hear him say, but it sounds like he's far away. His hand wraps around my wrist and gives a little tug. That does it. My feet unstick, and I practically fall over the threshold.

And then somehow our lips are meeting. I don't know which one of us moved first, but I think it was me. Judging by how hard I'm gripping his head, my hands tangled in his hair, holding him to me, this has the markings of something I put into motion. Something I've been thinking about, manifesting.

His hands slide around my waist before one travels up my bare back to my neck. With a gentle squeeze he manages to pull my head back, and the split second of disappointment evaporates when his lips connect with my throat. Hot needy kisses map every inch of my exposed skin.

Imagine those lips somewhere else. My knees practically give out at the thought. He's undoing my carefully constructed tapestry, and I'm letting him.

I desperately want to wrap my legs around him, pull him into me, but this damn dress doesn't allow for that. And then as if he can hear my thoughts, his hands are grabbing the fabric against my thighs and he's bunching it up, exposing inch after inch of my legs until the bottom is clenched in his fists. Relief spreads through me when I'm able to hook my thigh around his hip.

Foster seems to realize that he can let go of the dress without impeding my movement, and his strong hands grip my thighs, lifting me so both wrap around him. My back hits the wall as he uses it for leverage, managing to get even closer to me, his length pressing where I want it most as he pushes his hips harder against me.

We haven't said a thing. Not a word has been exchanged since our lips met, and for two people who talk a lot it's remarkably quiet, save for our pants and barely audible sounds of pleasure as we grind into one another.

He stumbles away from the wall with me still wrapped around him, and we land heavily in one of his dining chairs. His lips return to my neck while his right hand grips my thigh so hard I may have an artist trace the outline, have it tattooed on my body so I can point to it and say, *this, this is where he claimed me.*

I can't even remember why I'm here. Surely there was a reason for putting this dress on other than to have him take it off. If I'm being honest with myself, that's the reason I got the dress in the first place. The thought of him ripping it off me was the selling feature.

When I jog my hips against him, my name slips between his lips. I don't know if it's a warning or praise, but I want to hear it over and over again.

He unlatches his hand from my thigh and moves both to my ass, pulling me flush against him, his shocked eyes meeting mine for the first time since the first kiss.

"You're not wearing..." I shake my head. "You weren't wearing any then, either?" I shake my head again, pulling my lower lip between my teeth as my eyes drop to his mouth. I want it back on me, desperately, but he stays where he is, still holding me against him, appearing to collect himself. He's about to be a gentleman. He's about to say this wasn't part of the deal, that I'd said I didn't want sex. We got carried away and that's all this is.

But that's not what happens. Instead, his right hand slides lower, his eyes glued to mine, taking in my every tiny breath and twitch. Studying my reactions, plotting his journey. And when he reaches his destination, that mouth of his tilts up in a cocky grin I haven't seen before.

"Is this for me, sunshine?"

I cannot believe that came out of his mouth. All I can do is nod as his fingers slide into me. A hissed *yes* leaves my mouth when he starts a slow rhythm.

"I hate to break it to you, Soph," he begins, "but I don't think we're going to make it to the opera tonight."

"The opera is fine, orgasms are better," I pant as pressure builds inside me. "Just don't stop doing tha—hey!" I pout as he pulls his hand away. But I don't have time to say anything else before he's standing, with me still wrapped around him and marching to his bedroom.

At the foot of his bed, sets me down then drops in front of me. "Say something now, Soph, because once I get started I won't be able to stop."

I clamp my mouth shut because there is no way in hell I'm stopping this man from doing whatever the hell he wants to me. I trust him in a way I've never trusted another person.

"Good," he growls, rising on his knees to kiss me before gently pressing me back into the mattress. His hands push my dress over my hips then return to my thighs which I spread voluntarily. I hear a soft "Mmm, that's my good girl," and then the feel of his lips on my inner thigh. There's a sharp pain as he nips at my flesh, followed by a wave of pleasure hitting me directly in my core, and then he does it again to the other side, getting the same result.

When I think he's going to really get started, his head pops up. "What?" I ask, concerned that I've done something to ruin the experience. Did I make a noise? Tense up? Do I smell?

"I want to make it clear that if you do want me to stop, I actually will. I said that because... well, I don't really know. But I know no means no, so if at any time you say no or stop or any other word like that, I will." He looks far too nervous for a man kneeling between my legs should. I won't stand for it.

Sitting up, I take his face between my hands and look him dead in the eye. "Foster, if you don't use that beautiful mouth on me in the next minute, I'm going to walk out the door." And then I do something I've never done before. I run my tongue across his bottom lip and whisper, "Now, be a good boy and get to work." Then I guide his head back between my legs, lying back when his breath ghosts across my skin. I don't know who this person is, but I kinda like her.

He wastes no time sliding his tongue through the evidence of my arousal.

"Fuck," I pant when he adds two fingers, curling them inside and hitting a spot I've only heard about in passing. "Holy shit." My hips jump and my legs tighten, locking his head in place.

My reaction only seems to feed his desire.

FORTY-THREE

FOSTER

This is the best day of my life.

Sophie writhes against my mouth as I devour her. The taste of her overwhelming every other sense. I'm trying to maintain my composure. I don't want to rush this, but the sounds she's making are driving every move I make. One more curl of my fingers has her tensing and mumbling incoherently as her heels dig into my back. The thought of having bruises from them makes me painfully hard.

"Fuuuuck," she moans as her body relaxes ever so slightly but I don't let up. I want to experience that again. No, I *need* to experience that again.

I'm so close, and just the thought of coming without even touching myself while she loses control on my tongue is all I need apparently because the minute she tenses again, I explode.

Tremors wrack my body as my ragged breaths bathe her thigh. I can barely make out the sound of our combined panting as blood pounds in my ears. I'm frozen in place, my forehead resting on her leg, as I try to catch my breath.

Her fingers sliding through my hair brings me back.

Tilting my head, I look up at her as she sits up on her elbow. She's flushed and her hair is a disaster, but she's stunning. It's a view I'll likely never forget. One that surpasses every fantasy I've ever had of her.

No one can ever tell me dreams don't come true because mine is splayed in front of me right now.

Sophie shifts, and her feet softly touch the floor. Still graceful even after two orgasms.

"You're very good at that, Mr. Walsh," she praises. "Mind if I have a go now?" she asks as if she needs permission.

"Um, well..." I can feel my face heat, but I force myself to maintain eye contact.

"Did you?" she asks as her eyes widen in astonishment.

"Mmm," I hum. "You make very good noises, Miss Hore." I rise up on my knees, my hands sliding up her thighs to where her dress is bunched around her waist. "You're perfect," I purr, pushing the dress higher so I can kiss up her abdomen after she flops back again.

I stop just before I reach her chest and pull the fabric back down. She sighs contentedly when I stand and drop a kiss on each cheek before finally meeting her lips. I really need to get out of these pants, but when I go to step away, she wraps her hands around my neck and pulls me back in.

"Do you like the taste of you, sunshine?" I ask before sucking her tongue into my mouth.

"Yes," she coos, hooking a leg around my hip and pulling me back down to her. "Want you," she murmurs against my lips, shredding every bit of self-control I have left.

I push off the bed and haul her up with me. When she's standing in front of me I slide my hands into her hair and pull her to me, this kiss wiping all the others from my memory, instantly. The minute she relaxes, I turn her so her back is to me and walk us toward the bathroom, my lips on her neck the entire time. At the door I stop and set one hand on her hip while sliding the other under the dress. I watch her clock the progression of my hand beneath the fabric, her eyes going wide when she sees the trajectory.

Her head drops back onto my shoulder when I touch her. "Look at you," I whisper, nipping at her ear. "Look how responsive you are to me." I slip my finger back into her and watch as she quakes, my cock already rebounding. "Do you want more, Sophie?"

"Yes," she begs, pushing her ass back into me when I add a second finger.

"Feel how hard I am for you, sunshine? You've had me in this state every day since you walked back into my life."

I can tell she's close by the way she's breathing so I speed up my fingers while sucking at the space where her neck meets her shoulder, keeping my eyes on our reflection. She's fighting it, I can tell. I can feel it.

"Let go," I command, and she does. I have to wrap my arm around her waist to keep her upright as the orgasm hits. "Atta girl," I murmur against her skin.

Sophie's gaze lands on mine in the mirror and I can't hold back the smirk that crosses my lips as I bring my fingers to her lips. She opens without hesitation, sucking them into her greedy mouth. Her eyes remain locked on mine the entire time and I have to work very hard not to come again.

She spins in my arms and before I know it she's backing me up toward the bed.

"No more teasing, Foster," she says as my ass hits the bed and she immediately straddles me. "I'm on the pill, but I need you to wear a condom." She swallows. "Not that I don't trust you, it's that I can't... I can't go through it again." She doesn't need to clarify what she means.

"Of course, Soph, whatever you want." And I mean that.

"Where?"

"Third drawer on the left," I say, nodding toward the bathroom. "Wait, let me, I want to, uh"—I gesture at my crotch—"tidy up a bit."

She looks down, pulling her lip between her lips shyly. "I'm sorry." The words say one thing while the tone says something totally different.

"Sure you are, sunshine." I stand and do my best to walk at a normal speed to the bathroom.

When I walk back into the bedroom, Sophie is on her back with her arm resting on her stomach, her right knee bent and crossed over her left leg, totally naked. She's the picture of relaxation as she watches me with a contented smile on her face. It's having the opposite effect on me. I feel like someone shot me up with adrenaline.

"Goddamn."

FORTY-FOUR

As Foster saunters toward me, butterflies travel through my bloodstream, tiny flutters of anticipation. He's got a towel around his waist, but he may as well have nothing on as it doesn't hide his arousal. And those tattoos are so much better than I ever expected. He's all sharp lines and divots in all the right places. He looks airbrushed, for fuck's sake.

"I'm not going to lie, I'm a tad disappointed I didn't get to take that dress off you," he says, crawling onto the bed. "I'd been imagining it since you took your coat off at the gala." He dips and kisses me, my entire upper body arching off the bed to meet him.

"I can put it back on if you want? Then you can peel it off of me."

He looks down at my body, his eyes traveling slowly over my skin and shakes his head. "Nah, I don't want you to cover this masterpiece up."

"What if it's your only chance to take it off me?" I challenge and bite back the laugh that threatens when a look of panic appears. "Relax." I slide my hand over his chest, studying the scene from *Lord of the Rings* permanently inked there. "I only mean that it may be ruined now. I definitely heard a rip. But if I'm being honest, I've never wanted to ruin a piece of clothing so badly."

His muscles seem to flex involuntarily under my touch. "Me either, if you wanna know the truth," he chuckles.

"I want to see you," I say as my hand traces along the top of the towel.

He wastes no time reaching down, pulling the fabric away, tossing it on the floor and then lying back so I can get a good look at him.

"Now when your friends ask, you can confirm that I am indeed a ginger everywhere," he jokes.

I love the fact he's making me laugh while we're both naked for the first time together. He's still so, I don't know, Foster.

I have never been one who likes giving head all that much, but I'm starting to realize that a lot of what I think I don't like is because of the person I was with rather than a personal preference. I'm curious now, so without a word I roll onto him and begin to kiss down his body. I take in the way his breathing changes and his body flexes. The way he touches me so softly I'm not sure if I'm imagining it.

"You don't have—" The words die as I wrap my lips around him. "Oh god, just like that." He keens, and I smile knowing that I'm the one making him react this way.

He doesn't let me spend too much time on him before he's hauling me up his body, flipping me onto my back and kissing me until I'm convinced I don't require air to survive. I just need this.

"Need," he pants, "to be"—his lips return to mine, stealing more breath—"inside you." And I nod because yes, I need that too. Everything with Foster, things that I thought were wants have morphed into needs.

I've never been so turned on by the sound of a condom wrapper before, but when I hear him fumbling with it all I want to do is pull him back to me, protection be damned.

Watching him settle between my legs is almost an out-of-body experience. Like I'm watching from the other side of the room. His lips meet mine a half-second before I feel him press against me, and when I tilt my hips he slides in. We both suck in a breath, not releasing it until he's fully seated.

"Fuck." The word is so quiet that I'm not even sure I hear him properly.

He's watching me, studying my reaction, and when I nod the tiniest bit he starts to move, one arm holding him up while the other hooks under my knee. He drops a kiss to my knee before his eyes are on mine again. "You feel so damn good, Soph."

"Kiss me," I beg and he acquiesces instantly. His tongue matching pace with his cock, overwhelming me in the most sensational way.

He pulls his lips from me and drops his forehead to mine. "You feel like you were fucking made for me," he breathes out, as he eases my leg down.

His hands slide up my arms, guiding them above my head, and he holds my wrists in place as his thrusts become more forceful. *This. This is what I've been missing out on.* When I lift my hips, changing the angle, his head drops to my neck, a gasp seizing his body.

"Fucking do that again," he demands, and so I do, relishing in his unbridled reaction.

Once he appears to gain control of himself again, his hands release my wrists to grip my hips as he sits back on his heels.

Foster's gaze drops to where he's fucking me, a look of awe crossing his face. "Sophie?"

"Mm-hmm?" I barely manage to say.

"Touch yourself."

I slip my hand down my body, enjoying how he watches me, practically losing it when I apply the tiniest amount of pressure. I've never come this much in a week, let alone in a day, and my body feels about ready to detonate again.

Those sharp eyes of his don't miss the slight hitch in my breath or how my thighs tense. A cocky grin appears as he releases my hip in order to pull my hand away, raising my fingers to lips.

Seeing my fingers in his mouth is all I need apparently because a scream from somewhere deep inside explodes out of me and my hand falls onto the bed as he pulls my hips tighter against him, his muscles straining beneath his skin.

He falls forward, panting against my chest. I could die like this, I think. The weight of him, his breath on my skin, the feel of him still inside me.

This is the happiest I've ever been.

"It's blasphemous." Foster levels me with a look that does not make me think he's joking.

"It's delicious," I argue, dipping my mild buffalo chicken wing into the ranch I had to beg him to add to the order.

"The fact that it's the default is blasphemous. I've come to terms with the fact that people have terrible taste. What I cannot get on board with is that I have to ask for blue cheese, otherwise wings will come with ranch now."

"Are you from Buffalo?" I ask, licking the ranch off the wing I'm holding so I can distract him from his little rant. His eyes widen, but my efforts are wasted.

"You know I'm not, but I did work with a guy from Buffalo in Korea, and he was as annoyed by it as I was. It's actually how we became friends," he says as he dunks his wing into the vat of blue cheese dressing he requested.

Foster's wearing the hot man's uniform of only gray sweatpants, and I'm in a pair of his running shorts and the shirt he'd never gotten around to buttoning up. When I'd said it was a poor choice to have me wear it due to my ability to stain any article of clothing with whatever I was eating, he'd said the idea of me staining this shirt while wearing it was too much of a turn-on not to partake in.

So far, I haven't gotten a speck of anything on it, which is some kind of post-sex miracle.

"Do you have other opinions on buffalo wing-related things, or is it just the dip?"

He lets out a deep sigh. "Don't even get me started on breaded wings."

"Oh, they are the worst," I agree.

"I knew I liked you."

FORTY-FIVE

FOSTER

I've been awake for half an hour, but I can't bring myself to move. Sophie's back is pressed to me, the smell of citrus and honey faint in her hair. I hold my breath when she starts to stir, her ass pressing into me the sweetest torture I can imagine.

She murmurs something in her sleep, and her ass moves against me again. I tighten my hold and drop a kiss to her shoulder. "Foster." The gravel in her voice doesn't help my situation.

"Yeah, sunshine?" I whisper in case she is actually still asleep.

"Fuck me awake." The rasp in her voice is still there, but her intention is very clear when her hand lands on top of mine and drags it down her body.

I sink my fingers into her and she relaxes in my arms, little moans of pleasure mixed with murmurs. "You touch me so right." "I love what you do to me." "Yeah, like that."

When I roll away I hear the little harumph of disappointment and knowing she wants me back right fucking now is not going to make this a slow and sensual awakening.

The box of condoms that had been in the bathroom is now spilled on the bedside table, all decorum lost in the heat of the moment when we'd gone to bed last night.

I set a land speed record putting one on before rolling back to where Sophie remains.

"This is gonna be fast."

"Good," she says, raising her leg and draping it over mine so I can slide closer.

She gasps as I push in easily. "You're so ready for me." I nip her shoulder. "I like that you were ready for me, sunshine."

"Always," she sighs. "Make me feel you all day," she challenges.

I answer by speeding up my hips and my hand, adjusting speed and forcefulness according to the sounds she's making.

"Fos—" My name dies on her lips as she breaks apart in my arms and I'm already thinking about putting her back together so I can watch her shatter again as I finally give in to the sensation that's been building since I woke up.

Pete's fifty feet ahead of me on our first training run. He told me this morning that he doesn't think he'll be able to enter a race this year, but maybe next. I agreed that planning for the future would probably yield better results. Then he'd taken off, leaving me in his dust as he shouted over his shoulder.

My night and morning with Sophie seemed to have zapped my energy. Not that I'm complaining. I can't wait to miss the opera with her again. I made coffee and some toast while she showered, working up the nerve to ask her to come to my dad's party. I expected a no since it was such late notice, but she'd said yes before the words had even left my mouth. She'd admitted that Cass had given her a heads-up that I may be asking so she'd made sure her night was free.

"Hey, Mr. Walsh." Pete's voice breaks me out of the memory. "Stop daydreaming and move your butt."

"That's not a very nice way to talk to the guy trying to help you, ya know," I call back but pick up my pace so I'm only a couple feet behind him.

"When we get back to my house," he pants. "can you stay for lunch? My mom is making tomato soup and grilled cheese sandwiches."

"Weird sandwich for someone who can't eat dairy."

"It's not dairy," he assures me.

"Goat?" He shakes his head. "Nut?" He nods.

"She buys it from the store because she said she doesn't have time to milk her own nuts." I snort, and Pete looks up at me like I've lost it. "What?"

"Oh, nothing, just thought of something funny."

"Milking nuts?"

"Yeah," I admit.

"Mr. Walsh?"

"Pete McGee?"

"If nuts don't have...ugh..." He mimes breasts, and I have to bite my tongue. "How do people get milk from 'em?"

"How do you think?" I can't resist digging into this a bit more. I'm fascinated by Pete's imagination.

He stops, and I watch his face scrunch up in thought. "I think... I think they rub them like this." He rubs his forefinger and thumb together really fast, his mouth set in determination. "And then it turns into a powder and um…"

"Go on."

"Well, they can't add milk because that means it's not dairy-free."

"Correct."

"Goat milk?"

"Have you had goat milk?"

"Yeah, I don't like it."

"Okay, so do you like nut milk?"

He nods.

"Well, then they probably don't make nut milk with goat milk."

"That's true. Water?"

"I think so. I've never thought about it before."

"Hey, Mr. Walsh?"

I roll my eyes as I look down at him. "Yes, Pete?"

"Race ya!" He spins and starts hustling back the way we came, his signature cackle trailing behind him.

"Huh, I've never actually thought about how they make nut milk," Sophie says, pulling out her phone and typing. "Basically blended nuts with water. Not nearly as fun as I thought it would be."

"Fun?" I ask, glancing over in time to see her shrug.

"Probably the wrong word. Speaking of fun, are you ready to have some today?"

There is a higher probability that fun will be had today than at a usual gathering that includes my family simply because Cass and Sophie will be there with me. "I'm cautiously optimistic about fun."

"That's better than dread." She smiles at me, and I have to squeeze the wheel to avoid leaning over and kissing her. "So, um, about last night." My heart stutters at what she might say. It was a mistake? It can't happen again? It was nice but... "You said some things that shocked me."

Oh my god, what came out of my mouth? I glare at the road, trying to recall what I could have said that would shock her. "In a bad way?"

"Oh god no," she says. "I like *everything* you did with your mouth. It hit me this morning that you cursed. Like you said"—she leans in and whispers—"fuck."

"Did I?"

"Oh yeah, a few times, in fact."

"I don't remember that." I remember her noises, her smell and the feel of her, the way she tasted, and that's about it.

"I can remind you next time." *Next time.* All my fears disappear as I repeat those two words to myself.

FORTY-SIX

Foster's uncle is droning on about some new boat accessory he got for some amazing deal when we walk into Marley and Bennett's place. Everything about that man in this house is wrong, and I tighten my grip in Foster's.

"Would you look at that? Still putting up with him, eh?" he goads. "Guess I owe Marcus twenty."

I lean closer to Foster, my other hand automatically wrapping around his upper arm as I gaze up at him. "It's him that has to put up with me."

"Hardly," he says, dropping a kiss on my forehead instead of acknowledging his uncle.

"Foster! Sophie!" I look toward the living room just in time to see Foster's dad walk through the doorway with his arms spread, a red tinge already dotting his cheeks.

"Dad's been celebrating since about nine a.m.," Cass stage-whispers next to me.

"Hey, you only get to celebrate sixty once," he slurs, pulling Foster in for a hug.

"Happy birthday, Dad," Foster says once he steps back.

"Glad you could make the trip up to celebrate your old

man. I know how much you hate spending time with that jackass." He laughs, pointing at Foster's uncle.

Foster laughs uncomfortably and avoids looking to where his dad is pointing. "Just happy to celebrate you, Dad," he says as he steps around him and leads me to the dining room where a buffet is set up.

"Sophie!" Mrs. Walsh sounds surprised when she sees me, but at least she looks pleased. "It's so nice to see you again." She hugs Foster then me. "Wasn't it so nice of Bennett to let us use his place? Have you seen the tent? Your sister and that quiet little friend of hers did an amazing job. The flowers, I mean, those are completely lost on your father, but they're stunning. If this whole dog thing doesn't work out, I could see her getting into the flower business."

"We arrived and came right in," Foster explains, reaching for two plates and handing one to me. "We'll grab some food and head out."

"Good," Mrs. Walsh says, squeezing his arm as she passes. "Marcus, you better not have put any of that heavy metal stuff on the playlist," she calls as she walks from the room.

"What quiet one is she talking about?" I ask while I scoop various salads onto my plate.

Foster shakes his head. "I have no idea."

"Cass would have mentioned it if she was dating someone, right?" Have I been a terrible friend? Maybe I've been too self-centered lately and she hasn't felt comfortable talking to me? She'd always maintained that she had no interest in a relationship with anyone.

"You're not a bad friend." Foster's warm breath brushes my ear.

"How do you know that's what I'm thinking?"

"Because I know you," he says, straightening up and

plopping potato salad next to four giant shrimp and then setting the plate down, turning to me. He grips my chin in his hand and gently eases my head up so I have to look at him. "There is nothing bad about you, sunshine." His amber eyes search mine. "Got it?" I nod, so lost in his gaze that I don't notice that anyone else has entered the room.

"Private moment alert!" someone taunts.

Foster drops his hand, and I miss it immediately. Every second he hasn't been touching me since I left his place this morning has felt empty. I hate it.

We find my parents in the tent chatting with Foster's grandmother, and I feel him relax when she looks up and waves at him.

"Oh good, you finally made it." She swats him away when he leans down, opting to stand and hug him, practically disappearing as he wraps his long arms around her. "Has he made the tea ring for you yet?" she asks, pulling me in for a tight hug of my own.

"He has not," I say accusingly, glaring up at him.

He holds his hands up. "I haven't had a chance yet, but I will soon, I promise."

"What tea ring?" my mom asks, hugging me tightly before moving on to Foster.

"It's this..." I try to come up with a description but can't think of what it would be like. "I don't know, pastry?" I look at Foster and his grandmother for help.

"It's a yeasted pastry stuffed with spices, brown sugar, and pecans," his grandmother says.

"Sounds delicious," my dad says, releasing Foster from a hug. "Please include us when you make it. Hello, my favorite daughter," he murmurs, pulling me in.

"Still waiting to meet the least favorite one," I joke.

"And you never will." He laughs, releasing me and

returning to his seat. "Go get some of that delicious barbecue and come back and join us. Cass and Florence should be back soon."

"Is Florence the 'quiet little one'?" Foster asks, looking around, easily seeing over the heads of all the other guests.

"She's pretty quiet, not so little. She's twenty-one," my mom says.

"Does she work here?"

"She came to help for the weekend. She's a friend from up in Marmot Point."

"That's where Teddy and Nellie are," I tell Foster.

"Ah." He nods in understanding.

"She's in school down this way but comes here every now and again to get away from the hustle and bustle of the city."

My dad scoffs. "That university town is hardly a city, but I suppose it's a lot more peaceful here."

"Peace is always wel—"

"Denver, you made it!" my dad shouts across as a friend of his walks in.

"So much for peace," I whisper to Foster, grabbing his hand and leading the way to the massive barbecue pit that's set up outside the open end of the tent.

"My god, what isn't here?" Foster says in wonder.

"Is your dad a big barbecue aficionado?"

"I mean, he likes it, but this has my uncle written all over it. He probably knows a guy or something."

He's mid reach for a chicken thigh when I hear the voice that I've learned to despise in the short time I've known it. "I knew he wouldn't go for the real meat."

Before anyone can say anything, I whirl around. "Oh, is that the fake chicken I've heard so much about?"

Phil looks at me, mouth slightly agape, a dumb look on his face. "No," he finally says indignantly.

"Then what precisely makes it 'not real meat'?"

"You know, it's the healthier option."

"Phil, I am a social worker and I hear a shitload of dumb stuff, but that may be the dumbest thing I've heard yet."

He stands there looking dumbstruck, and I enjoy it for about half a second before I see the look of shock on Foster's face. I can't decipher whether it's a good look or not and I automatically assume it's bad.

I laugh nervously. "Anyway, I'm gonna..." I reach for a set of tongs and put chicken on my own plate before turning and practically running to the table.

"What's got you spooked?" Dad asks when I sit down.

"Hmm? Oh, nothing," I stammer before realizing Cass and who I'm guessing is Florence are sitting at the table. "You must be Florence?" I stand and extend my hand.

She greets me shyly, her face half hidden behind a curtain of wavy brown hair.

"The flowers look great," I compliment, gesturing toward the arrangement at the center of the table.

"Thanks," she replies, sitting back down. "The university has an excessive amount of flowers right now so I got lucky."

"What are you there for?"

"Plant science."

"What does a plant scientist do?" Foster's grandmother asks, leaning on her elbows, giving Florence her full attention.

"I'm not sure yet. I'm specifically studying plant activity in harsh climates. Areas that seem a bit more inhospitable." She explains, lighting up as she goes on to tell us how much she's looking forward to an upcoming research trip opportunity on the east coast.

"Where's Foster?" Cass asks, turning in her seat to look around when her grandmother starts asking Florence more specific questions.

I take her lead peering around, expecting to see his head above the crowd, but he's nowhere to be seen. I stand. "I'll be right back."

His uncle is nowhere to be seen either, and as I make my way to the house I can hear elevated voices.

"She only said what everyone else was thinking," Foster says, and I stop dead, leaning into the side of the house.

"She thinks she has the right to walk into this party that I paid half for and get lippy with me? If you were more of a man, you'd have put her in her place."

"What the hell is that supposed to mean?" I lean forward the tiniest bit in time to see Foster's mom put her hand on his uncle's arm.

"Phil, not now. Let's go back and have some more food. Everyone seems to be really enjoying it." Her attempt to defuse the situation sets my teeth on edge.

"Oh, that's right, Mom, protect him and his bullshit views from any kind of confrontation."

"Foster!" she exclaims, her hand clutching at invisible pearls.

"What's going on?" Cass whispers from behind me, making me jump.

I shake my head and shush her, not taking my attention off the three of them.

"No, Mom, it's fucking bullshit. He's treated us with nothing but contempt since we were kids and has only gotten worse in the last five years. He acts like Cass is less than human because of who she is. He makes constant remarks about my job, which I happen to love, by the way."

"That's not t—"

"True?" Foster shouts. "That's nothing but the truth. And if he's not making those comments you're commenting on how I could have done so much more. Been so much more. But I'm happy. I love my job. I make a difference in the lives of kids who society deems to be unworthy in some way. My students smile every morning when they see me, and the only thing that comes second to is when Sophie smiles at me. Yes, the first person who stood up to your nonsense, Phil," he seethes. "She's brilliant and kind and everything you could never be because your heart is full of hate and bigotry. She's the polar opposite of who you are and what she did, what she said, only makes me love her even more."

Love her even more.

Love. Her. Even. More.

"Did he just—" Cass starts.

"Shhh." If Cass wasn't here, I'd have assumed I was hallucinating what he said.

"I knew you two were too good at pretending," she squeals, without keeping her voice down, and I watch in horror as Foster, his uncle, and his mom look in our direction.

"Can't even fight without having backup hiding around the corner, eh? Pathetic," Phil sneers.

Hate is not something I generally feel toward other human beings on a regular basis. But right now my whole body is filled with it. When I look at Foster, he's in shock. Wide eyes stare back at me, and I have the sudden urge to apologize. Apologize for listening in and for sneaking around. Apologize for setting this whole thing into motion and potentially ruining the entire party.

"Foster, I—" I begin, but he shakes his head to stop me as he begins walking my way.

He takes my face in his hands and looks down at me, his expression softening the longer he looks. "I've gotta take care of one thing, okay?" I nod, unable to look away. "Did you hear everything?" I nod again. "So you heard that I..." I'm nodding before he can even get the words out, already worried he's about to tell me he didn't mean it. "Then you should know I meant it, okay? I love you, Sophie Hore." The kiss he plants on me isn't one that should be seen by others. He should be kissing me like this behind a closed door so we can keep kissing. Just as I think I may start climbing him, he pulls away. "Cass," he says, looking past me at his sister.

"Yeah?" she asks, a hint of mischief in her voice.

"Would you mind holding Soph back? She looks about ready to take matters into her own hands."

"I don't need to be controlled, Foster." I pout as his hands fall, and Cass wraps her arms around me from behind. "She's tiny. If I wanted to get away, I could, easily."

"Try me, Soph, I dare you," Cass taunts, and I let my shoulders drop, utterly defeated. "Okay, big brother, go get 'em."

Foster drops a kiss on the tip of my nose, turns, and marches back to his mom and uncle.

"Mom, if you want the two—no, three of us—to ever show up at a family event again, he can't be there. He shows up and spreads his toxic worldview around, and I'm done with putting up with it. I'm done with doubting my career and whether or not I'm enough. I'm done wondering how the hell I could possibly prove to you that I'm doing what I want to do and that I don't want to be an engineer or lawyer. I'm so over trying to convince you that there's so much more to happiness than a piece of paper from a school and the issuer's name on a paycheck. Cass is happy in her life. Hell, look where you are right now. This is because of her. She's amazing at her job and she loves it, and that should be enough. *We* should be enough." He looks back at me and for the first time since we arrived, he looks content. "I'm where I want to be in every aspect of my life, other than standing next to this complete hodenkobold."

I try and fail to catch the cackle that bursts out of me and don't even care when I see Foster's smile.

"What the hell is a hodenkowhatever?" Cass whispers.

"I'll tell you later." I'm too distracted by the sight of Foster walking toward me, head held high, chest slightly puffed, hot as sin.

"How was that, sunshine?" he asks, taking my hand and leading me back to the tent.

"Hot," I breathe out.

FOSTER

"What is this place?" I ask, looking around the little A-frame cottage that sits at the back of the Hores' property.

Sophie walks into the little living room and turns on a lamp. "My great-grandfather built it when he had hired help, then my parents moved in when they got married. I spent my first four years here," she says, returning to me and taking my hand. "My mom thought that maybe we'd like to stay here tonight instead of in the house."

"Should I be at all disturbed about why she thought that?" I pull her into me, brushing hair off her face.

"I'm not," she says, rising to place a gentle kiss on my lips. "Can I ask a favor?"

"Anything."

"Can you just hold me tonight?"

"As opposed to?" I watch a delicious blush spread across her cheeks. "Sex?" I whisper

She rolls her lips, looking nervous. It's so different from the woman who asked me to, and I quote, "fuck me awake" this morning.

"I'd do just about anything if I am doing it with you,

Soph," I admit. The blush deepens further, and I can see her effort to keep looking at me. She wants to look away so badly.

"What's the exception?"

I wasn't expecting her to ask this so I have to think for a minute. "Something terrible. I don't want you to have to do anything terrible."

"I survived your uncle. I think I could deal with anything now."

I love you, I think.

"Think you can survive getting ready for bed and a night of extreme spooning?"

"I think I could win a gold medal in that event." She beams.

"Foster?" she asks, her voice vibrating through my chest.

"Mmmm?" I say sleepily.

"I think you should know that I..." she trails off, and I feel the inhale and prepare myself for those words I have dreamed of hearing from her. "I'm so happy," she finishes, and the little balloon of joy in my chest deflates a little.

I wrap my arms tighter around her. "I'm very *happy* to hear it."

"Mr. Walsh?"

"Yes, Sophie." I laugh at her impression of Pete.

"You're amazing, did you know that?"

"I don't know about amazing, but I'm starting to accept that I may be alright. Miss Hore?" I ask.

"Yes, Foster?"

"Will you go out on a date with me?"

"Obviously, you're on for P."

"Does today not count? It was a party after all." I enunciate the P.

"I guess you're right. What are we going to do when we run out of letters?"

I bury my face in her hair and breathe in deeply. Staying like this for the rest of time seems like a solid idea. "Start over again? Pick an alphabet from a different language? Greek, perhaps?"

"Food categories?" she suggests.

"Try different dishes until we've eaten them all?"

"Make different dishes?"

"You wanna cook more with me?"

"I'll do just about anything if I'm doing it with you, Foster."

"Oh my god!" Sophie squeals when she sees the tea ring on the table the next morning. "Did you make this?"

I shake my head. "As if I was going to leave the bed when you were in my arms," I say, wrapping my arms around her and pulling her back into me.

"Did your grandmother?"

"I don't think so. The pattern is different."

When we approach, there's a handwritten note next to the plate.

Good morning! I got this recipe last night and thought it would be a good time to test it out.

Coffee's fresh and there's cream and milk in the fridge. Enjoy!
Love, Mom

"No way," I whisper, rereading the note and studying the tea ring. "I cannot believe she shared the recipe with your mom." She'd only just shared it with me on Easter.

"Nancy Hore is pretty persuasive," Sophie says as she pulls a couple plates and mugs down from the cupboard.

Sophie does that thing again where she takes a bite of something delicious and moans, and all my senses zero in on it. A bomb could go off outside the door, and I wouldn't have a clue.

"What?" she asks after swallowing.

"You do this thing when you like the taste of something. This little hum moan thing, and I'm pretty sure it's the hottest thing I've ever heard."

"Oh yeah?" A wicked little smirk appears on her face, and I'm not sure if I should be terrified or turned on by it. I watch as she wipes her mouth and stands, approaching me slowly, a lioness stalking her very willing prey.

When she's standing in front of me she bends, her lips millimeters from mine. "I bet I could make it hotter," she challenges as she sinks to her knees, pulling the waistband of my boxers as she goes. "Hmmm." She peers up at me through those long lashes. "I guess that did do something for you."

"Everything about you does something for me," I croak, watching as she leans forward and takes me in her mouth. The taste of the tea ring on my tongue and Sophie's hot mouth around my cock is pure magic. This must be heaven because I can't think of anything better. Then she fucking hums.

"So, is this real now?" Sophie asks from the passenger seat, staring at her hand twined with mine.

"Sunshine, this has been real since you agreed to have lunch with me."

"That long ago, eh?"

"I've been in love with you since I was sixteen, even younger according to my grandmother," I admit.

"Liar." Sophie laughs. "I would have known."

"Sophie, *I* didn't even know. And when I finally realized, I was too stuck in my own head to do anything about it."

"Well, you're welcome," she says smugly.

"For what?"

"Being the one to do something about it."

FORTY-EIGHT

Pete's playing with something in his pocket in our session on Thursday morning.

"What's in your pocket today?" I ask from my beanbag.

"A talisman," he replies slowly.

"Oh?"

"Mr. Walsh gave it to me last night."

Foster had gone to Pete's after school for another running practice. I knew what the talisman was, and I knew Pete had been a bit resistant about accepting it.

"Do you mind telling me what it is?"

I watch as he slowly removes his hand. Flipping it over, he unfurls his fingers and reveals a rock with a tortoise carved into it. "It's a reminder that being slow is okay."

"Just being slow?"

He shrugs. "And steady."

"Like the fable of the tortoise and the hare?"

"Yeah. I want to be fast right now, but Mr. Walsh said that everyone gets fast at their own pace."

"He's right, everyone is different. We are all good at different things. Sometimes we are good right away, and sometimes it takes a long time and a lot of practice to get good."

"Are you still practicing things?"

Keeping my house tidy, remembering where I put something, not worrying what someone is thinking about me, tolerating spice... I could go on forever with this list.

"Cooking," I admit.

He looks at me with judgmental eyes. "That's a good thing to practice."

"I agree."

"Miss Hore?"

I love the way he says my name even when we're the only ones in the room.

"Yes, Pete?"

"Are you and Mr. Walsh boyfriend-girlfriend?"

The joy that bubbles up from somewhere deep within me leaves me smiling like an idiot at a ten-year-old. "Yeah," I say. "We are, why?"

"I'm glad."

"You're glad that we're boyfriend and girlfriend?"

"Yeah, because Mr. Walsh is happy all the time. He's always happy when you're at school."

"I'm happy when he's at school too."

"Miss Hore."

"Yeah, Pete?" I laugh.

"I knew he loved you."

"Oh?"

He nods, squeezing the rock. "His eyes told me."

"You know, Pete, you may have a superpower some of us only dream of having."

He sits up, suddenly very interested. "What superpower?"

"The power of perception."

When I'm back in my office, I replay what Pete said. *"I knew he loved you."* I think deep down I may have known too, but I have heard those words before, and the longer I sit with them the more I question them. I believed them the first time, and they led me down a very long dark road. *He loves you* was something I told myself on the hardest days. They kept me in place. Those three words blinded me to what was going on. What if I can never trust them?

"Nineteen fifty-three," Foster says, and I write it down. "Technically they're still at war," he whispers.

"Why is it so hot that you know that?"

"Because knowledge is sexy." He smirks back.

"Can a pub quiz be considered foreplay?" I ask, dragging my foot up his calf, earning me a look of warning.

"Absofuckinglutely," he growls, and I find myself overwhelmed with excitement that I single handedly seem to have broken him out of his no swearing cage.

"Which tsar was the last to reign in Russia?" the quiz master calls out.

Foster doesn't break eye contact when he mouths "Nicholas," and chills spread across my body.

"Which Canadian city hosted the World's Fair in 1968?"

I know this one, but I let him lean closer until his lips are brushing my ear. His hand slips over my thigh and trails up until his fingers run along the center seam of my jeans. I don't move, but I'm looking frantically around the dark room for any prying eyes. No one is paying attention to us; this is a serious quiz with serious competitors. They don't care about the way he's teasing me. They have no idea how he applies just enough pressure to make me slam my thighs shut, trapping his hand there.

"It was actually in '67, but Montreal."

I think I write it down, but I can't be sure. I know my pencil touched the paper, but what he says next has me dropping it and rushing from the pub, Foster hot on my heels.

His lips are on mine before I even have a chance to open the car door. Hands in my hair, a hard body pressing me into the door. Someone whistles in the distance, but I don't care. All that matters is how he's touching me, kissing me, driving me wild.

"We're doing R tonight," he growls. "I'm going to absolutely ravish you."

His hand has a vice grip on my thigh the entire drive to his apartment, and it's amazing we ever make it inside since we stop every five feet to make out some more.

Once inside he immediately bends me over the counter and gets my jeans off using some kind of sex-crazed sorcery and then he kneels.

To say he ravishes me is an understatement. By the time he's on his feet again I'm not even sure of my own name.

Hours later, with only the streetlamp illuminating the room, I trace the *Lord of the Rings* tattoo on his chest with my finger. I know I should close my eyes and go to sleep, but it's hard when he's here with me. Part of me is afraid that I'll wake up and this will all have been a dream. I'm terrified of opening my eyes again and seeing Gregory in his place.

Being with Foster is the opposite. He is the antithesis of Gregory and all he stands for.

"What are you thinking about, sunshine?" Foster asks quietly.

"How grateful I am for you."

His arm tightens around me, and I feel a soft kiss in the exact same place he'd kissed me the first time. "Same."

While Foster spends Saturday morning with Pete, I bustle around my house, trying to put everything in its place before my parents arrive for brunch. As I throw a tote of random things into the corner of my room, I take a minute to look around. Piles of things here and there. Some big, some tiny, but it doesn't matter the size; they all cause me anxiety. Things that have proper places, but I can't seem to ever put them in those places. A constant battle.

I've spent the better part of the week staying with Foster, and I see myself fitting in almost too well there. There's a small pile of my laundry in the one corner and two chapsticks, three books, and two half-consumed glasses of water next to the bed on the side I sleep on.

He hasn't said a word. No passing remarks that make me paranoid about what's to come. I can't stop myself from worrying, though. You don't spend five years burying passive-aggressive comments under the rug without tripping over it now and again. It takes a lot of mental power to stay in the here and now once he's snoring softly beside me. While he sleeps, I worry. If this implodes, it's not a matter of years ruined. It's our shared history tainted forever.

Five minutes before my parents are set to arrive, I pull all the ingredients we need to make brunch out of the fridge. I have no doubt they'll show up with bread my mom whipped up this morning and probably some butter. My stomach growls at the thought.

I hear my dad's voice instead of a knock. "Favorite daughter!" he calls from the front door. I hurry out to greet them.

"Favorite father!" I throw my arms around him and sink into the best hug around.

"No Foster?" my mom asks after hugging me.

"Deal-breaker?" I wince.

"Of course not, but we always like seeing him. You two didn't..." She mimes breaking a stick, and I laugh.

"No, he's training a student. He'll be here later."

"What kind of training?" my dad asks as he carries bags through to the kitchen.

"He's helping him train for a marathon. What's with all the bags?"

"Oh, isn't that the nicest thing? He's a good egg, that one," Mom gushes as she starts removing loaves of bread and tins from the bags. "I brought some things for us to try for the book. I dropped things off to Cass, and to Marley and Bennett as well. I figured between all of us we can start narrowing it down."

"So we aren't cooking brunch now?"

"Nah." Mom shakes her head. "I thought this would give us time to chat too."

"Chat about what?"

My dad looks between us and clears his throat. "Your mom and I were talking after you left last weekend, and it dawned on us that how you are with Foster was never how you were with the other one."

"The oth—Gregory?"

"We don't really need to say his name."

"Okay."

"I, we didn't see it. I was so confused when you told us you'd broken up because things seemed so good. I mean you never let on even, and I'm not saying it's your fault," Mom adds quickly. "Only that I wish I'd..." She runs her hand over her stomach like she's feeling for something. "I had a feeling early on, but you were beaming and I ignored it. I should have said something."

"I wouldn't have listened," I assure her. "It took me months to see the truth."

"I wish I'd known for sure."

"*We* wish we'd known," Dad says quietly.

I wish they had to. If they had, then maybe I wouldn't have spent five years in a relationship that got worse so gradually I didn't realize it until recently. My parents and I have always had open communication, and I'm realizing now that I let them down. The tears start before I realize, and I feel both of their arms wrap around me.

"I'm sorry we failed you," my dad whispers, and the tears fall harder.

FORTY-NINE

FOSTER

I don't expect to walk into a family hug. Or to see Sophie's tear-stained face and red eyes look up at me. I don't know what else to do other than join in. Nancy and Karl both back away slowly, leaving Sophie for me to hold.

No one says anything while I stand there with her, swaying gently. When she releases a long shuddering breath, I loosen my grip a little so she's able to pull back.

"You're crying," she says, raising her hands to wipe my cheeks.

"So are you." I smile sadly at her.

"Why are you crying?" she asks, her forehead pinching in concern.

"Because you are." I shrug. "This isn't on purpose." I laugh, gesturing to my face. "This is very much an involuntary response to your sadness."

Sophie wraps her arms around me and buries her head in my chest.

"I love you, sunshine."

A little gasp draws my attention to where Nancy and Karl are standing at the counter, looking busy. But I don't miss the way Nancy wipes her eyes or the way Karl is trying and failing to hide his smile. Nancy notices me and shrugs.

"She loved you before she knew what being in love meant," Nancy says quietly.

She hasn't said it to me yet. I don't need the words. I see it when she looks at me. Feel it when she touches me, and I know in my bones she'll say it when she trusts her feelings more.

"She came home when she was what? Six?" Karl looks at Nancy for confirmation, and she nods. "She came home from your house and asked how old you had to be to get married."

"Karl said forty and then asked her why."

"And she looked me dead in the eye and said, 'When I'm forty, I'm going to marry Foster because I like his face.'"

"I did not," Sophie shrieks, pulling back. "No way in hell I said I liked his face when I was six."

Nancy bursts out laughing. "Oh, sweetie, you talked about Foster's face for a solid year."

"A whole year, eh?" I tease. "What happened after a year?"

"Oh, she thought boys were gross for a bit, and then she learned to keep some thoughts upstairs." Nancy laughs, tapping her head. "And now here she is all these years later, clearly still liking your face and trying new food left right and center. I've spent her whole life trying to get her to do that and then you walk in, and within a month she's an adventurous eater."

"Okay, let's move on, shall we?" Sophie grumbles. "Seeing as how I'm an '*adventurous eater*' now, we are taste testers today for recipes."

"This is the best day ever," I say in awe when I see all the things Nancy is plating up—muffins, scones, bread. Of course it's not the best day ever, since Sophie locked that up already.

"I need to put the finishing touches on some of the hot dishes. You take these out to the dining room and start. But you're going to be asked questions, so make sure you're paying attention while you eat."

Sophie groans. "I guess that's a small price to pay."

"The tomato, basil, and asiago scone was probably my favorite," I tell Nancy while she writes down notes. "It's a nice break from all the sweet you usually get at breakfast. I think I'd end up doing a whipped mascarpone or ricotta and some crispy prosciutto with it."

Nancy's head snaps up. "That's a really good idea. I have some fresh ricotta at home. I'm kicking myself for not bringing it."

"My favorite will always be the maple walnut scone," Sophie says, pressing her finger onto the crumbs left on her plate before licking them off. She catches me staring and offers me a tiny smirk. Is it weird to want to be someone's plate? Asking for a friend.

"That always surprises me," Karl says around a bite of cranberry orange scone. "You hate walnuts, and yet you'll gobble 'em up in that scone."

"It's a mystery." She shrugs. "I've had several labs reach out to see if they'd be able to study me."

"Okay, what about the hash and eggs?" Nancy asks, scooping some on each of our plates.

Sweet potatoes, greens, bacon, onions topped with

perfectly baked eggs. I watch as the yolk spills through the hash, my mouth filling with drool in anticipation.

"Oh god," I moan followed by the sound of Sophie choking.

"I think it's a winner." Karl laughs.

"It's really good, Mom," Sophie agrees after composing herself.

Nancy nods along to our praise and writes some things in her notebook, smiling the whole time.

When we're all stuffed to the gills, I convince the Hores to go hang out in the living room and I'll pack things up and do the dishes. I want them to be able to continue whatever I walked into earlier. By the time Nancy and Karl leave, I'm confident things are in a better place than they had been when I'd gotten here.

"So, I have a date planned for tonight," Sophie says while we plant the seedlings her parents brought.

"Sex?" I ask, smirking over at her.

"Maybe after." She flicks dirt at me. Knowing that I may get to sleep with this woman again has me smiling like a fool.

I brush my hands together, cleaning as much dirt off as possible before reaching for her. "What do you have planned for tonight, my love?"

She looks at my lips as she mouths "my love," a massive smile spreading, lighting up the shaded backyard.

"Stargazing," she says as her eyes flick to mine.

"Romantic," I murmur, slipping my hand around her neck and bringing her in for a kiss. "God, I love kissing you."

"Mmmm," she hums, pulling me back in.

Above us are stars, somewhere. There are unfortunately layers of clouds between us and those twinkly lights. Before us is an array of munchies, including a full fruit tray.

"I hope you still like ketchup chips," Sophie says as she pulls a bag out of the actual picnic basket she has packed.

"Sure do." I take the bag and open it, the smell hitting me immediately. "Cass used to send these to Korea for me. I got at least eight people hooked, which means I've spent a fortune on sending ketchup chips around the world."

"You're practically an ambassador. They should put you on the bag."

"Not sure that would be a big selling feature," I scoff, pulling out a couple chips and popping them in my mouth.

"I'd buy a bag with your face on it," she says thought-fully. "Plus with the red hair, you'd be a perfect ketchup chip ambassador."

"Well then, I guess we need to reach out to Lays and see if we can make this happen."

"Who should I be an ambassador for?" she asks, flipping her hair over her shoulder and looking at me sweetly. *Every fantasy I've ever had and will ever have?*

"Hmmm." I study her, getting closer and dropping a kiss on her jaw then her nose. "Something sweet." Another kiss. "Something mouth-watering,." A longer kiss. "Something completely unforgettable." She giggles as I wrap my arms around her and pull her on top of me. Stars are great and all, but I'd much rather gaze at Sophie. I'd rather do everything involving Sophie.

"We're going to miss the stars," she murmurs against my lips but doesn't pull away.

"They'll be there tomorrow, and the day after that, and so on," I move my lips to her neck and soak in her little sigh of contentment.

"That's a good point," she says, sliding her hands into my hair and holding me still as her lips trail along my jaw and down my neck.

I breathe deeply, willing my body to behave, which is taking an astronomical amount of effort, seeing how Sophie's body is on top of mine.

In the end we never saw any stars—not in the sky, anyway.

FIFTY

Maya and Davis are putting us to shame as they move around the dance floor with a fluidity I can barely imagine let alone accomplish. I've stepped on Foster's foot no fewer than six times, and his hand is so sweaty it's almost impossible to maintain our grip. How I thought I'd do better with the tango than I had with line dancing is beyond me. I blame Foster and his damn enthusiasm.

"Maybe don't pick a tango for your first dance," Maya leans over and whispers while we watch the instructors demonstrate the next set of moves.

"Oh, we won't." Foster laughs, pulling me tighter into his side, his fingers sneaking below my shirt, lazily caressing my skin.

The way he takes that exchange in stride, without stammering or making excuses about how it's too soon to be discussing such things, warms something deep within me.

I manage to miss most of the demonstration because I'm too busy looking at Foster. I'm beginning to realize that I've never felt like this for anyone. I thought I was in love with Gregory, but I never missed him the way I miss Foster when he's not in the same room with me. I never found myself smiling stupidly while thinking of him. My heart never raced at the thought of seeing him soon.

"Ready?" Foster asks, holding his hand out to me.

"Are your feet?" I joke, laying my hand in his and letting him pull me into his body. This part is seamless; my body doesn't fight any aspect of getting closer to him. But then my feet don't do what they're supposed to do. I'm like a newborn foal out here trying to keep a rhythm on ice.

Eventually, Foster and I move into a slow waltz type dance while Davis and Maya dance dramatically around us. We tried and that's the main thing, but now I'm quite content to rest my head next to Foster's and match my breathing to his.

Intimacy, I think. *This* is what I've been missing. These quiet moments where we simply exist in this little bubble together.

While T is technically Foster's letter and we have kind of learned a very basic tango, I couldn't help doing a little add-on after we get back to Foster's apartment.

He's sitting on the stool at the counter, blindfolded, waiting patiently for what's to come. Me on the other hand, I'm fidgety as all hell while I open little containers as quietly as possible, worrying that this idea is beyond dumb and won't play as seductively as I hope it will.

"Ready?" I ask, stepping in front of him with the first tiny cup.

"I was born ready," he says confidently.

"You don't even know what this is?" I laugh. "Hold out your hand."

I set the cup in his hand and direct him to smell. He raises it to his nose and gives a tiny sniff, his lips turning up immediately.

"Do I get to taste it?"

"If you'd like."

"I'd like."

This is where I hope things don't turn weird. I've been imagining this since he told me about his favorite challenge on Top Chef. Long before touching him became a possibility. Dabbing my finger into the golden liquid I then apply a dab to the center of my bottom lip before leaning in and kissing him.

When his lips meet mine, a tiny sound of satisfaction leaves them. His tongue sweeps across my lip, and I feel his smile as the sweet honey settles on his taste buds.

"Honey," he murmurs against my mouth. "The one from the farmers' market." He kisses me again, tasting my entire mouth this time. "Wanted to make sure I got it all."

"You're very thorough, Mr. Walsh." I push back gently, wiping my lips just in case there's any honey left and reach for the next cup.

Foster gets everything right. Mind you, it's all sauces, which he claims are easier than herbs and spices, but he's definitely not complaining.

"Last one," I say, handing over the cup and watching him smell. He's smiling before it even reaches his nose.

"Mmm, I can't wait to taste this one." He hands the cup back, and I apply the maple syrup quickly because as fun as this has been, I am very ready to get on with the evening.

He's kept his hands to himself throughout the game, but the minute my lips meet his, they're around my waist, pulling me into him.

Twenty minutes later, I'm the one with the blindfold on as Foster's tongue dances across my skin. The combination of not being able to see where he's going next and the stroke of his tongue unravels the fabric of my being.

All I can think right before his tongue dips between my legs and I release a moan that could wake the dead is that *Top Chef* could never.

"Now this was a good idea," Maya squeals as we walk through the aquarium.

I'd seen an ad for an adults-only after-dark night at the aquarium a couple years ago, but Gregory had rolled his eyes and told me it was childish. How he worked that out was beyond me when the event was eighteen-plus. So when I saw a post about it last week, I bought four tickets immediately. At first I didn't even factor in the alphabet, but when I'd mentioned it to Foster, he'd nodded and said that underwater was a solid choice for U.

So here we are, walking hand and hand through a tunnel while sharks swim lazily above our heads. It's far more peaceful than I had anticipated. No kids allowed probably helps.

"Soph, can you take a picture while there's no one around?" Maya asks, practically throwing her phone at me and pulling Davis into the center of the tunnel. Considering he was supposed to be a fling, Maya sure looks at the man like he's her world. "Okay, now you two." She takes her phone back and motions for us to go stand where she and Davis had been.

"Do you trust me?" Foster asks.

"Of course," I reply, curious why he'd ask me such a thing.

I think he's going in for a kiss, but his head moves to the

side and suddenly I'm spun around as his one hand supports my shoulders and his other drops to my thigh.

He dips me dramatically, and then his lips cover mine in a kiss that would leave me on the floor if he didn't have his arm around me.

I'm faintly aware of a hoot coming from somewhere nearby, but I block it out and focus completely on all the places Foster is touching me. This is one of the times hyper-fixation benefits me. Everything around me seems to fade away as I zero in on the way his left hand grips and loosens over and over again. The way his tongue explores my mouth. The feel of his heart beating wildly beneath my palm. I want to stay like this. Just him and me in this under-water world.

"Okay, you two, I got like six hundred pictures, let's move along," Maya calls.

Foster pulls back a little bit but only so he can look down at me. "What?"

He shakes his head and pulls me the rest of the way up, kissing me quickly before Maya and Davis join us to continue through the tunnel.

"Oh my god, it's so much harder than I expected," I grunt. "Oh shit, I'm so sorry," I apologize to the pottery instructor who got the bulk of my splattering clay. At least he's wearing an apron.

"Happens all the time." he says with a chuckle. "May I?" he asks, gesturing toward the elongated lump on my wheel.

"By all means." I raise my hands in surrender and

vacate the chair. I watch as he works to reshape what I ruined and do my best not to make a remark about what it looks like. Foster catches my eye, and I have to look away to keep from laughing, focusing extra hard on someone else working on my vase.

"Alright," the instructor says, standing from the chair. "Slow and steady this time."

Foster leans into my space. "I'm kind of glad you didn't do that well."

"Oh? Why is that?"

He raises an eyebrow at me. "I was getting a bit jealous of the clay." The loudest, most obnoxious snort leaves my body. "Hot," he whispers, going back to the vase he's nearly finished.

"Wedding at a winery," Foster says as he backs into an empty spot. "This seems almost too convenient."

I'm about to answer but the way he grins over at me freezes my tongue, and all I manage is a little hum and a starry-eyed smile. Not long ago I was planning on attending Yasmine and Miguel's wedding with someone totally different. But as I sit here staring at Foster, I can't even picture who. It feels like it was always going to be Foster.

"Ready?" he asks, one hand on the door handle while the other gives my hand a quick squeeze.

I manage to blink out of my stupor and nod. I have never been more ready.

Yasmine is crying as she practically drags her father down the aisle toward her future husband. When I look back at Miguel, tears sting my eyes. He's standing so tall, so proud as he watches the love of his life walk toward him, tears streaming down his own face.

Foster's hand in mine tightens, and I look over to see that he too has tears running down his face. He barely knows Yasmine and Miguel, and here he is openly crying at their wedding. *I adore him,* I think, looking back in time to see Yas kiss her father on the cheek and hand her sister her bouquet with one hand while reaching for Miguel's with the other.

The officiant does their thing while the small number of us in attendance laugh and cry some more. No one thought this day would come—well, no one except Yasmine. I'd smiled along to all her plans for the future with the guy she'd fallen for as a teenager, but I'm ashamed to admit that I hadn't had the hope she did. I was scared of her hope and what would happen to it if things didn't turn out for them. Terrified of what an unsuccessful transplant would do to my friend. I get it now, though—if it had been me and Foster, I wouldn't have had anything but hope.

"I love a short ceremony," Maya sighs as we walk toward the barrel room for cocktail hour. "This is exactly what I want," she adds quietly so only I can hear her, her gaze sliding to Davis as he and Foster grab us drinks.

"Nothing big and flashy?"

"Oh, I didn't say that. Everything will be big and flashy, but the boring stuff will be short and sweet." She winks.

"Mmm." I nod. "Like Davis."

Her responding laughter echoes off the walls.

I can name almost everyone in the room. Thirty guests, all family and close friends. It's exactly what I'd want except I want to get married at my parents' farm, down by the cottage. I want to kick off my shoes and dance barefoot all night long. And I want to do all of that with the man handing a glass of wine to me, wearing the same blue suit he picked me up in for that first friend date.

"What?" Foster asks, grinning at me before popping a stuffed mushroom into his mouth. His eyes close, and he makes a noise I've only ever heard him make in bed.

"Seems like I have competition," I whisper and watch as his cheeks darken.

He leans down, his lips brushing my ear. "Nothing stands a chance against you, sunshine." His lips meet the sensitive skin right below my ear, and I feel the need to grip the high-top table in front of me.

During dinner, Foster insists I try everything on his plate he thinks I'll like, and as usual he's right. Celeriac puree is delicious, who knew?

There is a first dance shortly after dinner, and we all stand in a circle around the bride and groom as they sway to Echosmith's "Surround You." When the last verse begins, they both gesture for their guests to join them. Foster wraps his arms around my body and pulls me in close. I let myself enjoy how right this all feels. A relaxing evening with my friends and my... Foster.

FIFTY-ONE

Sophie watches me go to my underwear drawer, and her mixed expression alone is worth it.

"I can't tell if I'm concerned, excited, or terrified," she says.

"Your face also can't seem to figure it out." I chuckle, pulling the box that arrived three days ago out of the drawer.

"This isn't where you tell me you have your own collection like that one we found in the trunk, is it?"

"No, but what if I did?"

I don't, but I'm curious what she has to say about it.

"I'd say to each their own, you do you."

I hold the box out to her and watch her take in the words. It's a discreet box. Nothing about it would give away what's inside.

"Inside and Out?" She reads out, flipping it over to see the back. "Is this a... sex game?"

I take the box from her and rip the plastic off. "It's a deep dive into intimacy."

She crawls onto the bed and sits cross-legged. "I, the longest letter in the alphabet apparently."

I sit down on the edge of the bed and set the box between us. "We were playing the intimacy game long before we got to I, sunshine."

She nods. "Yeah, I realized that randomly one day while I was doing dishes. I must have scrubbed a single mug for fifteen minutes while I thought back to all the times you asked me questions or the way you looked at me. How you made me lunch and cookies. The way you held and still hold my hand. All these little things that seemed so"—she shrugs—"mundane? But things he never did, not even in the beginning. Did you know he never asked me how my day was? He'd tell me about his the minute he got home, and then that was it. That's so incredibly fucked, right?"

"It's definitely fucked." She blushes as her gaze lands on my mouth. "Do you like when I use that word, Soph?" She nods, and I can't help leaning back to kiss her. "Only with you."

"How romantic." She giggles, and I drop a quick kiss on her lips.

"So, you up for this X-rated box of questions?" I tap the box.

"I'm up for anything with you, remember?"

"Well, this is..." Sophie flips the card over as if she's looking for more information.

"What?"

"It's not what I was expecting, but that's fine. Okay, Foster, what is something you are afraid of?"

"That's..." I start.

"Right? Should we skip it?"

"No, it's a game of intimacy, not sex. One thing, eh? The uncertainty in my career. That one day I won't be able to support myself..." I pause, unsure if I should vocalize my whole fear. "Or my family doing it. Now your turn. What's something you are afraid to tell others?"

My stomach sinks when she actually looks afraid to tell me, but then I watch her sit up a bit straighter. "I'm afraid I won't be able to have kids." I watch as she entwines her fingers and squeezes, collecting herself. "My mom struggled for years before she finally got pregnant, and I'm scared I've wasted my one chance. And I know, there are countless ways to be a parent, but... it's silly." She shakes her head, smiling weakly.

I reach for her hands, wrapping mine around them and drawing them up to my lips. "There's nothing silly about that, Soph." I kiss her knuckles. "That's a genuine fear, and you're allowed to feel it." I want to add that we'll cross that bridge when we come to it, but of course it's too soon for such a conversation, even if I know deep in my bones that she's the one I'll be having it with.

After setting her hands down gently, I draw a card. "What are two things your future self would thank you for?"

Sophie looks away, squinting as if she can see the answers in the distance. "Choosing to do my master's and..." She looks back at me, eyes searching my face, a small smile appearing. "Asking you to be my friend date."

"I'm very happy you asked me."

"What about you?"

"Well just to be a contrarian, not doing my master's and going back to school to be an EA and..." I could say saying yes to her that first time, but no, it was earlier than that. "Sharing my lunch with you that first day." Her responding smile erases all the pain and worry from her face, like the sun peeking out from behind a thick layer of clouds.

She pulls another card. "If you could switch places with one other person, who would it be?"

"Why would I want to switch places with anyone? It means I wouldn't be here with you." She rolls her eyes at me. "I'm serious," I insist.

"Play along. You'll still be here with me no matter who you say."

"Fine. Bennett, probably. That guy's life seems pretty decent."

"I'd say Bennett too." Sophie cracks up.

"Oh, okay, this one is a bit risqué,"

"Shoot."

I take a deep breath, feeling the nerves start to creep in. "What is your favorite way that I touch you?" She's red instantly, and my nerves disappear. God, I love that blush.

"Whoever wrote this question probably thinks everyone is going to answer this in a sexier way, but for me, it's when you're holding my hand and your thumb brushes back and forth over the back of my hand. I don't even know if you know you're doing it but it's like you're reminding me you're there."

Well, damn, I had kind of hoped for something a bit hotter, but I have to admit that's probably the best answer she could have given.

She stares at me expectantly. "Right, um... When you trace my tattoos with your finger. It makes me even happier that I got them."

I slip the card back into the box and hold it out for her.

She giggles and looks up at the ceiling. "What fantasy would you like to check off your list with me?"

"Can I be very honest without you saying it's a cop-out?"

Her eyes narrow suspiciously. "Okay."

"You've always been my fantasy. Like the chance of being with you in any capacity other than as friends was as likely as walking through a portal into Middle Earth." I inch closer. "Kissing you, really kissing you, was an out-of-body experience. Being inside you." I moan as I tip my head back. "If I die tomorrow, I'd die a very happy man. And I know that's something people say, but I mean it because I got to experience life with you in so many ways."

"Please don't die tomorrow," she whispers.

"Oh, sunshine, I'm not going anywhere. I've got way too much time to make up for where you're concerned." I pull the card from her hand and toss it away. "Too many future plans with you I don't want to miss out on. Too many places I have yet to taste you," I dip my head, running my tongue along her collarbone, smiling when she whimpers. "Too many sounds I still want to hear you make. Too many days of letting you know how beautiful you are left to live." I murmur against her lips, soaking up the sigh she releases as my body covers hers.

Sophie wakes me up the next morning with soft kisses and a mug full of coffee. "You're going to be late for training."

"Donkey balls," I curse, sitting up quickly and swinging out of bed. I stop dead when I see that Sophie is wearing only my Nyx Avalon concert shirt and her boy shorts, and I think my brain glitches. "How am I supposed to leave when you wake me up looking like this?" I gesture down her body. "This is not fair."

"Use it as motivation to be very, very efficient today," she stresses, walking toward me. "Because while you copped out on a fantasy, I have one I'd like to make come true later on."

Holy Sasquatch's snatch, she's going to be the death of me.

FIFTY-TWO

While Foster is off with Pete, I have a chance to prepare for date Y. After grabbing my half-packed suitcase from the car, I start packing the rest with Foster's things. I had casually asked about any sct plans he may have for the long weekend, and after he had said no, I went ahead and booked a yurt in the middle of the forest.

Finding date ideas that start with Y is harder than I expected. I'd thrown out a yellow theme early on and had spent a week flip-flopping between forcing myself to do yoga and a Yogi Bear marathon and then like magic, I'd seen an acquaintance from the university post about a rental yurt. I reached out, and she said bookings wouldn't be starting until next month, but she'd happily let us stay if I was able to get to campus to pick up the key.

So after I've packed, I jump in my car and head to campus.

Campus is quiet due to it being Saturday, but since the summer term is shorter, there are still students and staff dotted around, working at tables in the atrium I pass through to get to the faculty offices in the humanities department. The atrium was my favorite place to study. It's also where I met Gregory for the first time. In line at the café, he'd bumped into me, and I'd dropped my coffee. He'd been almost over the top with his apologies. He'd offered to replace it, then insisted I order something fancier than a coffee. I hadn't wanted anything fancy—I liked my simple coffee—but I'd done it. He'd brought that up a lot to people in the beginning. Passing it off as if he was saving the poor student from having to drink boring cheap coffee.

I had done what he had wanted right from the start. I hadn't had a chance.

My phone vibrates in my hand, and I look down to find a picture of Pete, red-faced, crutches blurry as he runs to Foster.

"Sophie?"

Ice travels down my back. I know that voice too well.

He's standing there in a polo and chinos, his Saturday uniform. Why is he here? He always hated being here on the weekend. I wish Foster was with me. Wish his hand was in mine keeping me centered.

Gregory steps toward me, and part of me wants to turn and run back to my car. Get back to Foster. But there is another part of me that wants to ask a question and is dead set on not leaving until I get an answer. That is the part that wins.

"Did you ever love me?" I ask. He stops immediately, clearly caught off guard by the question.

"I..." he begins and then looks away. He's going to say no. Going to laugh at how gullible I was. How young and stupid. "I did until I didn't."

I blink back at him. "What?"

He takes another step. "I never lied about loving you, not in the beginning."

"When... when did you stop?"

He shrugs. "I don't know. Gradually things that I used to find cute weren't cute anymore."

"Things I couldn't..."

"Things that would never change because they were part of you. Things I couldn't change about you." *Despite his attempts*, hangs in the air between us.

"You loved who I could have been, not who I was," I say quietly.

"Maybe that's right." He chuckles as if five years of my life were nothing to him.

I square my shoulders and force myself to look into his eyes. "I'd like to thank you, Gregory."

"For?" That cocky grin appears as if he's expecting me to compliment him. He's used to that from people.

"For showing me what love isn't. For demonstrating so wholeheartedly how I never want to be treated again." My entire body is shaking, and I wouldn't be surprised if my face is as red as a beet. But I feel something shift inside me. Like a door creaking open.

I see his mouth open, but I'm done now. His time is up, and I lift my hand to stop him. "Nope," I say.

A smile lifting the corners of my mouth in triumph, I leave him standing there to stew in a word he's certainly not accustomed to, and continue down the hall, each step becoming lighter than the last.

"Honey, I'm home!" he calls when he comes through the door. I close the book I've been failing to read for the past thirty minutes and make my way over. Making sure to give

Gary proper time to greet Foster before I throw myself at him. "God, I love coming home to you," he rasps against my neck as he presses me against the wall.

"Mmm," I hum. "I'm also a big fan of you coming home to me." I gently pry his lips from my skin. "But we have somewhere to be."

"Is this related to your fantasy?"

"You remember that, eh?"

He pulls back, his lips quirking to the side. "Remember it? I haven't stopped thinking about it," he whispers, leaning down to kiss me again.

"It's not actually, but..." I stop to think because maybe it would work... no, probably not, but maybe. There's no balcony, but there *is* a deck. In a forest against a tree—oh, maybe that appeals to me too. I wince thinking about the bark. That could be painful.

"Hey, where'd you go?" Foster stares down at me, searching my eyes for some kind of clue.

"Just thinking. Fantasy talk later. Go shower quickly, and we'll leave."

"Wanna join me?" He pulls me toward the bathroom.

I shake my head. "No time for that, shoo." I pull my hand away, watching as he turns and pouts at me from the door. "Oh, stop it."

His responding grin grows as he gives me a once-over. "Can you blame me?"

"Yes, hurry up."

I can hear him laughing even after he closes the door, and I get to work gathering the suitcase I'd hidden in the closet and throwing the prepared food into a cooler.

"What's up?" Foster asks when I get back inside to find him standing in the living room, a towel low around his waist, his hair standing on end every which way.

I'd reply, but I can't seem to make my lips move. He's a tattooed ginger Adonis. I know the strength in those arms and the feel of those abs beneath my touch. I've kissed each of his tattoos, traced them with my fingers and tongue. I'm the nightly beneficiary of all the ways that beautiful body can move.

"I need you to get dressed, now please," I falter, my voice almost an octave lower than normal.

"Should I be worried about how cagey you're being?" he asks, taking a step toward me.

I hold my hand up and take a step back. "No, it's a good reason, I promise, but you really need to get dressed."

He doesn't stop, not until his chest meets my outstretched hand. He wraps his hand around my wrist and lifts it, laying a gentle kiss on my palm, chiseling away at my resolve. How he can do that with his lips on the palm of my hand, is beyond me.

"Only because you asked so nicely," he says, dropping my hand and pulling me in for a searing kiss that all but forces me to slide my hands into his hair and pull him in more.

I'm lost in it, floating somewhere beyond the physical world. The feel of his hands sliding over mine, pulling them away from his head brings me back into my body.

He steps back, letting my arms fall to my side, the sensation of his damp hair stamped on my hands.

"Sorry, sunshine, I've got somewhere to be, apparently." He grins and backs away from me, smirking the whole way to his bedroom.

"Okay, well, this is very cool," Foster says, admiring the interior of the yurt before sitting on the edge of the bed and reaching for me.

I could say no, could tell him we have a hike to do before it gets too dark, but I have a hard time convincing myself that climbing a hill is going to be better than climbing him. Sexual mountaineering will always win out if the mountain is Foster.

When I stop between his legs, he doesn't do anything other than set his hands gently on my hips, his thumbs skimming over the skin there. Eventually his arms wrap around me and he pulls me in, resting his head on my stomach. It's not what I was expecting, and it takes me a minute to recalibrate.

Running my hands through his hair I gently ease his head back. "What's wrong?"

He shakes his head and smiles at me. "Nothing. I can't believe I get to do this."

"Hug me?"

"Hug you." His hands slip under my shirt and skim across my skin. "Touch you." He pushes the fabric higher and presses his lips to my stomach over and over again. "Kiss you."

I think I'm melting, physically disappearing into the floor until I feel his arms around me and my view changes. The top of his head disappears, and I'm left looking at the ceiling of the yurt before his face comes into view and his lips meet mine. I'm vaguely aware of the way his hand is traveling down my body, disappearing under the waistband of my tights. "Fuck you," he murmurs against my lips. I like this list of things he's reciting. I like what he's doing physically even more.

His kisses become more demanding as his fingers go to

work. A gasp escapes as I break away from his kiss, tipping my head back as my hips arch greedily into his hand. "Need..." I barely get the word out as his fingers dip into me, a tease of what's to come.

ABC

"Pete let me know this morning that he thinks he should start with a shorter race," Foster says as we make our way carefully down a steep, rocky section of the hill.

"So no more marathon dreams?"

"No." He turns, holding his hand out for me once he's made it past the worst of it. "I think he is still very much wanting to do that one day, or thinks he does. But he's impatient." He grins at me. "I've been trying to work on that with him for two years now."

When the terrain levels out he keeps my hand in his.

"I think when someone has been told by society that they can't do something for most of their life, waiting to prove people wrong may become a bit of a burden." I walk along the trunk of a fallen tree, balancing easily with Foster's assistance. "I mean, we live in such an instant gratification society now that waiting for anything is hard. Imagine deciding you're going to do something and then being told you can't yet and you'll have to train for a while first. Painful." I hop down from the log and pull Foster to a stop. "What you're doing with him, for him, is really great. Most people would have said some lovely empty things and then let him do it alone. He'll remember this forever. You'll be the guy who not only told him he could do it, but helped him do it."

God, I want to kiss the smile he smiles at me and never

stop. "I think he'll do it. It may take a long time, but he'll do it."

"And when he does, we'll be at the finish line screaming like maniacs."

Foster raises his hand and tucks a lock of hair behind my ear. "I can't wait for that day, sunshine. It's going to be a big one."

FIFTY-THREE

Leaving the bed when Sophie is half wrapped around me is hell, but sticking with my running routine is something that is important to me, so I'm up the minute my alarm goes off.

"Stay." Sophie's sleepy voice rasps, her hand brushing across my back.

I'm tempted to lie back and pull her into me. "I'll be back soon," I whisper, kissing her hand and watching as she offers a lazy smile and immediately falls back to sleep.

Running a trail through the forest is a bit different than the usual running I do down decently managed sidewalks, but I manage to make it back to the yurt without twisting anything.

Sophie is sitting on the deck in one of the Muskoka chairs, holding a coffee and staring out at the calm lake. She hasn't noticed me yet, and I stop to take in the view and a few deep breaths. Eventually she turns her head in my direction, and her smile is a beacon, leading me back to her.

"Good run?" she asks, reaching for my hand.

"It was." I bend and kiss her quickly. "I'm going to shower very, very quickly."

She pulls me back as I begin to rise. "Good," she murmurs, her lips connecting with mine.

"Some of these feel quite...vain." Sophie glares down at the card she's pulled from the box.

"But they work both ways, and therefore we both benefit."

"I guess. Okay, Foster, what are three things that made me attractive to you?"

Only three things? This is going to be hard to narrow down. "First, your smile. Yeah, that one right there." I point at her mouth as the corners tip up. "Your laugh, which is good because it goes well with your smile. And..." I study her for a beat. "Your hair."

"My hair? As in my generic blonde hair?"

"The way it catches the light. It's s—" I start to say.

"Sunshine," she says slowly.

"Sunshine," I confirm. "Now, do me." I sit up expectantly, breaking the tension.

"Oh, I plan to," she says, her eyebrows bouncing along with her shoulders, making me laugh.

"Let's finish this round, then you can *do me* all you want," I assure her.

She sighs and leans back on her hands. "Well, as my dad said, apparently I really liked your face when I was six. Turns out I still really like your face." She giggles. "Like, I really, really like your face."

"Great face, got it. What else?"

"Your kindness. You've always been kind. Even when you teased me as a kid, it wasn't malicious. Now watching you work with the kids." She fans her face, "Hot. And..." She studies me, her gaze eventually landing on my mouth. "Your smile, specifically when you look at me. I mean, it's always great, but it gives me butterflies. Like it's a goddamn butterfly conservatory"—she gestures around her entire body—"everywhere."

"Everywhere?" I creep forward, expecting her to inch away, but she doesn't. "Even here?" She cracks up when my finger presses into her shin.

She nods. "Especially there. You give me shin tingles like no one else."

Sitting back, I draw another card. "What sense is the most sensual to you?"

"Out of the five?" she asks, and I nod. She thinks for a minute as if going through experiences with all of them. When she licks her lips I already know what she's about to say. "Taste," she says confidently. "Your turn."

I could say taste, but when I think about the feel of her skin under my fingertips. The way mine reacts every time she touches me, the choice is clear. "Touch, hands down."

"Touching or being touched?" she asks.

"They're equally sensual if you're involved." She rolls her eyes and slips the card back into the box. "What? I'm serious. If I had it my way I'd spend all my days touching you."

"May make it hard to do your job."

"We'd adapt." I shrug.

The next question is a big one, and I visibly tense as I decide whether or not I should ask it.

"Is it a dirty one?" Sophie scoots closer, and I pull the card into my chest. "Oooh, it is, isn't it?" She reaches for me, and I cover the entire card with my hand, completely blocking it from her grasp. "Come on, you ordered me to sit on your face last night, Foster. Ask me the question."

Oh yes, let's do that again. Instead of asking this question, maybe we can reenact everything we did last night. The way she moved against my mouth as she leaned back, her nails digging into my thighs. How she'd begged me to fuck her harder against the railing of the deck, her cries echoing through the woods. But no, sex is nothing compared to this question.

"Where do you see yourself in five years, Sophie?" I ask, my heart thumping rapidly against my ribcage. I want the ground to open and swallow me. I want to be sucked into the sky. I want to evaporate. All those things would be better than waiting for this answer.

She doesn't make me wait. "With you. Happy, eating cookies at two a.m., watching *The Fellowship of the Ring* for the seven hundredth time, at least one dog trying to take over our bed. Still arguing about blue cheese versus ranch whenever we get wings. Watching you cook for me in nothing but those gray sweatpants. Waking up every morning with a smile on my face because your face is the first I see and I happen to like it even more than I do now."

Holy shit. She hasn't said I love you yet, but that felt like a bigger declaration.

I know I need to respond, say something equally lovely, but all my words are jumbled in my mouth. All my thoughts fully scrambled. Sixteen- or fourteen- or however-old-I-was-when-I-actually-fell-for-her-year-old me is screaming at me to do something, say something. But I just sit, mouth agape, staring at the woman of my dreams who says things that seemed impossible a couple months ago.

"Was that too much?" she asks, pulling her knees to her chest and looking worried.

All I can do is shake my head while I grasp at coherent thoughts falling like feathers through my mind.

"Are you going to say anything? Technically it's your turn. You don't have to say anything about me. I didn't say that so you'd say anything back. I won't be upset if you talk about winning a marathon or getting your entire back tattooed. Maybe in five years you'll be back in Korea, running a school. Or you'll have a whole running club for kids who have been told they can't do it. I can actually see you doing that, for the record. You'd be very good at that. Oh god, I made it awkward by being too honest, I'm sorry. I, fuck, I should have just said something like attending an alumni gala without needing a fake date or having a house without doom piles everyw—"

I cut her off with a kiss. I'm buying time, sure, but hopefully it stops her from worrying. She relaxes into me, and the kiss turns from desperate to slow and sensual. *This.* This is what I want to be doing. I give her one last long kiss before resting my forehead against hers, catching my breath, trying to slow my heart rate down.

"Kissing you whenever I want to. Holding your hand whenever you're near me. Waking up to sunshine even on cloudy days. Cooking for you. Laughing with you. Sharing all my good and bad days with you. Taking on the world by your side. Proving to you that you're worthy of every good thing life has in store. Showing you every single day what it is to be truly loved because you are the most loveable person I've ever known. Calling you mine and being yours. Being with you, Sophie, that's where I see myself in five years, because the alternative is unthinkable. Not loving you is unthinkable." I take a breath, and when I pull away and finally look at her, there are tears streaming down her face. "Don't cry, sunshine." I smile, wiping them away.

"They're happy tears."

"I guess those are allowed."

"Wow, they should put a warning on the box." She laughs, wiping her face, collecting all the tears I missed.

"Caution, may cause fits of truthfulness and sappiness."

She holds up another card. "This will be a nice palate cleanser. Foster, what is your favorite kind of foreplay?"

"Easy. Pretending to date you, or pretending I didn't desperately want to date you. It was like being edged for weeks on end. Why do you think I came without even touching myself?"

"Oh? Is edging something you're into?"

"If you're the one edging me, it sure is."

Her eyes trail down my body, her lip slipping between her teeth before they make their way back to my face. "Noted."

"What about you?"

"When you kiss or lick me right"—she runs her fingers along her collarbone—"here."

"Really?"

"Mm-hmm. No one had ever touched me like that before. It seems so small, but it's all the small things with you." A smile appears for a second but is quickly replaced by what appears to be worry.

"What's up?"

I watch as her fingers twine around each other, squeezing and releasing again and again. "It's all so good. With you, I mean. I keep having to push this annoying little voice down." She taps her temple.

"What's it saying?"

"Not to trust it," she admits quietly.

"Have..." I swallow, trying to collect myself, going over

our time together. "Have I done anything that gives that little voice power?"

She shakes her head. "He didn't either, in the beginning. I didn't even see it happening. Not until I was out and really started to look at things. Then I just felt incredibly dumb. I know I'm not." She stops me before I have a chance to contradict her. "But that doesn't mean I don't feel like I am. And I know, logically I know, I shouldn't listen to the voice. You're not him. You've never done a single thing in all the years I've known you that would make me think you're even capable. For one, you're not a narcissist." She laughs before releasing a deep sigh. "Also, Cass would never have pushed for this if she didn't believe you were right for me."

"It doesn't matter what anyone else thinks though, Soph. All that matters is what you think and feel."

"My god, this was supposed to be a fun game, and I keep taking it to this heavy place. What's your favorite foreplay? When you touch me here. What about you, Sophie? Proceeds to trauma-dump while making the man I'm very into worry I'm about to call the whole thing off. When really what I'm trying to do in the most awkward round-about way ever is tell him I love him t—."

"What?" I shout, making her jump but at least it stops her spiraling.

Her blue eyes meet mine as her head tilts to the left, her lips moving back and forth as if she's trying to contain words she hasn't said yet.

"Back up a sec. You what?"

"I love him. Him being you. I love you."

"Yeah?"

She nods slowly back, her eyes never leaving mine. "I have my whole life, it would seem. I was just afraid to admit it."

"Good. And for the record I'm not worried you're going to call the whole thing off."

"No?"

I shake my head slowly. "I'm not him, and I'm never going to be him."

FIFTY-FOUR

"So you have no idea what he's planning for your last...?" Maya trails off as she reaches for a fresh slice of pizza.

"Date?"

"Oh, are we allowed to call them dates now?"

"I think we both know they were always dates."

"I mean, I did, but you were adamant that they were not. Fake-dating fakers is what you two were."

"Sorry it took me so long to trust my feelings." I roll my eyes. "They needed a while to redeem themselves. But then it was like... I had spent years pretending I was fine, pretending I liked everything. And then I was getting all this time with *the guy* and I was pretending to pretend. And well, I'm very glad he seemed tired of pretending too."

Maya rolls her eyes at me and groans. "Sophie, that man was never pretending. He was being *the guy* we all know you deserve. Anyway, all that matters is that you put that poor man out of his misery and you did something for yourself. It's a win-win," she says, her eyes softening in a very un-Maya like way. "So, what's on deck for the last date?" Davis and Foster are out bonding, so we're eating pizza and pretending to watch a reality show neither of us actually cares about.

"No, not our last date. It's just the last in this round of themed dates," I correct her.

She holds her hands up. "You know what I mean." She rolls her eyes. "He's probably not taking you to the zoo."

"No, he already told me that was not happening. But um…" I start to say as we make our way to the living room. "So, there's this thing I wanted to ask you about." I don't know why I'm nervous. Maya and I talk about everything. Hell, I knew way too much about Davis before I even met the man.

"Is this about sex?" she asks, a bit too excitedly.

"Well, yeah, I guess so."

"Is it weird?"

"Is what weird?"

"His dick. Does he have a weird dick or something?"

I blink back at her. "What? No! This has nothing to do with anatomy."

"Oh, well, that's good. Although," she says with a sigh, "a weird dick can do glorious things." When she grins over at me I feel my cheeks heat.

"Anyway, so, with…"

"Shithead?" I laugh because Maya has taken to using the poop emoji whenever he comes up instead of his name.

"Yeah. We, well, the sex wasn't exactly…"

"Normal?"

"Maya, let me finish."

"Sorry, I'm impatient. Please continue."

"It wasn't exactly exciting. He, well, it always felt like I was there for him to use. He'd"—I mime him thrusting—"then it would be done and I'd lay there for a little bit wondering what all the fuss was about. I'd suggest things in the beginning, and he'd say 'sure, yeah, let's do that,' but we'd start the same way we always did and ultimately end that way too. It was like the minute something felt good for him, it erased the conversation."

Maya stares back. We haven't discussed this part of my relationship. I've been keeping it locked inside because looking back it's all blanketed in red flags. It's stupidly obvious.

"So like, you never... he never got you there or helped you get there, or fucking cared if you did?" She purses her lips looking as if she's ready to physically fight someone.

"I think we've established that he didn't care about anything but his own needs. That wasn't exactly specific to any one part of his life. He also didn't tend to care if I wasn't in the mood," I whisper and have to look away.

"Oh, Soph." I feel her move and her arms wrap around me. "I'm sorry."

I pull away because that's not why I'm bringing any of this up. I don't want to talk about him or what he didn't do for me or what he did to me while he was too busy doing everything for himself.

"With Foster, well, it's... I'm asking for things," I say slowly. "Demanding them, really. And he does them enthusiastically. Then he asks for things, and I'm excited to do whatever."

Maya looks like she's about to say something like "bless your heart" or "you sweet summer child," and I brace myself.

"So you're enjoying yourself," she states.

"Yes," I admit, feeling my face heat by several degrees.

"What's your question?"

"I don't know, sometimes I feel a bit like I'm maybe asking for too much or being too out there, but it's like anything I've even wondered about I say out loud and then he does it."

"There is nothing 'out there' about asking for what you want, Soph. Sounds like you're living your best life right now. You're with this guy who is madly in love with you rather than madly in love with the fact you're in love with him. Have you felt uncomfortable with anything?"

"God no," I sputter. "And that's what worried me a bit."

Maya shrugs. "You're two adults in a consensual relationship, and it sounds like you care about each other's pleasure versus only your own. Embrace it, my friend. If he's willing to try every little thing you want and vice versa, as long as you're being safe and it makes you happy, don't let those little worries in, okay?"

"Okay." I sigh.

"So it's good?"

I flop back against the couch with a dramatic groan. "It's so good."

"I knew it would be. Your chemistry is too powerful for it not to be extra-explosive in the bedroom." She takes a bite of pizza, and I know what she's about to say before she even opens her mouth. "Maybe buy some backup lamps."

The week after a long weekend is always the longest in history. Every hour drags by, or maybe that's how it feels waiting to find out what Foster has in store for Z.

"You're in a good mood today." I laugh as Pete practically skips out of his classroom. I take a peek through the door hoping to catch a glimpse of Foster, but he's nowhere to be seen.

"Mr. Walsh is helping Debra Donahue in Mr. Johnson's class."

"Oh, that's nice of him. I wasn't looking for him, though," I say as casually as possible.

"Miss Hore?"

"Yes, Pete?"

"I think we both know you were." The little shit grins up at me and winks, except Pete cannot wink so it's more of a regular blink with a very exaggerated head nod.

"Okay, fine, I was. You caught me."

He grins, nodding. "That's because I'm perceptive."

"How is training going?" I ask as he flops onto the bean bag across from me.

"We didn't train yesterday."

"Oh?" Strange, Foster was later than usual getting back because he said he was going to train with Pete. Alarm bells ring in the back of my mind. Why would he say that if that's not what he was doing?

"I have a giant blister," Pete says, leaning down to untie his shoe. "It's really gross."

"You can keep your shoe on. I know what gross blisters look like," I insist.

"Are you sure you don't want to see it? Mr. Walsh said it's a reward for how hard I'm working. It's a blister to be proud of."

"I bet it is. So Mr. Walsh saw your blister last night then?"

"Mm-hmm," he confirms. "He said we couldn't train, but that maybe I could help him with a project instead." I'm about to ask what the project is, but he holds out his hand to stop me. "I can't tell you, I pinky-promised."

Well then, Foster didn't lie about where he was going

and in fact was up to something that's probably going to make my heart melt right out of my body.

"I won't ask. That's between you and Mr. Walsh."

"It's good, the project." He leans forward. "Really good." He does his Pete wink again, and I laugh.

"Okay, I believe you. Now tell me how things are going at school. Did you do well on your last spelling test?"

"I got perfect. And," he says quickly, making me jolt, "I got the bonus word right."

"That's amazing, Pete. What was the bonus word?"

"Cornucopia."

"Oh wow, that's a good one."

He nods, his face scrunching. "I don't know what a cornucopia is though."

"What do you think it is?" After Foster's foray into nut milk with him, I'm curious to see what his mind does with this.

He shrugs. "A world made of corn? Like Zootopia but with corn."

"So corn characters or buildings?"

I watch him think. It looks as if he's building the entire world in his mind. "I think corn characters."

"And would they all be full cobs?"

His face somehow scrunches even more, his lips moving this way than that. "Do you think a corn cob could be a firefighter?"

Well, no. "Do you?"

"I would worry they'd pop." He lifts his hand and spreads his fingers, making popping sounds.

I can't hold the laugh in anymore. "It's kind of a disturbing world you're creating, Pete."

"Maybe a city made of corn instead."

"But what happens if it gets hot? Would houses start popping?"

"Miss Hore?"

"Mmhmm?"

"What's a cornucopia?"

"It's a big horn full of fruits and vegetables. Usually they're common around Thanksgiving."

"So... there's no corn?"

"Well, there could be corn inside."

"I like our idea more."

"Me too," I agree. "Way more interesting."

After dropping Pete back off, I catch a glimpse of Foster in another classroom. I pause to watch as he listens to the student he's sitting with. She seems a bit agitated, but he remains calm taking everything in stride. Eventually, the student seems to collect herself and her head bends as she begins writing something, Foster's lips moving the whole time, occasionally pointing at something on the page.

He's well regarded by the teachers and his fellow EAs in this school. Sometimes I worry he'll give in to the naysayers. Pursue something he's not passionate about just to get them off his back. He's capable of being whatever he wants to be—aside from anything involving blood, of course. But he's doing what he should be doing, what he was born to be doing. I believe that deep in my soul.

People like to talk about how professional athletes and artists have a gift, but I see that whenever I see Foster with his students. The kind of patience he has and his ability to take everything in turn isn't taught, it is something he was born with.

"Miss Hore?" Principal Wong comes around the corner, and I jump.

"Oh," I lay my hand on my chest, laughing nervously. "I didn't hear you coming."

She smiles at me. "I've perfected a stealth approach. Can I help you with something?"

I glance once more at Foster. "No, I was dropping Pete off and procrastinating before I have a call with my supervisor."

"He's very good at calming nerves," Principal Wong says when she sees who I was looking at.

This is incredibly unprofessional of me. We don't kiss or touch here. We still have lunch together every day, but that's as intimate as we are. And now the principal has caught me practically drooling all over the floor while staring at my boyfriend mid-day. *My boyfriend.*

"That he is. Anyway, I'm going to take that call. I'll see you later, Principal Wong."

"Sophie," she says as I'm about to round the corner. I turn back slowly, like a kid about to be reprimanded. "Good luck with your call." The smile she's sending my way is big, bright, and real.

"Thank you," I croak before scurrying back to my broom closet.

I'm in shock as I hang up the phone. Did Principal Wong know what the call was about? Is that why she was smiling at me like that?

There's a knock on the door.

"Come in," I call, a stupid smile plastered to my face.

"Hey," Foster says, slipping in.

I'm up and wrapped around him in seconds. I can't help

myself, seeing him right now is the cherry on top of the last twenty minutes.

His arms tighten around me and I get a little lost in the feel and smell of him. "Did you enjoy the show today?" he asks when he drops his arms and steps back.

"What show?"

"The one starring me and Debra Donahue."

"How did you know? You never even looked up."

He pulls me back in, his lips coming to rest near my ear. "I can feel when you're near, sunshine."

I scoff. "You cannot."

"Can too," he argues. "I have Sophiedar." He crosses his arms and leans back against the door. It's unfair how good he looks doing something so damn basic.

"Do you have Principal Wongdar too? That woman moves like a panther."

He shakes his head, his bottom lip trapped between his teeth as his eyes travel down my body. "Just you."

FIFTY-FIVE

FOSTER

It was impossible not to notice Sophie standing outside the classroom. She's wearing a blouse with multicolored chickens today. It's so loud it enters a room before she does. She was talking to the principal when I looked up, but I don't need to tell her that.

She's practically vibrating, and I'm even more interested to know why Principal Wong suggested I check in with her.

"What's up? You look like you could jump over the moon right now."

She bites her lip and looks back at her phone before clapping her hands together. "I just got off a call with my supervisor. She said Hazel, the one I'm covering for, won't be returning when her maternity leave ends because she'll be in a different region."

"So," I prompt, watching as she takes a deep breath, relaxing under my touch.

"I'm no longer on a mat leave contract. I'm permanent— or I will be once I sign all the relevant paperwork."

"Soph!" I pull her back to me and lift her right off the ground with my hug. "That's amazing, congratulations."

"Thank you," she murmurs into my hair.

"I feel like I need to come up with something better for Z now. We need to celebrate."

She's shaking her head before I even got the last word out. "No, I only want to be with you. That's enough for me." She slides back to the floor, her hands coming to rest on the side of my face. "Don't change a thing. I've been looking forward to this for a week."

"You don't even know what it is. You may hate it."

"Impossible," she says defiantly.

"You're very confident, Miss Hore."

"You've done nothing to sway that confidence in you, Mr. Walsh." She stares back, and I either need to leave or do that thing where we swipe everything off the desk and go at it. I reach back, and when I feel the doorknob, I turn it slowly. "I don't trust the look in your eyes right now, so I'm going to wait for you in the car."

I can hear her cackle all the way down the hall as I hurry out of the building. We've done a very good job not allowing things to get heated while we're at school. Keeping work and what we are separate is important to both of us, but there are some days where the presence of her is almost too much to ignore. Happy Sophie is irresistible, and while I have a good handle on my self-control, she likes to test it.

Sophie drops me off at my apartment and heads home to do some homeowner things, as she calls them. Walking through my door without her right there feels wrong though. She's basically lived at my place for the last two weeks. Little Sophie mementos are dotted around the apartment, proof that she has been here and that she will be here again soon. Gary is the number one reason we're usually here and not over at her house. She's made a couple comments though about what room he'd probably like and how she's got a few squirrels he could have stare-offs with. And while we've both acknowledged that this feels like it, we aren't changing our addresses just yet.

As usual, Gary demands my attention the second I'm through the door. When I pick him up he climbs up and flops over my shoulder, his paws stretching out behind me. He only started doing this recently, as if he's trying to get closer to Sophie when she comes in behind me. But she's not here to scratch behind his ears and coo as she leans in and rubs her nose with his.

Sophie shows up half an hour before she said she would, dressed in tights and an old sweatshirt—comfy, like I requested.

"I couldn't wait any longer. I'm sorry if this throws things—oh," she squeaks as I pull her through the door and into my arms, our lips colliding.

"I think we've waited long enough, sunshine," I breathe, running my nose along hers and feeling her relax against me.

She pulls back, her gaze sweeping over my face. "Hi," she whispers.

"Are you ready for Z?" I ask as Gary yowls from the stool he's perched on.

"So ready," she says confidently, sliding by me to see him. "Hey, buddy," she drawls, bending so he smooshes her nose with his entire face.

Wrapping my arms around her waist, I rest my head on her shoulder. "He was not impressed when I walked in without you."

"And to think he didn't seem to want to share you with me at first."

"I think he knows you're not going anywhere."

She turns slowly in my arms, smiling serenely up at me. I think she's about to say something but ends up using her lips for something else.

The kiss probably would have evolved into more, but the sound of water boiling over has me jumping away from her and running to the stove.

"Crap!" I grumble as the pasta starch burns onto the burner.

"Damn, sorry," Sophie says from behind me as she takes in the mess.

After quickly wiping the pot and sticking it on a fresh burner I turn back to her, cupping her face and pulling her mouth back to mine. "Worth it," I hum.

Luckily I'm able to separate myself from her lips before the water boils over again.

"Four-mushroom, pea, and sausage orecchiette," I say, placing a plate in front of Sophie.

She bends, smelling the food then sits back sighing. "You spoil me."

"Well, don't say that until after you've tried it," I chuckle, sitting down across from her with my own plate.

"Is this part of the Z?" she asks.

"It is, although it won't make sense until after."

"How intriguing." She smiles, taking her first bite. She reacts the way I dream of her reacting to everything she puts in her mouth. Eyes closed, a small smile, and a slight swaying as she hums her approval. "So good," she moans, and I have to take a very deep slow breath to keep myself in check.

Now that I know she's happy, I can dive into my own. It's good, rich and garlicky, but it's missing one thing for me. I open the chili oil I put on the table and spoon some on top, turning the dish red. Sophie watches with wide eyes as I take a bite.

"Now it's perfect," I say, offering her a bite.

"I believe you." She declines a taste. "I've never had this kind of pasta before. It's kind of adorable. Is that weird to say about pasta?"

"Orecchiette means 'little ears' in Italian, so it is kind of adorable. Or kind of disturbing," I say.

Sophie laughs, picking up a piece and studying it. "It's both, definitely both."

We chat about our weeks, touching on things we haven't yet and retelling stories we have definitely shared already but neither of us seems to mind. Sophie could tell me the same story every single day, and I'd happily listen.

When we finish eating, she insists on helping me clean up so we can get to the Z portion of the night faster. Technically we're already in it, but I'm curious about what her reaction will be when I tell her.

"Zombies," I say, sitting on the couch, turning on the TV and watching as her jaw drops.

FIFTY-SIX

"Zombies?" I repeat. "Like..." I groan, staggering toward where he's sitting on the couch.

"God, I love you." He reaches for my hand and pulls me down next to him and then kisses me in a way that doesn't leave me doubting his words.

I love living without doubt. I didn't realize how prevalent it had been in my life until recently and how freeing it has been to not have it seep in through every crack that appears in my confidence. Foster has been like an emotional caulk. Sealing every place that pesky doubt was able to get in before. Keeping my foundation strong.

"Isn't this that show you and Davis were talking about?" I ask when I see *The Last of Us* appear on the screen.

"It is."

"Didn't you make a point of saying this show was not about zombies?"

"You don't miss anything, do you?" He sits back, shock all over his face.

"I miss plenty. Half the time I'm in my own head, but when you're talking I'm dialed in."

"They aren't zombies in the traditional sense, but they may as well be."

"It's a fungus, right? That's why they're not zombie zombies?" He nods and something clicks. "Did you pick that pasta because it was called little ears and…" I gasp. "All the mushrooms. Fungus!" I practically shout, bouncing on the couch to face him. "You made a zombie fungus pasta for dinner? Why is that so damn amazing and gross and delicious, all at the same time?"

He shrugs. "The theme is strong tonight, if not a little off-putting."

"No," I insist. "This is amazing. You planned something low-key and intimate, made the perfect dinner to go along with it, and you're sharing something with me that you love. This is the best way to end the alphabet." I curl into his side, relaxing as his arm wraps around me and he rests his lips on the top of my head before hitting play.

At the end of the third episode, when I'm an absolute mess from probably the best hour of TV I've ever seen, Foster gets up to prepare dessert. When I say I'll help, he tells me to stay put. Gary crawls into my lap and I give him some much-needed attention.

"Strawberry cheesecake," Foster says, setting two slices of cake on the coffee table.

"Okay, well, this is a less disturbing ingredient." I reach for the dessert. "Did you make this?"

"I did," he says, sitting back down beside me.

"Is there anything you can't make?" I ask in wonder.

"Caramel," he states bluntly. "I've ruined several pots trying to make that stuff."

"Oh well, at least that's not something that you have to make daily."

Foster watches intently as I take my first bite, those sharp amber eyes not missing a thing as the creamy cake coats my tongue. I do my best to not moan. I do my best to keep my eyes from rolling back into my head. I fail at both and hear a soft stuttered breath from Foster.

"I'm going to let you finish that, sunshine, but when you're done, I'm afraid we'll have to continue watching the show later."

"Oh? Why?" I ask innocently, licking my lips so I can watch him squirm a little more.

He lets me finish every bite. Lets me dab up every crumb and every speck of strawberry. But the minute I set my plate down on the table again, his hands are on me, dragging my body onto his. When his lips meet mine, it's like a sigh of relief involving my entire body. This is all I want to be doing. I'm convinced at this point that his kisses could sustain me. They are toe curling, spine tingling, thirst quenching, and overwhelming. They are all the things I've read about but never experienced until Foster.

Everything with Foster feels like more, and I feel greedy for not being able to get enough.

"Tell me what you want, Soph," he pleads, his voice already breathless as he strains beneath me.

I'm still trying to get used to someone caring about what I want. And not just caring—no, he wants to know; he *demands* to know. It's enough to make me cry.

"Oh, god, what?" He pulls back, horror shining back through those beautiful eyes. "What did I do?"

I shake my head, frantically wiping the tears away.

"Nothing. Well, no, everything, but it's good. These are good, overwhelmed, joyous, blissfully happy, very turned-on tears." The worry begins to disappear from his face, a small smile appearing in its place. I take his face in my hands, holding him steady so he's staring back at me. "You. You're all I want. You're all I've ever wanted."

A tear slips down his cheek and I bend to kiss it away, his hands tightening on my waist as my lips connect with his skin. "Don't cry," I whisper against his cheek.

He draws my head back smiling. "These are good, overwhelmed, joyous—" He can't make it through my speech before his lips are back on mine. "Blissfully happy, fucking turned-on tears," he finally grits out when my hands slip beneath his shirt.

The kiss is interrupted when I pull his shirt up and over his head and then I sit back and admire the view in front of me.

"Fuck, have I mentioned before how hot you are?" I swoon. When I manage to pull my gaze from his chest, I catch the blush spreading, like an ink stain to his hairline. Lifting my right hand, I trace the hint of color over his ear with the tip of my finger.

His eyes flutter shut, his head tipped back, mouth slightly open as I comb my fingers through his hair. His hands shift to my thighs, squeezing in time with the movement of my hands. I look down again and watch his chest rise and fall, an idea forming at the back of my mind.

"Stay put," I purr against his lips before sliding off his lap, a sound of protest rising from deep within him.

It takes me no time to find what I'm looking for. A bowl of red sits on the counter with a spoon partially submerged. I grab both, and when I turn back toward the living room the look of realization that crosses Foster's face has me nearly throwing the bowl down and throwing myself at him.

He grins wickedly as I come to a stop in front of him. "What you got there, sunshine?"

Saying nothing, I straddle him again, holding the bowl to the side as I lean forward and take his bottom lip between my teeth. When I pull back, his lips chase mine, but I don't give in. I lay my hand on his chest and push him back and tip his chin so when I hold the spoon above him he knows what to do.

The red liquid steadily drips toward his mouth, most landing inside but the odd drop sliding over his lip and down his chin. I repeat the process a few times until the drops travel down his neck onto his chest. That's when I set the bowl aside, slide to the floor, lean forward, and lick up his body. His breath catches the minute my tongue touches him, his hips jumping beneath my chest so I can feel exactly how turned on he is.

Foster's hands land in my hair, and in one swift motion I rip them away, sitting back, my hands around his wrists. "No touching, Mr. Walsh." His eyes widen and a tiny surprised laugh escapes, but he nods his agreement. I release my grip, moving my hands to the waistband of his sweatpants and pulling them down. "I love how hard you are for me," I murmur, tracing a finger up his length, watching the way it follows my touch. "So responsive," I use his words on him, listening to the tiny sounds he makes in response, watching as he fights to not touch me.

Reaching for the bowl, I drizzle more onto his skin, watching it trail down the lines of his body before finally allowing myself to go back in. I collect the strawberry juice on my tongue, and when I pull back, let it slip through my lips onto his cock before taking him in my mouth.

A faint "Fuuuuck" comes from above me, and I smile as he pushes himself further into my mouth. I hum my approval as he begins a steady rhythm, fucking my mouth. I watch his fist clench out of the corner of my eye, imagining what that hand will do to me when I finally let him touch me. With one final hard suck, I release him and crawl up his strawberry-stained body. His hands remain on the couch, his breathing ragged, eyes clenched shut as I rock into him.

"Foster." His eyes pop open, revealing pupils that are blown wide. "Touch me." I don't need to ask twice.

FIFTY-SEVEN

FOSTER

I've got her shirt and bra off in no time, and then she's on her back, bared for me. There are so many things I want to do with her at this moment, and I need to pause so I can settle on one of them. The strawberry coulis is practically screaming at me from where she left it on the table, and I treat her body like a canvas, splattering and dripping the viscous red liquid from her lips to her bellybutton.

Sophie watches every move I make, and every so often I see her tongue nearly sneak out for a taste of the rogue coulis that sits in the center of her bottom lip. "That's mine, sunshine," I warn her when I think she's about to give in and I watch as her tongue curls back in her mouth. That tongue that just did delicious things to my body.

I briefly admire my handywork, committing the way the coulis looks on her pale skin to memory, before dropping to swirl my tongue around a nipple, sucking it into my mouth, letting her sounds of pleasure wash over me. She whines when my tongue leaves her skin, her back arching as if trying to convince me to return. I don't need convincing.

Her fingers wrap around my hair, pulling at the strands, a satisfying sting traveling across my scalp.

"Please, Foster," she begs and my hands get to work on her tights while my tongue licks the last of the coulis at the base of her throat, right at her collar bone. It's like I touched her with a live wire. Her legs wrap around my hips and she drags me against her, impeding all progress I was making.

I'm able to pull my hands away before my body crashes down onto hers. "Fuuuuck," I gasp as she writhes beneath me. It's impossible to ignore the heat coming off her body and it only makes me desperate to get closer, to be closer.

"Want you," Sophie gasps as my cock slides over her clit, the sensation of the fabric between us only adding to the need to get out of these pants.

I sit back, pulling her up with me in one swift motion, then I'm on my feet, charging toward my bedroom. I've never been so happy to have a small apartment as I reach my bed in six strides.

After I lay her down I step back to look at her. Her hair is fanned out around her head, fucking sunshine blazing back at me.

"Wait." Sophie sits up, her hands landing on mine as they curl around the top of her pants. I try to stand and step back, but her grip keeps me frozen in place. "Um." She suddenly looks nervous, her eyes dancing around the area around me but never landing on me.

"What is it, Soph?" My voice is calm, despite my racing heart and the raging erection I'm sporting.

"Rip them?" she asks then shakes her head. "Rip them," she says again as a demand and not a question.

I stare back, not entirely sure I understand what she's asking me to do. "Rip..." I look down at her tights, my mouth instantly watering because I know what they're hiding. "Your pants?"

She nods once and then several more times, more emphatically. "Please," she begs.

A small laugh escapes because what the hell. "Sorry, it's not funny, that wasn't a 'haha, you're hilarious' laugh. That was a..." I look to the ceiling trying to figure out what I'm trying to say because I feel like she may be about to jump up and run from the building. "'A holy fuck, that's the hottest thing I've ever heard from the most beautiful person I've ever met and I can't believe my fucking luck' laugh."

She smiles up at me laughing herself, throwing her arm over her face. This should be awkward, these little moments we have in the midst of sex. But they aren't. They feel like us. Like two people so comfortable together that we can laugh about the ridiculous moments while half naked. The fact that her laugh is as much of a turn on as her telling me to rip her pants open is something that squeezes something deep inside of me. A vice grip on my consciousness, a threat to not mess this up because it's never going to get better than it is with Sophie Hore.

"Look at me, sunshine." My voice sounds like it's being dragged across gravel, but the demand in it isn't lost on her as she drops her arm and her eyes find mine. "You want me to rip these right"—I run my finger along the seam between her legs, hearing her breath stop as I apply the tiniest bit of pressure—"here?"

Her "yes" is cut off as I rip the seam, watching her face the whole time and relishing in the look of relief that spreads across it.

"No underwear again, eh? This is becoming a habit." I spread my body over hers, keeping my hand at the new opening in her tights. "I like it," I growl, sliding my fingers into her and capturing her gasp in a kiss.

I pull away when she's on the edge and roll toward the nightstand, reaching for a condom. The bed shifts, and then Sophie's reaching for the foil packet and pushing me down onto my back. She tugs my sweats down just enough to uncover my cock, and I watch in awe as she rips the packet open with her teeth before covering me with a confidence I haven't seen before.

"Breathe, Foster," she orders, and I realize I haven't taken a breath since her hands wrapped around me. "Such a good listener," she purrs against my lips when I take a gulp of air into my lungs.

All the air I took in leaves my body as she sinks down onto me slowly, her eyes on mine the whole way. She begins to unravel me as she gives her hips a little swivel, and I have to grab her and hold her still.

"Need a minute," I breathe out, my jaw clenched tight as I work at getting a handle over my body. Sophie is too much at any time but right now, seeing her like this, in control, uninhibited, it's beyond.

She remains still, her fingers trailing over the Fellowship marching across my chest. It's not exactly helping matters, but I'm not about to stop her.

When I reach a place where it doesn't feel like I'm about to go off the minute she moves again, I lift my hips, watching her expression go from contentment to pleasure. A stuttered breath paired with her nails creating little crescents on my chest has me thrusting up harder.

"So good," she chants, falling forward so we're chest to chest. My hands hold her hips in place so I can keep up the pace I've set that she's so clearly enjoying. Her pants next to my ear, little moans and gasps filling the room, wipe every thought that isn't about her from my mind.

"Harder," she urges, the word cut off as her back hits the bed, and I bring my mouth down to hers for a kiss that reprograms every part of my brain.

"Hold on, sunshine," I whisper before giving her what she wants.

She says something but it's incoherent, letters and sounds jumbled together as her back arches, her neck straining with a moan I can see but can't hear.

"Touch yourself?" It comes out as a question and I clear my throat and try again. "Touch yourself, gorgeous."

I watch as she sucks two fingers into her mouth and then follows my direction. Nothing on earth could have prepared me for this version of Sophie. My sweet sunshiney girl knows what she wants and she does not hold back. The feeling of her tensing around me mixed with the view below me, creamy skin with criss-crosses of sticky strokes from my tongue leaves me no choice as I splinter into a million pieces.

Gathering her up, we hold one another as the aftershocks rock our bodies.

The sound of laughter has me pulling back. "What?"

"We are so sticky," she cackles, and I join in when I look down to see how our skin slowly pulls apart.

"We should probably shower," I suggest.

"Together?" she asks demurely, as if she hadn't recently demanded that I fuck her harder.

"Obviously."

FIFTY-EIGHT

SOPHIE

"That's amazing, Mom!" I squeal after my mom shares that the recipes for the book have all been approved and the cookbook is officially moving forward.

"Congrats!" Foster adds from the passenger seat.

"When can we celebrate? Are you two able to get up here any time soon?" My mom's voice crackles through the line. The phone reception at their place is still trash, but she still would rather call and hear every other word than resort to texts or email.

"In a couple weeks," Foster says, reaching for my hand and squeezing. "We'll be up that way for dinner with my parents, but I'm sure we could make something work."

"Are you staying for the weekend? The cottage is yours if you need it."

"We can do that," Foster agrees.

We've been done the alphabet for a couple weeks, and nothing has really changed, other than plans automatically being for both of us. Friends and family have adjusted to say "you two" and Foster and I speak in "we's" more than "me's" now.

We're on the way back to his apartment after grabbing some ingredients to make a recipe from Cyprus. Since ending the alphabet, we've started on popular dishes from different countries. So far we've had meat pie from Australia and egg biryani from Bangladesh. Foster wanted to make all of them from scratch, and as much as I would love to watch him cook and eat whatever he's willing to make me, some of the dishes can take hours and I'm not that patient. There are better things I can think of to do with him for hours. So we compromised and agreed to do half at home and half at a restaurant.

"Dinner is on the Friday night, so we could always do something on Saturday," I suggest.

"That works. I'll see if Marley and Bennett can come too, and obviously Cass is invited. She's here half the time, anyway." My mom laughs then swears as the sound of something metal echoes through the phone.

"You okay?"

"Oh yeah, just knocked a knife off the counter, missed my foot by an inch, no harm done." I roll my eyes at Foster who looks somewhat concerned. "Anyway, I'll let you two get back to whatever it is you were doing. I'll call when I have all the details. Love you!"

"Love you too," I say before hitting the end call button on my steering wheel.

"Another family-filled weekend around the corner. You going to be okay with that?" I ask Foster.

He shrugs. "I love your family so that's not going to be an issue."

ABC

"Here," Foster says, handing me a beautifully wrapped box.

"What's this for? A very late birthday gift?" I joke, looking up from the box to find Foster looking nervous.

Pushing back the white tissue paper, I reveal what looks to be a photo album. I look up at him, an unasked question on my lips, unshed tears in my eyes.

"Open it," he says, gesturing at the book.

The first page has a giant A, messily colored in. Below it is a picture of me and Foster from the gala. "How did you get this?" I ask, running my fingers over the image, the memory of his hand on my bare skin making my skin heat.

"It was on the website. I reached out to the photographer to see if I could get a better copy to print."

The next picture is one of me holding the fake drink from the April Fools' barbecue upside down over Foster's head.

Each page has a letter in the same style as the first followed by a picture.

I run my fingers over the image of Foster dipping me at the aquarium, smiling at the memory of how that moment felt. How something slid into place that day, filling the emptiness I'd been dealing with for months.

The last picture is a selfie of us doing our best zombie faces. Or it was maybe the second one he'd taken, but at the last second Foster had turned and licked my cheek. My mouth is wide open as I laugh and despite my expression, it's hot. I can practically feel his tongue on my skin as I look at the picture.

I flip back to the cover, and try to keep it together. But the tears come despite my best efforts, "The ABCs of You and Me" blurring in front of me.

"Um, Pete made the letters. I'm shocked he kept it a secret from you," he babbles nervously.

"Foster." I sniff. "This... it's the best gift I've ever received." I burst into tears, and he gathers me up.

It probably seems ridiculous that I'm nearly hysterical over this gift. But I spent years getting expensive shit from a man who had clearly never listened to a thing I said. Gaudy designer bags, a car that was totally impractical for my needs, lingerie that made me feel self-conscious and not at all sexy. Everything was for *him*. Things he wanted to see or wanted other people to see and know he was the one who provided them for me. Every gift that man had ever given me was for himself, and I'd been made to feel ungrateful for not jumping with delight with each one.

As I look at the beautiful, simple gift in my hands, all I want to do is jump for joy, but my body can't seem to move. Probably because Foster is holding me so tightly, whispering "I love you" and "don't cry, sunshine" against my temple. I'm trying not to cry because I know that when he pulls back he'll have started crying too. I know that no matter what kind of tears I shed, he'll shed them along with me.

The very best part of Foster Walsh is that he never saw me as someone he needed to fix. He was there. He showed up day in and day out without complaint. He's the sun and the moon, always lighting my life so I'll never be stuck in the dark again.

FIFTY-NINE

FOSTER

Two Months Later

"Come on, Mr. Walsh," Pete pants ahead of me.

He had started to fade under the late August heat, but then he heard the cheering and it was like his body immediately recharged.

I hear her before I see her, her voice carrying down the road cheering as loud for me as she is for Pete. There are other voices calling Pete's name too, no doubt his mom and sister, but when they come into view, my feet nearly stop moving.

Standing beside Sophie are Nancy and Karl, Marley, Cass, my grandmother, and my parents. My mom is shouting that we can do it while my dad does his obnoxious fingers-in-mouth-whistle thing. Sophie is jumping up and down, her hands cupped around her mouth, and I have to remind myself that I'm doing this for Pete and not for me, which means I can't finish this thing at a full sprint right into her arms.

Pete is engulfed by his family the second his feet cross the line, his mom lifting him off the ground and swinging him around, his legs flailing in every direction while his sister jumps back to avoid being kicked.

No one is lifting me off the ground, but Sophie launches herself at me, wrapping her legs around my waist, hugging me tightly.

"I'm sweaty," I protest, but she only squeezes me tighter.

"I'm so fucking proud of you," she whispers before letting her legs drop and sliding back to the ground. "So, um…" She steps back gesturing at my parents.

My mom steps forward, looking guilty. "Sophie invited us, I hope that's okay," she says, glancing at where Sophie is standing with her parents.

"Of course it's okay. I'm just shocked you're here."

"What you did for that little boy is…" I watch her swallow, her lips quivering the tiniest bit. "Really wonderful."

I shrug because her reaction seems excessive, but when she hugs me the emotion of them being here hits me. "I'm sorry it took us so long to see how special you are, baby." She's full-on crying into my sweaty shirt now, and I do my best to comfort her as my dad wraps his arms around us both.

"I'm just gonna stay over here," I hear Cass say from my left side then she makes an "umph" sound as my dad grabs her by the shirt and hauls her in for a family hug. "Oh my god, you're disgusting," Cass whines when her arm touches mine.

ABC

"I guess I know why you were so frantic about cleaning the house." I laugh as I pull Sophie into me and away from the veggie tray she's been painstakingly organizing for the last ten minutes.

It's the first time we've gotten a private moment since I left for the race this morning. Sophie had been a stress case last night, worrying about how clean the house was, and I couldn't figure out what had brought the panic on. The house is always fairly tidy aside from what she calls doom piles and I call Sophie piles that accumulate now and again randomly.

"Your family was coming. I didn't want them to think you moved in with a slob," she says, her fingers dancing over my chest, over the new tattoo that's just for her.

"Not a word that belongs in the same stratosphere as you, sunshine," I whisper, kissing the top of her head. "And I happen to like your Sophie piles. They remind me of where I am and who I'm with."

"Only you could romanticize my least favorite ADHD trait," she murmurs

"All your traits make you the person you are, whether you like them or not." I take her hand in mine. "You don't have to like them, but I do. I love every single piece of you. Even your weird love of ranch with your chicken wings."

"Baby's up for grabs," Karl calls from the living room, and I chuckle as Sophie drags me toward him.

She drops my hand the minute she sees the newborn, reaching out. "Gimme, gimme," she begs, and her father gently transfers Emma into her arms.

She sways slowly, staring down at Marley and Bennett's daughter.

"She's going to be a good mom." Marley nudges me, smiling at Sophie and Emma.

"Mm-hmm," I agree, but only because I know it's what Soph wants to be one day. For now she's quite content with being Aunt Sophie.

The contented look she gives me when she finally pulls her gaze from Emma is like a love bomb to the chest. I don't know what's in store for us as far as a family goes, but I know there's no one else I want to explore that future with.

She kisses my cheek as she slips the sleeping baby into my arms and then steps back, humming approvingly as she takes in the view. I know exactly what this view does to her, the evidence clear as day in the dreamy look on her face. I'd hold a million babies to see that expression more.

"I cried for an hour straight when I saw him hold her for the first time," Marley reminisces, pointing to where Bennett is chatting with my parents. "Never thought I'd be that person, but goddamn, that man." She sighs.

When I look at Sophie, I expect to see her looking at Bennett too, but her eyes are on me. "I love you," she mouths, sending my heart off to the races.

"I love you," I murmur back, not even trying to keep my smile at bay. We don't keep our feelings hidden anymore, even though I'm not sure we ever did. We were both just in denial when the other showed them off.

SIXTY

Six months after the 5K

When Foster pulls up outside of the Post-it diner, I look over, confused. "Craving some bereavement fries?"

"Something like that," Foster says as he pays for parking on an app. "Shall we?" he asks, sliding his phone into his pocket and opening the door.

He meets me on the sidewalk and immediately takes my hand, leading me into the diner. It's even less busy than last time, despite the fact it's dinner time and we're in a popular area.

"Reservation for Walsh," he tells the very bored-looking hostess.

"This way," she says without even looking at the table map on the stand.

"Good thing you got a reservation," I whisper as we head toward the table we sat at the first time we were here.

"One can never be too careful," Foster replies.

The second he sits down, a waitress appears next to the table. "What can I get you?"

"Oh, well, we haven't..." I start to say while Foster asks for the exact same thing we had the first time.

After she leaves, he smiles serenely at me. "What's going on?" I ask, suddenly incredibly suspicious.

"Nothing," he says, drawing the word out a little too much for me to believe it.

"You're bad at lying," I hiss.

He shrugs, avoiding eye contact with me as he looks around at the walls. "You say that as if it's a bad thing."

I join him in looking at the notes, seeing a few I recognize from last time, but a few I don't. At least I know people have been here since then.

"Ha." Foster laughs, pointing to a note above our table. "'The only thing that sounds worse than nut milk is nut cheese.'" He reads it aloud, and I actively gag.

"That person doesn't want anyone to have an appetite," I say as our drinks are placed on the table.

"I've never gotten the appeal of cheese made from nuts. Just don't eat it, ya know?" I stare back at my beautiful innocent-minded man.

"What?" he asks, genuinely confused.

"Foster. Nut. Cheese." I enunciate each word. He looks back at me with one eyebrow raised. "Does that not make you think of like... dried..." I don't even think I can say it. "Nut milk? Like thick, crusty..."

"Ew, Soph, why?" he groans, hiding his face in his hands.

"You're the one who read the note," I protest. "I'm simply telling you what it makes me think of."

"It's a good thing the food here sucks because I don't have much of an appetite now."

"Exactly." I nod. "I'm going to wash my hands and try to think of something else."

The fries arrive right after I sit back down, and they're as mediocre as the first time. The mozzarella sticks, chicken tenders, and spinach dip are a bit better, and the flatbread tastes like it had been in the freezer even longer than the last one.

By the end of the meal Foster looks as fidgety as I do on a regular day. He's never like this. If he's nervous it usually shows on his face, but his whole body appears to be vibrating.

"Hey." I reach across the table, sliding my fingers over his. "You're acting kind of weird. I like weird things, but I'm kind of worried. You're not going to break up with me, are you?"

His eyes go wide. "Oh god, no, no, sorry. I don't know what's up with me. Do you wanna..." He gestures to the front of the restaurant.

"Yeah, but maybe I should drive?"

"Sure," he murmurs, sliding out of the booth so fast he bumps his hip and releases a soft curse. "Actually, can I show you one thing?" He takes my hand and pulls me to the back wall. Weird considering he seemed so anxious to get the hell out of here.

He drags me in front of him and points up at the notes. "'Did you know Bon Jovi's singing about a steel horse and not a stale horse?'" I read.

"To the left." His hands direct my head to a blue note with writing I definitely recognize.

At ~~16~~ 14, I fell in love with a girl.
I'm ~~28~~ 29 now and still falling.

Marry me, sunshine?

I read it again and then again, and when I finally turn around, there's Foster down on one knee. A ring held out in front of him.

He's opening his mouth when I shout "Yes" and dive on top of him.

"I had a whole speech planned, ya know," Foster says as he unlocks the door, already poised to grab Gary before he has a chance to escape.

"You can say it to me now, if you want," I murmur, somewhat distracted by the emerald on my finger. "You know, this is the exact same color as—"

"The dress," he finishes. "I decided that first day that if I ever got to buy you a ring, it would be that color just so I could see it on you forever. Sorry if that's selfish," he says guiltily

"I don't believe you have the ability to be selfish, Foster Walsh." I grab his hand and pull him into the living room before pushing him back onto the couch. "That's one of the things I love most about you," I claim, climbing onto his lap.

"Feels kind of selfish asking you to be mine." He lifts my hand and kisses right behind the ring.

"Then I guess I'm just as selfish for saying yes so that you're mine," I say with conviction. "But really, I feel lucky that I get to do life with you. I love our ABCs, one, two, threes, and every other silly list we make for an excuse to spend time together." I pull his hand to me this time and kiss the back of it. "I get to be your wife. Mrs. Foster Walsh. Unless you want to be Mr. Hore."

I watch his smile jump with a trapped laugh. "I'll be Mr. Hore if you want me to be. I'll be whoever you want me to be, Soph."

"Just be you. That's all I ask." I lean down and press my lips to his, moaning as his tongue slides alongside mine and his hands grip my ass, pulling me harder against him. "Thanks for keeping the clouds at bay," I whisper.

He pulls back, eyes searching my face. My god, I really like his face. "Anytime, sunshine."

FOSTER'S THANK YOU COOKIES

1 c browned salted butter
1 c packed brown sugar
3/4 c white sugar
2 large eggs
2 1/2 c all-purpose flour
1 tsp baking soda
1 dash of vanilla (measure with your heart)
1 bag/1.5c of dark chocolate chips/chunks/mix of the two
1 tbsp sea salt

Brown the butter, you'll want to add a bit more than 1 cup
as it'll evaporate. Watch carefully it'll go from taking forever
to burnt real quick! Take off the heat and let cool to room
temperature.
*tip, brown more than one batch so you don't have to repeat
when you make another batch*
Preheat oven to 375F (190C)

Cream together butter and sugar, beat on high until the

mixture is fluffy and pale (or mix by hand for a very long time)
Add vanilla
Add eggs and beat on high for 2 minutes
Add flour and baking soda and mix on low speed until just incorporated
Add in chocolate chips and mix by hand

Roll dough into balls, flatten on baking sheet, sprinkle with salt.
Bake for 11 mins or until cookies are lightly golden. Ovens vary so just keep an eye on them. Bake longer if you like a harder cookie. (No judgment)

Transfer to a cooling rack and let cool for at least a couple minutes.
EAT!

ACKNOWLEDGMENTS

Cassandra, as always, I likely never would have started this journey without you. Thanks for going on it with me and for all the proofing!

Cristina, never in my wildest dreams did I think you'd become one of my closest friends. I thought you were far too cool for me, and truth be told, you are, but you're also just as unhinged as I am and not to get too Anne Shirley, but you're definitely a kindred spirit.

Jess, thank you for your insight into the life of an educational assistant. Your expertise helped immensely while crafting Foster. I am over the moon that he has your approval. Curious how many reads you'll end up doing of this one.

Hayley aka Sophie's #1 fan! Your enthusiasm for this character was unmatched and it helped guide me throughout the writing process. Thank you so much for alpha and beta reading this and for your phenomenal feedback. *Insert THAT gif here*

D, thank you for your gentle assistance with bringing Pete to life and for answering all my CP questions.

The pesto chicken sandwich from Station 1 in Grimsby. That sandwich fueled this book and inspired Foster's Pasta.

The Yogurt Squad - Christina (*Chrissykata_bibliophile*), Hayley (*thepaperback.stack*), Dawn (*dawnsworldblog*), Kae (*reads.with.kae*), Kate (*the.girl.who.reads.blog*), Ashleigh

(*Teatime_with_a_book*), Nicole (*Kauffeetablebooks*),
Stephanie C (*Naturally.caffeinated.reader*), Erin (*girlwell-read*), Melanie (*mels_reads*), Jess (*borgin.andbooks*), Katie (*chronically_kd*), Dana (*danish_mustardreads*), Emily (*read.-donuts.sleep.repeat*), Tracy (*readingwithtracy*), Megan (*_megs_reads_*), Melanie (*shelf_ishly_lit*), Michelle (*mls.adip*), Kaley (*Kaleys23*), Sylvie (*sylviesbook.nook*), Jenn (*burlingtonbiblio*), Jordan (collecting_rainbows), Kelly (*miss_kellysbookishcorner*), Becca (*coffee_pages*), Stephanie (*Stephs_cozycorner*), Taya (*tays_booknook*), Olivia (*liv_love_read_*), Haylee (*haylsbookshelf*), Maggi, and Court. Thank you for always being as enthusiastic for tiny sneak peeks of tattoos as you are for the finished book.

Fries and Beavers, an incredible group of Canadian indie authors, I'm honoured to get to call you peers and friends.

Sarah, you challenged me with this book, especially with Sophie but I'm so glad you did. It's not exactly a fun road, but it is a necessary one and I'm thrilled I have you to travel down it with.

Alpha and betas, Jamie, Alex, Ramona, Whitney, Erin C, Dana.

Aunt MJ, I'm always honoured that you read my books early.

Catherine, Baillie and Kerri ladies... I love you so fucking much. This book is for you too.

Readers, you make this all worth it. Every read, review, DM, post give me life. Thank you for spending time with the people from my head.

Greg, which is not your real name, thanks for the reminder of how important romance is in society, especially in this current climate. The fire you lit under my ass is eternal and I don't think that was your intention but alas, I'm petty. Also my dad said he feels sorry for your wife.

Ally, your talent blows me away. I cannot believe I get to have you designing my covers, every time you send me something it's a pinch myself moment. THANK YOU!

My family, I'm so incredibly fortunate to have such loudly supportive bunch behind me. You are the antithesis of Foster's family and I'm so glad.

Kail, the best sister and friend a girl could ask for. As I said in the dedication, this was all for you. I hope one day you find your Foster... if that's what you want.

Sean, please refer back the acknowledgments in AUP and YITM. Everything remains the same. I don't know what I did in a past life to deserve you but it must have been spectacular. There is quite a bit of you in the men I write, their patience and goodness come straight from my life with you. My goal is to never take those qualities for granted. Thank you for never making me doubt myself.

ABOUT THE AUTHOR

Megan McSpadden dreads talking about herself almost as much as seeing a snake on a hike. But she knows we all must do hard things so here it goes. Megan lives in Hamilton, Ontario with her husband, two dogs, two cats and unruly garden.

When not writing she can usually be found photographing families (don't worry they pay her to do it), yelling at her beloved Toronto Maple Leafs, dreaming of traveling somewhere else or cooking something her husband will ask her to make again but knows she won't because Megan doesn't do recipes. Megan enjoys writing romance that will make you laugh one minute only to cry the next. Don't ask why because she doesn't know.

Keep up-to-date by signing up for my newsletter!

Stay tuned for Nancy and Karl's story, Deck the Hores, coming late 2025!

ALSO BY MEGAN MCSPADDEN

An Unexpected Path

Years in the Making

www.ingramcontent.com/pod-product-compliance
Lightning Source LLC
Chambersburg PA
CBHW031738180726
48283CB00005B/1560